TELL IT TO THE
SPACE MARINES

"So, what are we going to do about it, Major?" Ostrowsky asked. "Sit here like good little POWs until they decide to let us go?"

Garroway had already given the problem considerable thought. "Our mission orders don't quite cover this situation," he said slowly. "But I do know that we still answer to the people who cut our orders Earthside . . . and we're not fulfilling our part of the bargain sitting here on our duffs doing what the UN tells us to do." He looked at each of the others at the table in turn, measuring them. "We're supposed to be safeguarding American interests here. Well, it seems to me those interests are under attack, and it's our duty to fight back."

"Fight back," Alexander said. He shook his head. "Damn, Major, I don't see how you can even think about that. We have no idea where we are, we have no weapons, and we can't call for help. Sounds impossible."

"No," Garroway said. "It sounds like a challenge."

Avon Books are available at special quantity discounts for bulk purchases for sales promotions, premiums, fund raising or educational use. Special books, or book excerpts, can also be created to fit specific needs.

For details write or telephone the office of the Director of Special Markets, Avon Books, Inc., Dept. FP, 1350 Avenue of the Americas, New York, New York 10019, 1-800-238-0658.

SEMPER MARS

BOOK ONE OF
THE HERITAGE TRILOGY

IAN DOUGLAS

AVON • EOS

This is a work of fiction. Names, characters, places, and incidents either are the product of the author's imagination or are used fictitiously. Any resemblance to actual events, locales, organizations, or persons, living or dead, is entirely coincidental and beyond the intent of either the author or the publisher.

AVON BOOKS, INC.
1350 Avenue of the Americas
New York, New York 10019

Copyright © 1998 by William H. Keith, Jr.
Published by arrangement with the author
Visit our website at http://www.AvonBooks.com/Eos
Library of Congress Catalog Card Number: 97-94881
ISBN: 0-380-78828-4

All rights reserved, which includes the right to reproduce this book or portions thereof in any form whatsoever except as provided by the U.S. Copyright Law. For information address Avon Books, Inc.

First Avon Eos Printing: May 1998

AVON EOS TRADEMARK REG. U.S. PAT. OFF. AND IN OTHER COUNTRIES, MARCA REGISTRADA, HECHO EN U.S.A.

Printed in the U.S.A.

WCD 10 9 8 7 6 5 4 3 2

If you purchased this book without a cover, you should be aware that this book is stolen property. It was reported as "unsold and destroyed" to the publisher, and neither the author nor the publisher has received any payment for this "stripped book."

SEMPER MARS

BOOK ONE OF

THE HERITAGE TRILOGY

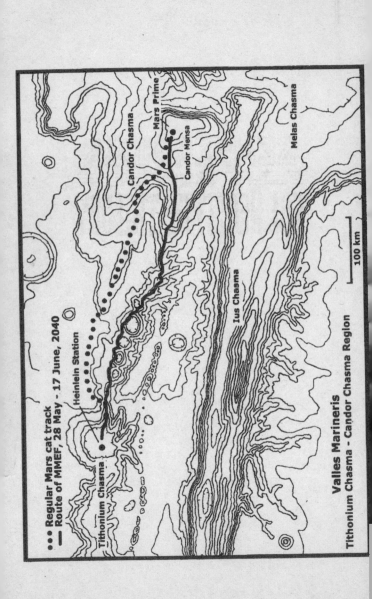

••• Regular Mars cat track
─── Route of MMEF, 28 May - 17 June, 2040

Tithonium Chasma

Heinlein Station

Candor Chasma

Mars Prime

Candor Mensa

Ius Chasma

Melas Chasma

100 km

Valles Marineris
Tithonium Chasma - Candor Chasma Region

2039

PROLOGUE

Office of the Chairman of the
Joint Chiefs of Staff (CJCS)
The Pentagon, Washington, DC
0950 hours EDT

"Christ, CJ! You can't let them do this to us!"

General Montgomery Warhurst teetered between radically opposing strategies, storming and pleading. The five-star admiral seated behind the broad and brightly polished oak desk before him was not only his commanding officer, but his friend. He and Admiral Charles Jordan Gray went way back. They'd been middies together at the Naval Academy, Warhurst in the Class of '08, Gray in the Class of '07. Since their postings to the five-sided squirrel cage, they'd attended one another's social affairs, had barbecues in each other's backyards, and shared the same wry disdain for Beltway politics. For them, the old Marine–Navy rivalry was a seal on their friendship, banter and laughing bluster over a couple of beers.

But, by God, Warhurst wasn't going to let them kill the Corps, wasn't going to let C. J. Gray kill the Corps, not if he had one thin, ragged breath.

Gray gave him a sad smile. "What's the matter, Monty? Trying to save your job?"

1

"That's not funny. I may be commandant of the United States Marine Corps, but every Marine is a rifleman first. I'd resign in an instant if it would change this. You know that. I'd give my life for the Corps, CJ. I goddamn would."

The smile vanished. "Jesus, Monty, I know how you feel, but—"

"Do you?" Warhurst gestured at the four-meter flatscreen dominating the wall behind Gray's desk. The display repeated in hand-high letters the document called up by the admiral's wrist-top. The words "HR378637: The Unified Military Act" showed at the top of the neatly formatted document in punch-to-the-stomach bold. "The BBs've been whittling away at us for years now, cutting our appropriations until we're damn near running on empty. Now it's . . . this."

Warhurst stopped himself. He was breathing hard, and he could feel the rising flush in his face, feel the blood hammering at his temples. His meds monitor would be kicking in any second now if he kept this up, but, damn it, the BBs—Pentagon slang for "Beltway Bastards"—never failed to raise his blood pressure.

And now they were trying to kill the Corps. *His* Corps! . . .

"There's not a damned thing I can do about it," the admiral said, shaking his head. His gaze flicked to the left, to the large, 3-D image of a grinning civilian on the wall to his right. "Archy's backing this thing, and that means it'll have the president's approval."

"Severin is a political hack. He's also an Internationalist—"

"May I remind you that Archibald Severin is secretary of defense, which makes him *our* political hack. That means you, me, and the rest of the Joint Chiefs answer to him . . . and after him the NSC and the president. They pass the word, and we snap to attention, say 'Yes, sir,' and politics never rears its ugly face."

"Everything in Washington is politics, CJ, and that includes the Pentagon and everyone in it. You know that as well as I do."

"Maybe. But the final word comes from a document you may have heard of: the Constitution, remember? It says we work for the politicians. Not the other way around."

"I never suggested any different. But this Unified Military Act *is* political. You know it. I know it. And there's a political way to fight back."

"And what might that be?"

"Public opinion."

The admiral groaned, shifting in his chair. "Jesus, Monty—"

"It's worked before. Truman? A century ago?" President Harry S Truman, a former artillery officer in the Navy, had come *that* close to shutting down the Marine Corps in the years immediately after World War II, declaring it to be unnecessary. Public opinion, however—the opinion of Americans who remembered names like Wake, Tarawa, and Iwo Jima—had secured a place for the Corps, by law, in the National Security Act of 1947. And that wasn't the first time Washington politicians had tried to kill or dismember the Corps. Congress alone had tried it on no fewer than five separate occasions between 1829 and the 1940s.

And each time, public opinion, in one way or another, had played a part in rescuing the Corps from the budget cutters' hatchets.

"I know that look," the admiral said. "You've got something in mind, or you wouldn't be in here waving your arms at me."

Warhurst bent over, picked up the briefcase he'd set on the thick-carpeted floor when he'd entered the CJCS's office ten minutes before, and set it on Gray's desk. Touching the lock points, he opened it wide and extracted his PAD, which he slid across the desk, screen up.

Gray picked the thin panel up, his touch awakening the screen. He frowned as he read the document displayed there.

"Mars? You want the Marines to go to . . . *Mars*?"

"To safeguard American interests there, CJ. The same

way the Marines have safeguarded American interests all over *this* world.''

Gray touched the turn-page corner of the PAD. ''How big an operation is this?''

''The logistics are laid out on page five,'' Warhurst said. ''I'm suggesting one platoon, twenty-three men. Plus an HQ element. Thirty men in all.''

The admiral paged through several more screens. ''Very complete.'' He looked up at Warhurst, one white eyebrow askance. ''And it's certainly topical. But you *can't* be serious.''

Warhurst reached across the desk and tapped a touch-point on the Personal Access Device. There was a moment while the PAD searched for the office's network channels, and then the flatscreen behind the admiral's desk flashed to a new set of uploading images. Gray swiveled in his chair to watch the display, which tinted the room with its ruddy glow.

Red sand and ocher stones littered an uneven, rolling ground as far as the eye could see, beneath a sky gone eerily pink and wan. An American flag hung from a mast in front of a cluster of pressurized domehuts, a tiny symbol of national defiance stirring listlessly in the thin wind. On the horizon, miles away but looming large enough to seem much closer, was the mountain. It reminded Warhurst sharply of Ayers Rock in the Australian outback, monolithic, vast, and red in the distance-chilled sunlight. The surface was sand-polished and smooth, its original angles, planes, and swellings worn down by the wind erosion of five hundred millennia, but the features were still discernible.

Or so some said. There were still voices—and powerful ones, at that—insisting that the so-called Cydonian Face, the Face on Mars, was a natural feature, a kind of cosmic prank elicited by shadows, coincidence, and the irrepressible human will to believe.

This despite the latest reports from Cydonia Base.

''In five more months,'' Warhurst said, ''*Columbus* will cycle past Mars and deliver her payload. They used a sealed hab payload, as was their right by the International Space Commerce Treaty . . . but Intelligence tells us the passengers include fifty soldiers of the Second Demibrigade, Legion Étranger—French Foreign Legion—in the service of the United Nations. That's more soldiers than we have scientists on Mars, right now . . . and they'll be armed, where our people are not.''

Admiral Gray turned away from the flatscreen, scowling. ''I needn't remind you, surely, that the administration is fighting for its life, right now. And trying like the devil to keep a low profile where the UN is concerned.''

''I'm well aware of our current . . . foreign policy,'' he replied. The way he said it added the words *lack of* in front of the word *foreign.*

''And how is sending thirty US Marines to Mars supposed to defuse a situation that is just a step or two short of outright war?''

''Maybe it doesn't,'' Warhurst said. ''But maybe the president would like an option that doesn't have us ducking for cover every time some two-bit dictator in South America or Asia sneezes and blames us. Maybe stationing troops on Mars to safeguard our interests— and we're still allowed to do that, I remind you, under the charter—maybe that would convince Geneva to back off and cut us some slack.''

Gray tapped several touchpoints on the PAD. The image of America's xenoarcheological station on the bitterly cold and windswept Cydonian plain remained on the wall flatscreen, but Warhurst's proposal came up on the PAD display. ''Hmm. And, just incidentally, it ingratiates the Marines with the American public, eh?''

''Maybe the American public is tired of getting kicked around by those two-bit dictators, too, CJ.''

''Maybe. And maybe Congress won't want to shut down the Marine Corps while thirty Marines are on their way to protect our people on Mars.'' Suddenly, he grinned, a cold and lopsided showing of teeth. ''My God. SECDEF and State are going to shit their pants when they see this.'' He paused and shook his head. ''Damn it, Monty, why the stick up your ass? Maybe Archy and the rest are right, and it's time to let the Corps retire, with dignity. With honor. Warfare has changed in the last century, you know . . . or haven't you been paying attention? Marine amphib ops like Inchon and Tavrichanka are things of the past. We'll never see a major amphibious landing again, not when satellites and space stations make secrecy impossible in any deployment. Do you want the Corps to end up as nothing more than the Navy's police force?''

"There are still a few things us Marines do that the other services don't," Warhurst replied. He looked down at the desk top for a long moment. "I'll tell you, though, CJ. The reason, the *real* reason, doesn't have that much fact or experience or science behind it. You know I have a son in the Marines. Ted's planning on making it his career. And his son, my grandson, Jeff. Eleven years old. He commed me just the other day to tell me he was going to be a Marine. Like his daddy. Like me. What the hell am I supposed to tell him, CJ, if they kill the Corps? The tradition? It would be like killing part of who we are."

Gray sighed. "There aren't any easy answers, Monty. You know that. The UN is pushing, pushing hard, to reduce all national militaries to a minimum."

"I'll let the politicians worry about disarmament," Warhurst said. "What I don't want to see is my son's face . . . or Jeffie's, when I have to tell them that the Marines are being shut down, that their country doesn't need them anymore."

"A hell of a note," Gray said, "proving we need them by sending them to Mars."

"The Marines," Warhurst replied, "always go where they're needed."

2040

ONE

Cycler Spacecraft Polyakov,
three days from Mars Transfer
1517 hours GMT (shipboard
time)

This wasn't the first time the Marines had ventured
into space, not by a long shot. On February 20, 1962,
Colonel John Glenn, United States Marine Corps, had
become the first American in orbit, thundering into space
atop a primitive Atlas-D booster. Of course, Navy astronauts were quick to point out that Alan Shepard, a former US Navy aviator and test pilot, had been the first
American in space nine months earlier, even if his suborbital flight—with a full five minutes in zero G—had
also been the *shortest* spaceflight in history.

Major Mark Alan Garroway did not think of himself
as an astronaut, even though he'd been in space for
seven months, was drawing astronaut's flight pay, and
was watching now as Mars drifted past the command
center's main viewport. He was a passenger—in effect,
he was extremely expensive cargo—aboard the *Polyakov*, one of four cycler spacecraft set to shuttling between Earth and Mars in the past decade. He was a
Marine, and as far as he was concerned, sharing bridge

7

watches with the ship's three officers—two Russians
and an American—did not make him an astronaut. *That*
distinction was reserved for the glory boys and girls of
NASA's Astronaut Corps and the Russkii Kosmonaht
Voiska. Marines liked to boast that *every* Marine was a
riflemen first, and that any other job description—
whether that of AV-32 pilot or combat engineer, of electronics and computer specialists like Garroway or the
goddamn commandant of the whole goddamned Corps—
was at best a minor elaboration.

Garroway was still less than enthusiastic about this
mission, even after seven months in space. The routine
had swiftly become tedious, especially after the magnif-
icence of the blue and cloud-smeared Earth faded to
nothing more than a brilliant, blue-white star. It was the
sameness of life aboard ship, day in and day out, that
ground away at his nerves, convincing him that this
time, finally, once and for all, when the mission was
done and he got back home, he was going to retire from
the Corps at last. That tour-boat concession in the Bahamas was looking better and better with each passing
watch. Kaitlin, his daughter, had been accusing him of
going soft, lately, in her frequent v-mails. Well, maybe
she was right. It was hard to stay gung ho for twenty-
five years in a Corps dying of slow starvation . . . and
with nothing much to show for it but a ticket to Mars
and a hell of a long tour away from home.

Mark Garroway was the second-highest-ranking officer in the Marine Mars Expeditionary Force, a thirty-
man unit comprised of a single, specially assembled
weapons platoon on special deployment . . . very special
deployment. General Warhurst himself had put this op
together, a last-ditch attempt at saving the US Marines
from the Washington compromiser corps. Tradition
might dictate that Garroway was a rifleman first, but he
rarely thought of himself as such these days. He was
forty-four years old and had been in the Corps for almost
twenty-five years. A mustang, he'd started out as an enlisted man, an aviation electronics specialist. When he'd
re-upped after his first hitch, however, the Marines had

paid for him to finish his interrupted tour at college, including stints first at MIT, and later at Carnegie Mellon University in Pittsburgh, and his area of expertise shifted from straight avionics to the obtuse, complex, and frequently highly classified electronics found in military communications, robotics, and AI computer systems. By then, of course, he'd received his commission, and he spent most of the next ten years working on classified programs at half a dozen research labs, from Aberdeen, Maryland, to Sandia, New Mexico, to Osaka, Japan.

His communications electronics expertise was the reason he was a part of the MMEF. Technically, he'd volunteered as a CE Tech for the Marine Mars Expeditionary Force, but no less a Corps luminary than General Montgomery Warhurst had personally requested that he accompany the expedition, and so far as Garroway was concerned, a request by the commandant of the US Marine Corps was a direct order—a politely disguised one, perhaps, but a direct order all the same.

Garroway's primary responsibility on the mission was to oversee the maintenance of the Marines' computers and electronic gear—especially the microcomp circuits that controlled their battle armor, commo gear, and assault rifles. Vital work, certainly, but considerably less than a full-time job. If it hadn't been for the fact that he was also Colonel Lloyd's executive officer, his second-in-command, Garroway thought he would have gone mad from the boredom by now.

His eyes followed the stately drift of Mars past the control deck's windows. He still hadn't accustomed himself to the strangeness, the *alienness* of the world. At the moment, it looked like a small and seriously diseased orange, its overall yellow-ocher coloration interrupted by patches, streaks, and smears of dark browns and grays. The north polar ice cap was a slender glimmer of sun-dazzled white. That band of black and dark red along the equator was almost certainly the Valles Marineris . . . the Valley of the Mariner Spacecraft. Despite over a year of study, he could recognize little else in the way of surface features save the polar cap and the three dark smudges of the Tharsis volcanoes.

And then the *Polyakov*'s slow rotation carried the planet past the edge of the window, and he was looking at stars and emptiness once more.

To his left, Commander Joshua Reiner reached up and tapped one of the monitor displays on the console above his workstation in that annoying way people have of trying to chivvy delicate electronics into proper operation. "Hey, Garroway?"

"Yeah?"

"We got a fault in camera sixty-two. No picture." Reiner tried upping the gain on a volume control. "No sound, either."

"Is the thing on?"

"Yup. Readouts say it is, anyway. Must be a loose connection."

Garroway snorted. Trouble with electronic systems was always dismissed as "a loose connection," even when the whole system was solid-state, with no wires to come loose in the first place. Pivoting his seat, he took a look over Josh's shoulder, verifying that the system was on, but without sound or picture.

"Huh. I see what you mean." The control-deck console was receiving a visual feed, but the screen was black. The sound, though, appeared to have been switched off.

"Storm cellar," Reiner said, identifying the location of the dead camera. "It's done this a few times before. Probably nothing major, but we have to log the failure for maintenance, y'know?"

"I'd let it go," Garroway replied, leaning back in his seat. He was pretty sure he knew what the problem was. "See if it fixes itself."

"Um. Trouble is, old L&M's on his way up there."

"Eh? Why? When?"

"He's logged for . . . let's see." With a few taps on his keyboard, Reiner called up a schedule on one of his monitors. "Here it is. Platoon weapons assembly drill, RSHF, 1530 hours."

"Oh, shit," Garroway said, glancing at the digital time readout on a nearby bulkhead. He'd prepared that schedule last week but forgotten that a drill was on for today.

"Yeah. And you never know if he's gonna want a vid record of the drill."

"Yeah, roger that." He pushed back from his console. "I'd better get up there before he does. Cover for me here?"

"You bet."

Garroway walked across the control deck, ducked low, and stepped through the open hatch into the transport-pod accessway. He moved carefully; spin gravity at the control-deck level was currently only about two-tenths of a G, and a careless move could send him slamming into the overhead.

"L&M" stood for "Lloyd and Master," the wry sobriquet of Colonel James Andrew Lloyd, the MMEF's commanding officer. The name was strictly unofficial, of course, used only behind his back by those who had to work with him. Lloyd was a stickler both for regulations and for proper form. His weapons drills aboard the cycler spacecraft had made him notorious; what, the ship's astronaut crew frequently asked one another in Garroway's hearing, could possibly be accomplished by drilling Marines in disassembling and reassembling their weapons in zero G? It wasn't as if they would need to accomplish the feat on Mars, where one-third gravity kept the inner workings of their M-29s conveniently anchored.

Technically, Lloyd held no more authority aboard the cycler than any of the other Marines—or the civilian scientists, for that matter. The ship's commanding officer was *Polkovnik* Natalia Filatinova, and she was the one who set the standards by which the men and women in her charge behaved. Nevertheless, old L&M wouldn't like it if the storm shelter was used for . . . *unofficial* activities.

Garroway touched the transport-pod call key mounted on the bulkhead between two lockways. Several moments dragged past, and then he heard the chunk-*hiss* of a connection being made, and the sealed airtight door swung ponderously open.

A man clambered out, tall and dark-skinned, mustached, clad in a NASA-blue coverall. Two mission patches adorned his left shoulder: the light blue flag of the United Nations, and the circular sword-on-Mars emblem with the letters OEU:AE.

Organisation des Nations unies: Armée de l'Espace. The United Nations' Space Force.

"Monsieur Colonel Bergerac," Garroway said, stepping aside to clear a way for him.

"Hello, Major." The man's English was perfect, his eyes cold. "Going down? Or up?"

"Up, monsieur."

"Ah?" He questioned with eyebrows and a cocking of the head.

"An electronic fault. Nothing serious." Grateful that the French colonel seemed uninterested in pushing the question further, Garroway ducked through the lockway and into the transport pod beyond. A touch of a keypad sealed the lock behind him, and then, he was climbing up one of *Polyakov*'s three two-hundred-meter arms.

He didn't like Bergerac. The man was a cold fish, and he clearly didn't like Americans, a dislike made sharper by the current state of cold-war standoff between the United States and the United Nations. Intelligence had reported the suspicion that Bergerac and the three officers traveling with him to Mars were carrying sealed orders of some kind for the UN troops already there, and Garroway was inclined to believe it. The man acted as though he was brooding over some dark and enjoyable secret.

He felt a mild giddiness as the transport pod continued rising up the strutwork tower. There were no windows, so he couldn't gauge his progress visually, but he could feel the spin gravity dwindling away to almost nothing. *Polyakov* was designed like a three-bladed propeller on a slender shaft. The strutwork blades supported the hab modules, control deck, and labs some two hundred meters out from the central spine, where one revolution in forty-five seconds mimicked the 0.38-G surface gravity of their destination. On the inward leg of the cycle, the ship's rotation would gradually be increased to two revolutions per minute, working the Earth-bound passengers up to nine-tenth's of a G by easy steps.

At the hub of the cycler were the supply modules, fuel, air, and water tanks, the docking bays for cycler shuttles, and, at the end of a long boom extending five hundred meters clear from the rest of the ship, *Polyakov*'s GE pressurized-water 50 MWe fission reactor.

And, because of the sheer mass of its shielding, *Polyakov*'s storm cellar was also mounted on the spine, just down the hub from the multiple docking collars, core transport-pod accessway, and main airlock. Only rarely was the big module referred to by its official name, the Radiation Shielded Hab Facility, or RSHF. Usually, it was called simply the "storm cellar," and with good reason . . . even if the cycler's out-is-down spin gravity dictated that *Polyakov*'s crew had to go *up* to reach it. Solar flares were infrequent hazards of flight, but when a small patch of the sun's surface suddenly brightened by a factor of five or ten times, spewing high-energy particles out in a deadly cloud, there was no way that a spaceship en route between worlds—locked by fuel requirements and the laws of physics into its slow-arcing orbit—could turn around and return to port . . . or even take evasive action, for that matter. The storm cellar was the one compartment aboard ship large enough and heavily shielded enough to give the cycler's crew and passengers a chance of surviving if they were caught by a bad flare.

It was also, by reason of its relatively remote location, one of the very few places on board a cycler where someone could leave the crowded hab modules and find a little precious privacy. . . .

"Storm Cellar"
Cycler Spacecraft Polyakov
1524 hours GMT

Sex in zero G, David Alexander thought, was wonderful . . . though it could be even more exhausting than its tamer, gravity-leaded incarnation. The novelty of no up or down, no on top or underneath, as the coupling pair twisted in a thin, hovering mist of drifting sweat droplets, brought an exotic newness to this most ancient of recreations.

Carefully, he leaned back a little, so he could focus on the dozing face of his lovely partner, framed in a golden splash of hair adrift in zero gravity, and as he did, he felt—again—that tiny, nagging pang of guilt. Alexander was married, but not to this woman. It had taken a lot of loneliness—and the rather heavy-handed rationalization that his marriage to Liana was all but over anyway—to get him to the point where he'd surrendered to the very considerable temptation. Mireille Joubert was a beautiful woman and an intelligent one; she clung avidly to the European notion of cosmopolitan maturity that saw nothing wrong with two adults enjoying recreational sex, whether either of them was married or not.

Mireille Joubert. Her first name was difficult . . . and a delight. She'd had to coach him on the pronunciation, which came out something like mere-ray. He turned his gaze to a drifting wad of clothing a few meters away, remembering fondly how frantically the French woman had shucked off her jumpsuit. Two emblems adorned her suit's sleeve—a blue UN flag, and a round patch displaying the Cydonian Face. He could just make out the words embroidered around the patch's rim: *Expédition Xenoarchéologique de l'Organisation des Nations unies.*

He frowned. There were some who would say that their lovemaking was treason. Well, screw that. Mireille Joubert was his colleague, on her way to Mars to assume her new position as director of the UN archeological oversight team there, a small group of men and women assigned by Geneva to monitor US discoveries and excavations at Cydonia.

He didn't really give a damn about the political situation, and his only interest in the reports of UN troops on Mars—or of the Marines, for that matter—was to marvel at the stupidity of sending soldiers to the red planet instead of more scientists. He, for one, intended to work closely with his UN colleagues, and the hell with international tensions. Technically, the UN team had no real authority on Mars, though their reports and recommendations could bring political pressure to bear back in the United States on the agencies and foundations sponsoring the Mars digs. Aerologist Dr. Jason Graves, already on Mars with the thirty-some US and Russian scientists on the planet, was the head of the Planetary Science Team. Alexander had worked with the man before and doubted that there would be a problem with his liaison with Joubert. *She* certainly didn't seem to think there was a problem with their fraternization.

Alexander started to ease his way from the woman's sleeping embrace, but the movement set them slowly tumbling, and she opened her eyes. "Mmm. You are wanting to do it again?" Her long, naked legs, clasped about his hips, tightened. He'd thought he was sated, but he could feel the stirrings of renewed interest as she moved against him.

"Do we have time?"

"Quelle heure est-il?"

He knew a little French. She had been teaching him. He glanced at the time display on his wrist-top. "Uh . . . almost fifteen-thirty." Shipboard time followed military and European usage, with a twenty-four-hour clock.

"Ah, well . . . I must go over the site plans with LaSalle at sixteen. . . ."

He sighed. "Perhaps we'd best undock, then." Zero-G sex, for obvious reasons, had picked up a lot of spacecraft maneuvering terminology. "Docking," "probe insertion," and "docking-collar contact" were favorites.

She pulled him closer, nuzzling his ear and enveloping his head in a sweet-smelling, drifting blur of golden hair. Her hips moved in interesting ways. "Oh, but we have *much* time yet. . . ."

He groaned—happily—then surrendered to warmth and growing hunger. He still felt clumsy with Joubert, even after . . . what was it? Five times. Or six. He wasn't sure. Their first time in the storm cellar, they'd used a Velcro strap to keep themselves tied together at their waists; *any* movement in zero G could have unforeseeable action-reaction repercussions, and when both partners were moving enthusiastically it was difficult to stay docked.

Joubert, though, was an expert at this sort of thing. Either she'd done it before, *lots*, he thought, or she was a damned fast learner. Superbly acrobatic, she used her legs to keep them tightly joined, flexing knees and thighs like an equestrian to give the necessary friction.

The motion started them turning again, a slow tumble through the mist of their lovemaking. Lazily, he reached out with one arm and caught a stowage-bin handle, checking their spin. Space was precious aboard a cycler. Much of the hexagonal chamber's interior space was taken up by supply bins anchored by bungee cord and Velcro to the room's inner surfaces. Fifty or sixty people could have squeezed into the shelter at once if necessary—hab compartments in microgravity acquire a third dimension that makes them far roomier than the same volume of space on Earth—but it would have been a ghastly exercise in claustrophobic conditioning. There were no windows, of course. Ports would have compromised the shelter's armor. He'd often wished that he could look out into space during one of these sessions. . . .

A metallic thump sounded somewhere close by.

Alexander reared back from Joubert, startled, his heart pounding harder now. The cycler was always noisy, especially here at the hub, where the rotors that kept the hab modules turning provided a constant background hum, and the effects of uneven solar heating on the stationary spine made a sound like far-off thunder. The sounds were muffled, though. Air pressure aboard the cycler was kept deliberately low, which meant that sounds didn't carry well. This had been close . . . and very loud.

There was only one thing it could have been—a transport pod docking with the hub spin-connector module. *Shit!* . . .

"Mireille, someone's coming!" he hissed, disentangling himself. "Quickly! Get dressed!"

Too late. The storm cellar's hatch leading to the connector mod was already swinging inward. Alexander recognized the lanky, backlit form of Major Garroway crouched in the opening, holding the hatch open but keeping his head primly turned away.

"If there's anyone in here pulling inventory," Garroway called loudly, "they've got about two minutes before Colonel Lloyd, Lieutenant King, and twenty-six Marines come barging in for weapons drill!"

"Right!" Alexander yelled back. "Almost done!"

Garroway pulled the hatch closed with a muffled clank, and the two of them were alone again . . . at least for a couple more minutes. They began grabbing for floating items of clothing. His T-shirt was carefully wrapped around the lens of camera sixty-two, mounted on a corner of the bulkhead. He decided to leave it in place until they both were more fully dressed.

With a rattling snort, he forced a sharp intake of air past blocked nasal passages. "What do you think?" he asked the woman. "Is the smell in here too bad?"

Polyakov was the newest of the fleet of four Earth–Mars cyclers, assembled in 2037, but she'd still acquired a zoo of ripe aromas from the tiny, claustrophobic communities that had accompanied her on two circuits from Earth to Mars and back. Fortunately, seven months of living aboard had dulled Alexander to the stench enough that he scarcely noticed anything now . . . and when he'd entered the microgravity hub of the assembly, nasal congestion settled in and pretty much killed whatever olfactory senses he might have had left.

Despite that, he could detect the heavy muskiness

hanging in the hot air, mingled odors of sweat and passion.

"Ohh, David," the woman said with coy amusement. "How *romantic*. . . ."

"We don't want them to know, do we?"

Joubert gave a delicate shrug, then folded her knees to her bare breasts and slipped both legs at once into her red panties. "And if they know," she said, "it is that they will simply be jealous, yes?"

"I'd kind of like to avoid that if we can," he said, reaching for white briefs adrift in the air.

She smiled, playful. "Ah. You are afraid your wife finds out?"

"It's not that." Well, not entirely. At the moment, he was more afraid of the teasing he was likely to get from the other Americans aboard *Polyakov*. Four Team scientists, plus thirty US Marines, and the one Navy guy, Reiner, who was with the ship's regular crew. That was a hell of an audience.

The compartment tumbled lazily about his head. He had his underpants on at last, but he was having trouble imitating the woman's casual flexibility with the coveralls, and he kept getting both feet tangled in the same leg hole. Damn it all. You'd think that after seven months he'd have managed to learn how to dress himself. . . .

Well, to be fair, he'd not had to dress in microgravity except for the few times he'd come up here with Joubert, one of the distinct advantages of having spin-gravity hab modules. How was it that she could be so graceful with no more practice than he'd had? Already dressed, she anchored herself from a handhold on the bulkhead, then grabbed his shoulder to brace him as he finally slid into the garment and zipped it up. Moving to the bulkhead, he untangled his T-shirt from the camera lens and switched the unit's sound back on. Swiftly, then, he used the T-shirt as a towel, trying to soak up some of the swirling mist of various bodily excretions in the air.

A second clang sounded from the next compartment. A moment later, the hatchway banged open and a file

of Marines in Class-Three armor began crowding bois-
terously through into the long, hexagonal chamber.

"Fall in! Fall in!" one Marine was shouting. He wore
a gunnery sergeant's chevrons on his sleeve.

"Whee-oo!" another shouted as he squeezed through
the hatch. "I do believe I smell fresh puss—"

"*As you were, Donatelli!*" the gunny sergeant, catching sight of Joubert and Alexander before the others did.
"There's a lady present!"

"Surely ya don't mean *me*, Gunny," a hard-muscled
woman Marine growled as she pushed into the compartment.

"He said 'lady,' Caswell. Not hormone-junky."

"Screw you, Marchewka."

"Silence! Fall in at attention!"

The crowd fell uncomfortably silent after that, each
Marine grabbing on to a handhold to anchor himself
more or less in line with the others. Alexander eyed
them with distaste ... ten or fifteen men and women
who were suddenly making the storm cellar as confining
as the inside of a walk-in safe. They carried rifles and
wore partial armor—breastplates and open helmets,
worn over dark green BDUs. The breastplate shells were
made of an artificial laminate that took on the color of
its surroundings, but that hadn't stopped most of the Marines from customizing the things with some artistic
touches of their own. *Mange la merde* was scrawled in
red on one Marine's armor. *Dirty UNdies* read another.
Alexander scowled. No wonder America's relations
were so bad with the rest of the world, if these were her
ambassadors.

Alexander decided that he and Joubert had better clear
out before the way was completely blocked. He took a
last, surreptitious look around to make sure there wasn't
any clothing adrift, then started moving toward the
hatch. Joubert followed.

"Gangway, people!" the sergeant snapped. "At ease
and make a hole! Civilians comin' through!" The line
of Marines hauled themselves back out of the way, giving the two of them just enough room to squeeze past.

Released from attention, several Marines whispered among themselves, and someone giggled.

"Uh . . . excuse me," one called out, "but did one of you lose something?"

Alexander paused at the hatch, turning in time to see a lacy, bright red bra drifting past the faces of grinning men and women. Joubert, with far more aplomb than Alexander was feeling at the moment, snagged the garment, and darted ahead through the hatch. Alexander followed, clumsily, as laughter exploded behind him.

In the connector module outside, Alexander came face-to-face with Major Garroway, who was clinging to a bulkhead beside the transport-pod hatch. The module, which was locked to the rotating hub collar, was turning slowly with a heavy, grinding sound, though here at the very center of rotation, the spin gravity at the walls was still practically nonexistent. According to the lights on the control panel, a second pod was on the way, carrying, no doubt, the rest of the MMEF section. The pods, which worked in tandem like Swiss Alpine elevated cars to preserve the cycler's spin, could carry only about fifteen people at a time. The second car would be here any moment, and then things would really get crowded.

With a loud clunk and the hiss of matching pressures, the second pod arrived, and the hatch opened up. Another line of lightly armored men and women spilled out, moving rapidly across the module toward the stormcellar hatch. Last out was a tall, ebony-skinned Marine in fatigues, wearing the silver eagles of a full colonel at his collar. "What are you doing here?" he demanded, glaring at the two civilians.

"Uh . . . inventory, Colonel Lloyd," Alexander replied. "Just . . . uh . . . checking the stuff the arky teams'll need at Cydonia."

Lloyd gave them a single brief, penetrating, and disdainful look, then followed the rest of his men into the cellar.

Alexander let the major and Joubert clamber into the waiting pod ahead of him. From the still-open door of the storm cellar, he heard Lloyd's familiar bellow. "All *right*, people. Enough skylarking!"

The cellar door boomed shut, cutting off the voice. Alexander clambered through the pod hatch and grabbed a handhold next to the major.

"Thanks," Alexander told him. "For the warning, I mean."

"Yeah." Garroway's voice was hard and cold. His eyes were on Joubert . . . or perhaps it was the UN flag on her sleeve he was staring at.

If he doesn't like it, Alexander thought viciously, *then screw him!*

Alexander hated the very idea of US Marines on Mars, hated the politics, hated the twisted, jingoist, nationalistic interests that pretended that such things were necessary. They had come to Mars to do *science*, vitally important science, with the discovery of the Cydonian ruins, and troops were only going to get in the way.

Well, maybe they'd be able to ignore them. After all, it wasn't like there was a *war* on.

TWO

VIDIMAGE—JANICE LANGE AT NET NEWS NETWORK ANCHOR DESK.

LANGE: "In Geneva, today, President Markham concluded his fifth straight day of talks with UN Director General Villanueva, announcing that, although much work remains before the outstanding differences between the United States and the United Nations can be fully resolved, he is confident that real progress is being made."

VIDIMAGE—THE PRESIDENT ADDRESSING A CROWD OF REPORTERS AND NETHAWKS.

PRESIDENT MARKHAM: "The United States of America is not now, nor has it ever been, engaged in any plot or cover-up involving the Martian artifacts. The joint US-Russian expedition to Mars is carrying out its research and investigations for the benefit of all humankind. We welcome the presence of UN observers and scientists at Cydonia. We welcome their assistance. The discoveries made there so far are . . . are astonishing in their implications for humanity, for everyone on this planet, and there's enough work there that needs doing for us to be very happy when anyone offers to lend a hand."

VIDIMAGE—DEMONSTRATORS OUTSIDE THE UN HEADQUARTERS SHOUTING, WAVING FISTS, AND DISPLAYING SIGNS READING "US MILITARY OUT OF SPACE!" AND "ALL POWER TO THE UN!" LONG SHOT OF PRESIDENT MARKHAM LEAVING BALCONY AS SOME DEMONSTRATORS THROW STONES AND UN POLICE STRUGGLE TO MAINTAIN A PERIMETER.

LANGE: "Large numbers of demonstrators protested the president's Geneva visit outside UN Headquarters."

VIDIMAGE: A PROTESTER, A WOMAN WITH A SIGN READING "US STAY HOME."

PROTESTER (in translation): "America's been grabbing the world's resources for years! Now they're trying to rape the other planets like they've raped the Earth! Well, we're here today to tell them that we're not gonna stand for it anymore!"

VIDIMAGE—JANICE LANGE AT TRIPLE-N ANCHOR DESK.

LANGE: "In other news today, Secretary of State John Matloff rejected as 'absurd' renewed calls for a UN-mandated plebiscite to determine the political future of the American Southwest. Representatives of the Hispanic America Alliance told reporters today that there would be no peace for America until the formal creation and recognition of the nation of Aztlan."

VIDIMAGE—RIOTERS IN DOWNTOWN LOS ANGELES OVERTURNING A POLICE CAR AND THROWING STONES, AS TROOPS MOVE IN BEHIND CLOUDS OF TEAR GAS.

LANGE: "HAA members seek the creation of the new state from territories in Northern Mexico and from the states of California, New Mexico, Arizona, and Texas. Armed confrontations in the region between HAA protesters and military and police authorities have so far resulted in at least two hundred deaths. . . ."

Cycler Spacecraft Polyakov
1546 hours GMT

"How's it working now?" Garroway asked, slipping
into the seat on the control deck next to Reiner. He
didn't like microgravity and was glad to get back to a
place where up was up and down was a place you could
sit.

The Navy astronaut looked up at the monitor. "Seems
to be fine, now. Vid and sound." He cocked an eyebrow
at the Marine. "Underpants?"

"T-shirt."

"Man, nice work if you can get it. Who was it?"

"Doesn't matter," Garroway lied.

It was an open secret with the cycler's crew that passengers frequently used the storm cellar as a place for
some precious, hard-to-get privacy. Different commanding officers handled the problem in different ways. Many
continued to adhere to the old policy, born of NASA's
long-standing dread of bad publicity, of forbidding sexual liaisons during extended space missions; others reasoned that liaisons were going to happen no matter what
the rule books said, and so long as they didn't create
problems for the crew or mission as a whole, they were
probably best ignored.

Normally, Garroway wouldn't have been interested in
how the other cycler passengers passed their too-
plentiful free time, but he was still angry at the realization that the storm cellar's occupants this time had
been Alexander and the Joubert woman. Damn it all, the
political situation was confused enough right now, without those two attempting their own brand of détente.

Reiner was obviously still interested in the identities
of the two up in the cellar, and Garroway decided he
wanted to avoid the issue. He moved his chair so that
he could peer across Reiner's shoulder at the screen.
"Let's have a look."

Colonel Lloyd was floating at the far end of the

crowded compartment, while the enlisted Marines were gathered into two lines running the chamber's length. Their torso armor had almost perfectly blended with the white bulkheads, with random, dark olive streaks where the active camouflage was picking up arms and legs from nearby Marines. Each Marine had his or her assault rifle hanging in the air in front of him, together with a small cloud of metallic pieces, rods, springs, and oil-glistening parts.

Reiner turned up the gain on the volume. ". . . faster, people," Lloyd was saying, his voice a drill-field growl. "Faster! The enemy is *not* gonna wait for you. Pick it *up*, pick it *up*!"

Hands flew as the Marines snatched pieces out of the air, each movement precise, smooth, and almost machinelike in its control. They appeared to be reassembling their rifles, and the number of floating stray parts steadily dwindled.

One Marine, Staff Sergeant Ostrowsky, completed the drill and brought her assembled rifle to port arms with a sharp *slap* as her hand smacked the plastic stock. Two more finished up—*slap-slap!*—an instant later, and then all of the Marines were bringing their rifles up to signal completion in a ragged chorus of skin on plastic. It was a remarkable demonstration, Garroway thought. In microgravity, even the slightest movement tended to give you a push in the opposite direction, and many rapid movements could accumulate a lot of drift or spin if you weren't careful. The Marines of the MMEF appeared to have mastered the art of balancing move with move to keep their bodies more or less motionless.

Lloyd waited until the last Marine snapped home the bolt and brought the weapon to port arms, then touched a button on his wrist-top. "Not good enough, people," he growled. "Not good enough by thirty seconds!"

"Damned robots," Reiner said. When Garroway looked at him, he shrugged. "Sorry, Major, but it seems like such a waste. Like close-order drill, you know? Great back when armies lined up in nice neat rows and had to go through loading and firing by the numbers, like two or three hundred years ago, but pretty useless in a modern war.''

''I'd say it's a pretty good exercise of self-control and discipline, wouldn't you?''

Reiner chuckled. ''Well, the next time I need a rifle stripped down and put back together in zero G, I'll sure as hell know who to go to. Shit, why's he making them wear armor in there? Ol' *Poly*'s been around her circuit two and a half times, now, and she hasn't been attacked by space pirates once!''

On the screen, Lloyd was grinning at the Marines with what could only be described as sadistic anticipation. ''All right, people. Since you keep falling asleep at this evolution, we'll try to make it a little bit more challenging. We'll do it again!'' Suddenly, the screen went black. ''In the dark! Ready . . . *begin*!''

The sound of clicking and snapping clattered from the speaker, until Reiner dialed down the gain once more.

Garroway thought about replying to the astronaut's jibe, something about discipline under pressure, or even about needing to learn how to work in the cumbersome armor without letting it turn you clumsy . . . but decided at last that it wasn't worth it. Reiner was Navy, and there were some things a squid just couldn't understand.

The fact was that Reiner had hit pretty close to the mark, talking about drills evolved from combat necessities centuries old. There'd been a lot of talk lately about the US Marines becoming obsolete, and scuttlebutt aplenty about the reason for this deployment. Garroway was pretty sure the MMEF was a political chip in some unseen, high-stakes game, a means, possibly, of keeping the Corps alive when a number of very powerful people and organizations wanted to kill it. And it was true that President Markham was beating the drum pretty loudly during his reelection campaign this year—''our brave young men and women, serving America's interests far from this blue Earth. . . .'' The United States was increasingly isolated in a hostile world, and her citizens were clinging tightly to symbols of American might, tradition, and security.

None of which addressed the real question. Was the Corps obsolete? Didn't the Marines simply duplicate functions now handled by the Army?

Well, maybe they did. What of it? Garroway was mildly surprised to find that he didn't really care, one way or the other, what became of the Corps.

It wasn't that he disliked the Marines. Quite the opposite, in fact. The Marines had introduced him to advanced electronics, paid for an outstanding college education, and let him work on some absolutely fascinating projects, from communications software to advanced AI. The trouble was that he'd pretty much reached the end of the opportunities that the Corps could provide. How, he often joked with his daughter, could the Corps possibly top a trip to Mars? In fact, he'd been passed over for promotion twice now, a sure sign that he was never gonna make it to light colonel. He was at the top of his field inside the Corps, but there was no place else to go. To realize his true potential, he'd have to reenter the world of civilians. His background would land him a position at Pittsburgh's Moravec Institute easily—he'd worked there for a time on a government-sponsored AI project, five years ago, and he knew some people who could pull some strings—but right now he was less interested in continuing with AI communications software than he was in the Bahamas . . . specifically in opening a charter hydrofoil and submarine tour boat service for rich vacationers. That was the extent of his ambition at the moment, a dream that had very little to do with the Corps.

More than one of the people he'd worked with over the past few years, people including Colonel Lloyd, had accused him of going ROAD—Retired On Active Duty—marking time, in other words, until he was a civilian once more.

Well, maybe that was true, in a way. It was a bit ironic, actually, that he should find himself a member of the MMEF, occupying a billet that a few thousand other Ma-

rines would have given their teeth for, and he didn't really
want to be here. Two more years—a planned fifteen-
month deployment on Mars, followed by a seven-month
transit home aboard the cycler *Columbus*—and he'd be
out of the Corps. With all the military cutbacks lately,
he shouldn't have any trouble resigning his commission,
and a month or two after that he'd be on the beach at
Nassau, alternately soaking up the sun and soaking the
rich tourists.

"Well," he said at last, after a long silence had
passed, "all the routine traffic is up-to-date. I guess I'll
head back to the hab." He stretched. "I still have five
minutes' shower credit left over from last month, and I
think I'm gonna luxuriate."

"Enjoy," Reiner replied. "And thanks for your help.
I don't know what we'll do if the cameras go out in the
shelter again on the Earth-bound leg."

"Oh, you'll manage, I'm sure." He jerked a thumb
at the monitor. "You won't have so many passengers
on board. Maybe the romantic ones can use their cubi-
cles, like normal folks."

"Nah," Reiner said, shaking his head. "Zero G is too
much fun."

"Oh? How would you know?"

"Classified information, Major. *I'll* never tell."

Garroway caught a transport pod and took it down to
the hab-mod level, where the spin gravity now measured
.38 Gs, the same as on the surface of Mars. There were
two hab modules attached to the outermost rack of the
cycler's A-arm. His quarters were in Hab One, which
was reserved for officers, female Marines, and civilian
passengers. The twenty-two enlisted male Marines were
quartered together in Hab Two's tiny open dorm.
Crowding was bad in both habs—worse in Two than in
One. At least the Marine officers were quartered two to
a compartment. He shared his semiprivate, closet-sized
quarters with the MMEF's supply officer, Captain Gregory Barnes.

As he stepped through the lock module into Hab
One's small rec lounge, he nearly collided with Mireille

Joubert. "Major! Hallo. I wanted to thank you for your, ah, timely warning."

"It was nothing." He'd not meant for his voice to sound cold, but it did anyway.

"It would have been most embarrassing. . . ."

"Excuse me, Miss Joubert—"

"It is *Doctor* Joubert, but I wish you would call me Mireille." She cocked her head to the left. "We have made this voyage all the way from Earth, seven months, now, and we have not had much opportunity to get to know one another. Perhaps it is time we did so."

Garroway raised an eyebrow. "I don't think that would be such a good idea, ma'am," he said, a little stiffly.

"Why? Because I work for the UN?"

"Isn't that enough?"

"I am not one of Colonel Bergerac's thugs," she said, lifting her chin. "I am a scientist, an archeologist. Whatever differences your nation might have with the UN, they should not affect you and me."

"Mmm. To tell you the truth, Dr. Joubert, I feel more kinship with Bergerac's 'thugs,' as you call them, than I do with you and your UN observers. In my opinion, it's misguided UN policy and the demands being made by your bureau that have created this crisis. Not my government. And not the MMEF."

"Did I say that it was?"

"The opinion the UN has about Marines on this expedition is well enough known, I think. As are the UN's opinions about American sovereignty." He gave her a wintry smile. "Funny. I always thought you French would fight to the death to keep your national sovereignty."

"And who says we do not, monsieur?" she flared back. "France is still free. Still sovereign . . . within very broad and liberal boundaries."

"If that's your story, you stick to it. Now, if you'll excuse me, they warned us back at Vandenberg that we shouldn't discuss politics with you people."

Pushing past her, he entered his cubicle and pulled the accordion-pleated door shut.

What he didn't need right now was to be reminded about politics. The political situation on Earth seemed to be worsening almost week by week, with the increasing pressure to cave in to UN demands. Russia and the United States of America were the last two major powers on the planet that had not signed the UN Reorganization Charter of 2025. That document called for the establishment of a United Nations government that would have jurisdiction over the national governments of the world, the gradual abolition of all national militaries, and new international laws and regulations governing the exploitation, shipment, and sale of the world's resources.

The reasons for the growing concern—no, the growing world *panic*—were easy enough to see. The problems had been around for a long time, growing steadily, growing as quickly, in fact, as the world's population, which currently stood at something just over nine billion people. Global warming, the subject of speculation as far back as the 1980s, had proved to be not speculation but hard fact for forty years or more. Sea levels had risen by half a meter the world over, and they were expected to rise by another meter or so before the century's end. Rising sea levels—and disastrous storms—had killed millions, and driven tens of millions more into refugee status. Precious agricultural land in Bangladesh and coastal China and the US Gulf Coast had been swallowed up by the advancing tides. As nations like the United States and Russia finally ended their dependencies on fossil fuels and polluting industries, the poorer nations of the world had finally reached the point where they could become rich . . . but only by embracing the air-, land-, and sea-destroying industries that the US and others were now abandoning. Acid rain generated by China was destroying forests in western Canada, and the Amazon rain forest was all but gone now, replaced by ranches and acid-pissing factories. The last of the oil was swiftly vanishing; other raw materials vital to civilization—copper, silver, titanium, cobalt, uranium, a dozen others—were nearly gone as well. Things were bad enough that the Geneva Report of 2030 had declared unequivocally that *all* of the world's nations had to be under direct UN control by 2060 if certain key controls on population and industry were to be successfully put into place.

No wonder the whole world was casting the US and Russia as villains, holdouts selfishly clinging to outmoded sovereignty simply because they feared a little thing like dictatorship. . . .

Garroway wasn't sure what the answer was, wasn't even sure if there *was* an answer. The US, though, had been arguing for years that two new factors were about to break the deadly cycle of poverty and scarcity on Earth once and for all, if the industrialized nations of the planet would just cooperate long enough to make use of them.

The first was the wholesale industrialization of space, where power from the sun could be collected on a never-before-imagined scale and applied to industries that should not be allowed to pollute or endanger the planet. In another few years, perhaps, orbital industries could start making a real difference in the mess on Earth. The question was whether or not they would be in time. . . .

The second factor, of course, was the discovery of artifacts on Mars, artifacts representing a technology that was old five hundred thousand years before humans had domesticated animals, developed an alphabet, or dreamed of riding ships into space. The Martian artifacts, the discoveries at Cydonia, in particular, in the shadow of that huge and enigmatic Face, were the reason humankind had at last ventured to the red planet in person.

They were also, unfortunately, the reason the Marines had been sent to Mars.

"Storm Cellar"
Cycler Spacecraft Polyakov
1602 hours GMT

"All right, people," Colonel Lloyd bawled. "I'm gonna have mercy on you poor slimeballs. Report back to the barracks hab and get squared away. You have one hour before I pull personal inspection. Then chow. Right? Gunnery Sergeant, take over this detail."

"Aye, aye, sir!"

"Dismissed!"

Lance Corporal Frank Kaminski looked at his buddy, Corporal Jack Slidell, and grinned. Slider grinned back, then reached above his head to one of the white storage modules strapped to the storm-cellar bulkhead and gave it a loving pat. The readout on the module said BAT-TERIES, GERMANIUM-ARSENIDE. "Hey, Ski!" Slidell called out. "Wanna quick charge?"

"Shit, Slider!" Kaminski said. He glanced toward the hatch, where Gunnery Sergeant Knox and Staff Sergeant Ostrowsky were ushering Second Section through to the transport pod. "Ice it, huh?"

Slider just laughed. "Yeah, I'll ice it. I could use a nice cold one." He rotated in the air, catching Ben Fulbert by eye. "How about it, Full-up? Ready to party?"

Kaminski glanced at the other Marines still in the storm cellar. Sometimes, Slider could be just a bit too brash for his own good . . . and if he screwed things for them now, just a few days out from Mars . . .

"Hey, Slider!" Ellen Caswell said, floating up next to them and catching herself with one hand on the bulkhead. "You and Ski got extra duty tonight, *capische?*"

"Aw, fuck," Slider snapped back. "Again? *Fuck* this shit. . . ."

"Fuck it yourself, Slider. You two can clean out the head cubicle before taps." She reached out and thumped his breastplate, right above the garishly scrawled *Mange la merde*. "The Man didn't like your graffiti. *Especially* with a French national present."

Slidell grinned at her around the wad of gum in his

mouth. "Yeah? And what was that Frenchie civilian doin' up here, anyway? Diggin' for buried treasure?"

"The head, shithead. Make it shine. And scrape that shit off your shell."

He tossed her a jaunty mock salute. "Aye, *aye*, sergeant, sir, ma'am!"

Kaminski sighed. After seven months, he was getting to know the tiny lavatory facility in the enlisted barracks *very* well. Slidell was his fire-team partner, and Corps discipline held both men responsible for infractions that reflected on the fire team as a whole. Hell, Fulbert and Marchewka were probably giving silent thanks that the shit detail hadn't hit the entire squad. Slidell had a peculiar talent for drawing fire.

"Ice it down, Slider," Kaminski said. "We're in enough trouble already."

"Shee-it," Slidell drawled as Caswell flexed her knees and launched herself across the compartment toward the hatchway. "What're they gonna do, send us to fuckin' Mars?"

Hang on a little longer, he told himself. *Things'll be better when you hit dirt.* Space was short, and tempers frayed in a situation where, paradoxically, there were too many people for the available space and too much work for the available people. The current TO&E for a Marine weapons platoon called for five-man squads—a pair of two-man fire teams and a squad leader—organized two squads to the section, two sections to the platoon. Kaminski was in First Squad, First Section; Slider, Sergeant Marchewka, and Lance Corporal Ben Fulbert were his squadmates, while Sergeant Ellen Caswell was both First Squad leader and First Assistant Section leader. Gunny Knox also wore two hats, as First Section leader and as Lieutenant King's assistant platoon leader.

With so small a force—a weapons platoon of twenty-three men and women, reinforced by a headquarters element of seven more—there was lots of double-hatting going on, and the Marines, rather than being mere passengers on the cycler transport, were expected to do their share of maintenance, cleaning, and general scutwork.

The real problem, though, was the fact that the MMEF platoon was so damned top-heavy in the ranks. The lowest rank aboard was E-3—lance corporal—and there were *lots* of corporals and sergeants, more than was usual for a typical weapons platoon. And when shit flows downhill in the military, it lands on the low man on the pole.

Part of the deal, in fact, was that all personnel in the MMEF would keep their current ranks until the end of the mission, which was expected to last the better part of two years, a measure designed by some desk-flying bureaucrat Earthside to keep the platoon from getting even more top-heavy than it was already from sheer time-in-grade attrition. Where they were going, there were no replacement depots or work pools to replace the lucky SOB who made E-4. That wasn't really as bad as it sounded. All of them were getting flight pay, hazardous-duty pay, and hardship pay enough to more than make up for the financial shortcomings of the arrangement. When they got back to Earth, most of the guys on their first hitch, Kaminski among them, would have their four in and have the choice of accepting a double promotion—Kaminski would have a shot at sergeant—or returning to civilian life with one hell of a nice separation pay packet.

Kaminski knew what *he* was gonna do. Four years for him was a great plenty. He would put in his hitch, and in another 745 days he would be out of here, out of the Corps and back to being a carefree civilian.

With lots of money waiting for him, too. Surreptitiously, he reached up beneath his breastplate, tugging at his BDU blouse to make sure the flag was still wrapped around his waist. Slidell saw the gesture and laughed. "Still there?"

Kaminski nodded. "Good thing, with all these damned PIs."

"You just keep it there, Ski, out of sight. Ha! Man, we're gonna clean up when we get back, right?"

"Aw, fer . . ." Kaminski shook his head. "Why don't you tell *everyone*, Slider?"

"Tell us what?" Sergeant Witek, one of the HQ element people, asked.

"Nothin'," Kaminski said, a little nervous. There wasn't anything *wrong* with what he was doing. But the other guys probably wouldn't understand. . . .

As far back as the Mercury program in the early 1960s, astronauts had carried small and easily transported items with them into space—toy space capsules, coins, even stamped envelopes that could be postmarked in space . . . items that would be worth a hell of a lot to collectors upon their return. This was a joint venture. It had been Slidell's idea to take something that might serve as a souvenir . . . and Kaminski's idea that the souvenir should be a flag, an American flag. He wore it day and night wrapped around his waist beneath his T-shirt, because if Knox or one of the other senior NCOs found it in his gear locker during an inspection, he'd be cleaning that lavatory cube all the way back to Earth, and likely they'd confiscate the flag, which would be worse. The idea was to have everyone sign it after the mission was over; Slidell claimed he knew a guy in San Diego who could put an artifact like that up for auction. God, a flag signed by fifteen or twenty of the Marines who'd actually been to Mars ought to fetch *thousands*. . . .

"All right, First Section!" Knox called out. "Hit the hatch!"

Making sure his M-29 ATAR assault rifle was securely strapped to his back, Kaminski joined the other Marines as they single-filed through the hatch and out to the transport pod. "Hey, Slider? What the hell do they want with US Marines on Mars, anyway?"

"Shit, why does the brass ever do anything?" Slidell replied. "To dump on the enlisted guy."

Which seemed as good an answer to Kaminski as any he'd heard so far.

THREE

Kaitlin Garroway took the second-floor door out of Herb Simon Hall onto the elwalk and headed for Schenley Park. Two exams down, three to go, plus her final project, and then she was off to Japan. She needed to work some more on her project this afternoon, but first she needed to clear her mind. After being closed up all morning, she was eager for the sight of trees and grass and blue sky.

The weather was something she really liked about Pittsburgh, the variety of the seasons, the spectacular explosion of fall colors, the sharp joy of spring after an icy winter. The dull sameness of the weather at Camp Pendleton in Southern California, where her dad had been stationed before his junket to Mars and where she'd lived before she entered college three years ago, had sometimes made her ready to scream. She laughed. Yukio thought she was nuts, but then his part of Japan was a lot like Southern California. Small wonder he hated the winters here.

Resting her hand lightly on the railing, she ran down

36

the steps from the elwalk to ground level and walked
down the hill into the park. What exactly did she feel
for Yukio? She'd liked him from the moment they'd met
last fall, in the Japanese Room of the International Center, and for the past few months, they'd been spending
more and more of their free time together. Kaitlin wasn't
scared of the words, "I love you," and had certainly
used them with Yukio, but did those words necessarily
imply a lifetime commitment? Was she *ready* for a lifetime commitment?

Maybe she didn't need to know. Maybe it was enough
to know that she loved him, that she enjoyed being with
him and talking with him about everything. Well, everything except politics, but then who *does* like to talk
about politics? Her parents had never agreed on politics—that's what her dad said, at any rate; her mother
had died before Kaitlin was politically aware—and they
got along beautifully. She and Yukio had just recently
started talking about the possibility of a long-term relationship, and now with their upcoming trip to Japan, she
found herself thinking about it a lot.

Yukio wanted to introduce her to his family, and she
knew enough about Japanese protocol to know what *that*
meant. She and Yukio both considered themselves to be
Internationalists, not in the sense of wanting the UN to
take over everything, but in the sense of being citizens
of the world. Would Yukio still feel that way if it came
to a choice between her . . . and his family? If his family
wouldn't accept her, would he be willing to live in the
States permanently? Come to think of it, suppose they
did accept her. Would *she* be willing to leave her country behind, to make a permanent home in Japan?

She shook her head. Too much serious thinking with
nothing in your stomach is a no-good way to make decisions. She really wished she could talk to her dad
about this, but somehow she hadn't been able to tell him
about Yukio, and she wasn't entirely sure why. She
hadn't even told him about the trip to Japan. Not that
she needed to, of course. She was of age, she had her
own passport, and she was paying for the trip out of

money she'd earned. But it had been a long time since she'd kept a secret from her father. She grinned. Usually the two of them kept secrets from others.

She reached her favorite tree, a sprawling black walnut, and sat down, first unhooking her PAD case from her hip belt. Taking her PAD out of its case, she carefully unfolded it and propped it up on her knees, keying it to download her v-mail. The usual departmental garbage—she'd have to check through it later to make sure she wasn't missing anything important. She still hadn't been able to write a filter good enough to catch everything she needed to see. She'd once accused Namir, the department head, of deliberately writing department memos so obscurely that a programmed filter wouldn't be able to extract the substance. "Well, if your filter isn't good enough, Kaitlin," he'd said with an irritating twinkle, "perhaps you'd better write one that is." Naturally, she'd risen to the challenge, but just as naturally, Namir had increased the obfuscatory nature of his memos. She grinned. She'd learned more about self-enhancing systems writing and rewriting those damned filters than she had in three years of classes. Namir's method was brutal, but it worked.

Hmm, what else? A few vids from friends, nothing critical. Nothing from Yukio, but that wasn't surprising. They'd planned to meet here after his exam, so the only reason for him to comm her would be to tell her that he couldn't make it. Notice of the Zugswang meeting tonight. She keyed in a reply, saying that she was planning on being there. A few games of chess would be the best preparation she could think of for her physics exam the next day. More study at this point would only fry her brain.

Ooh, great, a message from Dad. Kaitlin checked her wrist-top for the current time and then tapped a key to give her GMT, the Greenwich Mean Time that all spaceships and all space expeditions ran on. Only four hours difference now that Daylight Savings had kicked in, so it was late afternoon on the *Polyakov*. He mostly wrote her at night. When he wrote at other times, it was usually because he had something special to say, something beyond the trivia of day-to-day life aboard a cycler bound for Mars. She snorted. As if he didn't know full well that *anything* that happened on board the *Polyakov* was fascinating to her. She'd been space-happy since . . . since she didn't know how long. At least since she saw her first Vandenberg launch, but the genesis of her space fever was a lot earlier than that.

She remembered her mother reading to her a lot when she was little. Her dad had told her that a lot of the books her mother read to her were stories about spaceships and other planets and alien beings, books she later devoured for herself. Books by Heinlein and Asimov, Longyear and Brin, Zettel and Ecklar. It was infuriating. Here her dad was going off on a trip she'd give her eyeteeth for, not to mention certain other less mentionable parts, and *he didn't care*! He'd rather be on a beach in the Bahamas than on the sands of Mars! She was gonna have to comm that man a lecture. If he didn't learn to enjoy walking where no human had walked before . . . well, she wasn't sure what she'd do to him, but it wouldn't be pleasant, she could assure him of *that*.

She tapped on the vid icon on her PAD. It swelled and morphed into a waist-up view of a Marine major, with the stark gray wall of his hab behind him.

"The top o' the morning to you, Chicako," he said with a grin, "or whatever time it is when you see this." She grinned in return. The pet name her dad had given her when she was six and in love with everything Japanese meant "near and dear," and only he and Yukio were allowed to use it. "Well, it's been another exciting day in the old *Poly*, dodging asteroids and space pirates again. To keep from dying of boredom, I've actually resorted to some of those science-fiction books you gave me. The problem is, of course, that the realistic ones are boring and the unrealistic ones keep reminding me of how boring the real planet is likely to be. Take this one I've been reading lately, for instance." He held his PAD up in front of him. "*Red Planet* by that buddy of yours, Robert Heinlein."

Buddy of mine! Come on, Dad. He's been dead for fifty years.

"What I'm thinking is, if there were any aliens down there where we're going, like there are in that book, well, then this trip just might be worth something. But you know, Chicako, I just can't see that investigating rocks is worth the investment of thirty Marines. I can't help but feel that we're being used somehow." He shook his head and chuckled. "What am I talking about; of course, we're being used. We're supposed to be used. I guess what I mean is that we're not being used properly. We're not being used as a tool, we're being used as a pawn in some vast political game that I don't understand. But I can tell you, I don't like it."

He looked away for a long moment. "Something else I don't like," he said finally, turning back to face her. "This . . . uneasy dance we're doing with the UN. I know we have to let them use our cyclers by treaty, but why we're letting them horn in on our explorations on Mars is beyond me. Do they really think we'd hog all the goodies? I don't know."

"There's something that happened today I want to tell you about. It . . . it disturbed me, and I'm not entirely sure why. Maybe you can help me make some sense out of it. So long, Chicako. When next you see me, I'll be on the beach." His mouth twisted in a wry grin. "No ocean, unfortunately, but it'll be nice to have ground underfoot again. Till then." His face stayed on the screen for a full second and then dissolved into a string of numbers—the rest of his message was in code.

They'd started writing in code right after her mother died. A big, grown-up seven-year-old girl didn't really want to put down in writing that she was scared, that she missed her mommy, that she wished her daddy could be home with her instead of being stationed overseas. So her dad had taught her a simple substitution code so she could say all those things without anyone else knowing what she was saying.

Over the years their codes became more and more sophisticated, until now they were using a Beale code, guaranteed unbreakable without the book the code is based on. And that was the beauty of it. It could be any book; it was simply necessary that the two parties agree on the book and, specifically, on the edition of that book. For the Mars trip, the Garroways had agreed on a 2038 reprinting of *Shogun*, a twentieth-century novel about sixteenth-century Japan. Kaitlin had downloaded both the book and her own Beale code translation program to her dad's wrist-top before he'd left for Vandenberg.

Since then he'd used the Beale code routine for a part of just about every letter he'd sent her, but in the seven months that he'd been gone on the *Polyakov*, he'd only used it once or twice for more than a one- or two-liner. She paged down and estimated that, decoded, the message would probably run four or five paragraphs.

Kaitlin selected the text and ran her Beale code routine, wishing she could *talk* to him. V-mail was great, but there were still limitations. On the other hand, if he were here in person, he probably wouldn't talk about what was bothering him. He was a very private person. Maybe writing about whatever it was that had happened was the only way he could let it out.

As she began to read the translated text, she found herself growing cold. "Consorting with the enemy," he called it. Just because the woman was working for the UN? *What is this? It's not as though we're at war or anything.* She wondered what her father would think of her relationship with Yukio and was suddenly very glad she hadn't told him about her proposed trip to Japan.

A shadow fell over her PAD, and she looked up, startled. The backlit figure looming above her raised his hands in mock horror. "I didn't do it! Honest! Whatever it was, it wasn't me!"

She quickly tapped on the screen, hiding the message in the background. "Oh, it's just Dad," she said, as Yukio coiled down beside her.

"Ah."

Kaitlin folded up her PAD and tucked it back into its case. "And just what does 'ah' mean?" she asked.

He smiled. "It means that occasionally experiencing

a lack of harmony with one's paternal ancestor appears not to be an exclusively Japanese trait."

"Ah."

"Exactly." He began twining his fingers through her hair. "Have I mentioned lately that I love you, Chicako?"

She grinned. "Not since we got out of bed this morning, Snow Boy," she replied, using a rough translation of his name. She put her arms around his neck to greet him properly. "You're good for me, did you know that?"

"Mmm," he murmured as he responded warmly to her kiss. "You've said something about that a time or two before, I believe."

After a long moment, she pulled back. "You know, I'm kind of glad I stopped by the Japanese Room that day."

He nodded. "Me too. But we would have met eventually. It was fated."

Kaitlin looked quizzically at him. "Do you believe that? Do you really believe everything will work out for us?"

He turned very serious eyes toward her. "Those are two distinct questions, Kaitlin. Ones that do not necessarily have the same answer."

There was no response to make to that, so she made none. She knew what he meant; there was no point in going over it again. Instead she opened her belt pouch and pulled out the two quick-pak lunches she'd picked up earlier at the campus store.

"The landing is only a few days away now, isn't it?" Yukio asked as he produced two cold-bottles out of a hip pouch. He thumbed them open and handed one to her.

Kaitlin took a sip and then another. "Mmm, kiwi, that's good." She pressed a button on her wrist-top to check the calendar. "Yes. Three days. They should rendezvous with the landers Saturday morning."

"It is not a Japanese sentiment, but I . . . I envy

them.'' He tore off the lunch pack's lid and started to eat it.

Her mouth quirked in a wry grin. "It's funny, isn't it. Here the two of us are, dying to go into space. And there's my dad on his way to Mars, and he doesn't even want to be there! He keeps complaining about being bored!" She picked a processed seabar out of her lunch and started chewing on it.

"Is that what was . . . bothering you?"

She swallowed and took a deep breath. Might as well talk about it. "No. It was politics again. *Damn*, I hate politics!"

Yukio shrugged. "Politics is nothing more than two people trying to decide if they can share a bowl of rice, or if one of them will use his sword to ensure that all the rice is his. It is as much a part of being human as breathing."

"Well, then maybe being human ain't all it's cracked up to be. Why can't people just work together without all this stupid squabbling? Why can't we take care of each other instead of fighting over who gets the scraps?"

"It is not in our heritage to be kind to others when we haven't enough for ourselves. Altruism is not a survival trait, Kaitling."

She grinned at his deliberate mispronunciation of her name. Yukio was proud of his English, justifiably so, and this past year had delighted in adding English puns to his repertoire.

"Well, I'm not entirely sure what the bowl of rice is, in this case, but the guys with swords seem to be two of the archeologists. Actually, the problem seems to be that they're not using their swords but Dad thinks they should. I don't know. I think this metaphor is getting bent all out of shape." She finished up the seabar and started in on the edible packaging.

"There are lots more where that one came from."

She laughed. "Maybe I should just try to tell the story straight. Dad feels strongly that Americans should not be . . . intimate with UN personnel. In fact, he went so far as to call it 'consorting with the enemy.' Can you believe that?''

Yukio was silent for so long that she wondered if he'd heard her. "Yukio?''

He started. "I am sorry. I think my father would find your father's sentiment . . . not difficult to understand. There is considerable tension now concerning the possibilities of what may be discovered on Mars. I believe . . . I fear that it could lead to war.''

"But that's absurd! Whatever we find there, it's gonna take years to figure out even what it *is*, much less how we can use it! Why would we go to war over something like that?''

"Because people aren't always sensible, my love. Because a perceived advantage can be as strong a reason to fight as a real advantage.''

"What would Japan do? What does your father say?''

"If the UN and the US were at war?'' Yukio shook his head. "It is hard to say. We have treaty obligations to the United Nations, it is true . . . but my country is always loyal to itself first. I believe we will try to stay out of the fighting, if we can. I do not know what my father believes.''

"Well, maybe we can ask him in person next week.''

Yukio made no reply. Kaitlin let the silence drag on for a while, looking closely at him. Something was bugging him, but she knew better than to try to get anything out of him before he was ready to talk. He was a lot like her father in that respect. But she could sometimes get away with badgering her father when he was trying to keep things from her. If she did that with Yukio, he would just clam up even more.

"Kaitlin,'' he said finally. "I need to talk to you about our . . . proposed trip.''

Proposed? She'd thought it was settled. She clamped down on the questions she wanted to ask, giving Yukio the space to say things in his own way.

"I have received orders from the Space Defense Force. I must report to Tanegashima in twelve days.''

She was stunned. She'd known, of course, that Yukio

was technically in the military—he was here in the US, after all, to study the advanced electronics he needed as a space-aviation specialist—but he was supposed to be on a two-year study leave, or whatever they called it. They weren't supposed to suddenly call him back, not now when—

She stopped herself. *You're a grown woman, Kaitlin,* she told herself. *Start acting like one.*

"What's the reason for the sudden recall?" she asked in what she was delighted to hear was a calm voice. "Did they give any explanation?"

"My orders say merely that I am assigned to Tanegashima Space Base for a possible upgrade in my flight status. They don't even say how long I am expected to be there. But I received a vidmessage from my father. Because of his position with the government he frequently has access to information that is withheld from ordinary mortals. The impression I receive from his words is that this is a temporary assignment only, that I will be permitted to return here next fall to continue my studies. He implies that we are simply putting on a good face for our allies."

"Did you know that something like this might happen? I mean, I thought the deal was that you would complete your studies before going back into the service."

Yukio had finished his lunch, box and all. He picked up a small stone and began carving into the dirt at the base of the tree. "You say, 'going back into the service.' But, Kaitlin, I have never left. I am a *chu-i* in the Space Defense Force—you would say a 'lieutenant'—and I have always been under orders. I must follow those orders and fulfill my duty."

"Funny," she said, brandishing a dessert roll at him. "I always thought of you as chocolate creme, not *chu-i*."

Either he did not catch her pun, or he ignored it. He took a deep breath and looked straight at her. "We will have to cancel our trip, or at least postpone it. Perhaps you can come out later, when I know—"

"Why?"

Yukio looked startled, and then his face went cold and expressionless, and Kaitlin bit her lip. He seemed so Westernized, so . . . *American*, most of the time that she often forgot that he was still obedient to *shikata*, the way of doing things that is so distinctly Japanese. Interrupting a speaker when the two are equals was more than rude, it was disruptive of the *wa*, or harmony, that all Nihonjin strive for.

"*Sumimasen, Toshiyuki-san.*" She bowed her head, instinctively turning to Nihongo for her apology. The two of them spoke a mixture of English and Japanese with each other, but some things just didn't come out right in English. "*O-jama shimashita.*"

"*Daijobu, Chicako.*" He reached out and stroked her cheek. "I try to be open to Western ways, but sometimes I still just . . . react. After living here for a year I see much that is good in your openness, in your willingness to try new things, to change, but I find sometimes that I am still tied to the old ways. And the old ways must change if we are to take advantage of all the future has to offer."

"But there is good in the old ways, Yukio."

He nodded. "Yes. We must find a way to continue the growth of the past one hundred years without losing that which makes us what we are. It is . . . difficult.

"When we planned this trip, it was with the understanding that we would be traveling together, that I would introduce you to my family, yes, but also that I would show you around the country. This I can no longer do. I will probably be free from duty most evenings, but Tanegashima is six hundred kilometers from Kyoto. Even traveling by hydrofoil and maglev, it would be impossible for me to come home for anything less than a weekend."

"But couldn't I meet you there?" Kaitlin countered. She polished off the last of her package and washed it down with a slug of kiwi drink. "You're right, it's a long way from Kyoto, but your home's not the only possibility. If I couldn't actually go to the base, maybe

I could meet you at Kagoshima or Miyazaki. There are probably youth hostels there, same as there are in Kyoto.''

"But still I would be working, and I do not even know if I will have evenings or weekends off."

"When do you have to report? What day?"

"A week from Monday."

"Well, then we'd still have three days together, I'd get to meet your parents, your family, and after that . . . You seem to have forgotten that I have my own reasons for wanting to go to Japan."

Yukio picked up his stone again and continued his scraping. "You truly wouldn't object to being on your own in my country?"

She raised one eyebrow. "Is my Nihongo that bad?"

He grinned and tossed the stone at her. "You speak it fluently, and you know it."

"Precisely. So we leave next Thursday as planned. Right?"

"One final question. These are . . . dangerous times. Do you really think it will be safe for you to travel to a country allied with the UN?"

"The idea of war over Mars is ridiculous, Yukio. Mexico, I'll grant you, is a problem, with the Aztlan question and everything, but even if that flares up, I can't see Geneva putting Japanese troops on American soil to deal with it. Look, I know our countries are technically on different sides, but Japan has resisted the UN-sanctioned embargoes. We're still trade partners. I just can't see that there would be a problem. It's not as though we're talking about going to Colombia or France!"

Yukio shook his head. "I did not want to prevent you from going to Japan, but I wanted to make sure that you knew what the situation was."

Kaitlin grinned. "Yukio, my love, you couldn't have kept me from going to Japan if you'd tried, and that's not my Western individualism talking. That's *money* talking. Maybe rich kids like you can contemplate with equanimity losing a couple thousand bucks on a canceled SCRAMjet fare, but *I* can't. I've been saving up for a trip to Japan ever since I was old enough to rake leaves, and I'm gonna be on that Star Raker next Thursday, whether you're there or not.''

FOUR

United States Embassy
Mexico City, República de
México
1453 hours local time

Sergeant Gary Bledsoe, USMC, stood at his sandbag-
encircled post on the portico outside the Embassy
Residence, watching uneasily as the crowds gathered in
the plaza beyond the front gate. Many carried signs,
some in Spanish, most—displayed for the reporters and
vidcams—in English. YANQUIS HANDS OFF MARS! one
read. ALIEN TREASURES ARE FOR ALL! read another.
Some of the demonstrators evidently were voicing their
support for Aztlan, an Hispanic homeland to be carved
out of Mexico's northernmost states—and the US Southwest. Tensions with Mexico had been at the boiling
point since 2038, ever since the UN declared a plebiscite
to be held in August of this year; the United States had
already announced that it was not signatory to the agreement that had called for a vote on independence within
its own territorial boundaries.

Occasionally, a rock or bit of garbage sailed over the
high stone wall that fenced off the embassy compound.
Someone, Bledsoe could hear, was haranguing the

49

crowd in Spanish over a shrill and feedback-prone PA. He couldn't tell what was being said, but the crowd evidently approved, judging from the full-throated roar that followed each emphatic statement.

"Man, what's bitin' them?" Corporal Frank Larabee, standing at Bledsoe's side, said nervously.

"What's the matter? Don't you download the netnews?" Bledsoe said, his tone bantering. "They're afraid we're out to loot the Ancients' ruins on Mars and get all the good stuff for ourselves."

"Yeah? So what's that got to do with *us*?"

"The Ugly American, guy. Haven't you heard? We're getting uglier every day."

"Ugly?" Larabee patted his M-29 assault rifle. "I'll show 'em ugly."

"Easy there, Bee," Gary said. "I haven't heard a weapons-free, yet. You just be damn certain your toy's clean."

Both Marines were wearing their Class-Threes, lowtech, camouflaged helmets and kinevlar torso armor. Normally, of course, they'd have been in their Class-As, the full-dress blues with red-and-white trim that had been the uniform of Marines on embassy guard duty for well over a century now, but as the Mexican crisis had exploded into this ongoing riot, the orders had come down to go to battle dress.

The orders had also allowed them to carry loaded weapons, though they still had to wait for a release order to lock and load or open fire, even if they were fired on first. For a while there, a couple of weeks ago, the embassy Marines had been going around with unloaded rifles. The joke going the rounds at the time had been that the boxy, plastic M-29s weren't properly shaped to serve as decent clubs, so if a Marine was attacked, his best bet was to give his rifle to his attacker, then kick the bastard in the kneecap while he was still trying to figure out how the adtech weapon worked.

The M-29 ATAR, or advanced-technology assault rifle, was a direct-line descendent of the German-made G-11s of the last century, firing a 4.5mm ablative sabot caseless round with a muzzle velocity of over a kilo-meter and a half per second. With each bullet embedded in a solid, rectangular block of propellant, there was no spent brass with each shot, and no open ejection port to foul with dirt, sand, or mud. The weapon was loaded by snapping a plastic box containing one hundred rounds into the loading port in the butt, a "bullpup" design that resulted in a rifle only seventy centimeters long and weighing just four kilos. The '29 looked like a blocky, squared-off plastic toy with a cheap telescope affixed to the top and a pistol grip on the bottom . . . which was why the men and women who carried them referred to the weapons as their toys.

The caseless ammo was both the M-29's greatest strength and its biggest weakness. The lack of shell cas-ings to feed through an ejection port gave the rifle an incredibly high cyclic rate of twenty-five hundred rounds per minute, so fast that a three- or five-round burst could have the bullets on their way and dead on-target before the recoil had affected the shooter's aim. On the down-side, though, the firing chamber was easily fouled by chemical residues from the propellant blocks. The weapon used a clean-burning propellant, but there was always some gunk left over when it burned, and without an ejection port or shell casings, that gunk built up fast . . . fast enough to degrade the rifle's performance after only a couple of mags.

The Corps, which lived by the rule that the rifle was the whole reason there was a Marine in the first place, met this weakness with typical directness. Every Marine took a perfectionist's care of his weapon, learning to field-strip and clean it under the most extreme and dan-gerous of conditions, to do it fast, and to do it right. "Aw, he's got shit up his chamber" was by now well-established Marine slang for someone who didn't know what was what, who hadn't gotten the word, or who didn't know what the hell he was doing.

"She's clean, Sarge," Larabee said, replying to Bled-soe's warning. "Clean enough to eat off of. Uh-oh. Heads up."

Bledsoe turned to check the direction in which Larabee was looking. Captain Theodore Warhurst was emerging from the Residence. "Atten . . . *hut!*"

"As you were, men," Warhurst snapped. Like Bledsoe and Larabee, he wore fatigues, vest armor, and an old-style coal-scuttle helmet with a cloth camouflage cover. A service issue M-2020 pistol was secured to his combat vest in a shoulder-holster rig. "What's the word?"

"Natives are gettin' restless, Captain," Bledsoe said. He gestured toward the embassy's front gate, less than twenty meters away. "I don't hablo the Español, much, but it sounds to me like that guy with the microphone is getting them pretty riled up."

"Intel IDed that guy as a local SUD preacher. He could be trouble."

"Man," Larabee said. "*That's* all we need."

The *Solamente Uno Dios* was one of the noisier and more bitter factions competing for attention in the Federal District these days. Formed as part of the backlash against the myriad new religions and groups devoted to worshiping the Ancients as gods, the SUD was a startlingly unlikely coalition of Baptists, Pentacostals, and a few Catholics who found common cause in their belief that God, not aliens, had created Mankind and that the alien artifacts discovered on Mars should be left strictly alone. There were some things, SUD spokespersons declared every time a television or netnews camera was pointed in their direction, that Man simply was not meant to know, and other things that were explained so clearly in the Bible, thank you, that no further explanation was needed. There'd been several bloody clashes during the past few days between the SUD and some of the pro-Ancients groups, the International Ancient Astronaut Network and *Las Alienistas*, in particular.

Now, it seemed, the local SUDs were getting ready to take on the US Embassy.

"Just wanted to let you guys know," Warhurst said, keeping his eyes on the crowd beyond the high wall. "We're evacuating. Closing up shop and pulling out."

"Evacuating!" Bledsoe said, startled.

"That's what they tell me. We're passing the word in person, though, so our friends out there can't listen in on our platoon freaks. We've got Perries inbound now from the *Reagan*."

"All *right*," Larabee said. "About time we got clear of this shithole."

"What's it mean, Captain?" Bledsoe asked. "War?"

"Shit. You'll know when I know, Sergeant."

"Yeah, but *Peregrines*. I mean, are they fighting their way through Mexican airspace, or what?"

"I guess we'll find out when they get here, won't we?"

"If they get here," Larabee put in.

Warhurst chuckled. "We're talking TR-5s, Sergeant. Probably with Valkyries on CAP. They'll get here. I don't think the whole Mexican Air Force has anything more modern than a couple dozen old F/A-22s.

"In any case, Major Bainbridge wants you men to be on your toes. Those Peregrines' ETA is in another twenty minutes or so . . . and when they set down, the crowd could get a bit . . . eager."

"We'll be ready, sir." Bledsoe slapped the side of his ATAR for emphasis, a sharp crack of palm on plastic.

"I know you will. Carry on, Marines." He turned and disappeared into the Residence.

"Hey, Bled. Is it true what they say about that guy?"

"About him bein' the commandant's son? Sure is. I got the straight shit from Dolchik in Personnel."

"I'll be damned. He's not a bad sort, for the son of God."

"Well, I'll tell you. I'd rather have him at my back in a firefight than some of these new-Corps pukes."

"Roger that." They listened for several minutes more to the speech barking from the speakers outside the embassy walls. A final pronouncement sent the crowd wild, cheering and screaming and swearing and shouting, until Bledsoe thought they must be planning to knock down the walls by sheer volume alone. Another volley of garbage hurtled over the fence, bouncing and scattering across the lawn beneath one of the compound's spreading cypress trees but coming nowhere near the two Marines and their sandbag-barricaded post.

Bledsoe slung his rifle—with the crisis on, they were not required to remain rigidly at attention, soldiers on parade, as they would have been otherwise—and pulled his PAD out of the thigh pocket in his fatigue pants. When he touched the wake-up key, a keyboard and a display screen winked on, and he began tapping at the unyielding flat surface.

"Whatcha doin'?" Larabee asked.

"Linking in to the security net," Bledsoe replied. Several perimeter camera views were available over the general embassy net. "Ah. Here we go."

His PAD's display screen flickered from the logo of the embassy's local server to a low-res, real-time image shot from one of the small security cameras perched atop the compound wall. The scene looked out across the Paseo de la Reforma, Mexico City's Great White Way, a broad and skyscraper-lined boulevard that was now smothered in a seething, shifting mass of humanity. A short distance up the road, El Angel stood gracefully on her pedestal, a towering monument to Mexican independence; a dozen men had swarmed up her base to a vantage point well above the heads of the crowd. Beyond, the elegant but aging facade of the Maria Isabel Sheraton was nearly lost behind the surging mob.

Several rocks clattered off the embassy gate.

"Get a load of this," Bledsoe said, handing the PAD to Larabee. He pointed to the display. The security camera had clearly picked up a number of Mexican soldiers—in full battle gear—gathered in a small group in front of the Sheraton Hotel.

"Are they watching the mob?" Larabee wanted to know. "Or getting ready to join in?"

"Damfino," Bledsoe replied. "Maybe they don't know either. They might be there just to make sure the rocks don't get thrown at Mexican property."

"Yeah, but if a few gringos get dinged up, no big deal, right?"

Bledsoe set the PAD on top of the sandbag barricade and unslung his assault rifle. He didn't like the looks of that crowd—too many tough-looking and angry young men, and no women or children visible at all. If this was really a spontaneous demonstration, like the local sources had been saying, he would have expected to see a more broadly distributed mix representing the local demographics.

Not something that looked more like an army than a mob of demonstrators. . . .

United States Embassy
Mexico City, República de
México
1512 hours local time

"Come in."

Captain Theodore Warhurst opened the door and entered the large room—all deep carpets and oak paneling and framed photographs and oils—that was the office of Franklin R. Tibbs, the United States ambassador to Mexico. The scene inside was one of quiet, almost deliberate confusion, as aides transferred stacks of papers from gaping filing cabinets into boxes and piled them up. As Warhurst approached the desk, three more undersecretaries came into the room, hurried past him, and collected several of the boxes; the shredding machines down the hall were working continuously now, reducing American diplomatic secrets to unrecoverable confetti.

It was a curious statement about the culture, Warhurst thought, that government bureaucracies still depended on vast quantities of hard copy to keep their records and pass their orders, despite the omnipresence of computer systems that made such wholesale deforestation unnecessary.

Ambassador Tibbs, a heavy, florid man in a neatly tailored gray suit, was packing jewel boxes into his attaché case. Each small, flat box securely held a neatly ordered array of twelve CMC microdrives. The size of a pencil eraser, each color-coded computer memory clip looked, in fact, like a small jewel and was far more precious; a single CMC carried half a gig of storage.

"Hello, Captain," Tibbs said, looking up. His normally jovial features were sagging, his face creased and heavy. "You talk to your people?"

"Sir!" Warhurst said, coming to attention before the desk. "Yes, sir!"

"Aw, knock off the kay-det crap, Ted. Whatcha got for me?"

Warhurst allowed his rigid posture to relax, but only a little. He'd been gung ho, been *raised* gung ho, all of his life, and the ingrained training of a lifetime could not be easily discarded.

"The transport will be here in another few minutes, Mr. Ambassador," he said. "It'll touch down on the roof heliport. I'd like you to be on the first aircraft out."

Tibbs winced. "I wish we . . . we didn't have to do this. But my orders . . ."

"I don't see that we have any choice, sir."

Warhurst could tell that Tibbs was hurting, that he literally didn't know what to do next. A friend and confidant of three American presidents, the man had been assistant secretary of labor during Kerrey's second term, and secretary of state under Wood until his retirement in '35. Markham had appointed him ambassador to Mexico as a reward for years of service and generous campaign contributions.

He didn't look like he felt very rewarded at the moment. "I just . . . don't know how it came to this," he said, his voice so soft that no one in the room could have heard him but Warhurst.

"I'm sure there wasn't anything anyone could have done," Warhurst replied. "God knows, you've been in there pitching. Sir."

"I'm beginning to think those fanatics out there are right. We should leave that stuff on Mars where we found it. Of *course* it makes other countries nervous when it looks like we might try to grab it all for ourselves."

"That's not my department, sir," Warhurst replied carefully. He thought that Tibbs wanted to talk, that he was trying to relieve himself of some hard-to-discuss burden, but Warhurst had never been a particularly social man and didn't know how best to respond. "But it seems to me pretty senseless just to pretend there's nothing there. And if we can develop aldetech, well, everybody's gonna benefit."

Aldetech. Alien-derived technology. The word had been coined nearly a decade before to describe the expected commercial and industrial spin-offs from the fragments of lost technology discovered at Cydonia.

"You're right, of course," Tibbs said, nodding. "And if it wasn't us, it would be somebody else. The Japanese, maybe. Or the EU. They both have pretty aggressive space programs and could get to Mars by themselves in another few years, if they wanted to." He waved toward the office's windowless wall, in the general direction of the crowds outside. "It just seems to be such a fuss over, over *nothing*, really. It's not like we're threatening them, is it?"

"Well, it's always something, isn't it, sir? If it wasn't the UN afraid we were gonna grab the aldetech for ourselves, it would be Aztlan and the plebiscite." He made a face. "Or our refusal to disarm and become nice, docile members of the global family."

Tibbs sagged, the hopelessness of his situation, the *failure* clear in his eyes. Warhurst felt sorry for the man. He'd never liked Tibbs personally, and he certainly didn't share the man's politics, which leaned toward globalism and the new Internationalism more than he cared for. When President Markham had decided to take a tough, anti-Internationalist stance last year, defying the UN and their plebiscite and sending a Marine section to Mars to protect American interests there, he'd left many of the globalist and pro-UN people in the government dangling, especially in State, where the Internationalist influence had always been strongest.

As a member of the United States Armed Forces, as a Marine, Warhurst could have his own opinions about politics but couldn't take sides ... not publicly, not officially. If Tibbs was looking for forgiveness, understanding, or even simply a sympathetic ear, he wasn't gonna find it in the Embassy Guard detail. Still, Warhurst could sympathize with the man's impossible position, believing one thing, forced to carry out orders derived from an entirely different philosophy, and then being caught in the resultant back-blast.

"Anyway," Warhurst added, "you did all you could do. All *anyone* could expect."

Tibbs nodded, though Warhurst wasn't sure how much he'd heard. *Don't fold on me now, Ambassador,* he thought. *We're not out of this yet. Not by a long shot!*

"Do you need any more help here, sir? I can send up a couple of men."

"No, Captain," Tibbs said, straightening. "No. We're almost done."

Warhurst heard a sound, a distant, hollow thud, followed by something that might have been the popping of firecrackers muffled by walls and distance. "Okay," he said. "I'll send for you when we have the transports in sight. Meanwhile, sir, stay away from the windows. Stay away from any of the outer walls."

He turned and hurried from the room.

United States Embassy
Mexico City, República de
México
1518 hours local time

"Shit!" Larabee said. "Here they come!"

Bledsoe didn't need the warning. He was already on one knee, his M-29 braced atop the sandbag barricade as he covered the embassy compound's wall. A number of Mexicans, mostly young men, teenagers, in fact, were swarming up the wall and clambering across the top.

Some of them had guns.

"Outfield, this is Homeplate" crackled from Bledsoe's in-ear speaker. He keyed the transceiver attached to his combat rig. "Homeplate, Outfield. Go!" he replied.

"Weapons free. Repeat, weapons free!"

"Uh . . . copy 'weapons free.' Damn it, some of these guys are just kids!"

One of the attackers, straddling the wall, raised an old Armalite rifle to his shoulder and fired, the round shrieking off the bricks of the Residence a few feet behind Bledsoe's head. He shifted aim slightly and squeezed the trigger on his M-29, a light touch only that loosed a quick, three-round burst, exploding the gunman's chest before the recoil had time to kick the weapon up and back in his hands. The man pinwheeled back off the wall in a spray of scarlet. More gunshots, from the upper floors of buildings across the street, probed the Residence.

"Kids my ass!" Larabee growled. He fired his ATAR in short, precisely controlled bursts, knocking several more attackers off the wall. The yells and imprecations and shrieks from the crowd outside—shrieks of pain and of white-hot fury—grew louder and more shrill. He sprayed a long burst across the top of the wall, the sound like the riffling of a deck of plastic cards, but far louder. The high-velocity stream of rounds sent fragments of stone and bullet into the arms and faces of the attackers still clinging to the top.

Then they heard the growling of heavy armor, the rumble and clank of tanks moving down the street toward the embassy.

FIVE

FRIDAY, 11 MAY

Rattlesnake One
TR-5 Peregrine transport/
gunship
Inbound, east of Mexico City,
República de México
1519 hours local time

"Snakebite, this is Basket. Excalibur. I say again, Excalibur."

Lieutenant Carmen Fuentes, US Marine Corps, pressed her hand against her Mark III helmet, pressing its left speaker harder against her ear, trying to hear above the shrill whine of the TR-5 Peregrine's jets. "Basket, Snakebite," she replied over her helmet com. "Authenticate force release."

"Snakebite, Basket," the voice in her ear said again. "Authenticate Bravo-delta-delta-one-seven. Excalibur. I say again, Excalibur."

The release code and the word "Excalibur" were also glowing in green letters, winking on and off against the message display in the lower right corner of her helmet's HUD, the confirmation she'd been waiting for. Things had just turned nasty in Mexico City, and First Platoon, Alfa Company, was headed for a hot LZ.

Fuentes turned in her seat and caught the eyes of the rest of her platoon. They were all suited up in Class-Two armor, which made them look a bit like astronauts in EVA hardsuits . . . except that these suits used an active camo surface layer that mimicked the colors and shadows and light sources around them in an eerie shifting of ill-shaped reflections. The only thing Class-One had that Class-Two didn't, in fact, was the bulky full-support backpack that turned it into a space suit in fact as well as in appearance. She couldn't read the faces behind the dark helmet visors on either side of the Peregrine's troops compartment, but she knew every man and woman in the section was watching her intently.

"It's a go, Marines," she told them over her helmet's com system. "Mexican forces have opened fire on our people at the embassy. Basket has just relayed the codeword Excalibur. We go in, and we go in hot."

She'd been pretty sure that they would get the go-ahead this time. Fifteen minutes earlier, the Peregrine's pilot had alerted her that Mexican Air Force F/A-22s had tried to intercept them over the coast, and only the Marine AV-32s flying CAP on Operation Rattlesnake had stopped them from pulling an intercept. Maybe those F/A-22s had been ordered to simply escort the intruders out of Mexican airspace . . . but Fuentes didn't think so. The Mexicans had been getting cocky of late, certain that the entire United Nations was behind them in their dispute with the US, and they must have known that the only way to stop the relief flight was to shoot it down.

But that shooting would take some doing. Rattlesnake Flight consisted of four Peregrines and an escort of four Marine AV-32s, superb VSTOL fighters derived from the Harrier jump jets of the last century. All of the aircraft had stealth technology, and all had sophisticated antimissile defenses. There was a good chance that they would be into the Mexican capital and out again before the Mexican air-defense net could even get them pinpointed.

"So what do you think, Lieutenant?" Corporal Steve

Bellamy asked over the section's chat channel. "Is it gonna be war?"

"That," Fuentes replied with a singular lack of interest, "is up to the politicians."

Fuentes herself was about as apolitical as it was possible to be . . . but she hated the fact that some people had questioned her allegiance, and for no better reason than the ethnic origins of her name. She happened to be the daughter of legal Mexican immigrants, born in San Diego, California, and as far as she was concerned—at least until and unless the UN Aztlan plebiscite went through—that made her an American.

Hell, if the Southwestern US was suddenly torn away to become a new country, she wasn't gonna go with it. She'd already made up her mind to stay in the Corps and resettle wherever they sent her. She didn't like thinking about the rumor—an ugly possibility—that all Hispanics would be forced out of the US Armed Forces if that happened, or that they might even lose their citizenship. She was pretty sure that the other Hispanics in her platoon—Garcia, Ortega, and Carle—all felt the same.

In a way, she welcomed this current crisis with Mexico. It gave her an opportunity to show everyone just where her loyalties truly lay. She'd found it interesting as she thought about the problem over these past few days, however, that her primary loyalties weren't to the United States of America, though she considered herself a patriot and was willing to put her life on the line for her country.

Her main loyalties were to her brother and sister Marines.

She used the utility wrist-top jacked into her armor's dataport to open a window on her HUD's data display. Channel four showed a computer-generated map of the region northeast of the Mexico DF. The aerial relief flotilla had already cleared the Sierra Madre Oriental, flying nap-of-the-Earth up the Nautla Valley, then hurtling low across the plains of Tlaxcala. They were over Texcoco Lake now, hurtling toward downtown Mexico City at better than four hundred knots. Eighteen kilometers to go—at this speed, less than two minutes more.

"Everybody check your gear!" she called. "Ninety seconds!" She wished the Peregrine had a window so that she could see out . . . but, of course, every square centimeter possible of the aircraft's hull was coated in radar-absorbing polymers. She watched as each Marine in the platoon checked the armor and ordnance of the Marine at his or her left, then repeated the inspection to the right. Gunnery Sergeant Christopher Walsh checked her over, making certain that external armor snaps were locked, that grenades were secure, that she didn't have any "Irish pennants"—loose straps or cords dangling where they could hang up and trap her. Then she returned the favor.

"Nervous, Lieutenant?" Walsh asked her on the private channel.

"Hell, yes," she replied. It was her first time in combat, and Walsh knew that.

"Good," he replied, and she could just make out his grin through his dark helmet visor. "If you were sure of yourself, I'd request a transfer out of this outfit, effective yesterday. Don't worry, L-T. You'll show 'em!"

She was grateful that he hadn't patronized her with a "you'll do fine," and more grateful still that he recognized the spot she was in. Hell, in another couple of minutes, she might find herself shooting at her relatives.

But that was because they were shooting at her *family.* . . .

United States Embassy
Mexico City, República de
México
1520 hours local time

The Mexican civilians had stopped coming over the wall now; in fact, as far as Bledsoe could tell, all of the civilians had scattered and fled after those first few volleys. Bledsoe was still on his knees next to Larabee, bracing his ATAR on the sandbag wall, drawing a bead on a scrawny guy wearing officer's epaulets who seemed to be waving the attackers on from the far side of the barred front gate. He squeezed off another burst and watched the man tumble backward onto bloody pavement.

The initial rush had been beaten back, but the attack was far from over. Something large was growling unseen on the street beyond the gate, ominous and implacable. Moments later, an old Bradley AFV lumbered around the corner, striking the closed gate in a piercing clash and rattle of metal bars. A second M-2 Bradley followed the first . . . and a third.

"Christ!" Larabee yelled above the din. "They're sending in the whole frigging Mex army!"

A rotary cannon on the lead Bradley howled, its muzzle flash a flickering beacon on the turret. Both Marines hit the deck as brick and sandbag alike were pulverized by the stream of heavy metal. To the right of the main gate, a portion of the wall burst inward in a crashing shower of brick. The squat, hulking shape grinding through the breach was no Bradley, however, but an M1A2, one of the old Abrams tanks sold to the Mexicans twenty years before.

Abrams and Bradleys might be laughably obsolete by modern standards, but they were still deadly. Neither of the Marines was packing weapons that could challenge that kind of armor.

Reaching up, Bledsoe touched the transmit key on the Motorola strapped to his vest. "Homeplate, this is Outfield!" he called. "We've got heavy armor here, and they're knockin' on the goddamn front door!"

"Copy that, Outfield," a calm voice replied. It sounded like Captain Warhurst. "We see them. You can't do anything more out there. Come on inside."

"Rog—"

The world exploded. The Abrams had just fired its main gun, and the round had crashed into the front of the Residence and detonated somewhere inside, behind the front door. Bledsoe and Larabee, both already flat on the front porch, were lifted several feet and slammed against their crumbling sandbag barricade.

Groping through the swirling smoke, Bledsoe looked around for Larabee. The sandbags had been scattered as though kicked by a playful giant; Larabee lay on his back where the blast had flung him, off the porch, down the steps, and several yards out into the Residence front lawn. The front of the Residence itself, never designed to take such punishment, had partially collapsed, a jagged tangle of brick and beam and splintered wood, licked about with flame. The upper stories and the rear of the large mansion were intact, but a few more direct hits by that tank and the whole structure was gonna come tumbling down.

Mexican troops were spilling from the three Bradleys now, troops better equipped than the civilians in the first wave had been, with modern assault rifles and kinevlar vests similar to what Bledsoe and Larabee were wearing. Gunfire popped and chattered; Bledsoe groped for his ATAR, dropped when the Abrams had fired, and knocked down three or four running figures. The smoke was getting thicker now, and it was difficult to acquire and hold a target. The full-auto fire from the wrecked front of the building seemed to be making the attackers cautious.

But they would be charging across the lawn and up the steps of the Residence any second now.

Bledsoe knew he didn't have much time.

Rattlesnake One
TR-5 Peregrine transport/
gunship
Mexico City, República de
México
1521 hours local time

''Landing alert, Lieutenant!'' sounded in Fuentes's headset. ''Thirty seconds!'' She could feel the transport's nose coming up, could feel the change in pitch of the engines as they rotated to their straight-up, hover position.

"Roger that," she replied.

"We can see the embassy now," the Peregrine's pilot added. "Looks like there's a lot of shooting going on down there."

Her pulse raced. Had war broken out officially, or was this just another "incident," the kind that left widows and cripples in its wake? Had the Mexicans really been stupid enough to try a toe-to-toe slugfest with the United States?

Maybe they thought that with UN backing, they could win.

She punched in a combination on her wrist-top, then studied the low-res vid-feed from the TR-5's nose camera as it flickered in pale black and white on her helmet display. The embassy's broad, rooftop helipad was visible at the center of the picture; one of the AV-32s swept past her view from right to left, circling low, dropping smoke canisters that erupted in a dense, boiling gray-white fog around the embassy perimeter. There might be snipers nearby packing firepower heavy enough to bring down a Peregrine, and the smoke would hamper them when they tried to find a target. It would also screw up the enemy's laser range finders. There was already a hell of a lot of smoke in the area; it looked like the front of the Residence might be on fire.

Two of the Peregrines, moving according to plan, were making for the helipad, where they would start taking off the embassy's civilian staff. While a third circled the compound providing gunship support, the one carrying Fuentes's platoon would deposit them in the compound between the Residence and the front gate. They would hold the embassy until all of the civilians were away, then hightail it back for their transports and haul-tail for the Gulf of Campeche.

"Snakebite, Basket. Be advised that we have hostile MBTs and AFVs in the AO." A side window opened on the display, showing a freeze-frame image from a military satellite, looking down onto the embassy compound. Several vehicles were highlighted by winking red dots.

"Roger that." Tanks and troop carriers. Things were a bit more complicated than they'd expected. Just *frigging great*!

But then, she thought, main battle tanks were why God had invented Marine air close-ground support.

United States Embassy
Mexico City, República de
México
1521 hours local time

Bledsoe looked up as jet engines howled low out of the sky. The sheer relief, the *release* when he saw two Valkyrie AV-32 hoverjets sweeping low across the rooftops, sunlight glinting from their canopies, was enough to leave him weak and shaking. "Yeah!" he screamed at the sky. "Go! Go!"

The turrets of the Bradleys were pivoting to meet this new threat, but they were having trouble connecting with the targets. Vals were hard to see, even in broad daylight. Their active-camo hull coatings mimicked the surrounding colors of the sky almost as well as they absorbed radar, and with no vertical stabilizers on the flat upper surface, there was very little to catch the eye. When they dropped down low and started a head-on pass, they all but vanished, even if you knew exactly where to look.

The attack had at least distracted the Mexican troops for a few, precious moments. Bledsoe snatched at the chance, rising from his hiding place, sprinting across the scattering of sandbags, and throwing himself down across Larabee's still form.

Larabee was still alive and breathing, though he had a nasty gash down the side of his head, and blood was pumping from a neat, round hole in his thigh, just above his left knee. Bledsoe grabbed an M1 first-aid kit and fumbled it open, extracting a sterile gauze pad and stuffing it onto the wound, trying to stop the bleeding.

Then the Bradley AFVs opened fire with their rotary cannons, hosing the sky with streams of red tracers, trying to drag down the oncoming Vals. Bledsoe never even saw the Valkyries return fire; the armored fighting vehicles simply began exploding in a quick one-two-three succession, flame and jagged black chunks of metal whirling into the air. Another blast rocked the Mexican tank. The concussions were deafening; Bledsoe covered Larabee with his own body, sheltering him as the explosions thundered and the Marine Valkyries streaked overhead.

He looked up, blinking into swirling smoke. Two more Vals were circling in the distance, as a quartet of TR-5 Peregrines angled in toward the Residence.

Time to get the hell out of Dodge. Rolling off his buddy, he gathered the unconscious Larabee into a fireman's carry and started crawling back toward the embassy's shattered front porch.

Rattlesnake Flight
TR-5 Peregrine transport/
gunship
Mexico City, República de
México
1521 hours local time

In a swirling blast of deflected exhaust, two of the Peregrine gunships brought their noses up, tilt-jets howling as they swung to the upright, hover position, the aircraft barely moving as they drifted above the city streets in front of the embassy. A shoulder-launched rocket streaked skyward from the roof of the Sheraton; the aircraft's active antimissile defense system, reacting with a computer's superhuman speed, replied before the missile had traveled half the distance to the target, snapping back with a burst of radar-guided rotary cannon fire that detonated the SAM in an orange-black blossom of flame and smoke. The gunship's main battery cut loose then, its Zeus high-speed cannon buzz-sawing into the roof of the structure with a cyclic rate of six thousand rounds per minute. Under that firestorm of depleted uranium penetrators mingled with 6.2mm high-explosive rounds and green tracers in a 7:2:1 ratio, the roof of the hotel literally disintegrated in a black cloud of whirling chips and fragments. Windows exploded, walls buckled, and much of the upper two stories of the structure crumbled into an avalanche of shattered masonry, glass, and stucco. The line of green tracers, so thick and solid-seeming it appeared to be a bright streak of dazzling green light, played briefly across the target zone, then winked out.

The tilt-jet Peregrines pivoted slowly, like hovering, airborne dragons searching for prey. Most of the mob had dispersed by now, though a number of bodies sprawled motionless in the streets or crawled slowly for imagined places of safety. Three AFVs and a heavy tank were burning in front of the embassy. A second aging M1A2 grumbled from a side street, seeking shelter from the air attacks, perhaps, but the green bolt of solid-looking flame flared once more, touching the Abrams's turret at the engine cover. The fireball as the fuel tanks detonated roiled into the crystalline blue mountain air above the city like a black death's-head.

The Peregrines continued to take small-arms fire from the surrounding buildings. It looked as though most of the buildings had, in fact, been occupied by Mexican troops, though the Peregrine gunners were under orders not to initiate a slaughter of Mexico City's general population. They responded to the most serious threats, blocking incoming missiles and sending bursts of high-velocity cannon fire back at the shooters.

Enemy fire slacked off noticeably as the Mexican troops decided to stop calling attention to themselves.

Rattlesnake One
Mexico City, República de
México
1521 hours local time

Aboard the Peregrine, a red light winked on overhead.
"On target," the pilot's voice said in Fuentes's headset.
"Opening up!" With a growling whine, the Peregrine's
aft ramp cracked open, then lowered, admitting a blaze
of blue-white light from the outside.

There wasn't room to land a Peregrine on the Residence's front lawn. Instead, as the rear door eased open,
the aircraft's crew tossed four nylon ropes out the back;
almost immediately, the first four armored Marines were
fast-roping down the lines, hitting the ground hard and
moving fast, clearing the area before the next man down
the line hit the same spot. Fuentes followed Private Pe-
terson, stepping off the ramp and sliding down the rope
with practiced ease. The ride down was dizzying, with
the Peregrine hanging like a vast, black whale just above
their heads, the tilt-jets shrieking to left and right like
demented banshees.

Fuentes landed with pile-driver force, nearly sinking
to her knees, but then she was diving ahead, getting clear
before Gunny Walsh landed on her shoulders. She didn't
remember slapping the release on her M-29, but her rifle
was in her gloved hands and the liquid-crystal readout
on the stock showed a full load of one hundred rounds,
ready to rock and roll. She didn't see any immediate
targets; a Mex tank was burning cheerfully in a smashed-
out gap in the compound wall to her right; the smoking,
flame-blackened shells of a trio of Bradley AFVs were
scattered along the embassy's front drive farther on.

Near the front door of the embassy, she saw one Marine crawling with another man slung across his back.
"Bellamy! Kelly! Sanderson!" she snapped off. "Deploy right! Hold the wall! Gunny! Take the others! Form
a perimeter covering the main drive and the front of the
building!" Fuentes double-timed it across the lawn,
reaching down to help the Marine with his wounded

buddy. Both men were hurt, one unconscious with head and leg wounds, the other with blood smearing his face and the dazed look of someone caught too near an exploding round.

Another Marine appeared beside her, tall, lean-faced, with a captain's bars in dull black metal showing on his fatigue collar. WARHURST, T. was stenciled on his black combat vest. He helped her lift the wounded men and drag them toward the Residence. "Good to see you, Lieutenant," he said.

"Sir, Lieutenant Fuentes reporting," she told him. "First Platoon, Alfa Company. What's your situation?"

"We're okay now," he said, as more embassy Marines spilled out of the building and took charge of the two wounded Marines. He turned then to face her. "Now that you and some Marine air are here. They came over the wall three or four minutes ago . . . civilians, at first, or at least men in civilian clothing."

"A setup, you think?"

Warhurst nodded. "Definitely." He held up his hand as though spreading out a newspaper headline. " 'US Marines Slaughter Helpless Civilians at Demonstration outside Embassy.' It'll look great on Triple-N. Especially in Geneva."

She gestured toward a burned-out Bradley with her ATAR. "Civilians don't usually attack embassies with tanks or AFVs."

"Mmm, no . . . but they'll say they sent in the army to restore order. I doubt that anyone will question why the army just happened to have an armored division parked across the street when the trouble started."

Fuentes felt herself go ice-cold inside. She'd been responding to a provocation, following orders, even fighting the first battle of a war . . . but she'd not thought her actions could have possibly been construed as *starting* that war.

Gunfire continued to pop and crackle in the distance, but the area around the embassy was eerily calm at the moment. *God knows what they're shooting at*, she thought. *Or why.* Alien cultists, possibly, exchanging

pleasantries with anti-alien religious fanatics. The whole
world had been coming unglued lately. Maybe all that
had been needed to smash it apart was this one, last, tiny
nudge.

A roar from the roof of the embassy signaled the first
of the TR-5 transports lifting clear, hovering a moment,
then dipping its nose and banking toward the east. An
AV-32 followed, flying shotgun.

Warhurst touched the radio plug in his right ear, listening. "Okay," he said. "Roger that." He looked at
Fuentes. "The ambassador and his family are away.
Most of the civilians, too, and our wounded. Now we
just have to get ourselves the hell out of here."

The evacuation proceeded smoothly, with a choreo-
graphed precision that seemed to have been carefully
rehearsed. The remaining civilians, the embassy's CIA
staff, and the rest of the embassy Marines made it off
in the second TR-5. Warhurst helped get them all on the
tilt-jet before it lifted off and followed the first toward
the east and safety, but he remained behind on the roof
to see to the evacuation of the First Platoon Marines.

At Fuentes's signal, the last of her Marines outside
the Residence fell back from the walls, filing inside the
shattered building and making their way up the steps.
Fuentes found Warhurst standing on the embassy roof.
"Come on, sir!" she yelled. "Last plane out of this
burg!"

Something had caught his attention on the grounds
below, and he unslung his M-29. "Get the rest of your
people on board," he said. "We have company."

She joined him at the parapet, staring down into the
front of the compound. Under cover of the dense smoke,
more vehicles had moved close to the embassy walls,
and dark-uniformed troops were scrambling out and
spilling into the embassy grounds through a dozen different breaches.

"Now I know how Davy Crockett felt at the Alamo,"
he told her.

"Let's get out of here, sir!"

"You go. I'll—"

"Come on, Captain! Now!"

He nodded. "Okay! Go! Go!"

First Platoon's Peregrine was loading on the embassy roof now, with Sergeant Walsh hurrying the last few men across the helipad pavement to the waiting tilt-jet. Together, Fuentes and Warhurst sprinted for the aircraft. The engine whine was spooling up, the air above the pavement dancing and shimmering in the jetwash.

Fuentes had reached the TR-5, pounding up the lowered rear ramp before she realized that she was alone. "Where is he?"

Walsh looked about, then pointed. Twenty meters across the helipad, a small shed rose from the embassy roof, a shelter for the stairwell leading down into the building. Warhurst had positioned himself next to the open door and was leaning over the stairwell, firing his M-29 down the steps at unseen attackers.

Fuentes saw what must have happened. While the last of the Marines had been loading onto the transport, Mexican troops had raced into the embassy and come swarming up the stairs. Warhurst had known they were there already, or guessed it. He stood now on the landing, exchanging fire with the Mexican troops, keeping them from emerging onto the helipad.

"Captain!" Fuentes yelled. Her voice was lost in the roar of the engines. Biting off a curse, she touched her Motorola's transmit switch, choosing the command channel. "Captain!" she yelled again. "Come on! We'll cover you!"

"Roger that!"

Loosing a final long burst of gunfire down the stairwell, Warhurst turned and started running toward the Peregrine. He'd only come about three steps, however, when an explosion ripped the red metal door from the stairwell shed and knocked the Marine captain flat.

Fuentes started back down the ramp. Warhurst saw her and waved her back. "Get away!" She heard his voice over her transceiver. "Get the hell away!"

A machine gun opened fire from the roof of one of the neighboring buildings, striking sparks from the pavement between Fuentes and the downed Marine, smacking into the Peregrine with a chilling, metallic *thunk-thunk-thunk*. Instinctively, she dropped, searching for a target. The machine gun kept firing, aiming for the transport.

"We're taking hits!" the Peregrine's pilot called over her earpiece. "We're taking hits! We've got to *go!*"

"Go! Go!" Warhurst shouted. *"That's a goddamn order!"*

Mexican troops burst from the smoking stairwell shed, firing wildly. She saw Warhurst rolling over, saw him fire into the charge, saw him go under. Sergeant Walsh dragged her up the ramp as the pavement dropped away beneath her. The TR-5 was airborne, boosting itself into the sky as gunfire probed and chattered after it.

"You couldn't have gotten to him," Walsh told her.

"Damn them!" she yelled, battle lust and horror and frustration and rage all boiling from her in a nightmare of raw emotion. *"Damn them! . . ."*

One hundred feet above the embassy, the Peregrine's pilot banked the aircraft slightly, giving the Zeus gunner a clear field of fire. For three or four seconds, a solid line of tracers, like straight, hard, green lightning, licked at the embassy roof, smashing into and through the structure in a cataclysm of detonating HE rounds and depleted uranium penetrators. Fuentes, still watching from the half-opened ramp of the aircraft, saw dozens of troops trapped in that deadly beam, transfixed, then torn apart and scattered by that searing whirlwind of death and utter destruction.

The embassy roof, what was left of it, collapsed in flame and boiling smoke.

We never leave our own behind. . . .

But she had. Damn it, she had. . . .

SIX

Earth–Mars Cycler Polyakov
1417 hours GMT

"All right, people!" Colonel Lloyd bellowed. "Listen up! We got us a major change of plans, here."

Lloyd waited as the buzz of speculation and grumbling died away. Most of the MMEF's Marines had been gathered in *Polyakov*'s storm cellar, in full Class-One armor, with weapons and HUD helmets. Those not mustered in were watching through the unwinking eye of the television camera mounted on the bulkhead.

"What kind of change, Colonel?" Sergeant Ken Jacob called out.

"Yeah," Corporal John Donatelli added. "We gonna get to go kick ugly space-alien butt or not?"

The others chuckled, and several gave one another gloved high-fives.

"No, but I'm gonna kick some ugly Marine butt if you assholes don't simmer down."

James Andrew Lloyd knew he had a reputation for being hard on the men and women under his command. In fact, he gloried in that rep, cultivating the image of a hard-as-nails badass the way other men cultivated wealth or success. It had been that way for as long as he could remember. The United States, nearly a century after the Civil Rights Act of 1964, guaranteed equality for all . . . but there was still that unspoken assumption, strongest in the black, middle-class families like the one James— *never* "Jim"—had grown up in, that blacks and women had to work extra hard, had to go that extra kilometer, just to prove that they really had what it took.

James Lloyd had been taking that extra kilometer for a long time, now. Hard work and a no-nonsense attitude had led to his graduation *cum laude* from the University of Michigan, followed by both OCS and Marine Aviation Flight School. He'd flown a Harrier IV in Cuba in '24, led a platoon by airdrop into Colombia in '27, and seen combat since in Panama, Greece, and Andhra Pradesh.

While the fact that he was black had helped define his career, he rarely thought about it now. The Marine DI who'd run his OCS class had been black; an oft-quoted motivational expression of his was an old Corps theme: "There are no black Marines. There are no white Marines. There are only amphibious green Marines . . . and right now I want to see nothing but amphibious green *blurs*! . . ."

Colonel Lloyd thought of himself as amphibious green.

"Our original mission profile," he told them as the noise died away, "called for off-loading to a Mars Shuttle-Lander, followed by a descent to the primary base at Candor Chasma. Those of you who've read your mission profiles—maybe I should say those of you who can *read*—know that Candor Chasma is on the Martian equator . . . about five thousand kilometers from Cydonia, which is where we're ultimately supposed to be deployed.

"A new set of orders has come through from Earth, however. The MSL pilot has been ordered to take us directly to Cydonia. The bulk of our supplies and matériel will be sent to Candor Base, as originally planned. We will take with us what we can ferry along in the one MSL."

"Aw, shit, Colonel!"

Lloyd turned a hard gaze on the Marine who'd spoken. "You have a problem with that, Corporal Slidell?"

"Sorry, sir . . . but damn it, what about all our supplies and shit?"

"There is no effective difference in the new deployment," Lloyd said patiently, "at least insofar as our equipment is concerned. We would have had to off-load our gear at Candor, then repack what we needed to carry along aboard another MSL and redeploy by suborbital hop to Cydonia. As we needed spares or whatever, they would have been sent to us on the regular supply runs. We're just cutting out one extra hop for us." He studied Slidell's stricken face, wondering what was going through the man's head. "Be happy, Slider. The lot of you would've spent a day or two unloading shipping containers at Candor. Instead, you all get to sit on your fat, happy asses, guarding sand dunes at Cydonia."

"Yeah, but it ain't fair, jerkin' us around like that," Slidell said.

"Easy, man," Lance Corporal Ben Fulbert told Slidell. "Ice down."

"The Corps never promised you *fair*, Slider." Lloyd decided that he would have to keep an eye on the man. He seemed just a little too upset by the change in plans.

"Why the change, Colonel?" Staff Sergeant Ostrowsky wanted to know. "I thought everything had to channel through Mars Prime."

"When they tell me, Ostrowsky, I'll tell you. In the meantime, we follow orders." He hesitated before adding, "Let's just say that HQ is concerned about the friendliness of our reception. So we go in sharp, and we go in with Class-Ones. Questions?"

There were plenty of questions—there had to be with this crowd—but no one spoke up. Hell, *he* had questions, and none of them could be answered yet.

The change had come through only a few hours before, coded, and marked Secret and Eyes Only. INTEL BELIEVES UNFMC TROOPS SHIFTED TO MARS PRIME REGION LAST 72 HOURS, the report had stated. The United

Nations Force, Mars Contingent, numbered fifty men, almost twice the number in Lloyd's Marine platoon. If they'd shifted south from Cydonia to the Mars Prime base at Candor Chasma, it *could* be because they planned to confront the Marines when they landed.

Or possibly not. Bergerac, the UNF's new CO, was aboard the *Polyakov*. Maybe they were just getting ready to throw him a welcome-to-Mars party.

But Lloyd firmly believed that a little healthy paranoia was good for a man . . . and especially for Marines who planned to die in bed. That was why he'd ordered the platoon to assemble here in full armor, complete with weapons, HUD helmets, and full field gear. It made the storm cellar a bit crowded, and the deorbit was gonna be hell, but at least they would be ready, no matter what was waiting for them on the ground.

"Okay, people," he said at last. "We got thirty mikes before the shuttle docks. Time for weapons drill." He looked at his wrist-top, which had been attached to the outer sleeve of his gauntlet. "Ready . . . begin!"

Half an hour later, on schedule as dictated by the dead hand of Sir Isaac Newton, the first of a small fleet of approaching Mars Shuttle-Landers docked with *Polyakov*'s nonrotating hub. Though there were no windows in the storm cellar, there was a small television monitor with a feed from the control deck, and Lloyd was able to open a channel from one of *Polyakov*'s docking-bay approach cameras.

Harper's Bizarre—painted in grit-scoured red letters on the stubby craft's bare-metal prow—was the unofficial name of the first of the MSLs that slowly eased in to a capture and hard dock. The upper half of the forty-meter craft was a biconic hull, an off-center cone designed for atmospheric reentries, while the lower half consisted of two, stacked doughnut-clusters of spherical methane tanks and the close-folded complexity of a trio of spidery landing legs. The *Bizarre*, like the other MSLs on Mars, was a nuke, using a Westinghouse-Lockheed NTR, a Nuclear Thermal Rocket similar to the old Nerva designs, to heat the tanked reaction mass. The propellant of choice was methane, a liquid produced in quantity on Mars from atmospheric CO_2 and permafrost-melted water; the concept was known as NIMF, an unlikely acronym standing for Nuclear rocket using Indigenous Martian Fuel.

Once the green light showed for docking lock one, pressures were equalized and the MSL opened to *Polyakov*'s interior. As befitted one of the burgeoning Martian colony's workhorses, the *Bizarre* had a large and utilitarian cargo section, which for this trip had been fitted with a plug-in deck-chair module. Nothing fancy, but it had padding and straps enough to get human cargo from the cycler's orbit to the Martian surface in, if not comfort, then at least relative safety.

Lloyd's path through the docking collar and forward pressure lock brought him to a point where he passed beneath the feet of the MSL's pilot. "Marine Mars Expeditionary Force," he rasped out. "Request permission to come aboard."

"Granted, Colonel," the pilot called back. She was a slender redhead in a trim, lightweight pressure suit. "Find yourselves seats and get strapped in."

The rest of the Marines were already clambering in after him, muttering curses or sharp imprecations as their clumsy Class-Ones scraped or bumped against equipment, bulkheads, or the armor of other Marines. Class-One armor was almost as bulky as a full-fledged space suit, and with good reason. It was self-contained, pressurized, and—with a full-charged life-support pack and rebreather assembly—could keep a man alive in hard vacuum almost indefinitely . . . or at least until his food ran out.

All of the MMEF's armor had active chameleonic surfaces—coatings of a specially formulated plastic that "remembered" incident light and was able to adapt its color and texture within minutes to match the surroundings. The only parts of the suits that did not sport this constantly shifting surface were the helmet visors—normally dark to block ultraviolet radiation—and the traditionally camouflaged helmet covers. Those last were

something of an old Marine tradition, a holdover from
the second half of the twentieth century. Marine aviators,
though they'd worn flight suits and standard helmets
when they'd gone aloft in their old Harrier IIs or F/A-
18s or, later, in their F/A-22s and AV-32s—always wore
the US Marines' standard tan, brown, and green fabric
helmet cover . . . not for camouflage, but to show soli-
darity with their fellow Marines on the ground. It was a
tradition that went back at least as far as Vietnam, and
probably farther; Marines took extraordinary pride in the
close relationship between Marines in the mud and the
Marine aviators flying close support.

Lloyd found a convenient stanchion and hung on,
floating in an out-of-the-way attitude as the rest of the
Marines filed in. Overall, the evolution was an orderly
one . . . but he noticed one bit of confusion toward the
rear of the column.

Pushing off from his anchor point, he maneuvered to
the scene of the problem. An unarmored civilian had
infiltrated the column and had gotten tangled with the
armored troops.

It was one of the archeologists, Dr. David Alexander.

"Can I help you, sir?"

"Uh . . . I thought I would tag along on this shuttle,"
Alexander replied. "I understand you're going straight
to Cydonia, instead of to Mars Prime."

*The only thing faster than light is the damned ship-
board scuttlebutt,* Lloyd thought. "I'm not sure that's
such a good idea," he replied. "This is liable to be a
rough ride, with a hot reception at the end of it."

"Well, Captain Elliott said there was room."

"Captain Elliott?"

"Harper Elliott. *Bizarre*'s skipper. Turns out she used
to be a Navy aviator. Served on the *Reagan*, same ship
as my dad."

"I see." That put Lloyd in an uncomfortable position.
He didn't want to have civilians kicking around on his
assault boat, especially if things turned nasty when they
hit ground. On the other hand, it wasn't *his* assault boat,
not in the formal sense. Elliott was ship's captain, and

he didn't want to end up second-guessing the *Bizarre*'s CO.

Alexander seemed to sense Lloyd's dilemma and gave him a lopsided grin. "I'll promise to be good."

He sighed. "Very well, Dr. Alexander," Lloyd told the man. There ought to be room enough. "Find yourself a seat. But . . . if things are hot when we touch down, you get the hell out of the way, understand?"

"You expect things to be, uh, 'hot,' as you put it?"

"I don't expect anything, sir. But it's best to be prepared."

"Don't worry," Alexander said. "If anybody starts shooting, I'll be sure to keep my head down." The man spoke with a sardonic edge to his voice that told Lloyd he was being humored.

Colonel Lloyd did not like being humored, and he did not like the archaeologist's attitude, at once bantering and condescending. He almost—*almost*—wished that something would happen when they landed, just to teach the arrogant civilian some manners.

Not, he realized, a professional response at all.

                                                    1556 GMT
Mars Shuttle-Lander Harper's
Bizarre
Sol 5621: 1210 hours MMT

David Alexander had fought to get himself a window seat.

Not that there was terribly much to see through the narrow, thick-cut piece of grit-scoured transplas set in the circular port, but he felt he deserved a chance to see the Cydonian site from the air. The Marines, after all, didn't need to see the area they'd be guarding. It was just another deployment to them.

And besides, he wanted to see the Face.

He chuckled to himself. If Holst or that bureaucratic idiot Bahir at the Egyptian Ministry of Antiquities could just see him *now*. . . .

For a time, all he'd seen through the tiny port was the slowly revolving arms of the cycler as Marines continued to load their gear aboard *Harper's Bizarre*. Finally, though, with a short, hard shock, the MSL had cut free from the cycler, falling tail first away from the far larger spacecraft-station until Alexander, by pressing his face hard against the transplas and shielding it from the interior light with his hands, could see the cycler in its entirety. Two more MSLs were in the process of docking with the cycler as the *Bizarre* cleared the sweep of *Polyakov*'s arms. Then, with a gut-wrenching burst of acceleration, *Bizarre* spun to a new attitude that swept the other spacecraft from view.

Acceleration pressed him back against his thinly padded couch . . . building and building far beyond the meager three-tenths G he'd gotten used to over the past few weeks. He wasn't sure how long they were under boost; he'd forgotten to check his wrist-top when the *Bizarre*'s nukes cut in. He only knew that the weight pressing down on his body, on his chest and lungs, was unendurable . . . and that it went on and on and on, forcing him to endure, whatever he thought about the matter.

Eventually, they were in free fall again, but by that time he felt too tired to note the time . . . or even to look out the window.

After a while, acceleration resumed, and the sky beyond his tiny porthole began to glow.

The point of cycler spacecraft like *Polyakov* was that they occupied solar orbits that touched Earth's orbit on their inward swing and Mars's orbit on their outer. With some judicious use of gravity wells during each planetary swing-by and occasional kicks from their ion-electric drives, they could arrange to meet the planetary orbits when the planets themselves were there. It was necessary, however, to ferry the personnel and equipment brought out from Earth down to the Martian surface . . . and that meant a hefty delta-v burn, followed by aerobraking in the Martian atmosphere. The ride down was long, rough, and excruciatingly uncomfortable.

Alexander spent much of reentry trying hard not to be sick.

"Hey, uh . . . sir?" the Marine seated next to him said after a long time. "You see anything out there?"

Vaguely, Alexander realized that the man talking to him was the Marine he'd shouldered aside earlier in order to get the spot by the window. The name FULBERT was stenciled in black on the gray-and-white mottling of his chest armor. "Not a lot," he said.

Several more jolts slammed him in the back as *Bizarre*'s nuclear engines came up to full thrust. The shuttle was balancing down on its tail now. "Down" was aft, toward the rear of the ship, and Alexander was lying flat on his back with his knees braced above his chest.

"You're the new head archeologist gonna see the Face, right?" Fulbert said.

Alexander shook his head. He'd not associated much with the Marines for the past months, understandably enough, and his official mission had not been widely advertised, but it was impossible to live that long inside a couple of large, sealed tin cans without everyone learning something about everyone else.

"I'm just going with some new sonic imaging gear," he said, correcting the Marine. "Dr. Graves is head of the American team, and he's already at Cydonia. Dr. Joubert is going as head of the UN team, though."

Fulbert's face split into a broad and knowing grin inside the confines of his open helmet. "Man, *there's* a high-voltage outlet! I guess you two don't let the international shit get in the way of your workin' together, huh?"

Clearly, Fulbert was more interested in the salacious details of his relationship with Joubert than in the international situation. "She's a good archeologist," he replied, keeping his voice noncommittal. "She did some fine fieldwork in the Yucatán."

"Ha! I wouldn't mind doin' some fieldwork with her. Is that where you met her? Down in Yucatán?"

Alexander shook his head. "My specialty is . . . my specialty *was* Egypt." He found that the unfairness still hurt, even after three years. "In a way, I guess, we're enemies." He gave a wan smile. "Some folks with the UN don't care much for me or my ideas."

The Marine's eyes widened. "Egypt? You mean like, the pyramids and the Sphinx and all that?"

"That's right."

"So . . . you think there's some kind of connection? Between the Sphinx and the Face? Is that why you're on the UN's shit list?"

Alexander grimaced. The question always came up with the uninitiated. "The Sphinx at Giza and the Face at Cydonia have nothing, *nothing* whatsoever to do with one another." He'd long since lost count of how many times he'd gone through this. "The Face, as near as we can tell, is something like five hundred thousand years old. That's half a *million* years, okay? The Sphinx, I am convinced, is much, much older than the date traditionally assigned to it, but it is nowhere near that old. The idea that the same culture who made the Face also made the pyramids and the Sphinx is garbage . . . worse than trying to link the pyramids of Egypt with the pyramids of Mexico. Can't be done."

"Yeah? But I read that the UN was havin' to call out troops to break up demonstrations . . . and lots of those demonstrations were over the idea of aliens colonizing the Earth thousands of years ago. Things like the Sphinx are supposed to be proof the aliens were here, but the UN government doesn't like that."

Alexander sighed. As was often the case, the layman's view mingled a little fact with a great deal of fancy. "There were definitely aliens in the solar system half a million years ago," he explained. "They left traces at Cydonia . . . though you might be surprised to hear that there are still quite a few scientists who argue that the Face and the so-called pyramids on Mars are natural features."

"No shit?"

"Most of us think the Face, at least, was carved by someone . . . some*thing*, and the Fortress-Ship complex is obviously artificial, though after half a million years of dust storms and weathering, there's not much left of it. But there *is* room for debate. That's what science is all about, after all, testing hypotheses.''

"How come some scientists still think that Face-thing is natural? I've seen three-vids of that thing, and it gives me the crawlies.''

"Well, we still can't find a decent reason for a sculpture of an essentially human face to be carved into a mesa on Mars at a time when *Homo sapiens* was just appearing on Earth. The aliens, whoever or whatever they were, were *not* human. I guess it's easier to believe that the Face is a wind-carved freak of nature than it is to believe it could be a deliberately sculpted likeness of *us*.''

"Well, that's what all the nutcase new religions and shit are all about, ain't it? That the aliens tinkered with apes and turned 'em into people? Like in that old movie that everybody's talkin' about now, *2000*.''

"*2001: A Space Odyssey*,'' he said, correcting the Marine again. "And it wouldn't have been apes, not unless you count humans as a kind of ape. *Homo erectus* was the dominant hominid line on Earth half a million years ago.''

"Sure, whatever. But, like I was sayin', everybody on Earth, it seems like, either thinks the aliens were gods or thinks that we're tryin' to slip one over on 'em to take away their religion, or whatever, and the UN johnnies all seem dead sure that all the stuff about aliens visiting Earth back then is crap. Like it couldn't possibly happen, y'know?''

Alexander smiled. "I know.'' He'd been in the eye of that particular storm for a long time. In fact, he had his own opinions about some of the more improbable sites on Earth . . . not that aliens had *built* them, necessarily, but the possibility of alien inspiration and technical help was not unthinkable.

Still, it was dangerous territory to tread upon. The discoveries of the past few decades had transformed traditional science . . . but they'd also caused an explosion in the pseudosciences. The old "ancient astronaut'' theories had come back with a vengeance, spawning volume upon volume of crackpot ramblings, pop-science gibberish, and even a horde of new religions.

Hoping to end the conversation, he deliberately checked his wrist-top, calling up the time. Before the MSL rendezvous, everyone's personal computers had been updated to Mars time. The planet's rotation was slightly longer than Earth's and, therefore, could not be brought into synch with the GMT used aboard all spacecraft. A Martian day was called a sol; it was divided into traditional hours and minutes, as on Earth, but had an extra thirty-seven-minute catch-up period, called soltime, added after local midnight. The young Mars colony counted sols instead of days, beginning with the official establishment of the first permanently manned settlement—the base at Candor Chasma, now known as Mars Prime. Sol 1 was July 20, 2024, fifty-five years to the day after Armstrong had set foot on the moon. The current sol was 5621.

All of which meant that Mars Mean Time, or MMT, had nothing whatsoever in common with GMT. It was now, he saw, 1740 hours at Cydonia—late afternoon—and 2126 hours in Greenwich. Of course, for the next fifteen months or so, his only interest in what time . . . or day . . . it was on Earth would be when he had to calculate the arrival or departure time of another report.

"So," Fulbert said, still clinging to the conversation thread, "you don't think aliens did stuff on Earth? You know, the pyramids? Easter Island? All that shit?"

He decided not to mention his own reservations about the Giza pyramids, at least. "Easter Island? Certainly not! We *know* how the local population built and raised those great stone heads, because they showed us. No mystery there at all."

Turning away in another attempt to end the conversation, he pressed his face against the tiny port. He could see sky above—still a dark, purplish color at the horizon turning to jet-black overhead. Below, the Martian surface spread out beneath a curved horizon, a dusty, dusky ocher color tinted with streaks of rust and gray-brown.

They were still too high up for the smaller details of the surface to be visible, but he could see scattered, shadow-edged shapes that must be mountains or the jumble of chaotic terrain. He tried to orient himself. If it was late afternoon here, then north would be that way . . . but he didn't know if they were even descending in an attitude that would let him see the Face or the attendant structures. It was frustratingly like trying to recognize buildings or landmarks from the air while approaching a city's airport on Earth. For all he knew, the Cydonian ruins were on the other side of the—

He saw it.

My God! It's just like they all said . . . but so . . . so unexpected. . . .

It was smaller than he'd thought it would be, which was why he'd overlooked it at first. *Bizarre* must still be twenty or thirty kilometers up. He looked down on the Cydonian Face, and it returned his wondering stare with the same enigmatic and Sphinx-like skyward gaze it had worn for half a million years.

First captured by chance on two frames shot by the Viking 1 orbiter spacecraft in 1976, the Face hadn't even been noticed until the early 1980s . . . and then the image had been dismissed as a trick of the light and of the remarkable persistence of the human mind in imposing order and facial features on random shapes, be they ink-blots on a paper, or a mile-long landform in the desert. By the turn of the century, space probes had returned better images, and NASA had—with some reluctance—acknowledged at last that there might be something there worth investigating after all. That revelation, that *intelligence* had carved a mile-long face into a mesa in the Cydonian region of Mars, was the last in a rapid-fire barrage of discoveries that had completed at last the long-fought Copernican Revolution. Since the 1990s, it had been known that planet-bearing stars were common, and evidence of fossilized bacteria had been discovered on a meteorite gouged from the Martian surface eons before.

Humankind was not alone in the universe.

Those discoveries had spurred a long-awaited renaissance in space exploration. The first manned landing on Mars, a joint US–Russian venture, had taken place in 2019 at Candor Chasma; it wasn't until the second landing five years later that Geoffrey Cox, Anatol Kryukov, and Roberta Anders had stood at last in the shadow of that alien-carved enigma and wondered. . . .

Bizarre was lower now and starting to swing slightly in a clockwise turn. The Face drifted off toward the left; the "City" and the pyramids came into view to the right.

Alexander's heart was beating faster. There were mysteries enough here to keep ten thousand archeologists busy for millennia, mysteries still unopened, untapped, unknown. The beings who'd built this place were known variously as the Ancients or the Builders . . . but who they'd been, where they'd come from, what they'd looked like, all was still a frustrating puzzle. All that could be said with certainty was that they'd wielded powers that seemed like magic to the humans who'd investigated the ruins . . . and that they'd not been human.

When the Face was being built, humankind was in the process of evolving from *Homo erectus* into a primitive form of *Homo sapiens*. The knowledge of any power source more potent than fire was still half a million years in the future.

The "City"—its true purpose was yet unknown—consisted of four pyramids each the size of the Great Pyramid of Giza arranged in a perfect diamond pattern, surrounded by five titanic, mile-wide pyramids apparently carved from basaltic mountains. Six miles to the southeast, another pyramid, known as the D&M Pyramid after the initials of its twentieth-century discoverers, rose a full mile into the sky, almost two miles across, five-sided, buttressed . . . and apparently shattered on its eastern face by what might have been a meteorite impact . . . but which many now thought had been hostile action.

He glanced at Fulbert, squeezed into the seat to his

left, and smiled. Hostile action? Human Marines would be no match for whatever had smashed a mile-high pyramid carved from solid rock. Their assault rifles seemed pathetically toylike in the face of a weapon like that.

Of course, the Marines weren't here to fight *aliens*. . . .

"All right, Marines!" Lloyd's voice snapped. "Stand by for grounding! Helmet visors down and locked! Weapons ready!"

A clatter of snaps and clicks sounded through the passenger compartment, as the Marines locked their visors down and worked the actions on their rifles. If someone started shooting from the surface, the shuttle's hull might be breached and pressure lost, but the Marines might still survive the landing. Briefly, Alexander wondered what might be happening at the Cydonia base. Would the UN be stupid enough to try shooting them down? It seemed ridiculous.

Even so, he was glad he was wearing a pressure suit, just in case. Involuntarily, he glanced up at the overhead compartment where his emergency helmet was stored.

They continued their descent. Alexander could see nothing of the Ancients' complex now. Nearby mountaintops and mesas were rising swiftly, and the ground below was taking on a rocky, pocked-looking texture. His seat kicked him hard from below as the *Bizarre*'s main engines switched on. For several minutes more, he was aware only of the pounding of those nuclear thermal rockets as the MSL lowered itself toward the Martian surface. Dust, brick red except where the touch of low-slanting sunlight kissed it golden, swirled up past the window. There was the slightest of jars . . .

. . . and then the engine thunder was dwindling away.

"Okay, jarheads," Captain Elliott, the MSL's skipper, announced happily, "welcome to Mars!"

Throughout the compartment, armored Marines unbuckled harnesses and struggled to their feet. A ladder set into what on an airliner would have been the floor was now a series of steps going down the wall to the cargo lock below, and the Marines were swinging out of their seats and clambering down the ladder in surprisingly good order. Alexander stayed where he was, safely out of the way. He imagined that Lloyd must be shouting orders at them or counting them off by the numbers, but the Marines were all sealed up and their conversations restricted to their suit radios.

In seconds, the last of them had vanished down the ladder into the cargo hold and the hatch sealed shut with a bang. Alexander turned to try to see out the port, but little was visible except for dust, sand, and rock beneath an eerie pink sky. He could hear the throb of compressors as the cargo hold's atmosphere was tanked for later use and the compartment brought down to the near vacuum of the Martian surface. If somebody wanted to attack them, this would be a hell of a good time. . . .

"Looks like they have the welcome mat out for us, Dr. Alexander," Captain Elliott called down. "The natives are friendly. A little bent out of shape, maybe, but friendly."

Alexander hadn't realized how nervous he'd been. With a sigh of relief he began unbuckling, eager to get outside and see this place for himself, a place he'd been dreaming of for years.

Outside, as it had for millennia, the Face stared skyward with quiet and enigmatic aplomb.

SEVEN

United Orient Flight 372
95,000 feet above the Pacific
Ocean
1215 hours Tokyo time

Kaitlin Garroway peered out the cabin window at a
sky so blue it was almost black. A smattering of stars
was visible above a curved horizon. Each time she traveled on an HST she felt the same sense of mingled awe
and longing. Hypersonic transports didn't reach into
space, but it looked as though they were on the edge.
"Have you ever flown at this altitude?" she asked her
companion.

Yukio leaned over her shoulder to share the view.
"Yes, and a little higher. But still not into space. The
Inaduma fighter can reach orbit only with a very large
booster. So far I have only flown above thirty-five thousand meters in a simulator. Now if we'd taken the suborbital as I'd suggested . . ."

"My internal clock is gonna be no less scrambled
from this flight than from a forty-five-minute hop, thank
you very much, so what's the advantage? Besides, you
know I couldn't afford it. Those suborbs are for businessmen on expense accounts, not for college students."

"And you wouldn't let me pay your way."

"Certainly not. It's my vacation, and I'm going to enjoy knowing that my money paid for it."

"Independent-minded *gaijin*."

She turned quickly to see if he was serious. *Gaijin* was the word used to refer to a foreigner, but the connotation was more that of barbarian. Nihonjin, more than any other people she knew of, divided the world into two categories: people . . . and outsiders. Yukio's face was somber, but his eyes were twinkling, so she knew he was teasing her again. Still she wondered . . .

"Is it going to be a problem, Yukio?" she asked. "That I am my own person, that I have my own ideas and express them?"

"In other words, that you are not . . . a proper Japanese woman?"

She nodded.

Yukio leaned back in his seat and stared at the overhead light. "We have spoken of this before, and you know how I feel. We are part of a new generation, you and I, citizens of Earth."

"And yet there is *gimu*." The word meant duty, obligation.

"Yes. I have obligations, to my family, to my country. My military duty is just one part of this. I . . . I am having difficulty reconciling these duties with our vision of the world, of what the world is becoming, what it *must* become if the human race is to survive."

Kaitlin was silent for a while, considering her own duties. She had grown up assuming that she would enter the Marine Corps after college. After all, what better way to emulate her adored father? But during the last few years, and especially since she'd come to CMU, she'd begun seeing things in a different light. Exposed for the first time to the ideas of the Internationalist Party, she'd started to see her country as an obstacle to world peace and nationalism as an outmoded concept, notions that, understandably, horrified her father. It hurt her to realize that she was hurting him, but she couldn't not-think just to please his old-fashioned patriotism.

Things got further complicated when she realized that her father no longer had the same devotion to duty and to the Corps that he'd had when she was young. It worried her that he seemed to be just marking time until he could retire. She'd prefer a good, loud argument to the apathy she saw in him now. Occasionally things still ticked him off, like that incident with the two archaeologists last week, but most of the time he seemed content simply to put in his time. She wondered what he thought of the Mexico business.

That news had shaken her, not so much because of what happened as because of her reaction to it. She wasn't naive enough to believe everything she saw on Triple-N, so it hadn't surprised her when she found that the military newsgroups had a very different slant on the embassy takeover, claiming that the Mexicans were the aggressors and that what was supposedly a spontaneous demonstration had really been orchestrated by the Mexican Army. What *had* surprised her was her reaction to the Internationalist newsgroups. All of a sudden the talk of American imperialist aggressors sounded raucous and hollow to her, and she found herself vigorously defending the Marines . . . and getting flamed for it.

Not that getting flamed was unusual for her—she seldom held back on expressing her own opinions, regardless of how unpopular they might be—but that the attacks seemed so unreasoned bothered her. She'd thought of the Internationalists as a group of rational intellectuals; now she was seeing just as much unthinking prejudice in them as in, say, those who claimed the Martian Ancients were demons.

The Ancients.

"Yukio, who do you think the Ancients really were?"

"The Ancients?" He laughed. "How can I even take a guess? We know so little about them. What does your father say? Have they turned up anything new?"

Kaitlin shrugged. "They've only been there five days. He seems to be getting friendly with one of the archeologists, a guy named Alexander, and he's been filling him in on what the previous team had uncovered and where they're starting from now, but I don't think there's anything new and startling.''

The thought of her latest vid from her father made her grimace. She had a job lined up for later in the summer, and she'd told him all about it without specifically saying that it didn't start until the middle of July, so he assumed she was staying in Pittsburgh for the whole summer. If he knew she was going to Japan, he would have gotten all fatherly and protective, assuming that she couldn't take care of herself, and she just didn't want to have to deal with that. She always used her global.net account whenever she was outside of Pittsburgh, so he would be able to tell from her v-mail only that she was not at CMU.

"Anyway," she continued, "from all I've read on archeology, it's a long, involved, painstaking process. Alexander told Dad it might be years before they even knew the right questions to ask."

"So why do you think I might be able to answer those questions, when we don't even know what they are?"

"Well, of course we can't *know*. But we can guess, can't we? We can speculate. The idea of other intelligent beings, a whole other civilization, inhabiting this solar system long before modern humans even evolved . . . it's mind-boggling. I want to know who they were, why they came here, where they went."

Yukio grinned. "Then why aren't you studying exo-paleoarchaeology instead of AI systems design?"

Kaitlin shook her head. "I don't have the patience for archaeology. I want to go out there and *find* them, wherever they are. Even if that particular species is extinct, just the fact that they were there proves we're not alone. There must be others, thousands of other races throughout the galaxy. And I don't think we're going to find them by sitting here waiting for them to come to us. We've got to go to them."

Yukio gazed out into the deep blue of not-quite-space. "We're just on the edge of exploring the solar system. It will be quite some time before we are able to reach the stars."

"I don't know. If we can work the bugs out of anti-matter propulsion, we could be sending a ship to Alpha Centauri in, oh, twenty years or so.

"And I want to be on that ship."

0507 HOURS GMT

Kansai International Airport
Osaka Bay, Japan
1407 hours Tokyo time

Yukio held his hands casually in his lap to keep from gripping the handrests as the Star Raker came into its approach to the huge man-made island that was Kansai International Airport. He always felt a little nervous flying when he didn't have any electronic displays in front of him to follow course and speed and range. He didn't *know* the man in the cockpit, didn't *know* with certainty his competence and experience, the way he did with *Taii* Iijima, the Space Defense Force captain he usually flew with. For a veteran of thousands of hours of flight time, such nervousness seemed embarrassing, so he always tried to hide it. Usually he was successful.

A slight sound coming from his right made him turn his head to see Kaitlin looking at him as though she was trying hard not to laugh.

"Okay, now I really know you're a flight officer!"

"Oh? And why is that?"

"Dad says all flyers are like that, though the actual pilots are usually worse than side-seaters like you. Can't *stand* to have someone else in control."

Yukio grinned ruefully. "You found me out. And I thought I was hiding it pretty well."

She nodded. "You were. But don't worry, I won't let on I know your dreadful secret. It's just nice to know that you have at least one flaw."

The Star Raker came in for a textbook landing, and Yukio resumed his normal breathing pattern. The slide-walk in the International Terminal was bordered with gift shops, eating parlors, and communications stations;

signs in French, English, and Nihongo welcomed visitors, and holoboard advertisements bombarded them with sights and sounds as they made their way toward the baggage area. Travelers from all over the world came through Kansai, but there was a predominance of Asian faces. As he got off the end of the slidewalk, Yukio almost gave a skip. It was good to be home.

They took the Jet Foil across Osaka Wan to the mainland and then traveled by maglev to Kyoto. *One flaw, she said. How little she knows me, if she thinks I have only one.* He stole a glance at the woman on the seat next to him, seeing her as though with new eyes. By American standards she was beautiful, with long auburn hair curving around a thin green-eyed face. By international standards she was stylishly and appropriately dressed for travel, in a sleeveless one-piece jumpsuit with hip belt. By Japanese standards, she was neither appropriately dressed nor beautiful.

He thought about his name. Yukio was a shortened form of Toshiyuki; the nickname meant Snow Boy and implied one who goes his own way. When, Yukio wondered, had he ever gone his own way? He'd entered the Space Defense Force to please his father. He'd enrolled at Carnegie Mellon University because he was ordered to by the SDF. He'd agreed to this trip because Kaitlin wanted it, and he'd been almost relieved when he'd thought his new orders would make it impossible. Then he'd allowed himself to be persuaded again.

Yukio considered himself quite cosmopolitan, not Westernized to the extent of rejecting his heritage, of course, but enough of an Internationalist to be open-minded about Western ideas, Western culture . . . even Western women. In Pittsburgh Kaitlin had seemed perfect, exotic in the way that all Western women were, and yet familiar because of her love of Japan and Japan's culture. Now she seemed jarring, out of place . . . or was *he* the one who was out of place?

They took the subway from the maglev station and then walked the few blocks to the youth hostel where Kaitlin would be staying. She made a good impression on the clerk at the desk, bowing and addressing him in fluent and respectful Nihongo. Yukio had never stayed at a place like this, but he would guess that few Americans came here who would be able to converse with their host in the host's language . . . or who would wish to.

"I'm going up to change," she said. "I shouldn't be more than a few minutes. Unless you'd like to come wash up also?"

"No. I am fine. Thank you."

She gave him a strange look, then turned and walked up the stairs to her room. He mentally kicked himself. Ever since they'd landed at Kansai, he'd become more and more formal with Kaitlin. He knew that she felt it and was puzzled by it. The thing was, he was puzzled, too. He was well aware of the differences between American and Japanese customs. He was well aware that behavior that would be considered reprehensible in Kyoto was perfectly acceptable in Pittsburgh. But he'd thought of himself as a new Japanese, able to transcend his upbringing, to be a citizen of the world. He was finding that he was more tightly bound to tradition than he'd imagined possible.

He walked over to the comm station against one wall of the lobby. It was an old-fashioned one—audio only, no video, no net access—but sufficient for his purposes. He called home and arranged with Isoru Nabuko, his father's secretary, for a car to be sent to pick them up. "Is my father at home, *Hisho-san*?" he asked.

"Oh, yes, *Ishiwara-san*," the man replied. "Daijin Ishiwara returned from Tokyo two hours ago. He is eagerly awaiting your arrival and that of your honored guest." Nabuko chuckled. "I've not seen him so excited since you received your well-deserved promotion to the rank of *chu-i*."

Yukio asked that Nabuko convey his respects to his father, and then he hung up, wondering if the secretary knew that the honored guest in question was in fact a *gaijin*. He had not hidden the fact from his parents, but he didn't know whether the information had been passed on. Perhaps it had. Perhaps he was worrying unnecessarily. Perhaps he was the only one who—

"Is there a problem?" It was Kaitlin.

"Oh. No, certainly not. I was just thinking."

"Ah."

She was conservatively dressed, he was relieved to see, and holding a large, oblong box in her hands. "Did you call home?" she asked.

He nodded. "A car will be here in . . ." He glanced at his wrist-top. ". . . about a half an hour. Perhaps we can find a place nearby to sit down and have a drink."

"I need to get this wrapped first," she said, gesturing with the box. "The clerk here said there was a gift shop around the corner. All of those shops at the airport seemed geared for tourists, and I want to make sure this is wrapped properly."

Her thoughtfulness stung. Both the giving and the wrapping of gifts in Japan were high arts and were as cloaked in ritual as the tea ceremony. Kaitlin had a Western face, but her heart was Nihonjin.

Now if only his father were able to see her in the same light . . .

                                        0850 HOURS GMT

Ishiwara household
Outskirts of Kyoto
1750 hours Tokyo time

The limousine pulled up to the gate in front of Yukio's house, where a uniformed guard looked inside the car, then opened the gate, waving them through. Kaitlin glanced back to see him pick up a phone in the guard shack, presumably to announce them. The security measures—necessary, Kaitlin supposed, for the household of the minister of International Trade and Industry—were so impressive, she was surprised to find that the actual house was not large and appeared quite traditional. Yukio had told her that his father was conservative in mat-ters of custom, although he was something of a freethinker in the field of politics.

As they walked up to the front door, Kaitlin thought about the upcoming meeting. Back in Pittsburgh the idea of meeting Yukio's parents and younger brother had excited her. When her father had been stationed in Osaka in the early twenties, she'd come to love this country and its people. As soon as they'd arrived in Japan, her mother, a natural linguist and determined not to be perceived as a typical American, had arranged for language and culture lessons. Kaitlin herself picked up the language, not through formal study but from playing with the children of her mother's teacher.

Then her mother died, shortly after the end of her father's stint in Japan. For Kaitlin, studying Japanese became a way of remembering and honoring her mother.

And now she was being invited into a Japanese home for the first time in almost fifteen years . . . and she felt totally unprepared. Speaking the language wasn't enough—even knowing the customs wasn't enough. She was different, and she would always be different. Yukio's behavior proved that. At first she'd been hurt, watching him seal himself behind a wall of formality, but then she realized that it was simply that he was now home and acting accordingly. The misgivings she'd felt earlier reared up again. Was it possible for love to create a bridge between two cultures as different as theirs?

And if it *was* possible, was her love for Yukio strong enough?

Yukio slid the door open, and the two of them walked through into the *genkan*, the vestibule. "Toshi-chan!" a voice boomed down from the main level of the house. Three people were standing there, a young boy wearing a jean-suit and a T-shirt and an older couple in traditional garb.

"O-to-chan!" Yukio replied joyfully, confirming that the middle-aged man wearing Yukio's face was the senior Ishiwara. The suffix *chan* was used only among close family members; *o-to-san* was the more formal way to address one's father.

Yukio bowed to his father and slipped off his shoes, stepping easily onto the main level of the house and into the slippers that were waiting for him. Kaitlin followed suit, glad she'd remembered to change into slip-ons at the youth hostel. It was bad form to sit down to take off your shoes.

"Father, I have the honor to introduce Ms. Kaitlin Garroway."

Kaitlin bowed low. "*Konbanwa, Daijin-sama*," she said, using the title for a government minister. "I am honored by your invitation."

Ishiwara returned the bow. "*O-kyaku-sama*, you are welcome to our house."

Honored guest.

"Mother, Ms. Kaitlin Garroway."

Bows and greetings were exchanged again, and the process was repeated with Yukio's brother, Shigeru. Mrs. Ishiwara complimented Kaitlin's command of Nihongo, and Kaitlin politely disagreed. She knew her Japanese was flawless, but it would be rude to acknowledge such praise directly.

Kaitlin then bowed again to Yukio's parents and held out the package she had brought, resulting in still more bows and polite words. They would not open it in her presence, of course, so she would not be able to see their response, but with the Japanese simply the fact of a beautifully wrapped gift was more important than the gift itself. She wondered nervously whether she should have stayed with the gift she had originally bought for the Ishiwaras. Two weeks before, she had purchased a framed vidclip of a view of Pittsburgh from Mount Washington. During the course of the ten-second loop, the fountain at the Point sprayed into the air, birds flew past, and a tourist boat emerged from under the Fort Pitt Bridge. She and Yukio had taken a trip once on just such a boat. She knew that a gift from a foreigner that was representative of the foreigner's hometown was usually acceptable, and this had the added benefit of depicting the city where their son had been living for the past ten months.

But as she was walking through the Kansai Terminal, she'd noticed a shop selling models, beautifully detailed miniatures of various ships, aircraft, and spaceships. While Yukio was getting their bags, she slipped back, under the pretext of visiting the *O'tearai*, the honorable hand-washing place, to take a closer look. As she'd hoped, the shop sold completed models as well as model kits, and one of the models on display was a beautifully painted *Inaduma* fighter, complete with booster—the very spacecraft that Yukio flew in. She'd bought it on the spot, and that was the gift she'd had specially wrapped that afternoon, while the framed vidclip languished in her room at the youth hostel.

What was causing her misgivings now was the fact that the twelve-inch model was very expensive.

It wasn't that she couldn't afford it. For all she'd teased Yukio about his being a rich kid, she was not poor herself, and she had enough money in her savings to handle a few special purchases. No, the difficulty was that giving an expensive gift created an obligation to reciprocate equally. *She* felt that the gift was well matched by the honor of being invited to the Ishiwara home. The question was, would the Ishiwaras feel that way? She might never know.

The four of them walked down the hall to a room with a *tatami*-covered floor, so everyone removed their slippers before stepping onto the reed mats. Three times she was offered the seat of honor near the beauty alcove, the *toko-no-ma*, and three times she declined. The fourth time she knelt on the *tatami*. After a similar process of offers, polite refusals, and renewed offers, she shifted to a floor cushion, a *za-buton*.

As they'd walked down the hall, Kaitlin had noticed a room with a carpet and Western-style furniture, indicating that the Ishiwaras were used to entertaining foreign visitors. The fact that they were treating her as a Japanese guest instead—taking her to the Japanese living room rather than the Western-style one, continuing to speak Nihongo rather than switching to English—was an honor . . . and a test. So far she'd been doing all right.

The evening was young, though. She rarely got examination jitters, but she'd never had an exam on which so much depended.

Glancing at Yukio, she wondered what he thought of her performance. He had certainly come to life since arriving at his home. He was smiling, laughing, teasing Shigeru. This, she realized, was his world; this was where he belonged. As he glanced around, his eyes met hers and his smile faded. So. He too was wondering if she could ever belong here. Being an honored guest was one thing.

Being accepted as a member of the family was something completely different.

Slowly the evening wore on. After about an hour, they all moved to another room, which seemed identical to the first, with the addition of a low table in the middle of the *tatami*-covered floor. Here several hours of dinner were served by servants who were constantly refilling her bowls. The food was magnificently prepared, a feast for the eye as well as for the palate. Gradually she relaxed, telling herself to simply enjoy the experience.

"*O-kyaku-sama*," Shigeru said during a pause in the eating. "Toshi has told us that your honored father was going to Mars."

Kaitlin looked at the youngster and smiled at the eagerness in his voice. Yukio—Toshi, as his family seemed to call him—had told her that Shigeru was sixteen and just as space-happy as his brother.

"*Hai, Shigeru-san*," she said. "The cycler arrived in Mars orbit last week, and the shuttle lander ferried them down to Cydonia. I'm afraid my father is not as thrilled at being on the surface of the red planet as you or I would be. He prefers his sand with an ocean nearby. One that's not half a million years old."

"Both my sons feel strongly," Ishiwara said, "that our future is in space."

"And you feel differently, *Daijin-sama*?" she asked.

Ishiwara put his chopsticks down carefully on the *hashi-oki* and took a sip of *o-cha* before replying. "I would be more interested, Honored Guest, in your opinion. Both because you are an American and because of your connection with Mars.''

''I do not know that my opinion would be worth anything, Respected Minister, but I must agree with your sons. And for two reasons. However long it takes to uncover what is buried under the sands of Cydonia, it could change . . . everything. Whether it is new technology that we are able to make use of, or simply the knowledge that we are not alone in the universe, it will transform life on this planet.''

''You are . . . most persuasive. And what is the second reason?''

''A corollary of the first. The fact that the Ancients were there means that we are not alone. It means that there are others out there. If we stay put, nice and safe here within our solar system, well, then they might find us. The encounter might be . . . quite a shock. But if we are the explorers, if we go out and seek them, then . . . Well, I can't say we'll necessarily be ready for whatever we'll find, but surely it is better to be the seeker than the sought. In history it is the exploring nations that have grown, have developed, whether that exploration has been physical or intellectual. There are no more physical frontiers on this planet. For that . . . we have to reach out into space.''

''Japan has tried isolation before, Father,'' Yukio said. ''After the battle of Sekigahara we tried to wall ourselves off from the rest of the world, believing that if we continued to ignore them, they would politely continue to ignore us.''

''It didn't work, did it, Father?'' Shigeru asked.

''You are correct, *Shi-chan*, it did not. The world will not leave us alone, much as we may wish it. Many of my countrymen proclaim that everything that Japan needs can be found within Japan. That has not been true for a very long time, and it is becoming less true every day.''

''We need to expand into space,'' Shigeru said. ''And I plan to be a part of it. Wait and see. Ten years from now I'll be on Mars.''

Yukio laughed. "And I'll be there to welcome you!"

At the end of the meal, Ishiwara called for the limousine to take Kaitlin back to the youth hostel. Yukio accompanied her, but even with the glass up between them and the driver, his speech was polite and formal. He made a point of not sitting right next to her, which frustrated her even more. She was well aware that custom frowned on public displays of affection, but she hadn't quite realized that Yukio would be unwilling even to hold hands with her.

He did bring up the subject of where they might go during the next few days. Perhaps things would be better once they got away from Kyoto and the shadow of his father. At least she hoped so.

Because otherwise, it was going to be a very long and less-than-relaxing vacation.

FRIDAY, 18 MAY: 1810 HOURS GMT
Arlington National Cemetery
Arlington, Virginia
1410 hours EDT

Tombstones stood in rank upon gleaming rank on the eastern face of the hill, a seemingly endless forest of grave markers spreading in precisely ordered formation across the tree-shaded slopes of Arlington National Cemetery. At the top of the hill, half-hidden behind ancient, spreading oaks, the white-pillared expanse of the Custis-Lee Mansion brooded over the tableau on the hill below as it had since the American Civil War. It was said that the US government had originally buried Union dead practically on the doorstep of the mansion in order to discourage the Lees from ever returning to this place. Whatever the original reason, the nearly two centuries of fallen American heroes interred here had hallowed this ground.

Opposite, across the gray waters of the Potomac, the city of Washington, DC, shimmered beneath the early-afternoon sun. In the distance, lonely thunder rolled . . .

a SCRAMjet liner on final approach to Washington National, a few miles to the south.

General Montgomery Warhurst stood at attention at the front of a small crowd of mourners, which included as many Marines as it did civilians. Janet, Ted's widow, stood on his left, with twelve-year-old Jeff at her side. Stephanie, the general's wife, was on his right. Neither woman was crying, though their eyes were red. Jeff looked solemn; Warhurst wondered if he'd connected yet with what had happened.

Hell, he thought bitterly. *Have* you? Before him, a few feet away, the casket of his son rested above the open grave.

Chaplain Connell had completed his remarks and invocation.

"Comp'ny . . . ten-*hut!*" Warhurst and the other military personnel not in formation raised their hands in salute. A short distance up the hill, seven Marines in Class-As snapped to present arms, then in a single, smoothly oiled motion, brought rifles to shoulders, aiming out over the city.

"Ready . . . *fire!*" Volleyed gunfire barked, the noise sharp in the still spring air.

In ancient times, Warhurst thought, *volleys were fired to scare off evil spirits emerging from the hearts of the dead.* But there was no evil here, not in Ted's heart, not in the dead he was resting with. There was only sorrow, and a kind of bittersweet clutching for meaning amid words that threatened to lose all meaning.

Honor. Glory. Duty. . . .

"Ready . . . *fire!*"

A second volley exploded. Birds, startled, rose from nearby trees.

"Ready . . . *fire!*"

Warhurst's eyes were burning.

As the echoes of the third volley died away, a lone Marine raised a bugle to his lips and began playing the mournful dirge of taps. Two more Marines—Sergeant Gary Bledsoe and Lieutenant Carmen Fuentes, both part of the honor detachment—lifted the American flag from the casket and began folding it between them, corner over corner, fly to hoist, reducing it to a thick, white-starred, blue triangle with no red showing.

Taps wavered to its lump-throated conclusion.

Warhurst dropped his salute, the sound joining the sharp crack of other arms snapping to sides. Holding the folded flag before her, Fuentes pivoted ninety degrees, took two steps, pivoted again, the double right angle bringing her squarely in front of Colonel Brad Mackley, Ted's commanding officer. Crisp and correct, Mackley accepted the flag, did a sharp about-face, then paced off the four steps that brought him up to the crowd, directly in front of Janet.

"On behalf of a grateful nation and a proud Marine Corps," Mackley said quietly, "I present this flag to you in recognition of your husband's years of honorable and faithful service, and his sacrifice for this nation."

Mackley handed Janet the flag, then saluted her. "Port . . . *harms*!" a voice rasped out. "Order . . . *harms*! Detail . . . dis-*missed*!"

The crowd began breaking up, some of them wandering back toward the shady curve of Halsey Drive, others standing in small groups, talking. Several came up, saluted him, and said . . . something. He never heard the words. He wanted to say something himself to Janet and Jeff . . . but when he turned, he saw that Stephanie had led them away, her arm around Janet's shoulders. He felt . . . alone. And empty.

Warhurst closed his stinging eyes. You bring a son into the world, raise him, educate him, love him, grieve with him, rejoice with him. You watch him choose your own branch of the service, graduate from Annapolis, go on to his first command, be chosen for the honor of embassy duty. You see him get married, see him begin a family of his own.

And at the end, there was nothing to show for it all but a folded flag.

And the memories.

Warhurst drew a ragged breath. For a moment, he could have hated the tradition, the parade-ground finery, the solemn grandeur and the emotion-wringing symbolism. Ted had died in a fucking incident in a country that Warhurst didn't give a damn for, an *incident*, not even a real war. According to the latest netnews downloads, Mexico was charging that American Marines had fired on civilians, precipitating the regrettable attack by Army forces on the American embassy. Pundits, politicians, and bureaucrats would be arguing over the blame for months to come, but nothing had been settled.

What was it all for? What was the use? Damn it, his son was *dead*. . . .

The Marine Corps. The term "marine," of course, had its roots in seafaring tradition . . . a soldier who fought at sea. Since the founding of the Corps in November of 1775, though, the term had become synonymous with a very special elite, a force-in-readiness, a unit ready and able to fight *anywhere* at short notice.

Everywhere. On distant coral atolls. In disease-festering swamps. Now, possibly, thanks to him, even the surface of another world.

Or the roof of an embattled embassy in Mexico City, in an *incident*. . . .

He drew another breath . . . and another, willing the tears to recede. He would *not* give in to self-pity. There was too much at stake.

Ritual. Tradition. His son had died in the best traditions of the service.

The Marine Corps would continue.

He would continue.

Somehow. . . .

EIGHT

Mars Prime/Cydonia Prime: The two principal human settlements on __Mars__ during the first, exploratory phase of the colonization effort. Mars Prime was established July 20, 2024, at __Candor Chasma__ (5° S, 75° W), near the Martian equator, its location dictated by the interesting local geology and ease of access from orbit. Cydonia Prime was established November 1, 2028, at __Cydonia__ (40.9° N, 9.5° W), in order to study in place the __alien artifacts__ and __monuments__ discovered there.

By 2038, each base complex could support eighty to one hundred personnel. Dedicated structures included subsurface living, recreation, and storage buildings, labs, C^3 facilities, wells for tapping permafrost for water, and automated cracking and storage plants for the manufacture of methane fuel from water and atmospheric CO_2.

> —*Download from Networld Encyclopedia*
> *vrtp://earthnet.public.dataccess*

SATURDAY, 26 MAY: 0357 HOURS GMT

Pad One
Cydonia Base, Mars
Sol 5634: 1610 hours MMT

"I never thought I'd see the day," Garroway said, "when a couple of enlisted men would actually volunteer. *Especially* Slidell."

Gunnery Sergeant Knox shook his head, the motion just visible inside his helmet. "Man, if I've learned anything in twenty years in the Corps, it's never trust a Marine who volunteers for shit details."

"Slider isn't exactly the kind of Marine who volunteers for anything," Colonel Lloyd said. "I've been wondering about that guy. He's been looking for ways to get to Candor ever since we switched landing sites."

"So why've he and Fulbert been so damned anxious to get down there?" Knox wanted to know. "I heard scuttlebutt that they managed to smuggle some drugs out from Earth."

"That doesn't seem likely, does it?" Garroway said. "Not with the weekly medcheck." Once a week every person on Mars donated a drop of blood and a specimen of urine to the med-lab analyzers. The general medical monitoring of the expedition members' health was not aimed specifically at spotting drug use, but it would certainly detect it if it happened.

"Ah, who knows what goes through their minds?" Lloyd growled. "I've already e-mailed Barnes at Candor to let him know to keep an eye on those two."

They were standing outside the main hab at Cydonia, watching the preparations for a lobber launch. The two enlisted Marines in question, Corporals Jack Slidell and Ben Fulbert, had just climbed the ladder and boarded the ship, and in a few more minutes they would be on their way to Mars Prime, the big base at Candor Chasma on the Martian equator five thousand kilometers southwest of Cydonia.

It had been two weeks since they'd landed at Cydonia, two *busy* weeks as the MMEF Marines had worked to get settled in and check out the gear they'd brought with them. Most of their stuff had gone on to Mars Prime at Candor Chasma, and they'd had to manage with a lot of make-do.

The political situation was tense and growing worse. Colonel Bergerac, the new UN force commander, had vigorously protested the unannounced and unscheduled redeployment of the Marines to Cydonia. Only this morning had the last of the 2nd Demibrigade Foreign Legion troops assigned to the UN observers' force finally shuttled north again to Cydonia Prime, after their redeployment to Candor. It had made things uncomfortably crowded at Cydonia. With nearly thirty Marines, over fifty Foreign Legion troops, and over fifty civilians, the base's life-support systems were being severely strained.

For that reason, lobber shuttle flights between the main supply dump at Mars Prime down at Candor Chasma and Cydonia Prime had been increased.

Garroway looked up at the lobber resting on the charred strip of regocrete that served as launchpad and landing pad and wreathed in slow-curling clouds of steam. It was *Harper's Bizarre*, the dinged and battered-looking shuttle that had aerobraked them in from cycler orbit, but the crews at Candor had replaced her fuel stack and taken her down to her lobber configuration.

For trips to orbit and back, the shuttle rode atop a twenty-meter, double-ring stack of fuel tanks holding the methane reaction mass needed for high delta-v maneuvers, plus the broad, lopsided blister of the heat shield used in aerobraking. Now, however, the blunt-nosed biconic nose section housing cockpit, passenger compartment, and main cargo bay had been remounted on a suborbital boost platform. This was a single ring of smaller methane tanks nestled inside a wirework basket, swaddled in thermal blankets, and resting on four widely splayed legs. In this configuration, the shuttle was called a lobber and was used for point-to-point transport of personnel and cargo on the Martian surface.

"All personnel," a voice sounded over their helmet headsets. "Lobber Three is now ready for launch. Please clear the launch area."

"That's us, gents," Lloyd said. "Let's get inside."

"Roger that," Garroway said. There was little radiation hazard from the NIMF—the NTR engine was well shielded—but the plasma that seared out of the aft venturi was *hot*, nearly five thousand degrees, and deadly at close quarters.

"How're you settling in, Major?" Lloyd asked as they walked back toward the main hab.

Garroway grimaced, his gaze shifting to the bleak, brick red horizon with its oddly shaped mesas and black, pyramid-mountains. "Look at it, sir. The biggest beach in the solar system," he said. "But no ocean. No palm trees. No nude, sun-worshiper tourists."

"Hell," Knox said. "No *air*."

"I really do hate this place," Garroway said. "Sand with no ocean in front of it sucks."

"*Vacuum* sucks, sir," Knox pointed out reasonably as he opened the outer airlock door. "A physical fact."

"Shit, what're you two griping about?" Lloyd asked. "There's no vacuum here." He waved an armored hand. "*Lots* of air! You just can't breathe it!"

Garroway chuckled. He'd said much the same to Kaitlin in his last vidmessage, and he was expecting to be thoroughly roasted for it. She wanted to get into space so badly she could taste it; all he wanted was to get back to Earth . . . and start looking at Bahamian beachfront property.

He wondered what she was doing now.

0411 HOURS GMT

Site 12
Cydonia Base, Mars
1625 hours MMT

"There she goes," Dr. Craig Kettering said.

David Alexander turned, looking toward the south. A

dazzling flare of light emerged from behind the low, Quonset-hut shapes of the base habs, rising rapidly into the afternoon sky. Seconds passed, and then faint and far off, he heard the high-pitched crackle of the rocket's launch-thunder.

"About damned time," he said.

"There's the jolt," Dr. Devora Druzhininova said as she watched the main seismic readout panel. "Force two, this time."

"Just tell me when it's over," Alexander said.

Alexander, Kettering, and Druzhininova were standing next to the portable SIT console that they'd set up outside their Mars cat about two miles northwest of the Cydonian base, to the west of the enigmatic structures known as the Ship and the Fortress.

It was a place of titans. The popular press and some of the less responsible of the netnews services had christened the Cydonian Complex the Golden Plain of the Gods, and, at times, Alexander could almost sympathize. The Face, the mile-long Mt. Rushmore of Mars, as one account had called it, was not the only gigantic structure on this stretch of what once, long ago, had been a beach on a short-lived ocean. West lay the so-called City, four pyramids each easily the size of the Great Pyramid at Giza on Earth, centered on a still-buried gridwork of buildings, tunnels, and ruins. Those pyramids, in turn, were dwarfed by an encircling pentagon of much larger structures, natural mountains smoothed into pyramid shapes, each a mile across at the base.

To the east lay the Fortress, a structure believed to be the foundation of another mile-wide pyramid but with the upper two-thirds missing. The Ship, more enigmatic still, appeared to be a mile-long double-spiral tower that, millennia ago, had toppled across the Fortress and now lay half-embedded in the rubble. No one was certain what, exactly, the thing had been; the best guess was that it had been an enormous spacecraft, though either it was of extremely unusual design, or all that was left was a part of the twisted inner skeleton. So far, after sixteen years of digging and poking about the thing, nothing like engines, power plants, or living quarters had been found. It was like trying to guess the shape, color, and purpose of a long-buried automobile when all that you had to examine was a piece of rusted chassis.

That, of course, was what archeology was all about. Xenoarcheology, as it was developing on Mars, at any rate, had the singular advantage of uncovering ruins that had never been scattered, reused, or built upon by succeeding generations of inhabitants. In a way, that advantage was a disadvantage as well; excavations thus far at Cydonia had uncovered artifacts enough to fill storehouse after storehouse, far more than could possibly be shipped back to Earth, but scientists so far had been able to identify—*guess at*, actually, was the better phrase—perhaps one percent of everything catalogued so far.

And the *real* excavations hadn't even begun, yet. Since the first visit by humans to the site in 2024, archeological teams numbering from four to twelve had managed only to survey perhaps two percent of the entire complex. It was, Alexander thought, a task similar to sending a dozen people into Manhattan with instructions to visit, map, catalogue, photograph, and explore every street, building, alley, vehicle, ship, aircraft, and park on the entire island. The survey alone could take a century or more . . . and only then would the actual large-scale *digging* begin.

And the damned military had to keep sending troops instead of more archeologists!

There were now just twenty-five scientists at Cydonia, if you didn't count Dr. Joubert and the ten UN observers under her direction. Eighteen more were Russian or American support personnel. Now, at last count, there were more than eighty soldiers "protecting scientific and civilian interests," as they put it, and that, so far as Alexander was concerned, was an obscenity, a colossal fraud and waste. Twenty-five scientists couldn't begin to scratch the surface . . . and the UN people seemed more interested in the political ramifications of the research than in the actual fieldwork.

Hell, thirty more archeologists, geologists, and plan-

etary scientists would have been infinitely more useful
than thirty US Marines. As far as he could tell, the
greatest danger on Mars at the moment was the possibility that the Marines and the Foreign Legion UN
troops were going to start shooting at one another and
catch the scientists in the cross fire.

It was idiocy, stark, blatant, and simple. He hated it
. . . and the military mind set that thought in terms of
balanced forces, countered threats, and military expedi-
encies.

It hadn't always been that way. David Alexander had
been a Navy brat, the son of a Navy aviator. By the time
he was fifteen, he'd lived in three different countries and
seven different homes, and since he'd never known any
other life, he'd thought himself privileged. Then, in
2016, his father had died when the laser landing system
on the flight deck of the USS *Reagan* failed during a
night trap. His teenager's dream of being a naval aviator
like his father had died in the same fiery crash.

It wasn't exactly the military itself that Alexander
hated now. That would have been far too simplistic a
response to a tragedy that he'd come to grips with a long
time ago. He did dislike the whole idea of an organization that kept families apart and devoured resources
better spent on things more needful. Usually, he maintained a rather wry attitude about the military . . . unless,
of course, it interfered with his work.

Like now.

"Okay," Druzhininova said at last, looking up. "It's
dying away."

"It's about damned time," Alexander grumbled.
"Let's get this shot done, before something else happens."

"No more lobbers are scheduled for arrival today,
anyway," Craig Kettering said. "We should be cool
there."

Each time a shuttle landed or took off from Cydonia,
the shock caused enough of a seismic tremor in the
ground to thoroughly screw any seismic readings being
taken in the area for kilometers around. The Sonic Im-

aging Tomography display could pick up people walking within fifty meters, and when a lobber-configured shuttle lifted off, even two kilometers away, the ground could be ringing for minutes afterward. With all of the shuttling back and forth between Candor and Cydonia lately, *especially* with all of the UN troops coming north, it had been difficult to get solid periods of quiet for the multiple readings they needed.

"Devora?" Alexander asked. "You have a green on all charges?"

"Affirmative."

"Field team," he said. "Check in."

"All set, Dr. Alexander," Ed Pohl said.

"Clear," Louis Vandemeer added.

"Ready," Kettering said.

"And ready," Druzhininova said. "The console is armed and ready to fire."

Alexander gave a last visual check of the area. All four of the others were well clear of the blast site, a two-hundred-meter-wide region abutting the west side of the Fortress, just below the alien sprawl of the age-corroded Ship.

"Okay. C-Prime, C-Prime, this is Field One, ready to punch it."

"Field One, Cydonia Prime," replied the voice of Dr. Jason Graves. "We have you on-line, charge twenty-nine, site twelve. You may proceed."

Alexander took a final look to left, right, and behind, making certain that the work area was clear. "Okay," he said, turning to Druzhininova. "Let 'er rip!"

The Russian archeologist touched a winking green light on the field data display. There was a sharp, metallic *clack*, and the red-ocher ground in three distinct areas below the Fortress wall heaved upward, creating brief, miniature geysers of swirling red sand.

Alexander shook his head inside his helmet, grinning ruefully. Even after two weeks of this, he still wasn't used to a bang that was nothing at all like a proper *bang*. The three explosive charges they'd just detonated would have made an unholy racket had they set them off on Earth. On Mars, however, with an atmosphere something like one six-thousandth as thick as the air on Earth, sound traveled poorly, and only the deeper tones were preserved. The triple explosion had sounded like a clatter of garbage-can lids.

Still, it wasn't how the sound carried in air that mattered, but how it was transmitted through the cold, dense-packed Martian regolith and the permafrost beneath. "Let's have a look," he told Kettering.

"Nothing yet," Druzhininova said, looking at the screen.

Alexander checked the time function on his suit's HUD. He was tired. Maybe one more run, God and incoming lobbers willing, and then he'd be ready to call it a day . . . no, a *sol*, he reminded himself. It was 1635 hours, MMT, and sunset at Cydonia this time of year came at about 2000 hours.

Craig Kettering looked up from the SIT panel. "So, David," he said over the helmet radio. "What is it with you and that Joubert bi—"

Alexander made a slashing motion with his gloved hand. Although Kettering was using a suit-to-suit comm channel, Cydonia Prime's microwave mast was visible from here, and only about a mile away. It was more than possible that people at Cydonia Prime were listening in—or that the conversations of people in the field were being recorded for later analysis and discussion.

". . . uh . . . *babe*," Kettering said, recovering. "She *is* a babe, you know. . . ."

"We have a good, professional working relationship," Alexander replied, carefully neutral.

To his credit, Kettering didn't laugh out loud, or, if he did, he'd cut his helmet mike in time. It was no secret that he and Joubert hadn't been speaking to one another since their arrival on Mars, just as it apparently was no secret that they'd been romantically involved aboard the *Polyakov*.

At first, Alexander had thought she'd been upset by the sudden arrival of the Marines in *Polyakov*'s storm cellar, but since they'd reached Mars, he'd become convinced that it was something more.

She'd been angry, of course, when Alexander and the Marines had landed directly at Cydonia. She'd come to Cydonia on the next scheduled lobber flight, along with the first contingent of UN troops returning from their brief redeployment to the equator. When she arrived, she'd come in like a whirlwind, quoting regulations, demanding daily reports, and even suggesting that her position as senior UN field director on this expedition meant that the US and Russian scientists had to answer to *her*. Her attitude could change with lightning suddenness, from sweet to imperiously demanding.

He was beginning to suspect that their liaison during the long trip out had been one of two things. Either she'd been bored and found him distracting, or, worse, she was trying to use their sexual relationship to get concessions from him. When he refused to grant those concessions, their personal relationship had dwindled away as though it had never been. He wondered if he'd ever really known her.

Alexander's own directives were clear: treat the UN people with courtesy . . . but remember that this was an American operation, with UN people along as observers. Kenneth Morrow, the SECTECH himself, had talked to Alexander at length before he'd departed for Florida and the shuttle ride to orbit. Although the First Martian Archeological Survey was a civilian operation, it was funded completely by the government and came under the direct management and oversight of both the US Congress and the new Department of Technology. In other words, the UN scientists hitching a ride on the US–Russian cyclers could watch and they could conduct operations of their own—they'd purchased their seats, in effect, from NASA—but they didn't set policy and they didn't give the orders. Alexander was the senior archaeologist on the American team and as such answered only to Dr. Jason Graves, mission chief at Cydonia, and to Mission Control, back on Earth.

None of this had prevented Mireille Joubert from be-

coming a colossal pain in the ass, however. For over a
week, now as Alexander had continued his survey, she'd
demanded daily reports, demanded access to the survey
team's notes, planning meetings, and communications,
even listened in on their conversations.

Politics. . . .

David Alexander liked politics less than he liked the
military . . . especially when it collided with archeology.
Every time you tried crossing science with politics, you
got trouble. As an archeologist, Alexander was preoc-
cupied with facts. Unfortunately, facts tended to be inconvenient to politicians, and the two didn't play well
together.

He still couldn't think about his last assignment in
Egypt without a shudder.

Egyptology, once the most carefully reasoned and me-
ticulously researched of sciences, was currently a mess,
had *been* a mess since the turn of the century. For well
over a hundred years, archeologists and historians had
been confident about the order and the dating of Egyptian history . . . and in particular the identification of the
Giza Complex—three large pyramids, six small ones,
the Sphinx, and a number of associated ramps, road-
ways, temples, and tombs—with the Fourth Dynasty. In
particular, the Great Pyramid, largest of the main three,
had been known to have been built by the Pharaoh
Khufu, who'd ruled Egypt from 2590 to 2567 B.C., while
the Sphinx was believed to have been carved by Khafre,
his brother, successor, and builder of the second tallest
of the main pyramids.

All of that had been overturned during the past forty
years or so. The Great Pyramid's association with Khufu
depended on the writings of Herodotus—who had been
known to be wrong before—and some quarry markings
that were almost certainly recent fabrications, an attempt
by their nineteenth-century soldier-of-fortune discoverer
to have something of substance to show his investors.
The Sphinx, it had been discovered as far back as 1990,
showed geological evidence of dating to a time long before Khafre; the carving showed the unmistakable scal-

loping of rainwater erosion . . . and it had not rained that much on the Giza Plateau since eight thousand years *before* Khafre's day.

David Alexander's principal expertise wasn't Egyptology, but what he *was* expert at—Sonic Imaging Tomography—had a direct bearing on that highly specialized and bureaucratic subset of archeology.

The basic technique had been around for well over half a century. You set off an explosion underground, captured the sound waves scattered by buried structures, and used a computer to paint a kind of sonar picture of what lay hidden beneath sand, mud, soil, or water. Alexander's equipment differed from older models principally in the sophistication of the AI software that did the actual imaging. From three separate but simultaneous blasts, the Honeywell Talus 8000 computer at Cydonia Prime could create a three-dimensional hologram in the same way that separate light sources could be used to compose a 3-D holopic. Anything less dense than solid rock became transparent on the SIT display screen, revealing buried rooms, walls, even individual skeletons and artifacts, all in astonishing detail.

Alexander had been part of an expedition to Egypt in 2037, sponsored by the American Museum and the Smithsonian. After three weeks of work on the Giza Plateau, he'd announced the discovery of an astonishing and heretofore unknown labyrinth of underground passageways and chambers, including what appeared to be a long-vanished waterway, fed by the Nile, which extended from nearly thirty meters beneath the Sphinx all the way to a gallery of chambers far beneath the Great Pyramid itself. The structure was so elaborate, the complex so vast, that he'd confidently asserted this was proof positive, at last, that the Giza complex predated the Fourth Dynasty.

Alexander could still remember the face of Dr. Salim Bahir, Egypt's minister of antiquities, when he'd given the man his preliminary report. "Unacceptable!" the man had said, his fat lips pouting. "Totally and completely unacceptable!"

"I didn't make this up," Alexander had replied. "And it's easily testable. Some of those subterranean structures show evidence of being made of wood." That alone suggested that they'd been built long before this part of the world had turned dry! Trees had been in short supply in Egypt for at least nine thousand years. "Wood can be carbon-dated. And then we'll know! Just as soon as we open up the way into—"

"Excuse me," Bahir had replied, his manner stiff. "There will be no opening."

"What? But these underground—"

"I repeat, *no* opening. The Great Pyramids, the Sphinx, these date from our Fourth Dynasty. That is established scientific fact."

"So was the notion that the sun goes around the Earth. I think I've refuted the conventional dating."

The flat of Bahir's hand came down on his desk top with a sharp crack. "You have refuted nothing! You are a disseminator of vicious and anti-Egyptian propaganda! The Pyramids, the Sphinx, these, these antiquities are the very heart and soul of Egypt, of our culture, of who and what we are. You seek to tear these things from us, to give them to . . . to someone else. Someone you would claim occupied the Nile Valley long before the Egyptian people rose from savagery. This, Dr. Alexander, I will never allow. Not so long as I am head of this office."

He'd found himself under arrest a few hours later . . . and by the end of the week he'd been deported "for attacking the host nation's cultural institutions," as the complaint lodged against him with the World Archeological Congress had asserted.

It had been a blow to his career, though the increasing tensions between the United States and the UN had actually served to make him something of a popular hero at home. Politics, again. When the decision was made to send a tomographic imager to Mars, he'd been the obvious choice.

Cydonia presented tomographic scanners with a special problem: much of the complex was at least partly buried in the permafrost layer, which lay some two to three meters beneath the surface in this area. Permafrost is essentially frozen mud; at Martian temperatures, ice is an extremely hard material. Indeed, there were plans to begin constructing buildings made from permafrost bricks. The stuff was so hard it was difficult to distinguish between it and the materials the long-vanished Builders at Cydonia had used—mostly native bedrock, at a time when Mars had enjoyed an ocean of liquid water—the Boreal Sea.

"Hey! I think we've got something here," Kettering said. He pointed at the screen. "Is that an open space?"

"Too soon to tell yet," Alexander replied, studying the screen. "Wait it out. . . ." The features Kettering had pointed out were still little more than fuzzy gray shadows that suggested structures made of denser material than sand or ice, but they could be buried walls or buildings, or they might be sand-covered boulders. They did suggest an unusually orderly arrangement . . . a geometry of right angles, circles, and straight lines, and Alexander could feel his pulse quickening with excitement. It certainly looked artificial. . . .

"Look here," Kettering said, pointing at the SIT screen. "That's *got* to be a passageway, a tunnel or something, right up against the wall of the Fortress. And with an airlock at the surface."

"Or a ventilation duct," Alexander replied, "with air-conditioning or pressurization equipment at the top." He knew more than most the problems inherent in leaping to conclusions at the first encounter with new data.

Druzhininova was already using the display's keyboard to take a set of bearings. The Martian magnetic field was weak, about two-one-thousandths as strong as Earth's, making traditional compass navigation difficult to impossible, but navigation satellites in areosynchronous orbit let them pinpoint themselves, or visible landmarks, to within a few centimeters. All of the shapes and structures visible on the sonic display were now located on the computer's master navigational grid.

"There," she said, pointing. "Airlock or air conditioner, that's where it is."

Alexander looked at the spot where she was pointing—an otherwise unremarkable swelling in the ground where sand had piled up against the Fortress's western wall. There was *something* there.

In the sixteen years since humans had first stood at this site, literally hundreds of artificial structures had been found, and most seemed to suggest that there was a truly vast and labyrinthine complex of tunnels and interconnected chambers beneath the Martian surface. That was why they'd brought him here, after all.

"Whaddya say, Dave?" Kettering said. Alexander could hear the grin in his voice as he reached for one of the shovels resting in an equipment rack on the Mars cat. "What could it hurt? At least we can have a look."

Proper procedure called for flagging all new surface discoveries and bringing them up for review in the group research meeting held each morning. But as Kettering said . . . what could it hurt?

He hesitated a moment longer, then grabbed another shovel for himself. "Let's go check it out."

"Field Team, this is C-Prime," a woman's voice said in his helmet phones. "David? What are you doing?" It sounded like Mireille.

"Just checking something, C-Prime," he said. "Wait one."

"May I remind you that you are not to begin excavations until the site has been properly surveyed and mapped."

"Yes, you may. We just want to check something here."

Cydonia Prime was two kilometers distant. There was absolutely nothing they could do to stop the team from an act of what was certainly a breach of proper procedure . . . an act that Alexander knew he simply could not resist.

The hummock was perhaps a meter tall and four or five meters on a side, a mound of crusty soil against the Fortress wall that looked perfectly natural. Only the sub-

surface sonogram proved that a passageway ended right
. . . *here*.

Gently, he scraped at the dirt with the blade of his
shovel. The surface resisted at first, then crumbled away
in great, frozen clots of earth, revealing . . .

. . . a hole. A hole leading down into blackness beneath the Fortress.

"Christ!" Pohl said, standing just behind Kettering
and Druzhininova. "It's open!"

"Field Team, this is CP! What's open? What's happening? Answer!"

Gently, Alexander touched his gloved finger to his
visor, indicating silence, then tapped the side of his helmet. *Keep down the chatter. They're listening.* He didn't
want to debate each move with the UN archeologists.

It took only a few moments to clear away the opening.
Steps were visible. Apparently, some gray-colored, extremely hard material had been used to construct the
walls of the structure, and the floor had been cast with
steps. The tunnel was circular and about two meters
across.

A burning curiosity drove Alexander onward. He'd
expected a door, a sealed entrance, an airlock hatch. Apparently, the tunnel mouth had been open once, covered
over with . . . with mud, perhaps? Yes, almost certainly.
The mud had frozen, then dried, forming a crusty, easily
broken covering of regolith and packed sand.

"Field Team One! Field Team One! Respond,
please!"

Alexander reached up and switched on his helmet
light, the white beam showing plainly in the dust still
floating in the thin air of the descending tunnel. Carefully, testing each step, he started down the stairs.

According to the sonogram, this descending tunnel
should only extend down for about seven or eight meters, before entering a larger chamber of some sort. From
there the main passageway ran east five meters beneath
the surface.

The stairs were barely visible. The mud or whatever
it was that had covered over the surface structure evi-

dently had spilled down the stairway without blocking it completely. He had to bend nearly double, though, to get through to the bottom. Kettering and the others followed closely behind.

Carter must have felt this way at the opening of Tutankhamen's tomb. For the first time in how many millennia, a living being stood in this vault beneath the surface of Mars. He stood at the foot of the stairs, turning slowly, playing his helmet lamp across walls caked with the dust of uncounted ages. There was nothing distinctive about the architecture, no wall carvings, no decorations. The place was stark and utilitarian. He smiled. It might have been the interior of a military base, painted a bland conformist gray.

And then he saw the bodies.

There were four of them, and they all were huddled against a door to what Alexander knew was the southern passageway, the one leading to the nearby pyramid. The startling thing about them was that they looked *human* . . . a totally unexpected development.

"My God," Kettering said, awed. "*Humans! . . .*"

"They can't be," Vandemeer said. "Everything we've found indicates that the Ancients were nonhuman."

Alexander knelt carefully beside one of the bodies. It *was* still a body and not a skeleton, as he might have expected. The face was iron gray and hardened, the lips pulled back from clenched teeth in a death's-head rictus. The hair, long and braided, was the same color, matted with dust. He was wearing something that might have been a uniform, or worker's garb . . . without a proper context there was no way to tell. The device on one shoulder appeared to be a mission patch of some sort, though the colors were so faded it was impossible to make out what it might have represented.

Most disturbing, though, was the position the four had been in when they'd died. They were huddled together, some with arms still locked around their comrades. Two were reaching up with clawed, skeletal hands, resting against the sealed door, as though their last moments had been spent pounding or scratching at that barrier for admittance. One was partly turned, his blind face staring back toward the steps leading to the surface, as though watching for the arrival of whatever fate had overtaken them.

Careful not to touch any of the bodies—Alexander had the feeling that a touch, a whisper of breeze, even, would cause them to crumble—he searched for further clues. These people were technological, certainly. Each wore a metallic device of some sort on his right shoulder . . . a communicator, possibly. The more he looked, the more convinced he was that they were . . . not human, exactly, but very close. Their chins were less prominent than a human's, the jaw muscles more pronounced, the ridges above the vacantly staring eye sockets thicker, the eyebrows bushier. The eyes, unfortunately, were gone, freeze-dried into dust by millennia of near vacuum. He wished he could have seen the eyes. He had a feeling they would have been disturbingly like his own.

The problem with the Face, of course, had always been that it was so human-looking, even though, clearly, no human could possibly have carved it.

It might, in fact, have been a portrait of one of these dead men.

It would take more and careful study to be certain, but Alexander was virtually certain that he was looking at four members of genus *Homo*, species *erectus* . . . the hominids from which modern humans had evolved.

And the question, of course, was what the hell had they been doing on Mars?

He realized the increasingly frantic calls from Cydonia Prime had been cut off when he'd descended the stairs. These walls, evidently, blocked radio. "Pohl?" he said. "Go back up to the surface. Raise the base. Tell them . . . tell them they'd better get some people over here, that we've found something that's going to stand their hair on end."

It was, Alexander was convinced, a discovery in the same class as those made by Copernicus and Darwin, a find to revolutionize humankind's understanding of itself.

NINE

Human evolution/Brain size: The evolutionary tree of genus Homo is now well understood. *Homo habilis* gave rise, roughly 1.7 million years ago, to *Homo erectus*, who in turn gave rise to archaic populations of *Homo sapiens* 400,000 to 500,000 years ago. Besides the ongoing increase in average cranial capacity, principal changes included a general enlargement of the spinal cord, permitting better manual coordination. **Tool manufacture** began with *H. habilis* at least two million years ago, but tools remained primitive and coarse, little more than a few flakes struck from a pebble to create a sharp edge, until the greatly increased dexterity of *H. sapiens* permitted refinement and creative development. Speech was also a relatively late development.

It should be remembered that late *H. erectus* shared most of the traits of primitive or "archaic" *H. sapiens*, including brain size. Still, the transition appears to have been abrupt and is still poorly understood. Further study of the Martian data may . . .

—*Download from Networld Encyclopedia*
vrtp://earthnet.public.dataccess

Cydonia Base, Mars
Sol 5634: 2045 hours MMT

The last pale glow of the sunset had long since faded
from the sky outside, surrendering the desert below to
the star-dusted black of the Martian night. Inside the
common room, where Mark Garroway was sitting at the
table along with Colonel Lloyd, David Alexander, and
a dozen or so of the expedition's senior people, the harsh
and unrelenting glare of fluorescents gave scant warmth
to air swiftly turning chilly and damp. It was always like
this in these large habs, once the sun had set. Cydonia
Prime's environmental systems were being stretched to
their operational limits with the demands being made on
them just now. During the two weeks after *Harper's
Bizarre* had touched down, all fifty-four of the UN
troops had ferried back from Candor Chasma, along with
the new members of the UN science team, bringing the
complement on-station at Cydonia Prime to 138.

Both Colonel Bergerac and the UN archeological
team leader, Mireille Joubert, were present in the room
now. Joubert had called the emergency meeting, in fact,
apparently for the purpose of reading the riot act to Alexander.

"What do you mean," Alexander was saying slowly,
"we can't tell anyone on Earth yet? This . . . this is the
most incredible discovery in the history of—"

"Please, David, I *know* the importance, the possible
significance of this discovery. And that's precisely why
we shouldn't release it until we know more."

Dr. Graves laughed. "Until we know more? My God!
We've found four naturally mummified humans on
Mars! Isn't that worth at least the cost of an e-mail to
Earth?"

Garroway looked away as the argument continued,
distractedly studying the vaulting, strut-lined interior of
the building. Most of the habitats on Mars looked like
the interior of a Shuttle II's main fuel tank . . . probably

because most of them *were* Shuttle II fuel tanks, hauled out to Mars orbit by one or another of the cyclers, fitted with small, methane-fueled deorbit boosters, and lowered the last few kilometers to the Martian surface by parachute . . . a process far cheaper than hauling the building materials all the way out to Mars and then assembling them in place. This habitat possessed an upper and a lower deck—the lower given over to stores and a reserve of liquid water, the upper divided between living quarters, a rec facility, and the common room. Pressurized tunnels led to other habs nearby, including Ops, the big, pressurized ex–fuel tank next door that housed the communications center, the Central Operational Node or CON—essentially the facility's main AI computer—and the control center. The main tanks-turned-habitats were far more spacious than were needed yet within the growing colony, but they still lacked a few of the basic amenities . . . such as windows.

Not that Garroway was that interested in watching the sere and barren Martian landscape; he'd seen quite enough of it already during the past two weeks, as the Marines had gotten themselves settled in. But the interiors of the habitats were all the same, and, roomy or not, they forced your attention inward, to your own thoughts and to the people you were with. The idea of another year or more locked up in close quarters with Mireille Joubert was not exactly a solid inducement to emigrate to Mars. She might be nice to look at, but she'd become strident and overbearing since they'd landed. Worse, she was wielding the opinion that she was in charge of the expedition's science team like a weapon. Garroway generally tried to arrange things so that he could be where she wasn't.

Sometimes though, like during these department-head meetings, that just wasn't possible. Garroway had already decided his first day on the beach that the only way to keep his sanity over the next few months was to keep his head down and to say as little as possible. He allowed himself a private smile. The never-volunteer philosophy was generally the prerogative of enlisted men, rather than officers.

This was the worst such meeting he'd run into yet. He hadn't heard the whole story, but he gathered that Alexander had done something to put Joubert really out of sorts. The discovery—four beings that looked human or damned close to it—would seem to have been worth whatever risk or shortcut the man had taken, but Joubert had been raking him over the coals for it.

The funny part was, he didn't think she even had the authority to do so.

"A discovery of such potential," Joubert said, "demands extraordinary care in just how the announcement is made to the general public."

"We're not suggesting a release to the public," Alexander pointed out. "We're talking about transmitting text and images of what we found to Mission Control. They can decide what to say, if anything."

She rolled her eyes toward the chamber's ceiling. "Please, David, don't assume that I am stupid! I know how your press works . . . and your politicians. Transmitting this data to Earth is the same as plastering it all over every netnews download on the Web."

"I don't understand," Graves said. "What do you want . . . for us to just sit on this find? To run more tests?"

"Yes, just what more would you suggest, Doctor?" Alexander asked reasonably. "We don't have the equipment to run sophisticated tests, and I'm afraid that just touching those bodies will make them crumble away into dust."

"For one thing, we should try to establish scientifically what all of you seem to be taking for granted . . . that the bodies are human and that they are associated with the Builders."

"They're inside that room," Kettering said. He was leaning back in his chair, his arms folded across his chest. "The four of them looked like they were trying to claw their way right through that door. That looks pretty damned associated to me."

"And you can't seriously be suggesting that those bodies are not human," Dr. Patricia Colt said. She was Cydonia Prime's Life Sciences Department head, a rather broad job description that included the study of Martian parabiological soil chemistry, cataloguing microfossils, and running the base med lab.

"And why not?" Joubert replied.

"Everything we think we understand about xenobiology," Colt said, "suggests that when we meet extraterrestrials, they will look nothing like us."

"Hell, the big mystery that drew us here in the first place," Alexander added, "was the Face . . . and the question of what the representation of a human face was doing here. The fact that we found humans in that room suggests some extraordinary possibilities. If nothing else, it suggests that humans were here when this place was built. And that was . . . when, Dr. Graves?"

"It depends on the dating method you use. Somewhere between four and five hundred thousand years, though, is a close guess."

"The recordings shot by Dr. Alexander and his people," Colt added, "suggest that these . . . these people are not fully modern humans. Their facial features, the brow ridges, the receding chins, they show some characteristics that I would associate with archaic *Homo sapiens* . . . or even with late *Homo erectus*."

"In other words, people from half a million years ago," Alexander put in. "To find them . . . *here*. . . . That suggests to me that extraterrestrials took an interest in humans—or in what one day would become humans. They visited Earth in the mid to late Pleistocene, picked up some specimens of our ancestors, and brought them here." He laughed. "My God! We have here proof that there was direct interaction between the Ancients and the dominant hominid species on Earth half a million years ago. More than interaction! Those bodies are wearing uniforms and carrying devices that might be communicators or even small computers of some kind. There's at least a possibility that our own ancestors had a hand in building some of what we're seeing here, and it certainly casts an intriguing new light on the existence of the Face. We need to bring the rest of our colleagues back on Earth in on this as quickly as we can.''

''But that's just where you are jumping to conclusions! Don't you see? There are so many *other* possibilities!''

''Such as? . . .'' Graves asked.

''Those bodies might not be human at all. They could be aliens.''

''*Hardly* likely, Doctor,'' Colt said. ''The chances of a separate evolution producing a species nearly identical—''

''Let me finish! They could be humans, certainly, members of some ancient, lost civilization, one that developed space flight long ago in our remote prehistory.''

Alexander snorted. ''A global, highly technical civilization that leaves no trace of itself?''

''Our rise from the Stone Age spans, what?'' Joubert said. ''Six thousand years? Seven? The blink of an eye compared to half a million years.''

''Maybe. But in that 'blink of an eye,' as you call it, we've managed to pretty much tap out all of the easily accessible copper, tin, silver, gold, chromium . . . most of the elements necessary to produce a high-tech civilization. Not to mention draining most of the world's oil fields, polluting and fishing out the seas, creating vast garbage dumps, heating up the atmosphere enough to start the polar caps melting and paving over whole forests. Even after half a million years there'd be signs left of that kind of activity.''

''It still seems at least as viable an explanation as what you seem to be suggesting, that we were . . . were *tampered* with by aliens. That is what you're suggesting, is it not?'' She made a face. ''That smacks too much of the old ancient astronaut nonsense.''

Alexander folded his arms. ''I'm no von Danikenist, if that's what you mean. But Occam's Razor seems to apply here. We have people, beings, if you will, who—''

''We don't even know that those bodies have been here as long as the structures!'' she said quickly, interrupting. "Those poor men could have been brought here in recent times, by members of an alien expedition."

Alexander turned to the others, as several in the room groaned or chuckled. "In other words, ancient astronaut theories aren't even worth considering, but we *can* begin seriously investigating UFO abductions!"

"My point, gentlemen, and Dr. Colt, is that there are far too many possibilities for us to make any snap judgments! We should not recklessly broadcast this information to Earth. We should investigate further, gathering data, assessing further finds, and proceeding in a thorough, professional manner. *Not*," she added sharply, looking at Alexander, "conducting half-baked excavations on a whim. And not jumping to premature conclusions!"

"Which itself would be a violation of our mission directives," Alexander shot back, his face reddening. "I don't know how you people do things with the UN, Dr. Joubert, but we have been directed to keep our bosses Earthside apprised of all developments. As they happen! For one thing, that means if we all die tonight of a reactor malfunction, they'll still get something for their investment back on Earth. Besides, they have better brains and lots more of 'em back there. If anyone is qualified to draw conclusions from raw data, it's people like Dr. Soulter, Langley, Tom Hoskins at U of C, Dr. Samuels in Boston. Top people. Not dirt-beneath-the-nails diggers like us."

"The fact remains, Dr. Joubert," Dr. Jason Graves added, as Alexander's outburst subsided, "that you are not in command of the science team here. It happens that *I* am, and while I will be delighted to have you voice your concerns, the decision as to what may and may not be released to Earth, surely, is something to be determined by the American team."

"And I submit to you, Dr. Graves, that you are a geologist, an areologist, I should say, and not empowered to make *political* determinations about data recovered by this expedition."

"*Politics*!" Alexander spoke the word as though ridding his mouth of a foul taste.

"*Yes*, David. Politics! And I have been commissioned by the UN to serve as political officer for the UN contingent. In that capacity, I must insist that you at least listen to what I have to say."

Garroway exchanged a wry glance with Colonel Lloyd at that. He'd not realized the UN had a commissar on the team.

"And what is so political about what we've found?" Alexander wanted to know.

"Tell me, David," she said after a moment's pause. "Have you been listening to the news from Earth? It is bad, no?"

"I'm not sure I see how what's going on back there affects this decision," Alexander said.

"No? Then I suggest you review the netnews downloads of the fighting in Mexico City, the other day. An American Marine was killed there, I hear. Or the riots in Cairo, in New Delhi, in Tehran, Baghdad. Even in your United States, there are religious or quasireligious sects and factions that would be, shall we say, inflamed by news of what you have found here today. The careless dissemination of information such as this could cause a political and social explosion unlike anything seen before."

"Oh, come now, Dr. Joubert—" Graves began.

"We already have something like a quarter of the Earth's population convinced that what we are dealing with here on Mars is somehow demonic, that we are challenging proper beliefs in God, that we are overthrowing the established order, promulgating heretical doctrines, even intentionally corrupting all decent and God-fearing humans. We have another faction, smaller, perhaps, but even more vocal, convinced that the Ancients were gods of some sort who raised us up out of savagery, who gene-engineered our intelligence, who created us, in short. Some want to worship these, these outer-space *gods*! I tell you, the news that protohumans have been found here, amid the Ancients' ruins, could lead to a total collapse of civilization.''

"I think you're overstating things somewhat, Doctor," Graves said reasonably. "We humans have had our pet theories and prejudices overturned before. We're adaptable, after all."

"We may be, yes. But our cultures are not. Civilization is not. Civilization can be remarkably fragile, as anyone who has seen a food riot or cannibalism in a famine-stricken region can tell you. The United Nations World Cultural Bureau is extremely concerned about the threat of worldwide violence, violence precipitated by the irresponsible release of untested data such as this!''

Alexander was shaking his head, a grin on his face.

"What's so funny, David?" Joubert demanded.

"Ah . . . excuse me. I was just thinking that the Vatican must have thought something similar when Galileo wanted to publish his observations of the moons of Jupiter. Or when Copernicus published *De Revolutionibus*. I really thought that humankind had moved beyond such blinkered narrow-mindedness.''

"Not narrow-mindedness, David," Joubert replied coldly. "Responsibility. There is more here at stake than publishing credits in a science journal . . . or in making up for past professional mistakes.''

Alexander rose from his seat, and Garroway thought for a moment that he was going to strike the woman. He reached out with one hand and laid it on Alexander's elbow. "Easy, there, son. . . .''

The archeologist shook the hand off, then slowly, angrily resumed his seat. "That was uncalled for!" he said.

"I think not," Joubert replied. "You, David, of all people, would want to be careful about the information you present to a waiting world.'' She spread her hands. "And . . . I'm not suggesting anything like a permanent suppression of the data. Simply do me the favor of not making an announcement for, shall we say, forty-eight hours? Let me consult with my superiors in Geneva, and we can talk again after I've heard back from them. Two days more to gather further data and evaluate the site.

Isn't that fair? Especially given the importance of this find.''

Graves looked across the table at Alexander. ''What do you think, David? We could let her have that much, couldn't we? We'll need the time just to write up the reports and to check all of the digital scans.''

''I suppose so.'' He didn't sound happy. Garroway thought that Joubert's comment about his professional mistakes had touched a very raw nerve.

''Everybody?'' Graves asked, addressing the table. ''It's late, and we're all tired. Is there a problem with waiting two days before announcing this discovery?''

There were murmurs from the others, mostly in the negative. Colonel Lloyd raised his hand.

''Colonel?'' Graves said.

''I just wanted to say that . . . this isn't a scientific comment, but I do find the fact that the members of an American expedition are deferring to UN personnel with no jurisdiction . . . disturbing. It sets an unfortunate precedent.''

''In the first place, Colonel,'' Joubert replied, ''I'm not asking for you to defer to me. I just want a little time to consult with my superiors. Most likely, they will agree with Dr. Alexander, but if there is a problem, they should be allowed to share with us their views, no? As for precedent, I will only remind you that there is every possibility that future expeditions to Mars will be internationalized and, therefore, will come under direct UN jurisdiction and supervision. Your cooperation with my superiors could indeed set a precedent. A *good* one.''

The meeting broke up shortly afterward. After Joubert and the other UN people had left, Garroway turned to Alexander. ''I thought you had something going with Joubert?''

''Not anymore,'' the archeologist replied. ''That woman is bad, bad news.''

''Looked like you were about to slug her there, for a second.''

''No. I wish . . . but, no.''

"What was that crack about mistakes? You don't have to tell me if you don't—"

Alexander looked up at the doorway through which Joubert had just left. "Oh, there's nothing secret about it, but nothing really important, either. Let's just say I've crossed swords with some highly placed people before over discoveries that they'd rather didn't see the light of day. I guess she's done her research and found out whose toes I've been stepping on. I think she's looking for leverage, some way she can manipulate me."

Garroway chuckled. "I've heard it said that archeologists dig up other people's garbage. I didn't know that included skeletons in closets."

"Quite true. Very *old* garbage, usually, and you never know where the skeletons are going to turn up. Archeologists are diggers, Major. But sometimes, the things they dig up are inconvenient. Or culturally embarrassing."

"I'm still not sure I understand why she's so bent out of shape about this."

"Mmm. Hard to say, really. She's right that there are people back home who won't like what we've found here. And others who'll seize on it as proof that God was an astronaut."

"Yeah, I was wondering about that. What was that thing about ancient astronauts?"

"Oh, various writers, late twentieth, early twenty-first century, developed the notion that a lot of the strange artifacts and buildings and monuments on Earth couldn't have been built by primitive peoples . . . or at least, not by primitives working by themselves. They must have had extraterrestrials helping with antigravity or whatever."

Garroway laughed. "Seriously?"

"Oh, yes. Quite a few writers jumped on that particular wagon. Erich von Daniken was one of the noisiest. His willingness to attribute every cultural oddity or mystery to aliens pretty well soured the scientific community on the whole idea. Unfortunately, well, the discovery that the Face was an artificial structure of some kind gave an extra boost to his theories, gave them greater credibility. Probably spawned half a dozen star-child religions.''

''You believe this stuff?''

''Mostly, no. Most reputable scientists don't. The idea was popularized in a number of books, but the information was never scientifically presented, much of it was hearsay, and a lot of the facts were just plain wrong. Hell, back in the seventies, von Daniken's stuff gave the whole subject such a bad taste that most real archeologists stayed clear of the whole subject for fifty years.''

''No science, all air, huh?''

''Well, the trouble with most of those books was that they usually ignored the simple answer, even ignored the people right there on the spot who could still demonstrate how their ancestors built the whatever-it-was. The Easter Islanders are a great example.''

''I've heard about them. Big, stone heads on the beach. I didn't think aliens were supposed to have anything to do with them. They're big, yeah, but not so big you need antigravity to explain them. I thought the biggest mystery there was why the things were raised in the first place.''

''With the ancient-astronauts crowd, nothing is ever that simple.'' Alexander chuckled. ''Sometimes the ancient-astronaut guys really got carried away. One saw aircraft landing strips where the natives had cleared away dark surface pebbles to expose light-colored stones underneath. The Nazca lines, in Peru. They are incredible—huge drawings of animals and figures and geometric lines that can only be appreciated from the air.'' He chuckled. ''But don't ever try to land your airliner there.''

''Don't worry. I won't.''

''What I always hated about those theories was the way they could so casually dismiss the natural inventiveness, the creativity, the *cleverness* of us humans. We've done some quite spectacular things on this planet, you know, without a scrap of help from aliens with antigravity beams. Most of the evidence offered to support those theories is ambiguous at best.''

"Yeah, but you said 'mostly, no,' when I asked if you believed. What part do you believe?"

"Well, you know, sometimes I wonder if we didn't go too far in chucking everything those writers suggested. There are a few landmarks on Earth that probably weren't built by the people we've always assumed built them, and there's no decent explanation. The Temple of the Sun at Titicaca is one. The foundation at Baalbek in Lebanon is another. The complex at Giza, the Great Pyramids and the Sphinx, is a third. If aliens didn't build the things, it's at least possible they were inspired by, shall we say, visitors from someplace else. If I had to point to specific structures on Earth that I thought gave evidence that we'd been visited in the remote past, I'd point to those three." Alexander grinned suddenly. "Of course, don't tell my colleagues that. I'd be blackballed from the Loyal Fraternity of Diggers and Pot-Shard Hunters if they knew. Stripped of my official shovel and whisk broom and drummed out of the corps."

"My lips are sealed. But tell me, off the record. Is there really any chance that aliens built those places?"

Alexander sighed. "I wish I could tell you. I wish I *knew*. If I'd been doing archeology in the last century, I'd have to say that the chances were, oh, I don't know. Five percent. Once we demonstrated that the Face on Mars was no accident of light and shadow, the way they thought when they first photographed it from orbit, well, the chances went up quite a bit, you know? Fifty-fifty, maybe. Or better."

Garroway blinked. "Why so much?"

"Because now we *know* that, once upon a time, there were aliens in the neighborhood. We know we're not alone in the universe, and that one piece of information has already started to change everything about the way we look at ourselves, the way we think about our past and who we are and where we're going."

"Oh, I don't know about that," Garroway replied. "I think it's interesting, sure . . . but you don't see me joining any aliens-created-Man cults. I think most people will just, I don't know, accept it and get on with their lives.''

"Maybe." He didn't sound convinced. "With me, though, I can't help it, when I look at the stars now, thinking that there's some sort of a connection. Between us and the stars. Something more than just the fact that we're here.''

"Some of those groups back on Earth are claiming that humans are descended from a lost colony of aliens who got stranded here hundreds of thousands of years ago. Maybe what you found out there today supports that notion.''

Alexander laughed. "God, I hope not! That's one of the sillier ideas being bandied about right now. Man's place in Earth's evolutionary tree is very firmly established. Did you know that human DNA differs from chimpanzee DNA by something less than two percent?''

"No, I didn't know that.''

"It's true. Doesn't mean we're descended from chimps, of course. Just that they're relatives, with the same great-great-granddad as us. Not only that, but we're just too well adapted to the local ecology . . . from what we eat to the symbiotic relationship we have with bacteria in our guts. If early humans had come from another world, well, chances are they wouldn't even have been able to eat the local food. Even if their body chemistries were based on sugars and amino acids, there'd be just a one-in-four chance at best that they'd be able to digest the stuff they found growing here. Isomers.''

"Isomers?" Garroway made a whizzing motion with his hand above his head. "You lost me.''

Alexander was warming to the topic, growing enthusiastic. Garroway guessed that he was working off frustration accumulated in the meeting. "Some molecules have mirror-image versions of themselves. Same molecule, made of the same atoms, but structurally reversed. Biochemists talk about left- or right-handed molecules. Sugar, for example—we use right-handed sugar. That's where we get the name *dex*trose, in fact. We can't digest levo-sugars. They pass right through without doing a thing, because we've evolved to use the right-handed form. At the same time, we use levo–amino acids and can't digest the right-handed ones. And, so far as we can tell, whether a given planetary ecology evolves with right-handed or left-handed isomers of all the various organic molecules is purely a matter of chance. Toss a coin.''

Garroway nodded. ''Which is why you say we have a one-in-four chance of finding dextro-sugars *and* levo–amino acids on a new planet.''

''Right. And that's just for starters. There's also the problem of long-chain proteins that—''

''Whoa!'' Garroway said, holding up both hands. ''I never got beyond high-school chemistry. Organics leave me whimpering and sucking my thumb. But I get the idea. Humans may have picked up some hints and tips from aliens, but we *ain't* the aliens.''

''Eloquently stated, Major. I just wish we could find what the true extraterrestrial connection was.''

''Maybe we're about to find out,'' Garroway said.

''I know we are, Major. We've just scratched the surface.'' He pointed at the floor. ''The answers are *here*, under our feet. And I'm going to find them.''

Garroway was impressed by the man's determination, the sheer will in his voice. ''Yes, Dr. Alexander. I think you are.''

''And Mireille Joubert and her World Cultural Bureau and the whole damned UN can go to hell.''

They left the rec area together.

                                        1039 HOURS GMT

Communications Center
Cydonia Base, Mars
2253 hours MMT

Cydonia Prime's communications room was located in a partitioned-off portion of the command center. There wasn't much to see there—the computers used to maintain communications between people on surface EVA or in the Mars cats, the main workstation with a direct uplink to the areosynchronous comsat, and another unit that maintained a constant open channel with Mars Prime, again through the comsat. During the day, when teams were working out on the surface, the comm center was a busy, even a crowded place, but no one ventured out onto the surface during the night, when the outside temperature plunged to minus one hundred twenty Celsius or lower. A communications watch was maintained through the night, of course, with personnel rotating down the watch list from both the NASA crew and the US Marines.

A Marine was on watch this night, but that didn't bother Dr. Joubert. She smiled as the young man handed her a hardcopy printout. "Here ya go, ma'am."

"Thank you, Corporal." Turning, she walked through the partition door into the main command center. There were three or four people there, either on duty or chatting. Colonel Bergerac was waiting for her by the door.

"Colonel?" Joubert handed him the hardcopy. "It seems we have our reply."

Bergerac's bushy eyebrows raised as he accepted the sheet and glanced at it. ALPHA APPROVED IMMEDIATE was all it said.

"That was fast," he said. "Scarcely time for the light lag."

Earth and Mars were currently five light-minutes apart. The query, coded and inserted in the normal outbound comm traffic, had uploaded at 2136 hours. It would have reached Earth at 2141. Valle and the others must have been waiting right there at the Geneva command center to have made their decision and relayed it back in less than an hour.

"Soltime tomorrow," she said. "That will give our people at Candor time to get ready."

Bergerac nodded. "It will be good to have these American Marines out from underfoot," he said.

TEN

Mars Expedition/Communications: Reliable communications are vital for the safety, efficiency and productivity of the mission, and **Spacenet** has been adapted to the purpose. Established in 2024 as an extension of the existing **Internet**, **Spacenet** provides both broad- and narrow-band data transmission, including graphical and video interfacing through the **World Wide Web**. Primary Earthside nodes include the AI systems at **Kennedy** and **Vandenberg** Spaceports, as well as the **Marshal**, **Johnson**, and **Greenbelt** Space Centers. Spaceside nodes include the AI systems of each of the manned space stations, with the primary node in the **ISS**, as well as the **Fra Mauro** Node on Luna. All Mars communications are currently relayed through a PV-10K communications satellite in areosynchronous orbit. A secondary relay is located in the old MSC-1 system on the inner Martian moon, Phobos—currently inoperative.

—Download from Networld Encyclopedia
vrtp://earthnet.public.dataccess

SUNDAY, 27 MAY: 1159 HOURS GMT
Cydonia Base, Mars
Sol 5636: soltime +13 minutes
MMT

It was just past midnight, the time of the day reserved
for the so-called soltime, the extra forty-one minutes and
some odd seconds that brought the human reckoning of
time by hours, minutes, and seconds into line with
Mars's longer rotational period. Garroway had been
planning on hitting his rack early, but he was on edge
and sleep eluded him. It had been a long day—most of
it spent in a long series of diagnostics with the EVA
suits used by Alexander, Kettering, Pohl, Druzhininova,
and Vandemeer when they'd made their discovery at the
Fortress the day before. All five suits had flagged red in
pre-EVA checkout. With the chance—admittedly remote—that something about the site had somehow affected the suits, no one was being allowed to return to
the site until it could be checked out remotely, and that
was going to take time. There'd been nothing wrong
with the suits that he could determine.

Alexander had been furious, convinced that Joubert or
one of the UN people had sabotaged the readouts to keep
them from going back to the Fortress site.

The possibility that the expedition could be torn apart
by internal dissension or even UN sabotage was a serious one; building psychological pressures within any
small group of mismatched people cooped up together
far from other humans had more than once led to disaster.

Unable to sleep, Garroway walked over to the comm
center, where he commed a long vidmessage to Kaitlin.
After uploading it onto Spacenet, he went back to the
command center, poured himself a cup of coffee at the
mess, and sat down at a spare console seat with Dr.
Graves and Corporal Phil Hayes, who had the communications mid-watch. Hayes stood as Garroway came
closer.

"At ease, at ease," he said. "What's the good word?"

"Hello, Major," Graves said. "The corporal was just telling me about the problems you Marines are having on Mars."

"You having problems, Corporal?" Garroway asked.

"No, sir!" the Marine snapped back, resuming his seat but managing to remain at attention.

"It's okay, son," he said. "I'm not your CO, and I don't bite. What's the trouble?"

"Well, sir . . . the sand is hell on the rifles. It's more like a real fine dust or windblown grit, y'know? Gets into everything. Coats everything, worse'n mud."

"Which is why all of the weapons-cleaning drills on the way out, right?"

"Roger that, sir. Then, on top of that, some REMF back on Earth recalibrated all of ATARs, so we couldn't hit shit when we started range practice last week. We had 'em set for Mars gravity, y'know? Then when we started workin' with 'em here, we kept hitting above the bull's-eye. I thought old Lloyd and Master—uh, I mean—"

"That's okay. Go ahead, Marine."

"Uh, I thought the colonel was gonna shit, sir. We were all selected for this mission, y'know, on the strength of our quals Earthside, and it was looking like we were the worst damned shots in the Corps."

"You get that straightened out?"

"Oh, sure. It was pretty obvious what had happened. You know, no one in the Marines, no one in the ranks, anyway, likes these new electronic rifles. Too much gadgetry screws things up, y'know? Give me a rifle you could sight in with a sandbag and a screwdriver, like in the old days."

Garroway chuckled. Hayes looked too young to reminisce about "the old days."

"I was telling him," Graves added, "that it sounded like someone on Earth got his sums wrong."

"Exactly what I was thinking," Garroway said. The

M-29 ATAR was designed to accept PAD entries feeding it data such as air pressure, altitude, cartridge size, and gravity in order to precisely sight the rifle—supposedly a big improvement over the old-fashioned chore of taking it out to the range and sighting it in manually. "The gravitational acceleration on Earth is 980 centimeters per second squared. On Mars it's, what?"

"Three seventy-one and a bit," Graves said. "About a third."

"I can see how that would throw your aim off. Some supply officer probably looked at that 371 centimeters per second squared, said, 'Hey! This can't be right!' and changed it."

"Every rifleman ought to be responsible for sighting in his *own* weapon," Hayes said in the matter-of-fact way that professionals have when they discuss their tools. "Leave it to some supply officer back on Earth, and, see what happens? If there's a way to fuck it up, you know they'll find a way to do it." He didn't specify who *they* might be, but Garroway understood the feelings every soldier of every time and nationality had for the bureaucrats and bean counters behind the lines.

"You know," Graves added, "I'm reminded of something I read about the early space-station designs. The US Skylab, put up way back in the 1970s . . . apparently the crews had some real problems because the engineers back on Earth kept forgetting that there was no up or down in space. And these people were designing a space station, for chrissakes!"

"It's hard to shake our Earthbound prejudices," Garroway agreed.

"Tell me about it, sir!" Hayes said, laughing. "Didja hear about the boots?"

"Nooo. . . ."

"Some idiot, probably the same ROAD-SOB who fucked up the rifles, must've seen we were headed for a desert environment, 'cause he also saw to it we had thirty pairs of Boots, Mark I Desert, Marine Issue, Standard."

Garroway's eyes widened. "Desert boots? On *Mars*?"

"Swear to God! Like we could wear 'em with our Class-One armor! The colonel was fit to be tied when he heard. Anyway, I guess that's why Slider and Fulbert volunteered to go to Candor Chasma and give Captain Barnes a hand straightening the mess out."

"I'm *sure* Captain Barnes appreciates their help," Garroway said, grinning. "In fact, I—"

He broke off the sentence as the hatchway from the base common area clanked open. The first person in was one of the UN troops, wearing full combat armor and carrying a Sturmgewehr SG-32 assault rifle. The bullpup magazine was locked in place behind the pistol grip—in direct violation of standing station operational orders.

"What the hell—" Garroway started, but the UN trooper swung the muzzle of the stubby, deadly-looking weapon to cover him.

"Please to remain seated," the figure said, the voice harsh through the sealed helmet's external speaker. The accent sounded German; most of the Foreign Legion troops serving as UN security, Garroway knew, were German, serving under French officers, Bergerac, La Salle, and Dutetre.

Bergerac, in fact, was the next man through the hatch, though he was recognizable only by the name stenciled on his sand-scuffed armor. He held a SIG-Sauer P-940 in his gloved hand. "If you would please stand up and move back slowly from the console," he said, gesturing with his pistol. "And keep your hands where I can see them."

Two more soldiers entered, taking up positions flanking the door while the first man kept the two Marines and Dr. Graves covered at the center of the room.

"Please, no one make any sudden movements," Bergerac announced. He nodded, and one of the UN troops slung his weapon, moved past him, and began checking each American for weapons.

"*C'est libre,*" the man said when he was done.

"What is the meaning of this?" Graves demanded.

"Be quiet, Doctor. None of you is in any danger, unless my orders are disobeyed."

Another person in UN blues stepped through the hatch from the rec area. Mireille Joubert.

Garroway was not surprised. "You . . ."

"I *am* sorry, Major. But David's stubbornness has made this necessary." She was holding a small jewel case, which she handed to Bergerac. The tall French colonel opened the case, extracted a ten-gig RAM cartridge, and plugged it into a slot in the CON console. Then he began tapping out commands on a keyboard.

"Just a minute, now!" Graves said. He stepped forward and was immediately blocked by a burly young UN trooper, who stopped him with the blunt muzzle of his weapon shoved against the geologist's stomach. "But he can't *do* that!" Graves protested, backing off.

"On the contrary, Doctor," Joubert told him. "We can. And we have. At this moment, every American and Russian on this base is being taken prisoner."

Garroway's eyes narrowed. She could be right; the Marines' mission was to provide security for the US science team . . . but that was pretty vague. It was the middle of the night, and there was no reason for a heightened alert. Most of the Marines would be asleep in the barracks hab. The only exceptions would be the various people on watch—such as Hayes, here in the comm center—and the fire and security watches. That amounted to . . . what was it? Eight people out of thirty? No, out of twenty-seven, with three Marines at Candor Chasma. And all but two of them inside during the bitter Martian night.

Maybe the guys outside would notice something was wrong. Garroway had helped draw up the watch-standing bill for the week. Who had the duty outside tonight? Kaminski and Groller, he was pretty sure. He looked at the radio console. If someone could just get a message off on the working frequency . . .

"Forget about putting out a warning," Bergerac said, following his glance. "I've just uploaded new communications codes. That will keep your people from talking to one another . . . or you with Earth, for that matter.''

"You must be damned worried about those political repercussions you were talking about," Garroway told Joubert. As he spoke, he casually put his hands behind his back. Bergerac had demanded that they keep their hands out in the open, but he said nothing now as Garroway kept talking. "What are you trying to do? Bury David's discovery completely? Or just grab the credit for yourself?"

"You Americans concern yourselves far too much with the individual, or his accomplishments," she replied, "and not enough with the good of the community. In this case, the *world* community. We cannot allow this information to be released to the general public. Not until they've been properly prepared to receive it."

"I think there's something else you're worried about," Garroway told her. He kept his hands shielded from the UN people, his right hand cupped over his wrist-top. "You see a chance here to get sole access to the alien technology."

"That *is* a factor," she said. "Mostly, we cannot allow you Americans, or the Russians, to gain all of the benefits of what you learn here for yourselves."

"And you're not grabbing it for *your*selves?" He pressed the strap release on his wrist-top and let the device drop into the palm of his right hand. Carefully, betraying nothing with facial expression or movements of his arms, he tucked it into the waistband of his greens at the small of his back. He had a feeling these people were going to be nervous about their captives having access to computers . . . and maybe this way he could keep his.

It was the only plan going at the moment, the only thing he could think of.

"What we do," Bergerac said, "we do for all of Humanity. Not just for selfish and corrupt Americans."

The man sounded angry, and Garroway decided not to push the issue. The UN propaganda machine had been working overtime lately on the "greedy and corrupt Americans" idea, while mobilizing the rest of the world against them. The thought worried him. Once you reduce a person to a label—"greedy and corrupt" was as good as any—you're liable to have fewer qualms about arranging for that person's disappearance. If the UN troops were moving against all Americans on Mars . . . hell, what were they going to do with them? There were too many to guard easily.

At the moment, things did not look good. . . .

1211 HOURS GMT

Post 1, outside the hab
facilities
Cydonia Base, Mars
Soltime +25 minutes MMT

Lance Corporal Frank Kaminski's feet were getting cold, and he knew it was time to move on. Of all the duties assigned to the Marines at Cydonia, this was the worst. *Why,* he thought miserably, *am I freezing my ass off up here while Ben and Slider are taking it easy down at Candor?* The answer came immediately. *Because you were a pussy and didn't volunteer to go.* The truth was, he'd been afraid that Slider was going to do something stupid and get them all caught. *Man, I don't think I'm ever going to speak to either of those assholes again.*

After months cooped up inside the cycler, he'd thought he'd be glad to set foot on a planet again, with a real sky and the room to get out and move around some. Unfortunately, it hadn't worked out quite the way he'd expected. The habs at Cydonia were roomier than the cycler, of course, but they were all the same drab, stark, utilitarian design, obviously worked up by an architect who thought people *liked* living inside fuel tanks.

And outside was worse. You couldn't go out without wearing Class-One armor—the full rig, complete with fifty-kilo backpack and power unit. Even if that rig only weighed something like fifteen kilos on Mars, it still moved like fifty . . . and once you were walking, you had to be ready to dig in your heels to stop, or that backpack would keep on going and take you with it. He was used to wearing Class-Ones, of course, after long hours of practice, but it wasn't like really being outside. The information downloading over the HUD projected across his visor was comforting, but it still felt like he was playing video games inside a tin can.

At night it was really bad. The sky was so dark. Kaminski had grown up in a suburb of Chicago, and the nights there—between the city sprawl and the monster ultraplex at Woodfield—pretty much washed everything out of the sky except the Moon. Here, the blacknesses below and above the horizon were the same; you could tell the difference only by knowing that the horizon was where the dusting of diamond-hard, blue-white stars stopped. He'd never even seen the Milky Way before, but it arched across the sky like a long, fuzzy cloud. It made him feel . . . lonely.

Worse though, was the cold. Marine Class-One armor was designed to serve as a space suit, but it wasn't as well insulated as an EVA or Marsuit; it couldn't be, not and stay as relatively light and manageable as it was. The arsenic-gallenide batteries and the micro fuel cells provided power enough to keep him warm in the day— as well as processing the air he breathed and the water he drank—but at night, when the temperature plunged to 150 below, the ground got so cold it seemed to suck the heat right out through the soles of the boots. All of the Marines wore thermal socks inside their suits, but it wasn't enough, not on a long, four-hour watch in the icy darkness. Marines on outside watch kept warm by moving . . . and by spelling one another every twenty minutes or so inside the main hab's airlock.

His watch requirements were to patrol the general area around the main hab and the C^3 facility, with at least one stop per hour at the automated methane-cracking plant east of the base perimeter, the makeshift shuttle pad, and the well and freshwater storage tank to the south. It wasn't, he thought ruefully, as though *Martians* were going to attack . . . though the black hill they called the Fortress and the empty shell of the Ship, bulking huge against the stars to the north of the base, were eerie enough to have you believing in *anything* after more than ten minutes or so.

He'd just completed this hour's rounds, walking out to the fuel farm first, then swinging past the shuttle pad. Now he was trudging north through the sand, with the external lights of the base a welcome sight indeed. In their glare, he saw Groller, moving out from the shelter of the main lock. He waved, and Groller waved back.

He touched a control in the arm of his suit, switching on his armor's comm system. You were supposed to leave it on all the time, but on low-alert status, most of the Marines kept theirs switched off when they weren't using them to save the batteries.

As soon as he switched on, though, a blast of static crashed from his helmet speakers. Hastily, he tapped on the key that lowered the volume; the channel was completely blocked. He tried the backup . . . with the same result.

Damn. He saw Groller tapping the side of his helmet and knew that he was having trouble, too. That meant it wasn't a fault in the suit, then—for which Kaminski was grateful—but a screwup with the comm center. No matter. One of them could go inside and report it.

As he walked closer, he noticed another armored figure standing in the main lock. That was strange. No one else was supposed to be—

The figure in the lock was aiming an assault rifle at Groller. It took Kaminski a frozen instant to realize that the guy was firing the rifle; he could see the rapid flicker of the muzzle flash, could see him struggle with the weapon's climb as he loosed a burst at Groller's back on full auto.

Kaminski broke into a clumsy run, unslinging his ATAR as he surged forward through loose sand. In the cold, the upper layers of the sand tended to freeze, the grains sticking together in a brittle crust, and each step was an unsteady stride-*lurch* as the crust broke beneath his boots.

Amazingly, the gunman appeared to have missed his

target; Kaminski didn't know where that stream of rapid-fire lead had gone, but it had apparently sailed past the unsuspecting Groller without coming near enough to hit him. He remembered the problems the Marines had had on the firing range; maybe the gunman was having difficulty with the local gravity as well. Kaminski came to a clumsy halt, raised his ATAR, and sighted in on the gunman.

Directly aiming a rifle in a space suit is next to impossible, if for no other reason than that you can't get your eye close to the rear sight. The M-29, however, used a video low-light scan system that picked up the target picture through a camera lens mounted on the rifle's back and fed the magnified image to the rifleman's helmet electronics. In the green glow of his HUD's image feed, he could see only that the target was wearing UN armor and seemed to be trying to brace himself against the open airlock's seal for another shot. The laser rangefinder gave him a range of 243.6 meters. He dragged the crosshairs over the target . . . then cursed as the man ducked back out of sight.

Groller had seen him aim and obviously wondered what was going on. The Marine turned to look back at the main hab, saw nothing, turned again, his hands spreading in a *what-the-hell-are-you-playing at?* gesture.

Kaminski tried the comm channel again. Still blocked, and now he knew that somebody was jamming him. He started running again, signaling to Groller to get down, cursing wildly inside the ringing confines of his helmet.

The figure appeared at the airlock again . . . no, two figures, and one of them was cradling something long and vicious and deadly-looking, a rifle at least twice as long as an ATAR, and obviously much heavier and more clumsy. There was a green flash . . .

. . . and an answering flash against Groller's back-pack. A puff of white silently burst from the PLSS unit, propelling Groller forward and down.

Kaminski reached Groller an instant later. The other Marine was down on his hands and knees, wildly trying to reach behind him. It looked like his Number Two O_2

reserve tank had been breached; oxygen was spilling into the thin, cold atmosphere, the moisture in the tank freezing as it emerged in an icy fog.

Damn! He could exchange fire with the unknown attackers, or he could try to save Jim Groller. That was no choice at all. Dropping his rifle, he skidded in on his knees, one hand steadying his friend while the other groped for the emergency cutoff valve that would close the system before it bled Jim's precious air into near vacuum. *Shit!* The suit was breached too . . . the active camo surface was scorched away beside the burst O_2 tank, and frost was forming rapidly around a hole a little narrower than the width of a pencil.

"Damn it, Jim, hold still! Hold still!" The man was thrashing about so hard that Kaminski had to drive his shoulder into the man's side and knock him down, pinning him against the cold sand while he jammed the thumb of his glove against the breach. The armor was solid, if a bit slick with ice, and the pressure inside the suit was less than eight psi; he was able to stop the leak. One-handed, then, he began fumbling in his repair kit pouch for a self-seal patch.

When he looked up, several minutes later, he saw the two gunmen standing a few meters away, covering him with their weapons. The man with the assault rifle came forward and picked up the Marines' ATARs; the other kept them covered with his bulky weapon—which Kaminski now recognized as an H&K Laserkarabiner LK-36, a deadly and powerful man-portable laser weapon powered off of a backpack power unit.

Lasers were unaffected by gravity . . . which meant they usually hit what they were aimed at. Carefully, bitterly, Kaminski raised his hands, but only after he checked to make certain that the patch he'd just slapped over the puncture in Groller's armor was going to hold. The two UN troops closed in, then, urging both men to their feet.

It occurred to Kaminski as they were led back toward the habs that he and Groller had just become POWs.

And he'd not even known that they were at war.

ELEVEN

Marine Barracks
Cydonia Base, Mars
Sol 5636: soltime +34 minutes
MMT

Most of the Marines in the barracks area were asleep. The sole exception was Sergeant Randolph Gardner, First Squad, Second Section, who had the ten-to-two fire and security watch that night. He heard footsteps in the passageway, heard the hiss and thump of the pressure door opening, and centered himself on the hatch to give the challenge. He assumed, of course, that it would be Staff Sergeant Ostrowsky making the late rounds . . . or even Colonel Lloyd, checking to make certain that all of the watch standers were on their toes. He was not prepared for what he saw when the hatch swung open— the business end of an H&K pointed straight at his face.

"Do not give the alarm," the man at the far end of the rifle told him in thick, German-accented English. "Do not speak. Give me your weapon."

Gardner complied. His ATAR wouldn't have done him any good in any case; it was unloaded, as specified by regulations. The platoon's alert status was still green, which meant full weapons-safety protocols were in ef-

154

fect. He wasn't even wearing armor, save for the kinevlar vest he had on over his greens.

"Down on the floor!" the man said, speaking quietly but with a deadly will behind the words. "Hands behind your head!"

Gardner hit the deck, fingers interlaced behind his head as one of the intruders stood above him, well clear of any attempted heroics, a leg-sweep or a scissors. Other UN troops filed quietly into the barracks, moving almost silently, with only the occasional click of plastic on armor to warn of their coming. They fanned out through the barracks, taking key positions. Then, when all were in position, the man who'd first addressed him hit the light control panel.

The barracks lights came on, harsh and uncompromising. "Hey, what is this?" a male voice called.

"What the freakin'—"

A tall, severe-looking man in UN blues entered the barracks. "Fall in!" the man snapped. "All of you! At attention!"

Habit dragged a half dozen Marines out of their racks and up to the red tape line marked out on the deck . . . but others, realizing that what was happening was way outside of standard procedures, protested. "Who the fuck are you?" Sergeant Jacob demanded, standing in green T-shirt and white boxer shorts, hands on his hips. "And what the fuck are you doing in here?"

"Shut up and move!" the German barked. One of the UN soldiers rammed the muzzle of his short-barreled bullpup rifle against Jacob's side, propelling him toward Gardner's position. More soldiers emerged from the hab section partitioned off for the women Marines, grinning as they led them to join the other Marines. Ostrowsky, barefoot and wearing only a T-shirt and panties, was furious. "What the fucking hell is this all about?"

"I am Sergeant Ernst Stenke, of the Second Demibrigade, First Regiment of the Legion Étranger," he announced, "currently in the service of the United Nations Enforcement Arm. And for the moment, at least, you are all my prisoners."

A crash sounded from the far end of the barracks. It was taking three UN soldiers to subdue Colonel Lloyd, who'd been sleeping in the partitioned cubicle reserved for the Marine officers. No, *four*. Lloyd had left another one on the deck, clutching his left knee in what Gardner sincerely hoped was excruciating pain. Two of the UN troops had just slammed Lloyd facedown against a garbage can—the cause of all of the racket—while the third came up behind him, rifle raised above his head.

Gardner winced as the rifle descended sharply, butt down, connecting with a sickening *crack* against the back of Lloyd's skull.

"Anyone who resists," the sergeant continued, as they dragged Lloyd up the center aisle of the barracks, "or who does not carry out my orders precisely, will be subdued, then dragged. We do not wish to harm any of you, but you *will* do as we say!"

Gardner was finally allowed to sit up as the Marines were carefully counted and checked for weapons. There were twenty-three Marines in the barracks in all, counting Gardner and the unconscious Lloyd. Swiftly, efficiently, they were allowed to dress in twos or threes, with a guard standing by to check their greens and boots for hidden weapons, and then herded through the airtight hatches to the recreation area. There, they were deposited in the middle of the floor, seated with their hands up and their fingers locked behind their heads, all save Doc Casey, who was allowed to look after Lloyd.

Within a few minutes more, Bergerac, the UN commanding officer, led three more men into the room from the comm shack—Hayes and the major, along with one of the scientists who'd been at Cydonia when the Marines had arrived. During the next ten minutes, more UN troops brought in the rest of the American and Russian personnel from the station, most looking groggy and sleep-disheveled as they continued to pull on their clothing. There was confusion enough in their noisy entrance that several of the Marines took the chance to talk among themselves in quiet murmurs.

"What'dya think, Randy?" Corporal Theodore Miller, a young kid from Ohio in Gardner's squad sitting to his left, whispered. "Looks like some kinda military coup."

"Shut your trap," Sergeant Ostrowsky growled, her voice just loud enough to reach the two Marines. She was sitting to Gardner's right, and she was still furious. "We've got a war on our hands, here."

"Shit, Sarge. What makes you say that?"

"Stands to reason, doesn't it? You don't think they'd pull a dumb-ass stunt like this unless they had the full backing of the UN, do you? Oh, *shit*! They got Kaminski."

A pair of armored Foreign Legion troops were bringing Frank Kaminski into the room at gunpoint. That wasn't good. If the guys on duty outside had escaped the UN net, maybe they could've helped somehow. Groller's absence was worrying and a little hopeful. Was the other EVA security watch dead, or had he managed to get away?

And if he'd escaped, what could he do?

"Be quiet, all of you, if you please," Bergerac said, addressing the entire room. "By order of the United Nations Military Command and the UN World Cultural Bureau, I am assuming direct military control of this facility—"

There was an explosion of noise from the Marines, and from the scientists as well, people shouting, people starting to rise to their feet despite the threatening guards stationed close by.

"Quiet! *Quiet!*" He turned and rasped something to the troops near him, and a dozen rifle muzzles raised in unison, pointed at the Marines. For a panic-ragged moment, Gardner thought that one or another of the other troops was going to fire warning shots into the overhead . . . not a good idea with the next best thing to hard vacuum outside.

"You UNdies don't have any jurisdiction here!" Donatelli shouted above the commotion, using the popular Corps slang for UN troops or bureaucrats.

"I beg to differ. Now, all of you, *sit down*, and I will explain your position!"

"*I'll* show you some positions," Sergeant Jacob growled nearby, but, slowly, order was restored in the room.

"Now then," Bergerac continued, speaking as though nothing had happened, and despite the UN troops who still held their rifles aimed at the Marines like a firing squad. "As I said, we are assuming military control of this facility. The politics of this decision do not really concern any of you ... except insofar as this obviously changes the nature of your mission here. We do not have enough personnel to watch over you all the time, and so we are taking you to another ... place, where—"

He had to stop again as shouts, curses, and questions broke once more from the Americans before him.

"We will take you to a place where it will be easier to guard you. You will be our guests at this place for another three months, when the cycler *Champlain* arrives to take you all back to Earth."

Gardner let out the breath he'd been holding then. For a moment, he'd thought the Americans were all to be killed. Then he decided that it was premature to relax. The SS guards had told their prisoners in the death camps that they were being taken to the showers.

"We sincerely regret the necessity of this action, but be assured that we *will* carry out our program here, and you will not be allowed to stand in our way.

"You will be led in groups of three back to the common room," Bergerac continued, "where you will find your EVA armor already laid out. I assure you, all suits will have been carefully checked for weapons or other contraband. You will find your suits and you will put them on. There will be no talking. Any attempt at escape will be dealt with severely. Am I understood?"

This time, there were no protests, and Bergerac seemed to accept this as assent. "Very good," he said. He pointed. "You three! Let's go!"

Soldiers led Donatelli, Marchewka, and Hauser from

the room, and at that moment, Gardner wondered if he would ever see any of them again.

Mars Transport Shuttle
Cydonia Base, Mars
0605 hours MMT

The flight out of Cydonia was brutal, but mercifully short. The transport was so crowded with Marines—all of them encumbered in their Class-One armor—that there was no room to move or even shift to get into a more comfortable position. "Y'know," somebody said over the general comm channel, "if they wanted to get rid of all of us in a convenient accident—"

"*Ruhe!*" another voice barked. "Be quiet, all of you! No talking!"

The pilot—Garroway didn't know if it was one of the UN troops or a NASA pilot working at gunpoint—piled on the Gs for the liftoff from Cydonia . . . and the acceleration continued for a long time, long enough to convince Garroway that they were making a high-speed run to someplace rather than the usual slower, fuel-conserving suborbital hop.

He was sitting close enough to one of the shuttle's small observation ports that he could see a blur of ocher landscape below as they hurtled past. It had taken most of the rest of the night to secure the American prisoners, get them suited up, and to lead them three at a time out to the shuttle on its launchpad. The sun was just coming up, the light casting long fingers of black shadow from each rock or boulder or irregular fold of the chaotic terrain, but they were moving too quickly, and at too low an altitude, for him to tell where they were. At a guess, judging from the direction the shadows were pointing, they were heading more or less southwest, which made a certain amount of sense. There were only two major bases on Mars, Cydonia and Candor Chasma at the equator; they must be heading back for Candor Station.

The question, of course, was what was going to happen to them when they arrived.

He felt a growing discomfort in the small of his back, where the wrist-top he'd hidden there was trapped, pinched between him and the inside of his armor. They'd searched him again before he'd suited up, but he'd palmed the microcomputer when they frisked him, hiding it under hands clasped behind his head as they patted him down. By pretending to adjust his trousers before climbing into his armor, he'd managed to hide it again in his waistband. He wondered just how much stress the device could take, though, as several Gs slammed him back into the thinly padded seat.

Acceleration cut off, and for a long time after that they were in free fall, save for occasional violent thumps and kicks when the pilot fired steering jets to maintain attitude or to adjust their course. Their captors had made certain that all of the Marines were strapped down, and two of them sat now at the forward end of the compartment, as uncomfortable as any of the Americans as they kept an eye on their prisoners.

Garroway was wedged in between two Marines, with a third sitting half on top of him and half on the Marine to his right. In their armor, they were anonymous . . . but he could still recognize voices occasionally over the comm channel . . . mingled occasionally with the harsh, retching sounds of people being sick in their helmets.

The shuttle's cargo hold was designed to hold thirty passengers in something like relative comfort, and it could manage another ten, perhaps, with some crowding. That, however, assumed that the passengers weren't wearing bulky Class-Ones . . . or EVA suits. Most of the scientists, Garroway noticed, had been kept at Cydonia, but five had been packed into Mars surface suits and loaded aboard the shuttle with the Marines . . . the ones who'd discovered those *Homo erectus* corpses two days before. They'd nearly had to drag Alexander physically from the hab and chuck him into the lobber.

There were twenty-five Marines on board—Colonel Lloyd and Private Groller, both wounded, had been left at Cydonia under the care of Dr. Penkov, the Russian doctor at the base. That put a total of thirty prisoners aboard the shuttle, and the crowding was nightmarish with them all wearing armor or surface EVA suits.

After a small eternity of free fall, they were jarred by a sharp, dizzying swoop as the shuttle flipped end for end, and then acceleration hammered at them again when the main drive fired. The world tilted sickeningly, and then was obscured by swirling ocher dust as the craft settled in for a cushioned landing on its four hydraulic jacks.

They were down.

"Gentlemen, and ladies, we have arrived at your new home," Bergerac told them, climbing down the narrow ladder from the pilot's compartment. Had he flown the ship himself, Garroway wondered? No, he could see a NASA pilot behind him, seated at the console. The UN colonel must have been riding strapped to the bridge jumpseat.

With two UN guards urging them to move, the Marines and scientists clambered awkwardly down the center passageway ladder and into the shuttle's airlock bay. Since everyone had been suited up for the flight, the shuttle was already open to the Martian atmosphere. The loading ramp was down; in moments, Garroway stood with the others on the cold, still, and nearly airless desert.

This was *not* Candor Chasma.

That fact was beginning to register with the others as well. He heard several low-murmured comments, and several Marines exchanged words by touching their helmets together for a quick, sound-inducted comment or two.

Garroway had not been to Mars Prime, of course, but he'd read about the place often enough during the cycler flight out, and he'd seen plenty of video transmissions downloaded off the Spacenet. Mars Prime, the first permanent settlement on the red planet, lay close to the site of the first manned landing on the floor of Candor Chasma, one of the larger canyons in the vast and lab-

yrinthine complex of canyons known as Valles Marineris, the Valley of the Mariner Spacecraft. It consisted
of some fifteen hab modules, a large, permanent landing
strip, and water-drilling, fuel-production, and storage facilities even larger and more extensive than those at Cydonia. Compared to Mars Prime, the base at Cydonia
was a small and somewhat primitive frontier outpost.

This base was smaller still. Located on a valley
floor—Garroway could see the distant red cliffs, mostly
still lost in shadow but capped by gleaming gold, the
reflected light of the rising sun—it was a small outsta-
tion of some kind, consisting of a single hab partly covered over by sand and piles of bulldozed regolith. A
Mars cat was parked nearby, but Garroway could see no
drilling or fuel-production facilities, no storage structures, nothing, in fact, other than the hab, the cat, and
the grounded shuttle.

Lieutenant Russel King, standing nearby, turned to
him. "So what do we do now, Major?"

Garroway blinked at the platoon leader, unable for a
moment to reply. Until that moment, he'd not thought
about the command structure at all. But with Colonel
Lloyd wounded and left at Cydonia, he was the senior
officer of a section of twenty-four US Marines, plus five
scientists.

It was not a responsibility that Garroway had ever
imagined having to assume.

The other Marines were talking among themselves,
and with growing agitation. "What the fuck?" one man
said over the talk channel. "The bastards are just *leaving*
us here?"

Bergerac stood at the top of the ramp. "We are not
monsters," he told them, "or barbarians. We must have
full control of the Cydonian base, however, and for that
we need all of you out of the way. I'm sure you all
realize that we could have killed you . . . but instead we
are leaving you here, with plenty of food, water, and a
portable drilling unit for more water."

"I think we need some things clarified, Bergerac,"
Garroway said. "Are we prisoners of war?"

"Technically, of course, no state of war exists between your country and the United Nations, at least for the moment. Let us simply say that we are temporarily *reassigning* you to this outpost."

"Yeah, but for how long?" a woman's voice—Garroway thought it was Ostrowsky—called out. "You can't just abandon us here!"

"Silence in the ranks, Marine," Garroway rasped out. If he was in command, he would have to maintain order, starting now.

"How long," Bergerac said, "depends entirely on how long it takes to, eh, assess Dr. Alexander's finds at Cydonia."

"To hide them, you mean," Alexander called out, "or destroy them."

"Please, Dr. Alexander," Garroway said. He could see Alexander about twenty feet away, out of place among the armored Marines in his blue EVA suit. "Let's hear what he has to say."

"We are not vandals, Doctor," Bergerac added. "But we do intend to secure what technological assets we can from the Cydonia site. For the benefit of *all* Mankind."

"What the hell are you babbling about, Bergerac?" Alexander snapped back. "We haven't been holding out on anybody!"

"Yes, we could tell," Bergerac replied dryly. "So many papers published on the alien Ship. On the surveys. On the Builders' technology you've uncovered so far. What have we learned from you since you began studying these ruins? Nothing! Some of us believe that you are deceiving the rest of the world."

"The rest of the world, Colonel," Garroway said quietly, hoping to forestall another riposte from Alexander, "is deceiving itself. We've gone out of our way to accommodate you people here."

"Damn straight," Alexander added. "And if you wanted better access, you could build your own Mars cyclers."

"That is coming, Dr. Alexander, believe me. It is dangerous to leave you Americans, and your Russian friends, in sole possession of such a find, such a treasure trove as Cydonia. *We* will administer these treasures for the good of all, in accordance with the provisions of the RMT.''

The Revised Moon Treaty had been voted on and ratified by the UN in 2025, the same year that the Geneva UN Charter had been published, and five years after the United States had formally withdrawn from the UN. Like its predecessor, the Moon Treaty of 1979, the RMT discouraged private enterprise in space by forbidding private ownership or exploitation of any world or other body in space. Individual governments were forbidden to stake out claims—even of the fast-dwindling available satellite slots in geosynchronous orbit. The issue was one of many that had led to the American withdrawal from the UN, and the organization's relocation to Geneva.

The United States had never been signatory to the RMT, but it looked as though the UN was determined to enforce the treaty anyway.

"As for how long you will be kept here," Bergerac went on, "that depends on several factors outside my control. At worst, we will be forced to leave you until the next cycler flyby, which is scheduled for three months from now. With luck, however, we will have the situation . . . clarified sooner than that. At that time, we will arrange for your transport to Mars Prime, where you will remain until the cycler arrives."

"He can't do that!" someone said over the open channel.

"My God, what are we gonna do? . . ." That sounded like one of the scientists.

"*Shoot* the fuckers. . . ." That sounded like Ostrowsky.

Garroway was painfully aware that the discipline holding the men and women of his section was dangerously close to cracking; if they lost it, they would be at the mercy of their captors . . . and of the utter inhospitality of the Martian desert.

"You should find the outpost hab adequate," Bergerac continued, "if not exactly comfortable. The still is inside, and you have fuel cells enough to provide you with what power you'll need." He pointed. "That Mars cat has several of my men on board, never mind how many. It arrived here several hours ago to prepare the station for you, and to make certain there were no communications equipment or computers here. We cannot permit you to communicate at all with Earth, or even with other bases on the planet.

"They're here to keep an eye on you, at least for the time being. They will stay long enough to be certain that you are settled in and need nothing. If you do find you are lacking in anything, you may ask them, and they will communicate with me. I warn you, however, to approach the Mars cat one at a time only, and with a white cloth in your hand. You will not be permitted to approach the cat closer than about twenty meters . . . for reasons that should be obvious to you.

"And now, I must say *adieu*. We will see one another again, quite soon. Be assured of that."

Bergerac turned then and strode back into the shuttle, followed by the two guards, who backed up the ramp, their rifles still trained on the Marines.

"We can take 'em . . ." one voice said.

"Belay that, Marine," Garroway growled. If those UN troops started shooting now, half of his people would be dead or swiftly dying in the cold Martian air in the space of a second or two.

Then the moment was past, the hatch slowly closing. "Come on, people," Garroway said. "There'll be another time. Move back before they light that torch!"

The Marines and civilians turned and jogged toward the hab, putting as much distance between themselves and the shuttle as they could. A moment later, the landscape turned brighter, and Garroway's external mikes picked up a high-pitched, metallic shriek as the shuttle's main drive kicked in. He turned in time to see the shuttle climbing into the black, early-morning sky on a wavering pillar of superheated methane.

And the Marines were left alone in the desert.

TWELVE

Heinlein Station, Mars
Sol 5636: 0815 hours MMT

"I talked to Doc Casey," Garroway told the others at the table. "He didn't have all that much time to check them over, but he said he thought both the colonel and Groller were going to make it. The colonel probably has a concussion. Groller's worse. Depressurization injuries and third-degree burns in his side, but he should be okay, too."

"Thank God," Lieutenant King said. "What we have to do now is decide what we're going to do. Any ideas?"

"Don't know about you boys," Ostrowsky said with lazy indifference, "but I'm kinda partial to skinning the fuckers alive."

It was chilly inside the hab, cold enough that moisture was condensing on the inside walls and partitions. Most of the Marines had elected to keep their armor on for the time being, removing only their helmets, gloves, and backpacks, while his team still wore their EVA suits. Their breath showed as puffs of white when they spoke. The fuel cells were charged, however, and the heater units had been switched on. Sergeant Jacob, who'd checked the circuitry, had announced that the place should approach something like room temperature by midday.

It was also noisy. Most of the Marines in the room were on their feet, scuffing back and forth, talking loudly, even shouting, making as much of a racket as they could. It was possible that there were microphones hidden, and Garroway needed to discuss some things with his senior people that he didn't want to share with their UN guards.

Despite the cold, it hadn't taken the Marines long to get settled in. Like the habs at Cydonia, this one was little more than a large shell from a Shuttle II fuel tank, fitted out with an airlock, a floor, a few lightweight partitions, and a minimum of creature comforts. Perhaps half of the hab's volume was taken up with supplies— mostly packaged readymeals, enough for thirty people for 150 days.

If ever there was a splendid reason to escape a prison, Garroway thought wryly, that was it. Five months of readymeals, together with their edible packaging, was going to be a gastronomic nightmare.

Garroway looked at each of the people sitting about the small, plastic table in turn, feeling mingled fear and . . . pride. This was not exactly the sort of situation the Corps had taught him how to handle, but these were good people. Good Marines. The best. . . .

"So where are we, anyway?" King asked the others at the table. "Not Candor Chasma."

"No," Garroway agreed. "Not Candor Chasma. It has to be one of the outposts."

"Yeah," Lieutenant King said. "But which one?"

Garroway glanced up, his gaze sweeping across the large and mostly empty compartment—empty, of course, save for the Marines shuffling around and talking as loudly as they could. They couldn't possibly have found *all* of the listening devices hidden in the hab.

It had been a foregone conclusion that, since UN troops had stocked the place for them, they'd also left a remote mike or two and were listening in from the warm comfort of their Mars cat outside. Hell, what *else* could they do out there, except maybe play endless hands of cards?

And if hidden microphones were a possibility, of course, so, too, were hidden cameras. The AVT-400 series used in Marine recon UAVs, for instance, were smaller than the tip of a man's little finger, were powered by ambient light, and could transmit images on IR or UHF frequencies for a distance of half a kilometer. Without special electronic bug-hunting gear, the Marines might never find them all.

And so, as soon as they'd filed in through the airlock and started pulling off their helmets, Garroway had organized the Marines into bug-hunt teams, sending them throughout the hab in search of anything that might conceivably be a listening device or camera. Within twenty minutes, they'd turned up three cylinders the size of a wrist-top's power-up key, each less than half a centimeter long, one in each of the two living areas, and a third in the tiny 'fresher and shower cubicle.

As he'd sat at the table and mashed each cylinder in turn beneath his thumb, Ostrowsky had commented wryly that maybe the UN guys had just wanted to do some private peeping at the girls in the shower. Garroway had agreed with a laugh, but the spycams had him worried. There weren't many places in the empty hab to hide even cameras as small as these, but there could well be listening devices scattered all over the place; there were remote mikes as small as the head of a pin that would be impossible to discover without going over every square centimeter of all three rooms, walls, ceilings, and floors, with a magnifying glass.

After the bug sweep, Garroway had ordered an inventory taken of everything that might be of use in the hab . . . including anything that the Marines had managed to sneak in with them from Cydonia. He'd used hand signs, though, to indicate that only routine items like food or clothing were to be announced out loud. Everyone in the hab was aware that there were probably uninvited listeners.

Then he'd called the meeting of his senior staff, gathering them close around the plastic table where the secret inventory could be laid out and discussed. He was pretty sure there were no hidden cameras close enough to the center of the big room that hidden watchers would be able to see anything significant; there could be microphones in the deck under their feet, of course, but if they spoke indirectly, and in low-voiced whispers, where necessary, they could avoid giving too much away. Just to be on the safe side, he'd ordered the other Marines to walk around the inside of the hab, circling the seven at the table set up in the middle, talking loudly, swearing, laughing, or just plain scuffing their feet, making noise enough to drown out the whispers completely over a range of more than a meter or two.

Eighteen Marines could make one hell of a sonic scrambler when they put their minds to it.

The staff meeting included Dr. Alexander, the senior civilian scientist present. Besides Lieutenant King, the only other officer in the little band, he'd brought in his senior NCOs, Gunnery Sergeant Harold Knox and Sergeant Ellen Caswell, from First Section, and Staff Sergeant Kathryn Ostrowsky and Sergeant Ken Jacob from Second Section. He'd learned a long, long time ago that the real strength of the Corps was its noncoms . . . the experienced men and women who knew what needed to be done and how best to do it.

"Hell," Garroway said, his voice low. The others leaned close to catch his words against the noisy background. "I don't even know how many stations there are. Narrowing the choice down could be a bitch."

"There are twelve," Alexander told him. "Bradbury. Bova. Burroughs. Bear. Lots of 'Bs.' Clarke. Heinlein. Asimov. I don't remember the others. They're unmanned most of the time."

"How do you know all of that?" Ostrowsky wanted to know.

Alexander shrugged. "We had to familiarize ourselves with the remote hab facilities. They were originally set up to allow small teams of geologists, paleontologists, and archeologists to work in the field for extended periods of time.''

"I'm beginning to think the MMEF should have had a similar briefing," Garroway said. "The question, then, is which one we're at now.''

"We're close to the equator," Alexander put in. "That ought to narrow our selection down a bit, too."

"At the equator, huh?" King said. "Can you be sure about that?''

"I happened to look up," Alexander replied. "One of the moons—Deimos, the one like a bright star—was almost directly overhead.''

"Good point," Garroway said. "That tallies with how long our flight took, and the fact that I'm pretty sure we were going southwest. And those cliffs we saw outside suggest the Valles Marineris, too. That runs right along the equator. We could be inside the canyon chain, somewhere.''

"Hell, Valles Marineris is, what?" Caswell said. "Three thousand miles long? That's *only* as long as the United States is wide! We could be as far from Mars Prime as San Diego is from Washington!"

"No, we're close enough to Candor Chasma that the Mars cat could drive out here inside of a couple of days," Ostrowsky pointed out. "They couldn't have had more warning than that. That rules out the distant stations, like the one at Noctis Labyrinthus."

"That one's Bradbury Station," Alexander put in. "You know, I'd need a survey map to be certain, but I'd be willing to bet we're at Heinlein Station."

"Yeah?" Knox asked. "So where's that?"

"Damn, I don't have my wrist-top or PAD," Alexander said. "I really need something to draw on."

"Will this do?" Ostrowsky asked. She slid a pad of paper and a pen across the tabletop. "Found 'em in the stores.''

"Good enough." Alexander began sketching quickly. "Okay, here's the widest part of the whole Valles Marineris. We've got three big, oval-shaped, east–west canyons stacked north to south, small to large, like this.

Ophir Chasma up here. Candor in the middle. Melas to the south.

"To the west, we have two long, skinny canyons running in straight, east–west lines, like this. Ius Chasma comes into Melas Chasma, here. And Tithonium Chasma comes into Candor Chasma, so. Mars Prime is located on the Candor Mensa—a mensa is a kind of a plateau, flat-topped—smack in the middle of Candor Chasma, about here.

"Now, we've got several stations and outposts scattered around here, but the fact that we're on a canyon floor, and the canyon isn't all that wide—less than fifty kilometers is my guess—makes me think we're in Tithonium." He marked a spot in the northern of the two slender canyons west of Candor on the map. "Heinlein Station. I don't know much about it, except that it's supposed to be a single hab, and it was used by an areological team five years ago when they were surveying this part of the Valles. It's about 650 kilometers west of Candor Chasma."

King gave a low whistle. "That's almost four hundred miles. We can't do that on foot, that's for sure."

"No," Garroway agreed. "We're going to have to borrow that UN cat out there."

"You know, if we're that close," Knox said, "then we can probably figure our friends outside aren't going to stay there for the next three months, y'know? They wouldn't have enough supplies in that cat to last 'em that long."

"Shit," Ostrowsky put in. "Can you imagine sitting in a cat for that long, just watching POWs? Talk about the cat watching the mousehole. Not my idea of soft duty!"

"Right," Garroway said. "Their orders are probably to stay put and keep an eye on us until they know we're not going to cause any trouble. If we haven't tried anything in, oh, a week or so, they'll likely pull out and make tracks for Mars Prime."

"They might pop back in every once in a while to check up on us," Knox added. "Or maybe Bergerac has arranged to have another cat come out here every few days or so and change the guard.''

"That would make sense. If it wasn't tying up too many of their assets.''

"So what are we gonna do about it, Major?'' Ostrowsky asked. "Sit here like good little POWs until they decide to let us go?''

Garroway had already given the problem considerable thought. "Our mission orders don't quite cover this situation,'' he said slowly. "But I do know that we still answer to the people who cut our orders Earthside ... and we're not fulfilling our part of the bargain by sitting here on our duffs doing what the UN tells us to do.'' He looked at each of the others at the table in turn, measuring them. "We're supposed to be safeguarding American interests here. Well, it seems to me those interests are under attack, and it's our duty to fight back.''

"Fight back,'' Alexander said. He shook his head. "Damn, Major, I don't see how you can even think about that. We have no idea where we are, we have no weapons, and we can't call for help. Sounds impossible.''

"No,'' Garroway said. "It sounds like a *challenge*.''

He still wasn't sure what they should do, what they *could* do, when it came to that. He was just beginning to recognize the fact that he'd had it pretty easy in the Corps for a long time. He'd been comfortable, enough so that maybe what they'd been saying about him back on Earth was true ... that he'd gone ROAD.

Well, the hell with that noise. He wasn't going to just sit by and watch people who were looking to him for leadership get slammed aside by ambitious UN glory-grabbing sons of bitches. Reaching down, he opened a plastic kit bag and began removing several small items from its depths, careful to keep them shielded beneath his hands as he laid them out on the table. Their bodies should hide the stuff well enough from any remaining spycams. They would still have to be careful about what they said.

"It's fine to talk about fighting back,'' Caswell said.

She shivered and folded her arms across the armor of her cuirass. "But what can we do with . . . *this*?"

She nodded at the pitiful collection of artifacts on the table in front of them.

The inventory was actually a lot more impressive than Garroway had dared hope. The US Marines, it turned out, were an inventive bunch. Garroway first produced the wrist-top he'd smuggled out of Cydonia Prime. He didn't have a PAD, so he couldn't be sure it was still working after the rough handling it had taken in the shuttle, but when he strapped it on his wrist and touched the wake key, a winking point of green light showed that it was drawing power from his body heat and was ready to link. All he needed now was a display screen of some sort.

A surprising number of other Marines had smuggled various small objects out of their barracks. Sergeant Jacob had also managed to bring a wrist-top, though it was only an old, one-gig model, while Marchewka, Lazenby, Foster, and Donatelli all had pocketknives smuggled out in their shoes or hidden in unlikely parts of their clothing or anatomy. Doc Casey had walked right past the UN soldiers and climbed into his suit with a Mark I first-aid kit in his hand. Besides the usual pain meds, bandages, and other medical paraphernalia, Casey had squeezed a Marine combat knife inside. Lance Corporal Nolan contributed a length of number 4 steel wire, useful if they needed a garrote. Sergeant Radley had slipped some needle-nosed pliers into his shoe, while Corporal Hayes had palmed a five-gig memclip from the comm console. Kaminski's contribution was less practical but perfectly in keeping with Corps tradition. He'd somehow managed to wrap an American flag tightly around his body beneath his T-shirt.

The real prize, however, was contributed by Staff Sergeant Ostrowsky. When the UN troops had broken into the women's quarters, she'd managed to slip a Ruger-K Defender, a 2mm fléchette pistol, up inside her T-shirt. The Ruger was a tiny weapon—the sort of personal defense holdout weapon known as a pocket pistol—and could be concealed in a woman's hand; throughout the ordeal at Cydonia, even when she'd been forced to keep her hands behind her head, she'd managed to hold her elbows in such a way that she'd kept the weapon held snugly in place between her rather generous breasts.

The Ruger wasn't much of a weapon. Each of the five caseless sabot rounds in its magazine housed three 2mm fléchettes, deadly enough against an unprotected human if fired into throat or face at point-blank range, but useless against armor or even the protection afforded by a leather jacket, and next to useless at a range of more than a few meters. But it was something, at least. A beginning.

"Okay," Garroway said, dropping his voice to a whisper barely audible above the racket. "We have one ranged weapon, and that's close-up only. We've got to figure out a plan. How can we get in close enough to use it?"

"Make them come in here?" Jacob asked.

"Ah, they'd be stupid to do that," Knox replied. "At least, all at once. And we're gonna have to surprise all of 'em quick, so they can't radio for help."

"We're gonna need to sneak up on the sons of bitches," Ostrowsky pointed out quietly. "That could be tough. They'll have heat sensors in the cat."

"Yeah," Knox said, nodding. "Especially since we'll have to make our move at night. Our Class-Ones are pretty good at scattering heat plumes, but we're still gonna show up like torches if we go out there in the middle of the night, when the ambient temp's down to something like 150 below."

"Why do you say we'll have to move at night, Gunny?" Garroway said, thoughtful.

"Well, we sure as hell can't walk out there in broad daylight. . . ."

"I'm wondering about that." Garroway reached out and flicked his forefinger against Knox's torso armor, eliciting a hollow thump.

"You're thinking it'll be easier to mask our heat signatures out there at high noon," Ostrowsky whispered.

Garroway nodded. "Affirmative. We're close to the equator. Midday temperatures here can get up to a few degrees below freezing . . . or even higher. Thermal sensors work by comparing the contrast between the background temperature and what's being scanned."

"These tin suits still give off a hell of a lot of heat," Lieutenant King pointed out. "It's their main weakness. Besides, even their active camouflage won't provide a perfect blend with the environment, especially if we're moving."

"Well, there may be a way around that," Garroway said. "What we need to work out is a way to take down that Mars cat . . . and to do it before the bad guys can radio an alarm back to Bergerac. . . ."

2158 HOURS GMT

Heinlein Station, Mars
0935 hours MMT

"There's no more time for discussion," Alexander said quietly. "We're going to do it."

It was quieter now in the hab, though there was still an echoing murmur of people talking. Alexander had gathered the other archeologists about the plastic table at the center of the big room for a quiet, hurried discussion.

Significantly, it was the same group that had been with him yesterday when he'd discovered the vault and the mummified bodies—Dr. Craig Kettering, of Penn State; Dr. Devora Druzhininova, from the Russian Academy of Science; Edward Pohl, on extended loan from the Field Historical Research Foundation in Chicago; and Louis Vandemeer, from the Smithsonian. Everyone who'd actually seen the find had been packed off to this out-of-the-way outpost . . . probably on the assumption that if Graves and the rest of the US and Russian scientists could be kept out of the site, no one would be able to file a detailed report with Earth. Possibly they planned on manipulating those still at Cydonia, in order to suppress the find.

Suppress the find. *His* find. The knowledge that they were covering up his discovery, and the resultant frustration and anger, burned in his stomach and in his throat. It was happening again, damn it. He'd found a tiny crack in the wall that hid the past, just enough to let one slender shaft of light pass through and illuminate a piece of the Truth . . . and they were troweling the crack shut just as quickly as they could manage.

"We *can't*, Dave," Kettering said, "Don't you see? This could cause a war, a *shooting* war, right here on Mars! Remember what happened to the Sphinx? Napoléon?" The French invasion of Egypt at the end of the eighteenth century had been both a boon and a curse to archeologists. It had uncovered the Rosetta Stone and introduced Europe to the glories of Egypt's lost civilization.

At the same time, soldiers had shot off the nose of the Sphinx with a cannon, apparently just for fun.

"I can't lend my support to this," Vandemeer added, shaking his head. "It's just damned irresponsible!"

" 'Call   me . . . irresponsible . . . ' "   Druzhininova sang lightly, as though trying to ease the black tension hanging above the table. She had a thing for Western music, they all knew. Then she grew serious. "David is right, guys. By the time these people get done, we may never be able to figure out what the story is at Cydonia."

"But . . . what would be the point?" Vandemeer wanted to know. "They just want to make sure other countries have access to the technology we find. And, as for the, uh, discovery yesterday, it sounds to me like they're just concerned that, uh, sensitive information might be released too quick, maybe give fanatics the wrong idea. All they want is a *responsible* approach. . . ."

"Responsible my ass!" Alexander snapped. "I understand their concern, but so far we haven't found a hell of a lot we can use. Learning anything at all is going to take all of the resources of Earth for, for, I don't know, *centuries*, maybe, before we can make much out of it. And as for the discovery, it seems to me that they're not giving ordinary people credit for even a little common sense.''

"The fanatics'll make what they want out of things," Pohl said, "whether we provide the fuel or not."

"That's right," Alexander said. "Don't you see, Van? What we found out there says some *profound* things about who we are, where we came from. Things we've got to *know*! These bastards could scramble things so badly we may never get at the truth!"

"I'd like to know where these people get off setting themselves up as the arbiters of the dissemination of information," Druzhininova said.

"It's worse than what happened to me in Cairo," Alexander said. All of them were familiar with his expulsion from Egypt in '37, and the reasons behind it. "If we let them get away with this—"

"Are you sure," Vandemeer interrupted quietly, "that you're not just worried about your chances for publication?"

Alexander lunged to his feet, overturning his lightweight, plastic chair and nearly knocking the table aside. *"You take that back!"*

Druzhininova put her hand on Alexander's shoulder. "Easy, Dave."

Pohl stepped between him and Vandemeer. "Yeah, Dave. We're all in this together, right?"

"I'm not so sure about that," he said, his eyes still locked with Vandemeer's. He shook himself as the others released him. "I'll try to forget you said that, Vandemeer. But you hear me, and hear me good. You too, Craig."

"David . . ." Druzhininova began.

"It's okay, Devora." He kept his voice low and level. "If you two guys want to sit here and rot for the next three months, you're free to do so. But our military friends here are working out a way to block the UN bastards, and I'm going to help them every damned way that I can. If that means giving me a gun and charging that Mars cat out there, that's what I'm going to do. I'm sick of being shoved around, told what I can't dig, or told what I can't say, and I'm not going to sit still for it any longer, understand me?''

The odd part about it all was, Alexander still wasn't sure what he thought of this whole idea. He still hated the military . . . the regimentation, the spit and polish, the regulations, the dehumanization, all the aspects of military life that had grated on him when he was growing up as a Navy brat in Charleston, Pensacola, Portsmouth, Roosey Roads, and all of those other bases and stations scattered up and down the East Coast of America where he'd lived until his father had been killed. The thought that he was now voluntarily helping a bunch of US Marines was as startling personally as the find beneath the sands of Cydonia the day before . . . something that couldn't be, but was.

But he was going to follow through with the one, if that was what it took to uncover the truth about the other.

''I think you're making a mistake,'' Vandemeer said, ''but it's nothing worth fighting over.''

''That's where you're wrong, Louis,'' Alexander told him. ''The truth is *always* worth fighting for.''

THIRTEEN

Heinlein Station, Mars
Sol 5636: 1045 hours MMT

"So, you got your lines down?" Garroway asked. It was crowded in the hab's single, small airlock, with seven Marines and several bundles of equipment. "It's show time!"

"I'll have 'em eating out of my hand, Major," Staff Sergeant Ostrowsky replied.

"Just so you keep them drooling long enough for us to pull this off," he replied.

"Hey, not a problem," she replied, laughing.

He couldn't share her exuberant, almost cocky enthusiasm. There was too much at stake here, and far too many things could go wrong.

Ostrowsky was wearing one of the civilian archeologist's space suits. The name on the chest read DRUZHININOVA. It had been her idea, actually, and Devora Druzhininova had gone along with it. The Marines' helmet visors were nearly opaque with the HUD displays up. The civilian suits were lighter, and they sported goldfish bowl helmets that were transparent save for a slight blue tint to screen out the ultraviolet.

It meant that the UN troops inside the Mars cat would

be able to see that Ostrowsky was a woman. An *attractive* woman, buzz cut and all.

Sex, as Ostrowsky had reminded him, always sells.

The airlock's pressure matched the air pressure outside, and a red light winked on overhead. "Okay, radio silence, everyone," Garroway said. The hab walls would block the relatively weak UHF transmissions of their suits, but once they were outside the enemy would be listening to them. Turning, he touched the outer-hatch control. The door popped open, and they stepped out into the crisp, red-gold clarity of the Martian surface.

The scene was breathtakingly beautiful, gold sand beneath a cloudless sky that was pink on the horizon, but shaded to a deep and empty ultramarine overhead. All seven Marines—Garroway and Ostrowsky, Caswell, Donatelli, Foster, Jacob, and Kaminski—made their way in single file out of the airlock and around to the side of the hab that partly blocked the line of sight to the Mars cat, some fifty meters away.

They'd made several trips out through the airlock already, lugging along the pieces of the big Westinghouse portable drill unit . . . and some other things, carefully hidden with the bundles of tubing, condensers, heating coils, and batteries. The drill was portable in name only, a device weighing half a ton that could be assembled in an hour or so and had power enough to drill through tens of meters of hard-packed sand to reach the icy permafrost layer below. Once a hole had been opened, drill tubing with a heated head was lowered to the bottom and the permafrost melted to a thick slurry of mud and water. Most of the water vaporized as it melted into near vacuum; collectors at the drill head captured the vapor and condensed it into liquid, which was pumped into storage tanks for later use.

Such drills were responsible for opening Mars to large-scale human operations like the bases at Candor and Cydonia; besides drinking water, they provided both oxygen and the hydrogen for converting atmospheric CO_2 into the methane used by the shuttles. A wellhead had already been set up a few tens of meters to the north of the hab, but the Marines would be expected to start a new well right away; since all water on Mars was frozen, no one well site lasted more than a few days— a week at the most, depending on how many people were based at a given hab—and new wells had to be constantly sited and drilled.

The point was that the watchers would not find their work particularly suspicious. After a few moments, Ostrowsky left them, walking toward the cat with her arms out from the sides of her body, a white cloth in her right hand. "Hello!" she called. "You in the cat! Can we talk?" At least one person in the UN detail must speak English.

"Remain twenty meters from the vehicle," a heavily accented voice replied over the general talk channel. "What do you want?"

"A ride out of here," Ostrowsky replied. "For the women. I was wondering if we could strike a deal with you guys."

"What kind of a deal?"

"No deal," a second voice added. "We have our orders."

"Oh. Come on," Ostrowsky said. "You think us girls want to be locked up with these guys for the next three months?"

"You're Marines," the second voice replied. "Didn't you just spend months cooped up with them on the cycler?"

"At least we had *some* privacy! We had our own head! Look, there's gotta be something we can work out. If you could take us back to Mars Prime, maybe we could, I don't know, make it worth your while, y'know?"

"Well, you're going to have to be more explicit than that. Exactly what did you have in mind?"

"Well, gee, I don't know." Garroway could hear the slink in her voice, could imagine her shifting her hips in that lightweight EVA suit. "We could maybe work something out. But I gotta see you guys face-to-face if we're going to negotiate. I don't want . . . I mean, we've got people listening in, y'know?''

The other Marines continued their work, setting up the drilling rig's legs and connecting the fuel-cell array to the motor. As the banter continued, Garroway nodded to the others. Caswell, Donatelli, and Foster continued assembling the drill, while Garroway, Jacob, and Kaminski moved to a point where they were screened by the rig and found the armor sections that were waiting for them.

Marine Class-One armor could be broken down into eighteen separate parts. One was the front half of the cuirass, a single curved piece of kinevlar that covered the chest and torso. Earlier, several Marines had brought the portable drilling unit out and set it up around at the back of the hab, opposite the structure from the watching Mars cat. They'd brought out three cuirass front halves with the rest of the drilling and collection equipment, and left them piled with other equipment on the cold, hard ground.

Momentarily out of sight of the cat and its crew, Garroway, Kaminski, and Jacob dropped flat to the sand, each of them taking one of the torso armor sections. With the armor propped up in front of them then, they began crawling clumsily across the sand.

Active camouflage was an effect created by the layer of memory plastic coating the metal, requiring only sunlight or a trickle of body heat to work. Lying flat on his stomach, Garroway kept the cuirass out in front of him, bracing it by wedging the bottom edge into the sand, and holding it upright with straps wound tightly about his gloved hands.

In a sense, it was a high-tech version of a very old device . . . the shield. By keeping the half of an armor torso shell out away from his body, he was blocking the heat signature of his own suit. A careful scan from the Mars cat would almost certainly pick up the heat plume rising above his body in the cold, thin air, but with Ostrowsky out there talking to them, he didn't think they would be paying that much attention. The active camo on the outer surface, meanwhile, would blend in with the surrounding landscape. So long as he and the others moved slowly, without sudden jerks or movements, they stood a good chance of making it up close to the crawler unobserved.

"How many women are there?" another man's voice said, as the radio conversation continued. The exchange would help the Marines keep track of what was going on inside the cat.

"Five," Ostrowsky replied. "Four Marines and a civilian."

"I don't know," the voice came back. "That'd make it mighty crowded in here."

"Aw c'mon! You guys could think of *something*! . . ."

There were just two problems with this plan, one foreseen, the other a difficulty that Garroway hadn't even thought of until he was on his belly and slowly inching toward the objective. The foreseen plan was the trouble he and the other three would have seeing their objective. They'd allowed for that by working out their choreography with Ostrowsky. She was to walk to a point twenty meters away from the crawler's door; by keeping her in view and the crawler blocked by their shields, the strike team could close on the target even when they couldn't see it.

The unforeseen problem was worse. Garroway had forgotten how fiendishly cold the surface of the Martian desert was. The air temperature stood now, according to the readout on his helmet HUD, at minus fourteen Celsius, but the ground, hard-packed sand and loose gravel, was still a literal deep freeze. His armor's best insulation was on the soles of his boots, and the frigid ground seemed to leach the heat out through the front armor of his Class-Ones like a sponge soaking up a spill. He hadn't been on his stomach for more than ten minutes before he started shivering inside his armor. He'd already taken the precaution of disabling the thermostat of the suits—there was no sense in giving the UN heat sensors an easy target—and within a very few minutes more, all three of the slowly advancing Marines would be in danger of frostbite, or worse.

What the hell am I doing here? he asked himself. There'd been plenty of volunteers for this assault . . . and the more he thought about it, the more he knew that the role he'd assumed should have been given to someone younger, tougher, and possessing faster reflexes. He was feeling *old* . . . and the feeling grew worse the closer he crawled toward the objective.

"We might be able to work something out at that," a voice from the Mars cat said. "We're supposed to pull out of here in a day or two. We might be able to find some room for you women at that. *Maybe.* . . ."

"Well, okay," Ostrowsky said. "Let me go in and talk to the other girls, okay?"

Ostrowsky had promised to keep the soldiers in the cat talking until the Marines in the assault team had crawled to within twenty meters of their objective. Now she was walking slowly back toward the hab.

Garroway was shivering hard now, as he angled around toward the rear of the Mars cat. The cat's engine was in the rear, along with the radiators and waste-heat spills. From there, he and the others should be able to sprint the last few tens of meters to the vehicle without being picked up by its sensors . . . *if* they could rise from the icy sand and move now. Judging his position from the angle of the hab, he carefully lowered the shield, just enough to steal a glimpse of the Mars cat past its edge.

Right on target. He was looking straight on at the rear of the vehicle, from a distance of about fifteen meters.

There was still no indication that they'd been seen. Garroway looked about, checking the positions of the others.

Ostrowsky was clear. If they had anything on the ball, the UN troops would be searching the area for anything amiss . . . but with luck their IR scan wouldn't pick up the three Marines in the heat shadow of their own power plant. Garroway waited . . . waited . . . watching for some overt reaction, and when there was none, he dropped the armor segment, scrambled to his feet, and sprinted forward.

His body was so cold it was more of a lumber than a sprint, but he covered those last few meters and sagged against the Mars cat's starboard track. He spared a single glance for the hab, knowing that Lieutenant King was watching, was signaling the others to start the next phase of the plan. Working on the assumption that there were undiscovered listening devices still scattered about the hab's interior, several of the Marines should now be starting to discuss what they were going to do to get rescued. They wouldn't actually discuss anything; the idea wasn't to have the UN guards radio for help, but to gather around their radio, trying to make out what the prisoners were saying.

And in the meantime, Garroway, Jacob, and Kaminski had reached the cat's door.

Jacob was an electronics expert, like Garroway had been when he was an enlisted man. He held up his weapons—Radley's pliers and one of the smuggled pocketknives—and nodded his readiness. Garroway held Ostrowsky's fléchette gun . . . and hoped once again that he'd be able to work the thing if he had to. Even with the trigger guard removed, he was having trouble feeling anything at all through the fabric of his glove, and he wasn't sure he'd be able to manipulate the trigger.

With his other hand, he did a quick, three-fingered countdown, two . . . one . . .

Garroway hit the emergency airlock entry switch, which slid the outer door open immediately. Kaminski set one booted foot on the rung of the ladder going up the vehicle's side, then scrambled up to the roof, where the small sat dish hung on its yoke, aimed almost directly straight up. A couple of quick turns on the locking release, and the satellite dish swung easily in its mounting, aiming uselessly at the horizon.

Jacob was the first into the airlock. Both he and Garroway had worked on Mars cats before, during their mission training on Earth and in simulation during the cycler passage. There was a maintenance access panel in the tiny compartment to the left, and in seconds Jacob had popped the cover and was wrist-deep in the wiring on the other side. Garroway braced himself in the airlock's outer hatchway, Ostrowsky's fléchette pistol aimed head high at the inner hatch, just in case somebody tried coming through. Overriding the airlock's safeties, which prevented both hatches from being open to vacuum at once, was a relatively simple matter of cutting, stripping, and crossing four sets of wires, but the process took an eternity of seconds . . . and the UN troops on board would have known something was going down as soon as the outer hatch cracked open.

"C'mon!" Garroway said, keeping his eyes on the inner hatch. It was the first thing spoken since they'd left the shelter of the hab. "Damn it, *c'mon*!"

"Almost . . . got it . . . *shit*! Can't feel . . . a thing . . . through these . . . damned gloves . . ."

Kaminski dropped to the sand outside the airlock, Doc Casey's knife at the ready.

"Here she goes!" Jacob yelled, and then the inner hatch was sliding away as a swiftly strengthening wind blasted out into the airlock. A swirl of loose paper and garbage followed—a couple of readymeal packets, some plastic wrapping, an empty memclip case—and then the hurricane was past and an armored figure with a light blue helmet was swinging into view, framed in the open hatch.

Garroway had been gambling that however many men there were aboard the Mars cat, most would not have their armor on. The stuff was bulky and uncomfortable and made such essential details as urination a tedious chore—or forced the wearer to wire himself up with uncomfortable plastic plumbing. Someone, at least, would be in armor at all times in case of an emergency . . . but the whole plan would go seriously wrong if *several* of them happened to have been wearing their suits.

The EVA-suited man in the hatch, staggering a bit still from the shock of the abrupt decompression of the cat's cabin, was raising a French FA-29 assault rifle to his shoulder. Garroway was already in position, the

Ruger pointed straight at the UN trooper's helmet visor. He squeezed his hand almost convulsively; he felt nothing through the glove, heard nothing in the thin air but a sharp *snap*, but a white star appeared squarely in the center of the dark visor, and the soldier dropped his rifle, staggering back, groping at his face.

Garroway leaped into the cabin, colliding with the downed man as he thrashed on the deck and nearly falling. Regaining his balance, he swung left, checking the cabin's rear, then right, toward the control deck. He saw three other men, all down, all unarmored, all clutching faces or throats as they desperately tried to breathe.

"I'm in," he yelled over the tactical channel. "Four down! Jacob! Seal the hatch!"

"Working on it, Major."

The inner hatch slid shut a moment later, but it was too slow . . . too slow. The three unsuited men were still now, or nearly so. The suited man continued to claw at his visor. Garroway knelt beside him, trying to keep his hands away from the starred plastic. Several of the high-velocity fléchettes had penetrated the visor, their finned tails sticking out of the tough plastic like tiny arrows, but air was seeping through myriad tiny cracks. As the gas expanded, it grew cold, and a layer of frost was forming around the impact point. Water was condensing on the inside of the visor, and bubbling wildly through one of the larger cracks. The life-support indicator set into a pop-open recess in the man's chest armor showed his suit's pressure at a quarter bar and falling, his heart and respiration dangerously high and shallow.

Garroway fumbled at his armor's utility kit. If he could get a patch in place, he might save the man's life . . . but to do that he would have to pull the fléchettes out, and the suit would decompress completely in those few seconds, even if he managed not to shatter the plastic.

The man's eyes, just visible through frost and dark plastic, were panic-wide and bleeding. He clutched at Garroway's wrist as the Marine tried to tamp down a pressure seal around the cluster of fléchettes . . . but before he could complete the task, the man's life-support indicators flatlined.

"I think the poor bastard's had it," Kaminski said. Garroway started. He'd not realized the other Marine had entered the cat.

With the short, sharp fight over, Garroway felt numb, barely alive himself. He'd not been in a firefight for a good many years, and he'd managed to forget how terrifying the experience was . . . and how much he disliked it. He hadn't even been shot at, but his senses had been keyed to such a high pitch that now, as the adrenaline rush receded, he could hardly stand.

Kaminski was checking the other bodies. All showed the bruised faces, the blood at nose, mouth, eyes, and ears characteristic of explosive decompression.

Not a pleasant way to die at all. . . .

Garroway forced himself to keep moving, keep *working*, as he checked through the cat to make sure they'd caught all of the UN troops. The interior of the Mars cat was about the same size and shape as the inside of a large recreational trailer. There were four bunks aft, and a doorway leading to the supply lockers and fuel-cell storage. Forward was a tiny galley, a sitting area, and the forward command suite, which included the driver's seat and a small communications console on the cab's right side.

Sergeant Jacob was already sliding into the chair at the communications console. One of the dead men lay sprawled at his feet. "Hey, Major? Today's our lucky day!"

"What's that?"

"Doesn't look like they got a message off."

Garroway leaned over the Marine's shoulder, studying the main screen. The unit was set for satcom relay, and the screen showed the cryptic legend SATLINK ACQUISITION and the winking word SEARCHING. One of four smaller display monitors above the console showed an image—the inside of the hab module, as viewed from one corner of the room, high up near the ceiling. The fuzzy image showed Lieutenant King talking to three other Marines. They *had* missed a bug, then . . . though it fortunately had been positioned far enough away from the table that the UN troops wouldn't have been able to overhear their planning sessions.

"Let's see if we can get an uplink," Garroway told Jacob. The younger Marine's fingers flicked across the touch screen on the console, tapping in a chain of commands. A moment later, the SATLINK ACQUISITION line was updated with a CONNECT: MARSCOMSAT4 and a passcode entry blank.

Garroway stared at the screen for an unpleasant moment. All nonmilitary communications on Mars had used a programmed passcode; the human operators didn't need to enter a thing. If the computer was demanding a code entry now, it was because someone had added it. He'd seen Bergerac insert a computer memory clip in the com console back at Cydonia. "Try the standard passcode," he told Jacob.

Jacob complied, and a new line appeared on-screen.

PASSCODE INCORRECT; ENTER PASSCODE:_____

He'd been right. The UN had changed the access codes for all communications links on Mars, and not just the military ones, either. It only made sense. The key to any successful coup was communications; Bergerac and the Joubert woman obviously wanted to keep the takeover on Mars a secret, at least for now, and the only way to do that was to lock up the Marines and take over all communications on the planet. By changing and then controlling the access codes, they could do just that.

"What do you think, Sarge?" he asked. "Can you hack it?"

Jacob shook his head. "I could try, sure . . . but you know what kind of wall we're up against here, sir. Without a trapdoor or the code key back at Cydonia or Candor, I could sit here for a century or two typing in random alphanumerics and never get anywhere."

"Okay. See what you can do, anyway. Maybe you'll get lucky."

"Yeah, and maybe we can fly this thing back to

Earth,'' Jacob replied, but he immediately began tapping away at the touchscreen.

Kaminski had finished checking the bodies. ''I've got their IDs and stuff, sir,'' he said, holding out a handful of tags.

Garroway accepted them without comment, slipping them into a thigh pocket in his suit. They would be returned to Bergerac or some other senior UN representative when this was all over.

He was troubled on several counts, not the least of which was the blunt and bloody fact that if a war started now, he couldn't be entirely certain whether the UN had started it by imprisoning the Marine section . . . or whether he had by killing four UN soldiers. His orders—to ''protect American scientific and research interests on the planet Mars''—were unsatisfyingly vague when it came to reactions against hostile or *potentially* hostile UN moves.

He'd also just committed his tiny command to combat, and while he knew his next move would have to be to reach Candor Chasma, he wasn't quite certain yet just how he was going to accomplish that.

His first duty, though, would be to inform his superiors at the Pentagon about what was going on. He was alone and cut off as no military officer had ever been cut off before, tens of millions of miles away from reinforcements or relief. He knew well that he could expect no help from Earth, that his decisions on Mars would be dictated by what he had on hand and could hope to achieve with just twenty-five Marines.

But he was also painfully aware that his decisions here would affect American policy back home . . . and UN policy as well. If there was any way to keep US policymakers informed, he had to find it.

''Major?'' Jacob said. ''I'm not getting anywhere with this. We're locked out, and unless we find that code . . .''

''Understood.'' He thought for a moment. ''Okay. You and Kaminski start going through the cabin. See if they left anything written down that might help us.''

"They'd be pretty damned stupid if they did, sir."

"Agreed, it's unlikely, but we have to cover all the bases. Let me sit there."

"Aye, aye, sir."

He slid into the seat as Jacob vacated it and stared for a moment at the screen. Mars possessed no ionosphere—not in the sense that Earth did—and that meant that all radio communications were restricted to line of sight. There were microwave relays like the ones at Cydonia scattered about those regions where travel and exploration were common, but most parts of the planet relied on the handful of communications satellites in Martian orbit—the Ares Constellation of five low-orbit comsats, plus one in areosynchronous orbit, permanently stationed seventeen thousand kilometers above Candor Chasma.

Access to any of those satellites, however, required certain comm prefixes, codes, in other words, all of which would have been changed by now precisely to stop unauthorized personnel—like Garroway—from doing what he was about to attempt.

There might be, however, an alternative. When the first Mars Expedition had arrived in Mars orbit in 2019, a communications relay had been positioned on Phobos, the planet's inner moon. When Colonel Johnston and *Polkovnik* Reztsov had set foot on the sandy regolith of Candor Chasma and unfurled their respective nations' flags, the televised images and historic first words had been transmitted to a waiting Earth via that relay. It could only be employed when Phobos was above the horizon, but the minor worldlet made an easy visual target for a satcom dish.

That relay was still there. He knew it was and, better yet, he knew the activation codes. His original assignment on Mars, after all, had been to service and run computers and commo gear used by both the Marines and the civilians. Usually, messages to Earth were routed through one or another of the regular comsats, but during periods of heavy traffic to and from Earth it was always good to have a backup, just in case the available bandwidth was cut to unacceptable levels. The Phobos relay station provided an alternate means for reaching Spacenet.

His first step was to link his wrist-top into the Mars cat's display and call up his Beale code routine. It worked, and that was one less worry. Swiftly, then, he began typing at the keyboard, calling up a com request routine and checking to see that the crawler's satellite dish was still on-line after the rough handling it had received. So far, so good. He had the com routine up and running, and the tracking system indicated a lock on Phobos, now just fifteen degrees above the eastern horizon—which meant it was on the way down. With its seven-hour-plus period, Phobos was one of the handful of satellites in the solar system that rose in the west and set in the east. It also moved so quickly across the sky—a half a degree in about a minute—that you could actually see its drift with the naked eye. He had about thirty minutes before the moon set.

He touched a colored rectangle on his plastic console and pinged the relay. He had it! And now to compose the message. . . .

A message from Heinlein Station directly to Earth was out of the question. The UN would have people on Earth listening for any unauthorized transmissions inbound from Mars . . . and if they picked one up, they could almost certainly block it simply by jamming that frequency. They would have people at both Cydonia and Candor, too, who would come down hard on the Marines if they picked up his broadcast.

What Garroway was trying to do was a little more underhanded than phoning home without permission. He needed to tap into Spacenet, the electronic web linking all operations in space with one another and, through the primary node at the International Space Station, with Earthnet. He couldn't do it overtly, but he could squeeze a short message into a tiny packet of data that could be layered with routine, outgoing transmissions—the "housekeeping" talk between the computers on Mars and Earth that basically kept tabs on one another and ensured from moment to moment that all communications channels were open and functional. He couldn't send an open message; there might be watchdog routines running at Mars Prime or Cydonia specifically watching for anything tagged for Pentagon HQCOM, Washington or any other government or military installation on or near Earth. Hell, Bergerac probably had routines running right now listening for words like "Marine," "Lloyd," or "UN."

But he had one hidden ace . . . the Beale code link with Kaitlin. If he could slip the code—a long string of numbers—into the housekeeping traffic going back to Earth, he could address it in such a way that it would automatically be routed to Spacenet's e-mail service. The next time Kaitlin downloaded her mail, his message would be waiting.

He hated dragging her into this, but it was the only chance he saw. She should be safe enough, after all, in Pittsburgh.

FOURTEEN

It had been eight days since Kaitlin had seen Yukio, since he'd left for his base way to the south on Tanega Island, and now her v-mail was being flagged as undeliverable. She'd placed a long-distance call to the base, but all she got was a recorded vidloop, saying that no calls were being accepted at this time. She wished she knew whether the Japanese military routinely closed their bases to outsiders during a drill . . . or if this was an indication that something serious was brewing. There'd been nothing in the papers or on netnews to help her make sense of the situation. It was very puzzling . . . and a little disturbing.

She'd come to the temple this morning looking for a quiet restful place in which to think. To think about herself and Yukio, about their future . . . if they had one. They'd had a few days to travel around Japan before Yukio had to report to his base, and as she had feared, he'd become only slightly less formal away from Kyoto than he had been in his father's house. It wasn't just the absence of sex—she'd experienced dry spells before, and she could live with that. It wasn't even the lack of

194

those public displays of intimacy that she'd become accustomed to back home, holding hands, walking arm in arm, calling each other pet names. Being in Japan and speaking Japanese constantly made her almost *feel* Japanese. The day after they arrived, in fact, they'd seen a young couple holding hands on the maglev to Tokyo, and she'd been shocked . . . as well as amused at her own reaction. No, the problem went deeper than that.

She feared that Yukio was seeing her now as *hen na gaijin*, as someone who would never fit in, no matter how well she spoke the language or understood the customs. She remembered times before, back in the States, when they had discussed the difficulties that a mixed couple would face. He'd been the practical one, pointing out the problems foreigners still had in Japan, and the provincialism of large parts of the United States. She'd always countered with her belief that anything was possible . . . if they'd loved each other enough. And that was probably it. Yukio must have realized that his love for her wasn't strong enough.

A high bamboo fence bordered the path to the temple. She ran her fingers gently along the bamboo as she walked along, head down. Abruptly the fence came to an end as the path ran along the edge of the lake. She saw it first in its reflection and caught her breath, as she suddenly knew why it was called the Golden Pavilion. Three stories high and covered with gold leaf, the temple gleamed with a dazzling brilliance both above and below the water. She found a spot next to the water and sat down, thinking how strange everything was. Her love for Yukio was stronger than ever . . . just when it seemed that his love for her was fading.

She unclipped her PAD to check the netnews again. Nothing. More rumblings with Mexico. Anti-American and aldetech riots in Quebec and Paris. A new messiah in Rome who promised the aliens would soon return for the faithful. Nothing, though, to indicate why Japanese military bases might be going on alert. Well, time to check her v-mail. Something from CMU, her grades. Hey, all right! She grinned. Too bad Yukio wasn't here.

They'd always had a friendly rivalry going with their grades, even though he was taking graduate-level courses. Of course he always tried to claim that a B for a grad course was equivalent to an A for an undergrad, but she never bought that line. Not that he often got anything less than an A anyway.

What else? Hmm, something from her dad. Funny. She'd just gotten a long vid from him yesterday, and he usually didn't comm her more than once or twice a week. Strange, too, it was text only . . . and the whole thing was in code. What the . . . ? As she opened her Beale routine to decode the message, she found herself hoping it wasn't something stupid like that silly mix-up with the two archeologists.

It wasn't.

Kaitlin:

> *This is urgent, Chicako. Pass the following message on to Uncle Walt. You'll know how. The cat's probably watching the mousehole right now, so you'd better come to Japan for the return trip. Thanks!*
> *Love!—Dad*
> *Walt, you sorry-assed son of a bitch, listen up and listen good. The blue boys pulled a Pearl Harbor 1207 GMT 27 May. The boss is down, but okay. Forcibly relocated to Red Planet. Have capped guards and secured cat. Am marching on Derna, with complete openness.*

Semper fi.—Mark

She had to read the message through three times before she grasped it. Her mouth was hanging open as she worked her way through her father's circumlocutions. "Blue boys" would be the UN. Pearl Harbor . . . a sneak attack? Forcibly relocated . . . as in imprisoned?

But the Marines obviously didn't believe in staying where they had been put. A strange and unfamiliar feeling welled up inside her as she read about their escape. It took her a moment to recognize it as pride, both in the Marines . . . and in her father.

Something had happened to her father. The man who'd written this was not the same man who'd been planning to arrange an out after the Mars mission, the man who'd been just marking time doing his job . . . but not really caring. The man who'd written this was a man who was taking charge. She wondered what had happened to Colonel Lloyd; the message sounded as though Major Mark Garroway was the one in command.

She grinned as she figured out his cryptic reference to Heinlein Station. *So, Dad,* she thought, *I guess all that science fiction I gave you did some good after all.*

So now, what to do about this message? Obviously she needed to pass it on as soon as possible. But how?

Uncle Walt, of course, was Colonel Walter Fox. He and her dad had been buddies since before she was born, and she'd grown up thinking of him and his wife as uncle and aunt. In fact, it was Walter and Melanie Fox who'd taken care of her after her mother died, whenever her father was stationed overseas. The question was, could she risk sending this message in the clear? She had several other encryption programs, including one of her own design, but she didn't know what Uncle Walt had.

She took another look at the second part of the message, translating to Tokyo time. The UN forces had taken over at 2107 Sunday . . . yesterday. Her last message from Yukio was dated Saturday, and yesterday her messages started getting bounced. That was too much to believe of coincidence. The Japanese government must have closed the base in response to word from the UN. No, she didn't dare put this message on the net from inside Japan. She would have to go back to the States . . . and fast.

She thought about splurging on a taxi to get back to the youth hostel but then decided that the subway would be quicker. It didn't take her long to pack her bag and check out, and then another subway ride got her to the maglev station, where she got on the first direct car to Kansai. She immediately shut herself in one of two enclosed comm stations to check out flight times. *Damn!* By the time the maglev got to Kansai, she'd have less than ten minutes to make the next Star Raker for the States, and the first one after that wasn't for another four hours ... all of that assuming she could get a seat. The Star Raker coming over had been pretty full; she hadn't seen any empty places.

So. What other options did she have? It probably wasn't all *that* urgent to get this message through quickly. After all, what could they do ... send a message back saying, "Reinforcements on the way, ETA six months"? Still it would be important for them—she wasn't exactly sure who she meant by "them"—to know what the UN had done.

Besides, ever since she'd put the timing of the attack together with the closing of Yukio's base, she'd had an increasing feeling that it wouldn't be healthy for her to stick around here much longer. The words "enemy alien" came to mind, and she shivered.

So was there anything sooner than that second Star Raker? Ah, that would do it. It was only going as far as Los Angeles, but maybe she would stay with Aunt Melanie and Uncle Walt down at Camp Pendleton for a few days before heading back East. She checked the price and whistled. Well, what's the point in having an American Express account if you can't use the thing when you really need it? She connected to Reservations and pressed a button on her wrist-top to send her AmEx code through. Now she was all set ... except for one more little chore.

She'd decided to wait and do this on the maglev rather than in the train station because she'd wanted an enclosed comm station where she could take her time recording the message ... messages, actually. The first one was no problem; expressing thanks for hospitality received and sorrow for an unexpected but necessary departure was easy to do in Japanese. The second one, though, that was another matter. There was no estab-

lished custom for what she had to say to Yukio. She
wanted to tell him how much she loved him, but she
also wanted to set him free. Between his feelings of
obligation and loyalty to his family and his country and
whatever of love he still felt for her, he was being pulled
to pieces. She wanted . . . she *needed* to release him.

Several times she broke down in tears and had to erase
the message and start over, but finally it was done. She
played it back one last time, nodding in satisfaction. Yes,
she had walked the tightrope successfully. Making sure
her smile was in place before she pressed RECORD, she
added, "Look me up when you get back to the States.
We can have a cup of *cha* and talk about old times.
Sayonara, Toshiyuki-san." STOP

The messages complete, she took a deep breath,
opened her address book, and selected the Ishiwara
household. The minister would certainly not be in at this
time of day; probably his private secretary—what had
Yukio said his name was? Nabuko?—would answer.
Just as well. She wasn't sure she could face Yukio's
father right now.

The screen in front of her dissolved into an image of
a young man sitting cross-legged on a tatami behind a
low table with a PAD. She thought she'd seen him the
night she had dinner there, and he obviously recognized
her. Of course, it would be a large part of his business
to remember names and faces. After the initial pleasantries, she made her request.

"I find I must leave this beautiful country and return
to my home. I have recorded a message of farewell for
the Honored Minister. May I transmit it now?"

Nabuko bowed in assent, and she selected SEND. She
had embedded the message to Yukio inside the one to
his father, asking the senior Ishiwara to pass the message
along when it became possible to do so. As a government minister, he might even be able to get around the
difficulty of the base being closed.

"I hope your journey will be a pleasant one, *Garroway Kaitlin-san.*"

She bowed and ended the connection, then slumped back in the seat. Done. It was done.

0143 HOURS GMT

Heinlein Station, Mars
Sol 5636: 1320 hours MMT

He didn't want to see the Corps die.

Garroway had been a Marine for twenty-three years, now. He'd seen the Corps during the frenzied build-up during America's involvement in the Colombian Civil War, in '27, and again during the disastrous intervention in Andhra Pradesh six years later. He'd seen the BCs— the slang pejorative variously meant budget cutters, bean counters, or things less savory—come *that* close to strangling the Corps, particularly in the years since the fighting in southeastern India. The argument ran to the effect that amphibious operations were a thing of the past; indeed, the last large-scale combat amphib deployment had been at Tavrichanka in 2012, when the First Marine Division had waded ashore to save Vladivostok from the invading Chinese. The other major Marine interventions in recent years had been by helicopter or Valkyrie. The Army Special Forces routinely deployed the same way, and they had better and more modern equipment.

So who needed the Marines?

And that, Garroway was increasingly convinced, was what had been responsible for his ROAD-like behavior, his determination to put in his time and get the hell out. He could do a lot better on the Outside; hell, he had a standing job offer from Vince Mayhew at Moravec. He didn't *need* this shit.

Only now he was finding that he did . . . and that his dedication to the Corps had less to do with his oath to the country or the reason the Marines existed than it did with the people who were depending on him for leadership right here, right now.

Maybe the country didn't need the US Marines, but *he* did.

The entire group was gathered once again in the main room of the Heinlein Station hab, the Marines in rows seated on the bare floor, the five scientists by themselves off to the left. Garroway had started, an hour earlier, to try to put together some sort of inspirational speech, but nothing he'd written down had worked. He would just have to ad-lib this one.

"People," he said. "In the absence of specific orders from the military command authority, we have to assume that, as of this morning, we are at war."

He had their full attention now. There was not a sound in the hab, and every eye in the room met his.

"Our orders were to safeguard American interests on Mars and, specifically, to protect the civilian research outpost at Cydonia, which, as I'm sure you all know, was somewhat, ah . . . *controversial* in certain quarters. That outpost has now been taken over by the UN. Two of our people were hurt. In the absence of specific orders from Earth, I must assume that that action was a hostile one. By capturing the Mars cat this morning, we have made our first strike back against the enemy. We now have the means to leave our prison and to carry the battle to the UN forces occupying our facilities.

"I've discussed my intentions with a number of you this morning, so you know what I have in mind. It is my intention to take the Mars cat and march on Candor Chasma, 650 kilometers east of here. I intend to leave this afternoon, within the next hour, if possible."

A babble of voices rose from the Marines and from the scientists as well. Garroway raised both hands, motioning the room to silence. "The march," he continued, "will be difficult . . . and dangerous. Nothing like this has ever been attempted before, and we have only a very spotty knowledge of the terrain between here and there. Our biggest problem is going to be water, because, as I understand it, permafrost tends to be kind of patchy along the Valles Marineris, and we can't count on finding drill sites that will come up wet. We'll carry as much water as we can manage, but I'm afraid we're going to be on short rations for most of the trip.''

''Now just a damned minute!'' The protest came not from one of the Marines, but from Dr. Kettering, standing off to the side with the other scientists. ''You can't seriously be thinking of dragging us all across four hundred miles of Martian desert!''

''You are welcome to stay, Doctor,'' Garroway replied. He turned to face the Marines. ''In fact, this is strictly a volunteer-only mission. Any of you who want to stay behind may do so. There's plenty of food, and we'll leave the drilling equipment.''

That brought a startled reaction from some of the Marines. ''Sir!'' Ostrowsky said, raising her hand. ''You mean we're crossing the desert without water?''

Garroway exchanged glances with Devora Druzhininova, who silently nodded. ''I've discussed the plan with Dr. Druzhininova,'' he said. ''Maybe I should let her tell us about that.''

Druzhininova didn't leave the group of scientists. She simply folded her arms and began addressing the entire group. ''You all know that most of Mars's water—a whole ocean of it, in fact—exists beneath the planet's surface as permafrost . . . essentially frozen mud buried beneath anywhere from two to twenty meters of regolith.

''The permafrost layer is not uniform over the entire planet, however. It's much thicker in the north polar regions, especially north of about forty degrees north latitude, where the Boreal Sea existed once. Cydonia Prime depends on the permafrost left when that sea froze, billions of years ago. It's almost nonexistent around the equator, though. Here in the Mariner Valley, most of the ice was melted a billion years ago by the raising of the Tharsis Bulge to the west.''

''We've got water wells here,'' Lance Corporal Julia Higgins called out. ''What do you think that drill out back is for?''

''Subsurface fossil water. There are deep pools kept liquid by volcanism, even yet. Heinlein Station and Mars Prime are both positioned over fairly large water traps, but we can't expect to find more between here and there. I'm afraid we'll be limited to what we can carry . . . and what our suits and the life-support gear on the Mars cat can recycle." She looked at Garroway. "I wish I had happier news."

"That's okay, Doctor," he replied. "Lieutenant King and I have gone over the numbers. We'll be able to carry enough with us to last, if we're careful."

He paused a moment, taking the time to study the expressions on the faces of the men and women before him. Some looked afraid or worried, some determined. Most simply looked attentive, as though this were simply another briefing at the start of a rugged but routine training exercise.

He suddenly felt incredibly, inexpressibly *proud* of these people.

"I need to know," he told them, "how many of you are coming along."

Almost as one, people began standing up . . . Ostrowsky and Jacob making it to their feet first, but the rest within a second or two. They stood before him at attention, as though on the parade ground, and Garroway felt his pride swelling even more.

David Alexander and Dr. Druzhininova both crossed the floor and joined the Marines, followed a reluctant moment later by Edward Pohl; Craig Kettering and Louis Vandemeer remained where they were, arms folded, expressions shuttered.

Well, he hadn't expected the civilians to embrace this madness. He needed either Alexander or Druzhininova—he'd discussed the matter with them an hour ago—and was pleased that both of them, and Pohl, would be coming along. The other two should be safe enough here until someone came by to pick them up.

He did know that he wanted no one along who wasn't committed to the mission's success.

"Thank you, everyone," he said. "I knew I could count on you all. Be seated."

"What we're about to do," he told them as they resumed their places on the floor, "is going to be difficult.

It's never been done. But it's also not without precedent. How many of you remember Presley O'Bannon?''

Perhaps a dozen hands went up—mostly those of the older Marines, the NCOs and senior people. Some of the younger ones looked uncertain. Others wore blank expressions that suggested they'd read about the incident in their Corps manuals and promptly forgotten it. The O'Bannon saga was required reading for *every* Marine.

''Lieutenant Presley Neville O'Bannon was a twenty-year-old Marine from the Blue Ridge Mountains of Kentucky who, in 1805, commanded a detachment of seven US Marines on a march from Alexandria, Egypt, to Derna, in what is now the People's Glorious Jihad of Islamic Revolution. The march was led by Thomas Eaton, the US consul to Tunis and, besides the Marines, included about five hundred Arab revolutionaries and Greek mercenaries.

''That was during our war against what were then called the Barbary States . . . Tripoli, in particular, the worst of the lot. Eaton had hatched a plan to help an Arab exile named Hamet overthrow his brother, who was pasha of Tripoli at the time, and install a government friendly to the United States, ending once and for all Tripoli's habit of capturing American seamen and holding them for ransom.

''O'Bannon and his Marines helped Eaton achieve the impossible. They prevented an Arab mutiny along the way by seizing the expedition's food stores. When they reached Derna, they led a charge that carried the defenses of the city, which happened to be Tripoli's most important territorial holding. Two Marines died in the attack, and two more, including O'Bannon, were wounded. O'Bannon himself raised the Stars and Stripes over Derna's fortress, the first time the American colors were raised in battle in the Eastern Hemisphere. The action won for the US Marines both the line in the Marine Corps Hymn referring to 'the shores of Tripoli' and the Mameluke design of the Corps officer's curved dress sword.'' He grinned. ''And you Marines who didn't know all that have some studying to do!''

He paused as the men and women laughed, then went on, more seriously. "O'Bannon and his men accomplished an impossible march, six hundred miles across the Sahara Desert in something just over six weeks. We've only got four hundred miles to cross, and we have a Mars cat to do it with instead of O'Bannon's camels. I think we'll be able to do a bit better than he did!"

"So how long is it going to take us, Major?" Corporal Hayes asked.

Garroway took a deep breath. He'd had two answers ready, a short one based on the assumption that everyone would be able to travel inside the captured Mars cat, and a longer one calculated on the need for some to ride— or walk—outside. If only six or eight had volunteered, it would have been possible to make the trip to Mars Prime in less than two days.

But that, of course, would have raised rather serious additional difficulties; taking on the UN contingent that was probably stationed at Candor Chasma with eight Marines would have been chancy at best.

"If we're lucky," he told them, "we'll be able to complete the trip in about a week. Since we'll be facing extreme conditions, however, and uncertain terrain, I'm planning on the march taking at least two weeks, and quite possibly more."

"Major, you can't seriously be considering this," Vandemeer said.

"You two will be safe enough here," he told them. "The UN soldiers in the cat were supposed to report in every so often. When they don't report in tonight, someone will be on the way to check up on the place. When they get here, you'll be able to tell them, quite truthfully, that you wanted nothing to do with this scheme."

"We'll tell them where you're going!"

"Go ahead. They'll know as soon as they find out we're gone." He grinned. "Even with us following the Mars cat's tracks all the way to Mars Prime . . . well, it's a damn big desert!"

"Damn it, Major!" Kettering said. "You could be starting a war!"

"Those people have already started it, Doctor," Garroway said, nodding toward the airlock and the bodies of the UN troops now lying on the cold Martian sand. "All we're going to do is finish it."

FIFTEEN

PRA Flight 81
60,000 feet above the Pacific
Ocean
1605 hours Tokyo time

According to the data displayed on the seatback screen, the Pacific Rim Airlines *Amagiri* transport was nearly at its maximum altitude of sixty thousand feet. The countdown readout in the corner showed 30 ... 29 ... 28 ...

Kaitlin double-checked her seat restraints, then gripped the handrests firmly, not from terror but from excitement. She'd never flown a suborbital before, and this one—one of the Lockheed Ballistic 2020s, better known to the businessmen who flew them as Yankee Bullets—was just about to drop from the *Amagiri* and boost for space.

Space. She was excited by the idea, more excited than she'd thought she would be. Star Rakers employed on intercontinental runs typically cruised at 100,000 to 150,000 feet, but suborbitals actually grazed the arbitrary boundary of space—264,000 feet, or fifty miles. People who'd crossed that boundary were entitled to wear astronaut wings; PRA handed out gold-plated wings as souvenirs, she knew, as a promotion, to everyone who'd ridden one of their sub-Os. They could afford to, of course. She shuddered to think what her AmEx bill would look like next month, but it was worth it!

The countdown reached zero, and, for a few precious seconds, Kaitlin felt the elevator-descent sensation of free fall as the delta-winged sub-O fell from beneath the broad, twin-fuselaged wing of the *Amagiri* transport.

The rocket boost, when it came, surprised her by being so gentle. The acceleration built steadily, though, until she was pressed deep into her seat. What a ride! She remembered her father's v-mail description of the exhilaration he'd felt during his boost into orbit last year. "Like a real kick in the pants," he'd told her.

I know what you mean now, Dad.

The boost dragged on until she almost wondered if the pilot had made a mistake and was going to take them into orbit after all, but then she began to feel lighter and lighter and then . . . nothing. The engines cut out, and she was weightless. The screen readout on the seatback in front of her showed altitude in both miles and kilometers. They were passing forty miles, now, and still rising higher with every passing moment.

Though it might have been fun, she thought, to float about the cabin, she was glad for the seat restraints. She was also suddenly very glad for the tridemerin patch on her left arm as she heard the unmistakable sounds of someone across the aisle being sick. Pacific Rim attendants had offered the antispacesickness patches to all the passengers, requiring all who refused the medicine to thumbprint a waiver; apparently at least one of her fellow passengers had availed himself of the waiver option . . . and was now availing himself of his complimentary comfort bag.

Fifty miles . . . fifty-one! She was in space! There were no windows in the sub-O's passenger section, but a repeater screen at the front of the cabin showed a nose-camera view of the sky ahead, black above and black below, separated by a curved band of glorious blue radiance. The Bullet was passing the terminator now, plunging into night. She grinned suddenly. She'd actually made it past the magic fifty-mile barrier before Yukio! He'd be so jealous if he knew. *It'd be good for him!*

Now for Uncle Walt. She'd not wanted to transmit on one of the Japanese e-nets, not and run the risk of having her call intercepted. The suborbital, though, had a direct feed to a comsat, and the channel ought to be secure. Checking her wrist-top, she did a quick conversion in her head. With the eight-hour time difference, it would be about twelve-twenty at night at Camp Pendleton. She didn't want to wake him . . . but she didn't feel like hanging on to this message by herself for another eight or nine hours either. Tuning her wrist-top to the seatback screen in front of her, she pinged his home account. All right! He was in and hooked up. She transmitted a connection request . . . and in a few seconds was looking at the worry lines and prematurely receding hairline of one of her oldest friends.

Colonel Walter Fox broke into a huge grin when he saw her. "Kaitlin! So good to see you! How're you doing? What're you doing? Where are you?"

"That last is the easiest to answer, Uncle Walt," she said with a mirror grin. "I'm at, oh, about fifty-five miles up over the Pacific right now."

He whistled. "Flying high in more ways than one, aren't you, Chicklet?" he said, using his own mangled version of her Japanese nickname. "Those suborbs don't come cheap."

"Well, it . . . seemed important to get back to port right away. Listen, Uncle Walt," she said quickly, before he started asking questions. "I got a message from, ah, a mutual friend. I'd like to transmit it to you now."

He nodded and said nothing while the message was being transferred from Kaitlin's wrist-top to the suborb's communications relay to a communications satellite in geosynchronous orbit and then to a downlink station at Camp Pendleton and finally to Fox's wrist-top. He stared

at his display, raised his left eyebrow, then studied the
screen some more.

"Did our . . . mutual friend transmit this to you in the
clear?" he asked.

She shook her head. "No." Walter Fox knew all
about the Garroways' penchant for codes. There was no
need for her to be more specific, especially over a channel whose security she wasn't able to verify. Maybe she
was being paranoid—there'd been no indication that she
had been followed or was being watched while she was
in Japan—but, hey, just because you're paranoid doesn't
mean they're *not* out to get you.

"Good. Okay, what flight are you on?"

"PRA 81 inbound for LAX. Uncle Walt? Do you suppose I could stay with you and Aunt Melanie for a few
days?" She laughed, a mirthless chuckle. "My vacation
sort of got interrupted, and I'm somewhat at loose ends
right now."

"Mmm," he grunted, deep in thought. "Kaitlin, do
you know how to get a message back to . . . our friend?"

"Yes. The, ah, normal channels seem to be down, but
we have a back door."

"Excellent. Okay, this won't wait. Look . . . I'll talk
to you later."

And Kaitlin was left staring, dumbfounded, at a blank
screen. Uncle Walt wasn't usually so abrupt. He probably wanted to let the base commander know about the
message before it got any later. She was stunned,
though, and a little hurt, that he hadn't even responded
to her inviting herself over. Well, she could always
spend the night at an airport hotel and then call Aunt
Melanie in the morning.

Then she realized that his abruptness was a confirmation. She'd been right. Getting her dad's message
through *was* important. She was now very, very glad
she'd followed her hunch and taken the suborbital. If
what had happened on Mars was a prelude to war, and
if she'd stayed on in Japan, she might have found herself unable to leave. And she would have been the
only one on the planet to know what had gone down

... and she wouldn't have been able to do a damn thing about it.

In a surprisingly short time the descent warning sounded, followed by a period of gradually increasing weight and a growing shudder. The nose-camera view was beginning to show a pearly opalescence, deep red, tinted pink on the edges, as the Bullet plowed back into thicker atmosphere, killing velocity with a series of vast, computer-controlled S-sweeps across the northeastern Pacific.

She thought about what her father had always said, about the Marine Corps being like a family. She wondered what other members of that family would do when they found out about the takeover at Cydonia. Uncle Walt cared because he knew her dad, but what would *his* superiors think ... and feel? Would they care ... or was what happened to a few Marines a hundred million miles away not worth the risk of going to war?

She saw little of the actual landing—a sudden blur of city lights as the suborbital swept in over the coastline somewhere near San Jose, followed by a rapid descent and a final burst of power from the craft's traditional ramjets as it maneuvered into the LAX landing pattern. By the time the suborbital touched down with a bump and a squeal she had worked herself into a real state. Kaitlin knew just how precarious the survival of the Marine Corps was right now. Damn it, *nobody* cared. Her father's message would probably be ignored ... or dismissed as a fake. It was a peculiarly helpless feeling, knowing that Dad was in trouble on another planet, and there wasn't a thing she could do to help him.

As the aircraft came to a halt at the terminal, a warning sounded and display screens flashed in several languages, instructing all passengers to stay in their seats.

"Miss Garroway?"

She looked up at the flight attendant who'd just materialized by her seat. "Uh, yeah?"

He smiled politely. "Would you get your things and follow me, please?"

What? As she followed the attendant out the main door of the craft and into the transport tunnel, she heard rustlings behind her as the other passengers were at last allowed to move. Since when did she rate VIP treatment?

Then she wondered if her message to Uncle Walt had been intercepted by the Japanese government after all ... but she was on American soil now. Surely, they couldn't detain her here, no matter what the current UN situation might be.

Two Marines in khaki uniforms, a gunnery sergeant and a staff sergeant, were waiting for her in the terminal, and she felt a hot rush of relief. *Marines* she could handle.

"Miss Garroway?" the gunnery sergeant asked, and she nodded. "Please come with us, ma'am."

As she sat down in the waiting transfer cart, she turned to the gunnery sergeant. "Colonel Fox sent you, didn't he?" she asked.

"No, ma'am," was the uninformative reply.

"He didn't? Well, who did? Where are you taking me? What's going on here?" She was getting more than a little annoyed.

"Our orders come directly from Commandant Warhurst, ma'am. We're taking you to Terminal E for transfer to a military Star Eagle transport."

"The commandant! But why? What's going on? Where am I going?"

The man finally turned and looked at her. She had the feeling that he was as puzzled about his orders as she was. "Ma'am," he said apologetically, "we don't exactly know what's going on ourselves. But our orders are to take you by fastest available military transport to Andrews Aerospace Force Base and from there to the Pentagon. The commandant himself will be waiting for you."

Suddenly he grinned. "Don't know what you've done, ma'am, but I tell you, I haven't seen the brass this worked up since the Colombian War ... and believe you me, *that* takes some doing!"

TUESDAY, 29 MAY: 1830 HOURS GMT

National Security Council
Conference Room,
Executive Building Basement,
Washington, DC
1430 hours EDT

I never thought an electronics specialist would be the one to start a damned war, General Warhurst thought, as he showed his special pass and ID to a grim-faced Army guard at yet another checkpoint. He followed Admiral Gray through the x-ray scanner and into the bustling subterranean labyrinth that was the Executive Building's deepest basement levels. Still, given the high-tech nature of warfare these days, an electronics specialist and computer programmer was as likely to push the war initiate sequence button as anyone else, and maybe more so.

He thought about his son. He'd been thinking about Ted a lot, lately. It had been eighteen days since his death in Mexico, and eleven since the funeral at Arlington. Life, these past weeks, had become a vast and yawning emptiness . . . one that Montgomery Warhurst had been trying to fill with work.

He felt guilty about that. Stephanie seemed to be covering up her grief pretty well, but Janet was in a bad way; she and Jeff, Ted's son, were staying at the house in Warrenton for a while, until things could settle out. At least he had work, something to occupy his mind.

The nights were rough, though. He hadn't been sleeping much. . . .

This new crisis on Mars was almost welcome. *Any* distraction was welcome now.

Admiral Gray led him down a long and gleaming passageway, guided him left into a comfortably appointed lobby, then ushered him between two more sentries and through an inner door that would have done a bank vault proud.

The room was lavish enough, with its rich oak paneling, thick carpet, and executive-style leather chairs, but it somehow didn't match the mental image Warhurst had formed of the place when CJ had asked him to attend this morning's meeting. He'd expected something larger and grander, frankly, a corner room, perhaps, with a splendid view of the White House grounds next door and the Capitol Building beyond. The room was large, with a low ceiling lit by fluorescents concealed behind plastic panels. One wall, the one opposite the room's only door, was taken up by a floor-to-ceiling display screen which currently showed the NSC seal and was flanked by the American flag and a flag bearing the presidential seal.

There were no windows and, in fact, the entire room was a kind of vault more secure than any bank's. It was easier to maintain security here, of course, four floors down from street level in the warren of tunnels, passageways, and rooms that honeycombed this part of the nation's capital. For a good many years, now, the joke circulating through official Washington was that the city was like an iceberg; nine-tenths of the place was below ground, hidden where you couldn't see it.

And beyond the reach of laser eavesdropping devices or cruise missiles or remote-piloted microdrone assassins. Even the president, these days, spent more of his time in the hardened bunkers of the old Situation Room Complex beneath the White House than he did upstairs in the exposed Oval Office. *Especially* these days, with a dozen terrorist groups sworn to strike at Satan America, with the threat of war looming so large and desperately close.

"Have a seat, Monty," Gray said, gesturing. Other men were already filtering in and taking their places at the table. Admiral Gray had met Warhurst personally in the basement lobby and walked him through the security gates. Now, for the first time, he found himself inside the National Security Council's main conference room, a place he'd heard of often enough but never seen.

Since 1989, the National Security Council had been

organized into three subgroups; the NSC Principals Committee was the senior of these, tasked with coordinating and monitoring all national-security policy. Currently, it was chaired by Louis Carlton Harrel, the president's national security advisor. Its regular members included John Matloff, secretary of state; Archibald Severin, secretary of defense; Arthur J. Kinsley, director of central intelligence; Charles Dockery, the president's chief of staff; and Admiral Gray, chairman of the Joint Chiefs. Other people might attend at the president's invitation, and that was the case for Warhurst, who'd received a scrambled call from Harrel himself only two hours ago.

Harrel was the last to arrive, hurrying through the vault door with a wave to the guards to seal it off behind him. Warhurst didn't know the man personally. He was a tall, kindly faced black man in his late fifties who had the reputation for being one of the sharper and more aggressive of President Markham's personal advisors.

"General Warhurst," Harrel said, taking his seat at the head of the table. "Allow me to express, for all of us, our sincere regrets about your son. We know how you must feel, and we appreciate your being with us this morning, despite your loss."

Memories burned, but Warhurst held them in check. "Thank you, sir. My son gave his life for his country and for his fellow Marines, and I'm proud of him for that."

"We've asked you to come here," Harrel went on, "because of this remarkable message we understand reached us through the daughter of one of the Marines with the MMEF."

"Yes, sir. That would be Kaitlin Garroway."

"You've seen the message?" Matloff demanded. He was a lean, white-haired, hawk of a man in his sixties. He touched a key on his wrist-top, and the display screen on the wall lit up with the Garroway message.

"Yes, sir."

"Well, what do you make of it?"

"I'd say it's legitimate, Mr. Secretary. My people have already checked it out, and I've spoken at length both with Colonel Fox and with Garroway's daughter. Both are convinced that this is a genuine message."

"Now, Colonel Fox is Garroway's commanding officer, is he not?" Matloff said. "This, this first sentence of the message isn't exactly the sort of thing a military officer writes to his superior, is it?"

"Major Garroway and Colonel Walter Fox are old friends, Mr. Secretary. They were both mustangs, and they were stationed together several times, in Japan, and at Camp Pendleton. According to Fox, they maintained a good-natured rivalry, especially after Fox passed Garroway up on the promotions list. The, ah, language of that first line was intended to convince Fox that it was, indeed, Garroway who was writing it."

"Why all the damned cryptic gobbledygook, General?" Severin demanded. "It was my understanding that this message was transmitted in some kind of secret code."

"A Beale code, Mr. Secretary," Arthur Kinsley said with a smile. "I gather that Garroway used it to keep parts of his e-mail correspondence with his daughter private."

"So why use indirect language? I don't understand some of this stuff at all. Red Planet? We *know* he's on Mars. . . ."

"Beale codes," Kinsley pointed out, "are among the most secure codes there are, since, to crack one, you have to know which book is being used to provide page, line, and character numbers for the correspondents. Even so, any code can be broken with enough information. Major Garroway might have been afraid that the wrong people would intercept this."

"It's my feeling, Mr. Secretary," Warhurst added, "that the major was playing it safe. He's a careful man with a high security clearance for the electronics and communications work he does, and he's well aware of what codes can and cannot guarantee. The cryptic references are probably there just in case one of the UN security agencies had already cracked his code. He'd been using it throughout the cycler flight to Mars, after all, and it's possible that someone had picked up on it. His use of circumlocutions is designed to sidestep any automated search program set up at Mars, something set to flag any transmissions of the words 'Heinlein Station' or 'UN' or 'Candor Chasma.' His use of 'Red Planet' doesn't mean Mars, Mr. Secretary. That's the title of a book written almost a century ago by a writer named Robert Heinlein. Heinlein Station. 'Blue boys' means the UN. 'Complete openness' is 'candor,' as in 'Candor Chasma.' He's telling us exactly where he is going."

"Can you tell us, General," Harrel said, "what the devil 'Derna' might refer to? We've had our staff looking it up, and all they can find is the obvious geographical reference to the city in North Africa."

"The shores of Tripoli, sir." Warhurst managed a smile. "Any Marine would pick up on that right away." He proceeded to tell them briefly about Presley O'Bannon and his 1805 march through the desert.

"Your conclusion, then," Harrel said when Warhurst had finished the tale, "is that Garroway is marching from Heinlein Station across some . . . how far is it?"

"Almost four hundred miles," Kinsley replied.

"He's crossing four hundred miles of Martian desert to Mars Prime?"

"That is the way I would read it, sir," Warhurst replied.

"The real question then," Matloff said, "is what Garroway intends to do once he reaches Mars Prime. He doesn't make any cryptic references to his plans in this message, does he, General?"

"I think that's clear enough from the context, Mr. Secretary," Warhurst replied. "He says he 'capped' the guards at Heinlein Station. That's old-time infantry slang for 'shot' or 'killed.' The Derna reference suggests he plans on taking Mars Prime, the way O'Bannon took Derna."

"Damn it, General!" Matloff exploded. "What kind

of mad dog is this Garroway? We're not at war!''

"It would appear that Major Garroway believes differently, John," Harrel said gently. "What do you think,
General?"

"He obviously couldn't say much," Warhurst replied.
"But Garroway is not the sort of man who would run
off half-cocked. The Pearl Harbor reference seems clear
enough. The UN launched some sort of a coup and took
over the base. I, ah, must point out that the MMEF was
sent to Mars expressly to counter such a move on the
UN's part."

"It seems they didn't do the job they were sent to do,
then," the DCI suggested.

"It looks that way, sir. But I'd rather wait and hear
what Major Garroway has to say about it. The Marines
were probably not on full alert, and they were operating
in a situation where their precise responsibilities and operational parameters were not clear. They were there in
the hope that their mere presence would discourage any
hostile activity by the UN military forces stationed there.
And there is always the danger of mischance in war.
You can't prepare for every—"

"I repeat," Matloff interrupted, "we are *not* at war!
My people are negotiating with the UN right this moment at Geneva, trying to prevent this kind of mass in-
sanity!"

"What have we heard officially from Mars?" Harrel
wanted to know. "Last I heard there was some sort of
communications problem."

"Since Sunday morning," Kinsley said, "there's
been nothing from either Mars Prime or Cydonia Prime
but a COMMUNICATIONS DIFFICULTIES, PLEASE STAND BY
message. This sort of thing happens sometimes, nothing
unusual about it, but it does tend to corroborate Garroway's message. If UN forces took over our facilities on
Mars, they might drop a commo blackout for a time,
while they get things organized. Maybe they're preparing some sort of cover story."

"Or preparing a parallel operation of some sort here
on Earth," Severin suggested.

"But why?" Matloff said. "Why would the United
Nations want to do such a thing? Their people are on
Mars purely as observers—"

"Including those fifty Foreign Legion troops?" Severin said, interrupting the SECSTATE. "It sounds to me
like they've started doing a damned sight more than ob-
serving."

"I must insist," Matloff said, a bit stiffly, "that the
peace process here be allowed to continue, that it be
given a *chance*. We have the opportunity here to guarantee a lasting peace with the rest of the world!"

"For a moment there, John," Harrel said, "I thought
you were going to tell us that we were guaranteeing
peace in our time."

"I do not find that funny," Matloff replied. "Perhaps
you are not aware of just how serious our position is,
vis-à-vis the United Nations. Their trade embargo
against us has all but crippled our economy. Our only
allies are Russia and Great Britain, and both of them are
even worse off economically just now than we are. We
are a nation of some five hundred million people, gentlemen, against a world of nearly eight *billion*. We cannot play games here. If we are to preserve any shred of
our sovereignty as an independent nation, we must cooperate completely. We must work and we must compromise in order to establish a firm basis of mutual trust
with the other nations of the world. If we fail, if we
allow ourselves to be goaded into an ill-considered war,
we cannot hope to survive."

"I thought you said that there was no proof the United
Nations was acting in a hostile manner," Severin said.

"They have acted in a completely reasonable fashion
so far. If these rogue Marines on Mars drag us into a
war, however, I don't see how we can hope to survive
as a nation. Do you all remember what happened to Brazil?"

Brazil had been the first of the world's nations to feel
the full brunt of the United Nations after the new UN
charter had been adopted. Accused of continuing to cut
down vast tracts of fast-dwindling rain forest in direct

violation of several world treaties, Brazil had been invaded by UN forces in September of 2026. The rain forest, what was left of it, had been declared a "special world protectorate" and was now administered by a UN bureau operating out of Brasilia, in accordance with the terms of the Treaty of Rio.

The US had formally severed its long-unraveling ties with the UN in 2020 and was not involved in the takeover. Polls taken at the time had suggested that a large majority of Americans had disapproved of and mistrusted the UN's high-handed—some said dictatorial—approach to curbing various global problems. Many though, in particular the Internationalists, were more concerned with the fact that *something* had to be done about global warming and the biosphere die-off, even if that something violated national sovereignty.

"The president is concerned," Harrel said quietly, "with the demands the UN is making of us. Geneva has ordered us to hold a plebiscite within our Southwestern states on the Aztlan question, a plebiscite which, if held, might well result in the loss of a major portion of the American Southwest. They have threatened us over our space stations in orbit and our bases on Mars. They've threatened us over the whole question of technology gleaned from the Mars excavations. The president compromised on that one to the extent of allowing UN observers to travel to Mars. Their 'observers' turned out to be a few legitimate scientists and fifty armed men, a deliberate challenge to our control of the Martian excavations and our own facilities on the planet.

"Now, how long are we supposed to keep giving in and compromising and backpedaling before we find ourselves with our proverbial backs against the proverbial wall? I can tell you right now, Mr. Secretary, that the president is *not* going to yield on the Aztlan thing. He has already promised to share any alien technology that we find on Mars, and I can't see what further concessions he could make there, either. And if it's true that those UN thugs have just moved in and taken over our bases on Mars, lock, stock, and barrel, well, I can't see any room there for compromise either, can you?"

"Well then, perhaps it's time we started looking a little harder for compromise," Matloff said, "for some means of surmounting the difficulties that have separated us from the member states of the United Nations for so long. We *need* a unified world, gentlemen, for the survival of mankind, and I, for one, will not stand still for loose-cannon opportunists who are risking everything we have built!"

"Mr. Secretary, there's really very little we can do about Major Garroway at the moment," Admiral Gray pointed out. "He's something like a hundred million miles away, right now, and we don't even have a secure communications link with the man."

"I think we should concentrate our efforts on what we should be doing on this end," Severin said. "Garroway's actions could significantly impact the situation here."

Warhurst looked sharply at Severin. The SECDEF might be the next step up the ladder from the Joint Chiefs, but he was not himself a military man. He was a civilian, a politician who'd started off with one of the big defense contractors, a man whose lobbying efforts and financial contributions had been rewarded by a succession of cabinet posts. It was, Warhurst mused, the way Washington worked, but it left him uneasy to think that the lives of people, *his* people, depended on decisions made by men who cared more about covering their asses than they did about the lives of men and women farther down the chain of command.

"General?" Harrel said, turning to him. "Just what are the chances of Garroway and his people getting our facilities on Mars back?"

Warhurst spread his hands. "I wish I could answer that, sir, but I can't. The message seems to indicate that Colonel Lloyd is wounded or otherwise incapacitated, and we can't know how many more Marines might have been killed or wounded at this point. We don't know

Garroway's logistical situation—food, water, ammo . . . though chances are they have either no weapons at all or damned few. And, more to the point, perhaps, we don't know what he's up against. If the UN troops are split between Cydonia and Candor, he might, *might* have a chance of taking down one group before the other is alerted, but it seems like a damned slender chance to me. His best shot may be to grab something the UN needs at Candor and hold it hostage.''

"What?" Severin wanted to know.

"I don't know. The food stores, maybe. O'Bannon's Marines seized their expedition's food supplies to put down a mutiny among the Arab rebels in the party. Maybe that's his plan."

"That might make sense," Kinsley said. "Mars isn't like Earth, where you can live off the land. They've got major, centralized stockpiles of the stuff they need. Food. Water. Air. That makes them vulnerable."

"Where are the food supplies kept?" Severin wanted to know.

"There are stockpiles at both of the major bases, sir," Warhurst replied. "Candor and Cydonia. But the main stores are at the big base at Candor. I gather shuttles fly supplies out to all of the active bases every week or so."

"So does he have a chance?" Harrel asked. "I'll tell you, General, I've got to walk over and talk to the Man next door when this meeting is over. What do I tell him? Can a handful of US Marines take back our bases on Mars? Or at least get us something to bargain with?"

"They are United States Marines, sir," Warhurst replied evenly. "If anybody can do the job, they can."

"There have already been casualties," Admiral Gray pointed out. "Certainly UN casualties. Apparently Marines as well . . . at least Colonel Lloyd. We may already be over the brink on this thing."

"You're saying we can't micromanage things on Mars from here," the DCI said with a grin. "Kind of galling for us behind-the-lines types, isn't it?"

"I believe," Warhurst said, "that we can trust Garroway's assessment of the situation. He's experienced. He's well trained. He will take whatever action he feels is justified, given his understanding of the tactical and political situation on Mars. I don't think we should try second-guessing him on that. And if there's any way to support him, we should—"

"My suggestion, my *strong* suggestion," Matloff said, interrupting, "is to disavow Garroway's people. Immediately. If necessary, explain to the UN that some of our Marines may have, ah, misunderstood their orders . . . ah, may have interpreted them too strongly, in fact, and that UN forces on Mars should take measures to beef up security around the Candor site. . . ."

Warhurst was on his feet. "*You can't do that!*"

"Sit down, General," Admiral Gray said.

"Sir! With respect! We can't just—"

"We understand your concern, General," Harrel said. "I think, however, that it would be best if you would wait outside. Please."

"The Marine Corps has a tradition, gentlemen," Warhurst said. "A very old one. We never leave our people behind. *Never.*"

"That's quite enough, General," Harrel said.

Gray took Warhurst by the arm. "Come on, Monty," he said. "Wait outside until this is over."

"That . . . that *bastard* is about to throw away the lives of our people!"

He turned to glare at Matloff, but the man refused to meet his eyes . . . probably out of an instinctive sense of self-preservation.

Fists clenched, not trusting himself to speak further, Warhurst shook off Gray's hand and slowly walked for the door.

Beyond the conference-room door was an outer office and waiting area manned by a couple of Army Special Forces security guards standing at rigid and unresponsive attention. Furious, Warhurst paced the blue-and-white carpet for several moments, trying to organize his thoughts. When he'd told the tale of

O'Bannon and his Marines at Derna, he'd neglected to tell them the ending. The very day that O'Bannon's men stormed the fortress, an agent of the US State Department had signed a humiliating treaty that granted a $60,000 ransom to Tripoli in exchange for the freedom of captured American seamen and an end to hostilities, though news of the treaty didn't reach Derna for another week. Eaton and the Marines were forced to abandon their Arab allies by slipping quietly out of the harbor on an American ship.

There would be a fine comparison with history, Warhurst thought ... to have the diplomats resolve this whole business on Earth while Garroway's Marines were embroiled in a small war!

He cooled his heels in the outer office for another fifteen minutes before the members of the NSC Principals Committee began filing out of the vault door. Except for Admiral Gray, none stopped to speak or even look his way, and Warhurst had a sinking feeling in the pit of his stomach. They couldn't follow Matloff's advice. They *couldn't....*

But then, he knew Washington well enough to know that that was exactly what they would do, if they felt they had to.

Gray clapped a hand on Warhurst's shoulder. "That's got to be a first, Monty. I don't think I've ever seen a guest at one of these meetings go for a cabinet member's throat before."

"I apologize for my behavior, Admiral." The words came woodenly, without feeling. It was impossible to really mean them.

"I think everyone knew how you felt, Monty. And, well, they know about Ted."

"Sir, I—"

"Matloff can be a thoroughgoing bastard. If a war starts after all of the negotiating he's been doing here and in Geneva, he's going to look very bad. It could ruin his whole career."

"Oh, I'm *so* sorry for the man!" Warhurst managed to pack the words with acid. "So they're going to turn

our people over to the enemy to save his career. Is that
it?''

Gray didn't meet his eyes, and the sinking feeling got
worse. ''They're not turning them over to the UN, no.
But Harrel's going to tell the president that we should
adopt a wait-and-see attitude. Matloff, I'm afraid, is going to see the president later today and pass on his own
recommendations. Which is his right, of course. He is
the cabinet member tasked with maintaining peaceful relations with the rest of the world . . . however unreasonable they seem, sometimes.''

''So? What do you think the president is going to
do?''

''If I knew that, Monty, I'd be president.'' He
shrugged. ''Hell, Markham's pro-military, which is a
point in our favor, and I have the feeling he'd grab at
just about any chance, however slim, to get us out of
this bind with our honor intact as well as our territory.
But I also know that Matloff is right about the odds
we're facing. Our best hope, the *country's* best hope, is
for a settlement with the UN that gives them most of
what they want . . . and lets us maintain our sovereignty
a little bit longer.''

''Admiral, you can't agree with that . . . man.'' He sti-
fled the urge to use a stronger word, and it nearly choked
him.

''The trouble is, Matloff is *right*. Sooner or later, that
one-world state we've been hearing so much about is
going to happen, just to make sure food and resources
get properly distributed all over the globe, if nothing
else. When it does, the United States is going to lose an
awful lot of its power, its prestige, and maybe its territory as well. If it comes down to a choice between giving
up on what we've built on Mars, and having the UN
occupy the US the way they did Brazil, well, I know
what I would have to choose.''

''So . . . our people are on their own.'' He thought of
Ted, alone on the embassy rooftop as the transport lifted
off without him. He felt sick.

Gray hesitated for a brief moment, then dropped his eyes. "Yes."

"I'd like to work out a way of getting a message back to Garroway, sir. I know we can't send e-mail back the same way we got it, not without risking tipping the bad guys off, but Garroway's daughter may have a back door for us."

"That's a negative."

"But—"

"I said *negative*. Harrel was specific on that point, and he made sure to tell me to pass it on to you, loud and clear. If the president needs negotiating room on this, he can't have us undercutting his position by sending messages to Garroway."

"*What?*"

"If the UN intercepts our messages to Garroway, they could claim that Markham was negotiating with one hand and managing some kind of guerrilla operation on Mars with the other. We can't take that chance, Monty. We can't even acknowledge that we got his message in the first place. The fact that we know the UN pulled an offensive move against us up there when they don't know that we know what they did, well, that might provide us with some leverage in Geneva. As far as you and I and everybody else on Earth is concerned, we have no idea where Garroway is or what he is up to."

"You're abandoning him, then." The words were hard and bitter.

"Call it plausible deniability. Anyway, it's not as though we could do anything to *help*. The next cycler's due for Earth return next week, but we don't have time to put together a reinforcement mission. Even if we did, it'd be another eight months before they could reach him."

"Just knowing that you've got people pulling for you can help sometimes, Admiral. Right now, I'd guess that Garroway and his people are about as lonely as any US military detachment has ever been in history."

"Well, God help them," Gray said. "Because we

can't." He stopped and held Warhurst with his gaze. "I mean that, Monty. That's a direct order. No communications with Garroway until this matter is resolved."

"Aye, aye, sir."

In thirty-six years of military service, Montgomery Warhurst had never disobeyed an order . . . but *damn*, he was tempted to now.

SIXTEEN

It was, Garroway thought, one of the oddest-looking marches in the annals of military history . . . the Mars cat, a bug-faced, tracked monstrosity piled high with stores and armored Marines, grinding along at the pace of a man's walk and dragging behind it in a swirling cloud of dust a flat sled similarly loaded down with men and supplies.

The sled was the brainchild of Gunnery Sergeant Knox and Staff Sergeant Ostrowsky, who'd suggested the idea as a way of beating some unpleasant facts of life. The Mars cat was designed to carry six to eight people comfortably, but experiment demonstrated that sixteen could be jammed in with considerable crowding, a crowding made worse by the fact that none of the people aboard would remove their armor during the trek. Six or eight more at a time could ride on top of the crawler, clinging to plastic straps rigged from cargo-handling grips.

That left at least four more who would have to walk . . . and anyone moving on foot would drastically slow the cat from its usual fifteen to thirty kilometers per hour

228

down to the two to three kph that could be expected of
a human in full armor trudging along through the sand.
At one point, during the planning before they'd left
Heinlein Station, Garroway had been convinced that he
was going to have to leave at least four of the Marines
behind, simply because they couldn't afford to crawl all
the way to Candor at the speed a man could walk.

His two senior NCOs had suggested an alternative,
however. A number of carbaluminum pipes—sections
for the microwave relay mast that was to have been built
at Heinlein Station in the near future—were stored outside the hab. The interior walls of the hab were made
of foamboard, a lightweight composite-material used ex-
tensively in the cyclers and other MST-derived habs and
spacecraft for interior fittings. By wiring sheets of foamboard cut from the hab partitions to an X-framed rectangle of carbaluminum piping, a team of Marines had
managed to jury-rig a sled four meters long and three
wide and attach it to the Mars cat by its rear tow cable.

"Now, in the *old* Marine Corps," Knox had wise-
cracked, "we could go weeks at a time without food.
Just thinking about those old MREs was enough to keep
us going on spit and cusswords. But a tow-sled'll let us
carry enough food and water to see us through a couple
of weeks, anyway, and it means the people outside can
ride instead of walk." The sled would also carry some
of their bulkier equipment—fuel-cell-powered heaters, a
rolled-up plastic pressure tent, and spare tanks of liquid
oxygen and nitrogen.

The whole assembly looked bizarrely improbable
once it was loaded and yoked to the cat's winch. It was
a compromise and, like all such, was not perfect. The
drag sled slowed the cat considerably. Both because of
the strain put on the Mars cat's electric drive and for
safety reasons, the cat would not be able to make much
better than eight kilometers per hour, at the very best
. . . and in rough terrain, the Marines outside would have
to actually carry the sled like a huge canoe, portaging
their way across the steepest or roughest stretches.

Nor could they travel a full twenty-four and a half

hours a day. The period of the Martian night between midnight and dawn was far too cold for Marines to remain outside for more than two or three hours at a time, nor could the cat's engines take the sustained punishment of round-the-clock travel with that kind of load. They were going to have to stop and camp for at least six hours each night while the cat's fuel-cells recharged, and the people riding outside would all have to be cycled through the cat's interior every couple of hours in order to get warm and to recharge their suits' batteries.

They'd made only fifteen kilometers that first day, traveling southeast to pick up the opening in the encircling chasma walls that would give entrance to an extremely narrow and steep-sided canyon. According to maps found aboard the Mars cat, this was where the wider portion of Tithonium was squeezed down to a slender rille—actually a chain of deep fault-collapse craters puncturing the surface in a straight line all the way to the broad expanses of Candor Chasma, some 450 kilometers to the east.

They'd not set off, however, until a scant two hours before sunset, and moving at a slow and painful crawl, they'd managed about ten kilometers before the sun set. The Martian night swept down the valley with astonishing swiftness, the sky fading from pink to orange to deepest, star-strewn black within the space of a couple of minutes. The outside temperature began plummeting as well, from minus five centigrade to minus forty-five in the first three hours after sunset.

With nightfall, they kept going . . . but their speed was reduced even further. Garroway didn't want the cat to show lights, not with the very real possibility of a UN air search by lobber, and the two tiny moons shed almost no illumination on the dark desert floor. Marines took turns walking ahead of the Mars cat, scouting out obstacles like craters or boulders and slowly guiding the vehicle through the night practically step by step.

And they were still on the flat and sandy floor of the chasma; their progress would be slower still once they entered the rougher terrain of the canyon proper.

At some point around local midnight, Garroway had called a halt, set the watches, and let the party hunker down for a restless night. At the very best, at this rate of travel, Garroway estimated that they could make the passage from Heinlein Station to Mars Prime in four to five days . . . *if* they could average ninety miles per day— almost 150 kilometers—across almost four hundred miles.

He knew better than to expect that kind of average, however. Given the fact that they faced unpredictably rough terrain and the likelihood of things breaking down or simply taking longer than expected, he figured they would be lucky if they managed something on the order of ten to twelve days instead, and a much longer time was distinctly possible. Water was going to be a headache, with food and air nearly as bad. They were carrying as much extra water as could be held in a pair of large, pressurized drums, plus enough readymeal packets to last twenty-eight people for twenty days. The air recirculators both in the cat's cabin and in their suit PLSS backpacks would extend their breathing time, but they would need occasional recharges of liquid oxygen and nitrogen to make up for the unavoidable loss each time an airlock was opened or a helmet was removed. Garroway's best back-of-the-envelope calculation said . . . twenty to twenty-five days, depending on their exertion. If they didn't make it in that time . . . well, he could always call for help. That meant surrender, however, an option he was not willing to consider.

Not yet.

During the drive out from Heinlein Station, Garroway, King, and Knox had worked out a rotation schedule for the twelve people outside. Each night after they stopped, every person in the party would spend a two-hour security watch outside, the ones outside exchanging with the ones inside. It looked like no one was going to be getting much sleep on this trek, not with everyone taking a turn freezing in the desert each night.

Garroway had insisted that both he and King take their turns outside with the rest, and he volunteered for the first watch. Alexander had volunteered himself and the other two scientists too, but Garroway had turned him down. Marine Corps armor was designed to stand up to the horrors of the NBC battlefield and, with adequate power, could handle life support for literally days on end. The three scientists were wearing lightweight EVA suits with much weaker heaters and power units, and he didn't want to risk losing the civilians in his charge.

The Marine armor *should* be able to take the cold, though he had plenty of reason to question that the first night, as he stomped around outside, trying to stay warm in the pitch-black of the frigid Martian night. Class-One armor was rated at sixty below for four hours, but as far as he knew, no one had tested it yet at lower temperatures. He would have his people stick with two-hour watches, at least for now.

Garroway had a lot of time to think, he found, walking around on the desert with the other outside Marines, trying to keep his feet warm as his suit's heaters battled the frigid cold. No one spoke. They were officially on radio silence, though everyone had cables and jacks that would let them hard-wire into one another's intercoms if they wanted to chat. There didn't seem to be much to talk about, however.

When his watch had ended at last, he'd limped inside, found a place to wedge in between two other Marines, and fallen into an exhausted and fitful sleep. All too soon, King had used the suit intercom to wake him, alerting him to the fact that it was an estimated one hour before daybreak and time to get moving once again.

Soon they'd gotten under way, seeking to put as much distance between themselves and Heinlein Station as they could. Garroway was certain that the UN guards must have some sort of call-in routine, and that call-in was long overdue by now.

The first rays of a golden sunrise were just beginning to touch the floor of Tithonium Chasma as the Mars cat started to climb up a sandy ridge, snaking its way higher and higher up the eastern escarpment of the chasma.

During the night, Kaminski had attached his flag to the cat's whip antenna, and it made a brave sight as it fluttered in the thin wind above the vehicle's cab. Progress was slow, however, and at times the Marines riding outside had to dismount and carry the sled over rough spots, while the Mars cat ground forward with painful deliberation along the steepening, narrowing path.

By 0900, Mars time, they'd crested a saddle between the two cliff walls. The path cut sharply left and on up to the top of the cliff, where it emerged on flat and open terrain. That, Garroway knew, was the regular crawler route; radar beacons had been set along the path to mark it, and he could see the tracks the cat had left when it'd come this way a few days before. Directly ahead, though, the terrain turned ominous, plunging into a broken and tortured landscape of cliffs, craters, and boulders. According to the maps on board, that was the continuation of the Tithonium Chasma, a narrow and rough-bottomed canyon that ran arrow straight toward Candor.

Garroway tapped the shoulder of the crawler driver—it was Sergeant Caswell this watch—and pointed ahead. She nodded inside her helmet and, without hesitation, gunned the vehicle's electric motors with the foot pedal and sent them lurching forward.

Bergerac would expect them to take the fast and easy route to Mars Prime, the one over smooth terrain that would get them there in a day or two. By staying in the chaotic badlands of the canyon, Garroway was taking a fearful risk of breakdown or outright catastrophe if the cat slid off a cliff or got mired in soft sand. But the canyon also gave them their best chance of evading the patrols—both on land and in the air—that Bergerac was certain to employ. Marines *always* avoided the regular paths and trails when they could.

Garroway thought it worth the risk, especially since his comments to Kettering and Vandemeer about staying on the main track might well reach Bergerac's ears.

He just hoped he'd guessed right, because they were

less than a full sol into the march, and it was already beginning to take on some of the overtones of hell.

SATURDAY, 2 JUNE

International Space Station
344 kilometers over the North
Pacific Ocean
0915 hours GMT

It was called the International Space Station, and the fiction of global cooperation had been maintained over the years, despite the realities of world politics. The design once planned as Space Station Freedom, and later as the International Friendship Station, had eventually become Earth's lone orbital spaceport, a spindly, Tinkertoy collection of struts, modules, solar panels, and trusses circling the globe in low Earth orbit.

When construction had begun during the last couple of years of the previous century, the facility had been planned with a twenty-year life expectancy. By 2041, the station was definitely showing its age; it had always been easiest and cheapest simply to add new components to one end of the aging structure, rather than starting fresh with something new. The original station main module, called the Alfa Complex—leaking now through a dozen badly deteriorated pressure seals and valves— was relegated to storage of non–vacuum-sensitive supplies, while the docking facility was located at the far end, eighty meters distant. To either side, four sets of solar panels stretched like vast and glisteningly black damselfly wings spread from the slim and segmented white body.

Despite its age, the ISS remained the premier human facility in orbit, and a true spaceport. When the joint US-UN Return to the Moon mission was launched in 2012, the landers had departed from the ISS. Mars One was assembled there in sections by NASA workers berthed in a temporary hab adjoining the station, and

Columbus, the first cycler, was also assembled and launched from the ISS.

There were other stations in LEO as well. Japan and the ESA both had small, independent facilities in the same orbit, some fifty kilometers ahead of the ISS, while the United States maintained a half dozen free-flying stations either in LEO or in higher, polar orbits. The International Space Station, however, was by far the largest, eighty meters long, with solar panels spanning over two hundred meters, with a permanent crew of fifteen to twenty people, and room for as many as fifteen short-term visitors.

In keeping with its designation as a spaceport, its facilities included twelve Shuttle II fuel tanks now filled with water and cryogenic oxygen and hydrogen, fuel for the cyclers, the UN moonships, and the small fleet of tugs that serviced the other space stations in the vicinity and even made weekly treks out to the L-5 facilities. Most of the other LEO stations, in fact, were positioned within a few tens of kilometers of the spaceport, partly for convenience, partly for safety. The fleet of Mark IV space tugs stationed at the ISS were valuable both for routine repair and maintenance of all the orbital structures and for evacuations, if such became necessary.

What no one seemed to have considered so far, though, was what would happen if something went wrong with the ISS.

Colonel Paul Gresham was not particularly worried about structure failure at the moment . . . though the ISS carried an uncomfortably long list of things on its maintenance log that needed to be checked, replaced, or repaired. He was concerned, however, about the human components under his command. The political situation was getting damned dicey.

Gresham carried the rank of colonel in the US Aerospace Force, but he was currently assigned to NASA, had been, in fact, ever since he'd been accepted for the astronaut program eight years before. He was the commander of the ISS, a position that, by international agreement, was rotated among the senior members of the current station staff on a monthly basis. It was a cumbersome system, and one that never worked entirely to perfection. Last month, the CO had been LeClerc, with the ESA contingent. Next month, the position was due to rotate to Zhang Shu, of Manchuria . . . unless the scuttlebutt he'd heard was accurate and Zhang got recalled early. If that happened, chances were that his Russian counterpart, Kulagin, would get the job.

It was annoying having necessary work, tight schedules, convenience, and even safety all twisted out of shape by politics, but that seemed to be the price for running a truly international space station in the uncertain political situation of the day. The irony was that most of the people on ISS duty couldn't care less about politics. There was something about being able to float over to a nearby port and see the entire expanse of the glorious, blue-white Earth that tended to bring the people inside this little string of pressurized tin cans closer together, in a way that just wasn't possible on the ground.

Sometimes, he thought, it would be nice to just sever all ties with Earth. "Come talk to us when you have your problems worked out. . . ."

"ISS, I did not copy that."

Gresham blinked. Damn, he'd been up too long—almost three months now on this tour. He was starting to talk to himself and not even realize it.

"Ah . . . Hermes One-zero-one, you are clear for final approach and docking, over."

He was floating in the ISS command center, a somewhat larger than normal tin can mounted behind the station's primary docking module. With his feet slipped into the deck restraints, his head was positioned behind the two main windows that looked out across the DM and beyond, to the Hermes shuttle silhouetted against the spectacular, cloud-brushed turquoise glory of Earth.

Hermes was a European design, a smaller version of the old US shuttle orbiter. Launched from any of several spaceports, from Guiana to Zanzibar to the South Pacific on an Energiya-III booster—the Russians still made the biggest, most powerful, and most reliable heavy-lift boosters anywhere—the Hermes was the workhorse of the European space program, shuttling personnel and cargo to and from LEO with near clockwork regularity.

"Copy, ISS," the voice in his headset told him. "On final approach. Range four-five meters, approach one mps."

Gresham checked his own readouts. They matched those of the Hermes pilot.

"Roger, I copy that four-five meters at one mps."

In fact, rather more Hermes flights were made to the ISS each month than were American Shuttle II or Star Raker flights. For a time, US involvement in space had been on the decline.

Of course, the discoveries on Mars had changed all that. Hell, in another few years, if things kept going the way they were now and the international situation didn't turn into a war, the ISS would be a true city in space, and Gresham would be thinking about retiring to the Moon or Mars.

Hermes 101 was slated to bring up a load of fresh water, half a ton of other consumables—food, mostly— and a set of replacement solar panels for main arrays worn out by the constant sandblasting that years of circling the Earth brought it.

There were also four people on board, replacements for four of the six ESA scientists currently on the station. The ISS complement currently numbered six Europeans, two Japanese, two Manchurians, three Russians, and five Americans.

"ISS, Hermes One-zero-one. Range two-one meters, closing at point four mps."

"Copy, Hermes. Two-one meters at point four mps. Suggest you yaw one degree starboard and slow to point two mps."

"Roger, ISS. I comply. Yaw, one degree starboard. Range now one-seven meters, closing at point two mps."

Slowly, the blunt face of the Hermes grew larger in the window, its gently sloped hull white above and black below, a white acquisition strobe pulsing brilliantly above and behind its cockpit. Beyond, the blue Pacific was growing masked by clouds . . . the ocean vanishing beneath the vast, counterclockwise spiral of Hurricane Julio.

"Ten meters. Point two mps in approach."

"You're looking very good, Hermes. Bring her on in."

The shuttle's nose vanished behind the blunt projection of the station's docking module. The shuttle's airlock and docking tunnel were mounted vertically behind the cabin, in the cargo bay. Gresham now directed his full attention to one of the television monitors on his console, the one showing a camera angle looking straight down the docking collar, a view already blocked by the immense bulk of the Hermes orbiter. Slowly, slowly, the shuttle's docking collar slid into view, slowed . . . steadied . . . then grew larger as the Hermes began snuggling up closer to the far larger ISS. Gresham gave the final countdown. "Three meters . . . two . . . one point five . . . one meter. Point five meter . . . contact light! I have contact. I have five green lights on the capture latches. Hermes One-zero-one, you are hard-docked. Welcome to the International Space Station!"

"*Merci beaucoup*, ISS. It is very good to be here."

"I'm reading equalized pressures on both sides of the lock. You may come aboard when ready."

"We come."

Gresham shut down the console, removed his headset, and prepared to go and greet the newcomers. Visitors were always a high point at the station. "Hey, Colonel? Smitty." It was Wesley Smith, one of the NASA engineers on board, calling over his coverall's electronics. "I'm at the docking module. I, ah, think you'd—"

The transmission cut off. Puzzled, Gresham began pulling himself hand over hand across the control center. Nakamura and Taylor, the other two on duty in the control center, looked up.

"Probably a com failure. I'll be right back." Headfirst, he dove through the deck hatch and entered the spine passageway, the main highway that extended from one end of the station to the other. Twisting left, he pulled himself with three months' practice toward the docking module. . . .

. . . grabbed a handhold and yanked himself to an abrupt and bobbing halt. Four men in black armor with light blue helmets spilled into the corridor in front of him, moving clumsily in microgravity and with the burden of the assault rifles they carried strapped to their sides. A fifth armored man appeared, propelling Smitty—who looked terribly vulnerable and scrawny in his NASA blue coveralls—ahead of him.

"Colonel Gresham?" a voice said, slightly distorted through a suit's external speaker.

"I'm Gresham. What is the meaning of this?" Later he would realize how terribly trite that sounded, but at the time he could think of nothing more inventive.

"I am Colonel Cuvier, of the European Space Command. This facility is now under my control, and you and your people are my prisoners."

"*What the fuck do you think—*"

"Please, Colonel," the figure said, gesturing with an assault rifle. "It is war, and we have just . . . how is it you American military people put it? We have just taken the high ground."

More UN troops were clambering through the hatch from the Hermes shuttle now, and Gresham's mind leaped to the absurd image of boarders in a ship-to-ship action in the days of sail.

And there was not a damned thing he could do about it. No one on the ISS was armed, except for these armored troopers pouring through from what was supposed to have been a routine supply shuttle.

"Playing pirate, Cuvier?"

"No, Colonel. We are winning a war before it starts."

The way he said it sent a chill down Gresham's spine.

The Pentagon
1215 hours EDT

Kaitlin Garroway was beginning at last to recover from her jet lag. It had been a week since she'd returned to the US to be greeted by a whirlwind of meetings and conferences, first with Commandant Warhurst himself, then with various military officers and civilians who'd debriefed her on what she'd seen in Japan, whom she'd talked to, and what the more cryptic portions of her father's message might mean. She'd been as helpful as she could . . . and thank God that she hadn't seen much in the way of military preparations. She didn't want to be in the position of an American spy when the information she provided might be used against Yukio.

Fortunately, all she could tell them was that the base at Tanegashima had been closed to all outside communications, which they would have been able to verify other ways . . . and that the mood of the people, in particular, the people of the Ishiwara household, had not been notably belligerent or anti-American. She still found it hard to believe that Japan would join the UN crusade against the United States.

For the past week, she'd been staying at the Warhurst house out in Warrenton, Virginia, a twenty-five-minute maglev commute from the Pentagon. She'd protested that he didn't need to do that, that she could take a hotel or even return to Pittsburgh, but Warhurst had insisted.

She liked the Warhursts. She had the feeling that they were struggling to pull their lives together after the tragedy that had just overwhelmed them. Stephanie, Warhurst's wife, went out of her way to make Kaitlin feel at home. Over the course of the week, she found herself growing closer both to Stephanie and to Janet, their daughter-in-law, who was also staying in Warrenton, and even young Jeff was glad to have found a new chess partner. The Warhursts' sincere welcome warmed her, all the more once she became aware of the grief they all suffered. She'd known that an American had been killed during the embassy takeover in Mexico City . . . but not that he'd been the son of the commandant of the Marine Corps.

Montgomery Warhurst seemed to be carrying the loss well, though he did wear an air of quiet sorrow. Maybe that was why she'd finally agreed to stay in Warrenton for a while; she found it hard to refuse anyone who was hurting so. In any case, the commandant seemed to feel that she could yet be useful in communicating with her father, and if there was any chance at all of finding out what was going on on Mars, she was determined to grab it.

After a week, though, she'd begun wondering when she could get back to Pittsburgh. Not that it was urgent—her job didn't start for another month—but she was beginning to feel like a fifth wheel at the Warrenton place. She was surprised, then, when Warhurst called her early one morning and asked her to meet him at the Pentagon . . . for lunch.

All of her security clearances had been handled the week before. An Army lieutenant met her at the maglev station in the basement of the "five-sided squirrel cage," as her father liked to call the place, and escorted her to the office of the commandant. A Marine major received them in Warhurst's outer office.

"Kaitlin Garroway for the commandant," the lieutenant said, saluting.

"Very good, Lieutenant," the major replied—not saluting because Marines did not salute uncovered indoors. "Good afternoon, Ms. Garroway. Please be seated for a moment. The commandant is anxious to see you."

She ignored the hard seats he indicated and remained standing, while he touched a PAD screen on his desk. In less than twenty seconds, a door opened and General Warhurst strode out. Automatically, she stood at attention, sternly suppressing an urge to salute this man who commanded respect not because of what he did, but just because of who he was.

"Kaitlin," he said warmly, grasping her hand. "I'm

glad you managed to slip past those bastards downstairs this time.''

He was referring to the Intel people who'd grilled her last week. His irreverence drew a reluctant grin from her. ''It hasn't been too bad, sir,'' she admitted.

''Good, good.'' He led her into his office before saying any more. ''Well, the worst of it should be over now,'' he said as he waved her toward one of two comfortable-looking chairs in front of his desk. ''I just heard from Brentlow. Intel's finally decided that you're not a spy for the Japanese after all.''

She took a deep breath and expelled it forcibly. ''I was wondering, sir. Some of them were getting, well, pretty intense.''

''Hmm.'' He sounded distracted.

''Is something the matter, sir?''

''Well, it's not good. You know about the ISS, of course.''

She nodded. Even if she hadn't been a newshound, she couldn't have avoided learning about the UN's takeover of the ISS. Jeff had been talking about little else since Saturday, that and what was happening on Mars.

''In a way, the UN action was good,'' he said. ''It verified that what your dad told us was true, which might get some of the fence-sitters around here off their asses and off to work. Anyway, at 0225 hours this morning, our time, there was a launch from Guiana Space Center. Thirty-one minutes later, there was a SCRAMjet launch from San Marco Equatorial. Both of them rendezvoused with the ISS a few hours later.''

''Two SCRAMjets? What . . . oh!'' Her eyes widened. ''They're getting ready to meet the next incoming cycler!''

''No.'' He shook his head. ''We thought so too, at first. But now we believe that the first launch was a Mars Direct.''

Kaitlin knew a little about Mars Direct flights. The first three manned Mars missions had used the technique, in the years before the first cycler had been deployed.

"We're fairly certain that the new ship is a modified *Faucon* 1B, with a Proton booster second stage. It appears to be refueling at the ISS now. When fueling is complete, it will be able to launch for Mars on a trajectory that will get it there in about five months."

"And the SCRAMjet was carrying more troops?"

He nodded. "Almost certainly. Intelligence guesses another thirty UN troops, probably Foreign Legion from the Second Demibrigade. The same unit that already has a detachment on Mars."

"Shit!" She looked up, then blushed at her unguarded expletive. "Ah . . . excuse me, sir."

"S'all right. I feel the same way. And, of course, with the ISS in UN hands, even if your dad's people win through on Mars, we're not going to be able to bring them back."

The realization struck Kaitlin like a punch to the stomach. She'd forgotten. *All* outbound interplanetary insertions used the fuel stored at the ISS spaceport to top off tanks drained dry by their struggle up the side of the planet's fearsome gravity well. That must have been the reason the UN had captured the space station in the first place . . . so that they could be sure of launching their *Faucon*. For the same reason, the ISS maintained the fleet of tugs and high-delta-v transports that could rendezvous with incoming cyclers and transfer their passengers to a shuttle bound for Earth.

If the ISS was controlled by the UN, any cycler returning from Mars would depend on the UN's good graces to rendezvous with them and effect the transfer to Earth orbit.

A cold anger blazed in Kaitlin. "So we're just . . . abandoning them? Sir?"

The hint of a smile touched the corners of Warhurst's mouth. "Allow me to rephrase that. *As long as* the UN forces retain control of the ISS, we won't be able to bring our boys home from Mars."

"Ah." She wondered what unit would have the honor of recapturing the station. It was almost enough to make her want to be a Marine herself. She sat up a little straighter in her chair.

Warhurst appeared to be thinking something over. His brow was furrowed, and there was a hard set to his mouth. "We have a Marine unit going into training tomorrow at Vandenberg, for a possible strike against the ISS." He gave her a sharp look. "That *is* classified, you know. In fact, I shouldn't have told you."

"Uh . . . sure." She was confused. So why *had* he told her? She knew that Warhurst had an iron control when it came to revealing or concealing anything. His self-control in regard to his dead son was proof enough of that. She could not believe that it had just been a slip. . . .

"In any case," he continued, as though nothing out of the ordinary had occurred, "I'm afraid that there's not a damned thing we can do to help your dad on Mars. *Especially* with the space station in UN hands. But there may be something we can do here. To make sure he can get back. And, possibly even more important, to make sure he knows the score."

"Have you been able to establish contact with him yet?" Kaitlin asked. She'd been requested—ordered might have been the better word—not to use her back-door communications route until the political situation was clearer. She didn't like it; her question was a polite way of reminding Warhurst that she wanted to talk to her father . . . while at the same time she wanted to be careful not to get in the Pentagon's way.

He shook his head. "No. And that brings me, going around Robin Hood's barn, to what I really wanted to see you about. You told me that your father was assuming that regular e-mail would not be a secure method of reaching him, and I'm inclined to agree with his assumption. The bad guys would be stupid not to safeguard those channels. But you also told me that the two of you had an alternate means of communication to fall back on."

"Yes, through a newsgroup that we both like a lot. I can post a message there, and Dad could just search for messages from me. They can't shut down Usenet, and they wouldn't be able to check all the postings.''

"From your study at CMU, Kaitlin, I assume you would know about these things. Is there any way they could search for your user name in the Usenet postings?''

She grinned. "Even if they knew which of something like eighty thousand newsgroups to search, they wouldn't find me. I'd use my global-dot-net account, not my CMU one. That user ID is 'chicako,' not 'garroway.' ''

Warhurst didn't look as pleased to hear that there was a secure way to communicate with the Marines on Mars as she'd expected. Instead he frowned, tapping his fingers rhythmically on a lone sheet of paper on the top of his desk. "I would like to be able to use that channel, Kaitlin. I would like to tell your father that we're pulling for him, even if we can't do anything substantial right now. I even have the letter written.'' He stopped his drumming and laid his index finger on the paper. "Right here.''

"No problem, sir. I can—''

"I'm afraid there *is* a problem. I've been forbidden to communicate with your father.''

That statement hit Kaitlin even harder than the earlier one about the ISS, but she remained calm. By now she knew that Warhurst said nothing without a purpose . . . and that sometimes he intended to convey something different from the literal meaning of his words. "May I ask why, sir?''

The general sighed. "The feeling is that the president may need negotiating room. How the hell we're supposed to negotiate with the bastards, I don't know, but that's the idea. And the upshot of it is I can't use that channel of yours to communicate with your father. Even though I've got the message all written, ready and waiting to go.''

He stood up and started to walk around his desk. "Well, I guess that's it then. So. How about lunch?'' Without waiting for an answer, he added, "I'll tell Major

Garth to make reservations for us at the Szechuan Garden.'' And with that he walked out of the office, closing the door behind him.

Kaitlin grinned. He didn't need to talk to the major in person to tell him to comm a restaurant. He just wanted to leave the room for a minute. To leave her alone . . . with the letter.

As she reached over to the desk and picked up the letter, she felt a peculiar twinge, as though she were cheating on an exam back in grade school. She almost laughed out loud.

This time the teacher was ordering her to cheat . . . because the Marines take care of their own.

SEVENTEEN

Mark Garroway watched his daughter's face on the Mars cat's computer display with a sense of homesickness and longing sharper than anything he'd felt in his life. In that moment, he felt every one of the hundred million–plus miles between himself and his daughter and wondered if he would ever see her again.

He hated Mars. He hated the Marines.

No . . . not that. He couldn't hate the Corps, not really, even though the Corps was what had separated him from Kaitlin.

Outside the cat was the blackness of the Martian night, with a dazzle of stars directly overhead but cut off on all sides by the sheer cliffs rising above the crawler. A thin, hard wind was blowing down the chasm; the outside temperature was down to ninety-five below and dropping. His watch outside was coming up in another hour, and he could barely stand the thought of having to go stomp around in the bitterly frigid sands again, constantly moving to avoid freezing to death.

Ten sols had passed since they'd left Heinlein Station . . . and it felt as though their journey had scarcely begun. The terrain they'd been following through the narrow chasm was impossibly rugged, a tortured badlands of sand pits and boulders, an endless succession of craters drilled rim to rim into the crumbling regolith. Scouting teams now walked ahead of the crawler searching for safe paths; as often as not, Marines on foot ended up carrying the sled, hauling it by brute force up and down the crater rims. More than once they'd had to use the cat's winch and tow cable to drag the whole vehicle up a slippery, yielding slope that the sturdy machine could not otherwise have traversed.

This rift in the planet's surface, Garroway kept reminding himself, was one of the little ones, and yet Arizona's Grand Canyon could have comfortably fit inside. Its only advantage was that it lay on a nearly straight line with the Candor Chasma base, as straight as one of the mythical canals of pre-Viking, pre-Mariner Mars.

He shook away thoughts of the bleak, cold night surrounding the Mars cat and tried to concentrate on his daughter's face. He'd been using the cat's electronics to tap into Mars Prime's Spacenet server every few Phobos orbits, looking in on the Usenet postings that were regularly mirrored from Earth.

Usenet had grown enormously since its beginnings in the old Internet of the late twentieth century. Some newsgroups were still little more than written postings on static electronic bulletin boards, but most had benefited from new communications hardware and protocols and expanded to allow vidpostings, downloaded segments where you could actually see the person who was talking, along with maps, graphics, vidclips, or whatever else might help the presentation. He and Kaitlin both were partial to rec.humanities.culture.japan, a newsgroup for Japanophiles from all over the world. That was why he'd suggested that newsgroup as a posting place for any return messages in reply to his first message to Earth.

If the Pentagon wanted to reply, he couldn't expect them to drop an e-mail in his box in Candor's server. If the UN forces on Mars were serious about cutting off all communication between Mars and Earth, they would certainly cut off the e-mail conduit; at the very least, they would set a watch program over the mailboxes set to retrieve and delete any message from Earth for any of the Marines.

He doubted that they would cut off the Usenet postings, though. There would be no particular reason to do so; at the same time, they wouldn't be able to watch every one of the newsgroups posted onto the Spacenet. And, so far, he'd seen no indication that they were even aware of the unauthorized waking of the Phobos com relay.

Kaitlin's posting was there, as he'd hoped, as he'd almost feared, her image frozen with a familiar, wrinkle-browed expression that mingled worry with excitement. The date, time, and post lines at the bottom left of the screen indicated that the message had been uploaded about twenty-six hours ago.

He touched the hotspot on the console that brought life to the vidimage.

"Ah . . . okay. This is to the guy that said he'd meet me in Japan," she said. She seemed a bit nervous, as though she was being extra careful of what she was saying.

"I hope you're keeping up with the Cu-Ja postings, 'cause it looks like this is the only way I'll get to talk to you. There are a lot of folks here who want to get together with you, only there's, ah, no way they can see their way clear to do it right now. The situation is pretty confused, as you can imagine. There's talk about the Japanese joining the UN against the United States, and, well, the last I saw, it looked like that was going to happen. I know personally that some military bases there are on full alert. Like the one at Tanegashima."

Tanegashima? That's Japan's main launch center, on a tiny island fifty miles south of the southern tip of Kyushu. An alert there meant the Japanese may be preparing to do something with their Space Defense Force, and that was not good, not good at all.

"I've got a picture for you here. Translate it the usual way. And, well, until we can get together again, in Japan

or, or wherever . . . you take care of yourself, okay?''
There were tears glistening in her eyes. She said the final
words so quickly he almost missed them. "I love you."

Kaitlin's face vanished, replaced by columns of numbers. Anyone casually glancing at the page would assume it was an encoded picture or illustration of some
kind, one using a private algorithm to keep the content
private. In a sense, that was exactly what it was. Those
columns of three were almost certainly a Beale code
sequence. Garroway checked to make sure the memory
clip containing *Shogun* was plugged in on his wrist-top,
then touched a key, feeding a copy through the Beale
encoder/decoder program, and sending it back to the
screen as text. It took only a few seconds for the whole
message to appear.

Date: 5 June 2040
Mark:

> *Your daughter got your message through. Smart
> thinking. She's a sharp kid and obviously has a
> lot in common with her dad.*
> *I wish to hell I had better news. The official
> word is, no communication with you at all, just in
> case the president needs some maneuvering room
> with the UN. Though we still have some optimists
> in Washington, we are almost certainly going to
> be at war with the UN within a very few days. UN
> armies are reported massing in both Quebec and
> Mexico. We're tracking a number of French,
> German, and Manchurian arsenal ships off our
> coasts.*
> *Mark, I also have to tell you that three days
> ago—2 June—UN forces seized the International
> Space Station. Just this morning, a UN spacecraft
> lifted from Kourou. We think that it's a Mars Di-
> rect flight and that it's carrying at least thirty
> more UN troops. Could be you'll be getting com-
> pany in another five months. Whatever you do,*

you'll have to do it before those reinforcements reach Mars.

In any case, don't worry about Kaitlin. I've asked her to stay at my place in VA. She'll be safe there, if anywhere.

What you do on Mars is, I'm afraid, up to you and what you think you can get away with. At this point, anything you could do to put a wrench in the UN's plans would be desirable. Future communications can be via the same method you used with Kaitlin. We need to know why the UN is so interested in Mars.

Consider this a personal weapons-free order. By the time you get to where you're going, we very likely are going to be at war. Sorry to leave you on your own, but, then, anything more than one platoon of US Marines against the UN forces now on Mars simply wouldn't be fair. Good luck! We're all pulling for you.

Semper fi.
—Warhurst, Gen. USMC

Garroway blinked at the signature line. Warhurst? He'd sent his original message to Colonel Fox; he'd had no idea that it would get bumped clear up to the commandant of the Corps!

"Hey, Major?" Sergeant Ostrowsky called as she squeezed into the Marine-crowded lounge area of the cat. "You wanted me to let you know. Your watch outside."

"Thank you, Sergeant," he said. Carefully, he made sure the decoded message was saved on his wrist-top, then began shutting down the com center.

Warhurst was right. The news wasn't good ... especially the bit about UN reinforcements. It was funny, though, that just hearing from someone back on Earth helped. He found he could face going out into the bitter cold and loneliness once again.

Or was that the result of getting to hear his daughter's

voice again? He wasn't sure. It didn't really matter.

He reached for his gloves and helmet and began the laborious process of sealing up his armor.

FRIDAY, 8 JUNE: 2230 HOURS GMT
Net News Network
1830 hours EDT

VOICE-OVER, WITH SPECIAL LOGO: This is a Net News Special Presentation . . . Collision Course, the UN Crisis. And now, from the Net News Center in Washington, DC, special reporter Carlotta Braun. . . .

CARLOTTA BRAUN: Good evening. President Markham today responded forcefully to what he called 'a blunt ultimatum' by the UN General Assembly, denouncing that body for its 'unwarranted intrusion into the internal affairs of the United States' and its 'highhanded and hostile actions against American assets in space.'

VIDIMAGE—PRESIDENT MARKHAM SPEAKING FROM THE WHITE HOUSE BASEMENT OFFICE:
"At 10:45 Eastern Daylight Time this morning, I asked the Congress of these United States to recognize that a state of war now exists between the United States of America and the governing body of the United Nations.

"I wish to stress that we have no quarrel with any member nation of that body. This war was forced upon us by the hostile and unreasonable demands made by the UN, by their violations of American sovereignty, and by their takeover of the International Space Station. We call upon men of courage, vision, bravery, and goodwill in all nations to help us now as we face together this corrupt tyranny that claims to be a world government but so far has proven only that it is a world disgrace. . . ."

VIDIMAGE—A CITY SCENE SHOWING SEVERAL BUILDINGS IN RUINS, THEIR FACADES BLASTED AWAY, A GAPING CRATER IN THE STREET, AN OVERTURNED GROUND CAR. CIVILIANS AND NATIONAL GUARD TROOPS ARE DIGGING THROUGH THE RUBBLE, SEARCHING FOR SURVIVORS. THE SUBTITLE READS "ATLANTA."

CARLOTTA BRAUN: "The UN response was immediate and dramatic. By 11:30 Eastern Time, UN cruise missiles launched from Quebec, Cuba, and Mexico were striking deep into the American heartland. An estimated two hundred missiles were fired from various launch points, and while fighters from Aerospace Force, Navy, and Marine units succeeded in downing many of them, an as yet unknown number managed to get through."

VIDIMAGE—SEVERAL MORE CITY SHOTS IN RAPID SUCCESSION SHOW THE RESULTS OF MISSILE STRIKES IN OTHER CITIES, CROWDS OF CIVILIANS FLEEING IN THE STREETS, A PALL OF DENSE, BLACK SMOKE ABOVE DOWNTOWN CHICAGO, AND ONE QUICK VIEW OF A WINGED CRUISE MISSILE SWEEPING LOW ABOVE A CITY PARK, CAPTURED IN SHAKY FOOTAGE BY AN AMATEUR VIDCORDER OPERATOR.

CARLOTTA BRAUN: "Twenty-two major population centers have been hit so far, including Dallas, Chicago, Washington, Boston, Atlanta, and New York City. In addition, there are reports of heavy fighting at the US border, both along the Rio Grande River, in Texas, and north of Plattsburgh, New York, where elements of the Armored *Armée québecois* are reported to have crossed into the United States in a quick thrust south from Montreal. There are no official reports as yet, but casualties are said to be heavy.

"Government authorities stress that civilians should remain inside and off the streets. The bombardment thus far has been limited to high-explosive warheads, and authorities insist that, despite rumors to the contrary, there have been no nuclear, chemical, or biological strikes by UN forces. Damage, though widespread, is not considered serious, and there has been no reported disruption of critical services. Civilians are requested—''

NET NEWS IS EXPERIENCING TECHNICAL DIFFICULTIES. PLEASE STAND BY.

SATURDAY, 9 JUNE

Shepard Military Orbital
Platform (MOP)
1417 hours GMT

Colonel Peter Dahlgren had been a member of the US Astronaut Corps for nearly fourteen years. Before that, he'd been Aerospace Force, starting off driving F-22s and ending up as an ace test pilot working on some of the most advanced and highly secret flight development programs in the US government's arsenal. Most of his work in the last five years had been more or less routine—if that word could ever be successfully applied to working in space. He'd served on the ISS three times, once as station commander, and he'd been slated for a US lunar mission until budgetary and political problems had canceled that program.

Six months earlier, his high security clearance had gotten him a shot at another orbital mission—a tour aboard Shepard MOP, one of the handful of independent US LEO facilities. The tour had lasted six weeks, and upon his return to Vandenberg, he'd thought he was grounded for good.

Then war clouds had begun gathering, and he found himself assigned once again to Shepard . . . running the station's highly classified military payload.

Shepard Station was little more than a Shuttle II external tank fitted out with living quarters, a lab, and a docking module. It also possessed a 500 KW nuclear reactor, though this was a closely guarded secret. The *real* secret of Shepard, though, was the Hecate laser that filled most of the main lab compartment.

Hecate—named for the Greek deity who, among other

things, was goddess of the night——was a new weapons system with a software AI developed within the past few years at the Moravec Institute in Pittsburgh. Dahlgren had needed his astronomical security classification just to learn about the new device, a High-Energy Laser, or HEL, which had been put into orbit the previous year. The idea was to deploy a laser powerful enough to knock down missiles or aircraft from orbit, and so far it had worked well in tests against both static and moving targets in the Nevada desert.

Now, however, the Hecate HEL was about to be used for the first time in combat. According to the coded message beamed to Shepard that morning, cruise missiles were still striking targets across most of the continental US and causing heavy damage. It would be impossible to use one laser in a single fast-moving station in LEO to knock down more than a scant handful of the incoming cruise missiles, but the attempt would demonstrate once and for all the system's practicality ... and the value of an idea that had been argued vehemently over for the past fifty-five years. As Shepard Station drifted southeast across the Gulf of Mexico west of Florida, Dahlgren was floating in the lab, his face pressed against the rubber-hooded repeater screen for the station's Earth-watch telescope system. The telescope, slaved to Shepard's powerful look-down radar, was being operated by his companion aboard the station, Major Fred Lance, USAF.

"I've got a target, Colonel," Lance reported. "Matanzas launch, two minutes, twelve seconds ago. Heading three-five-eight, altitude approximately five meters."

"Lock us on, Fred," Dahlgren replied. The lighted display showed a dizzying sweep of water and cloud as the telescope, a relatively small device mounted on the station's outer hull, pivoted slightly. Green crosshairs centered a moment later on a white sliver in the center of the display. He pressed a touch screen point, and the image enlarged, giving him a detailed look at the target, which the telescope was now following automatically. The craft was apparently unmarked and painted off-white, a cigar shape with squared-off ends, a tail section like a miniature jet aircraft, and short, skinny wings amidships.

"You should be centered, Colonel."

"I've got him. Do we have a shot?"

"Looks clear to me. On your command. . . ."

"Fire."

A point on the cruise missile, hurtling along at just below the speed of sound two hundred miles below, grew suddenly and intolerably brilliant, a dazzling star so bright that Dahlgren blinked and looked away. When he looked back, the dazzle was still there, but dimmer as the telescope-camera CCD adjusted for the intensity of the light.

Lance was counting off the seconds. "Two . . . three . . ."

And then the cruise missile was gone, replaced in a literal flash by a tumbling cloud of broken debris that streaked ahead for several seconds more before impacting the surface of the water in a ragged burst of white spray.

"I have lost target, Colonel," Lance said. "Hecate at power off."

"Target destroyed," Dahlgren replied. He looked up and met Lance's eyes across the lab. "Nice shooting!"

Lance shrugged. "Hell, Colonel. Hecate did it. All I did was push the damned button. . . ."

And that, of course, was the beauty of the thing. Dahlgren looked up at the porthole in the hull a few meters away, at the drifting glory of sea and cloud. What Hecate had just done was truly remarkable. With little direction from the two human operators aboard Shepard, the sophisticated AI software had run a down-looking radar and, from an altitude of 320 kilometers, separated a speeding cruise missile three meters long and with a wingspan of less than a meter from the return of the water less than five meters below it. It had slaved an optical CCD telescope to the radar image for use as a visual target system and kept the target locked on despite both the target's flight north at five hundred miles per hour and the space station's drift southeast at its orbital velocity of nearly 18,000 mph.

And finally and perhaps most remarkably, it had fired the station's laser and held the beam dead on its tiny target for the seconds necessary to burn through the missile's hull and destroy it. Hecate was only a half-megawatt laser, and much of that energy was lost in the turbulence of the Earth's atmosphere below; the Hecate AI had used backscatter from the laser beam on the target to continually correct the beam's output and aim, keeping it locked on until the target was destroyed.

"Looks like we've got a winner, Fred," he said. "Find me another target before we complete this pass."

"You got it, sir. I've got another launch, same site, at one minute five seconds ago, bearing three-five-two . . ."

Dahlgren peered again into the hooded screen, watching as the AI software lined up the next shot. *Like shooting fish in a goddamn barrel.*

"Shepard, Shepard, this is Cheyenne Mountain," a voice called over his jumpsuit's com speaker.

"This is Shepard, Colorado," he replied. "Go."

"Shepard, we have an orbit change for you, execution in . . . seven minutes. Drop what you're doing and get set for a burn."

"Ah . . . Colorado," Dahlgren said. "We have a target ready for lock-on—"

"We copy that, Shepard, but this can't wait. Secure your gear and stand by to copy the burn parameters. Over."

"Roger that." Damn! What could be so all-fired important? That cruise missile streaking north out of Cuba was going to come down someplace, and people were going to die. Shepard couldn't intercept all of the missiles, but it could stop a bunch, each time it passed overhead. The idea was to force the bad guys to stagger their launches to times when Shepard was below the horizon, and give the air-defense boys time to regroup.

But evidently, Cheyenne Mountain had other things in mind.

Shepard MOP was not exactly a spaceship. It had all of the maneuverability of an elephant in free fall. Still, a rack of strap-on B-30 maneuvering thrusters attached to the external tank's framework gave them the ability to change orbit within certain fairly narrow parameters, enough to pass over a particular target on the ground at a specified time. If Colorado wanted them to engage in a burn within the next few minutes, it was because they had a particular destination in mind, one with a fairly narrow access window. That argued that they were trying to manage an orbital rendezvous.

Seven minutes wasn't much time. The Hecate laser was a delicate piece of equipment, and parts had to be strapped down before any delta-v maneuver.

"Let's hump it, Fred," Dahlgren called. Together, they began securing the laser. Two hundred miles below them, the cruise missile continued streaking north, just a few feet above the Gulf of Mexico.

EIGHTEEN

Office of the President
White House Basement,
Washington DC
1529 hours EDT

The president looked a lot older now than he had the last time Admiral Gray had seen him, less than twenty-four hours before. The familiar, easy, politician's grin, the engaging and confident manner, both were gone. Markham was slumped into the big executive's chair behind the desk, head supported on one hand, eyes bleak as he stared at the muted images flickering across the wall screen to his right. Net News had gotten back on the air again this morning, despite the cruise missile strike that had taken out its broadcast antenna in Silver Springs.

"So?" Markham's voice was muffled by his hand. "How are we holding, CJ?"

"We're doing better than we expected, Mr. President." Gray laid a folder on the president's desk. "Our air-defense forces, air national guard, naval air groups, and other assets, we estimate, have accounted for approximately four hundred cruise missiles, or roughly sixty-five percent of what they've thrown at us so far."

259

"You're saying over two hundred missiles have gotten through."

Louis Harrel, standing at Gray's side, nodded. "Two hundred fourteen, as of the latest count, Mr. President."

On the big wall screen, Carlotta Braun's dark features stared down at the three men, her too-red lips moving soundlessly. Abruptly, the scene shifted to an aerial view of Washington. The Mall was visible, a long green rectangle reaching toward the familiar, white-domed majesty of the Capitol Building. Something—a tiny, white something like a child's glider—was streaking along the Mall, chasing its own shadow on the ground. In a heartbeat, it streaked past the Air and Space Museum, passed Fourth and Third Streets and the Capital Reflecting Pool, and arrowed squarely into the Capitol's west side, detonating inside the Rotunda.

The explosion blew out windows, pieces of stone wall, and several Greek columns. The Capitol steps, mercifully, were empty of people, but the blast flipped several hydrogen-fueled cars parked on the drive below and lashed nearby cherry trees with hurricane winds. For an agonizing several seconds, nothing more happened. Then the huge dome seemed to settle slightly, cracked, then collapsed inward as chunks of white stone crashed down in a billowing avalanche into the gutted center of the building.

Braun's face reappeared, lips moving.

"They've been showing that same damned news clip for three hours now," President Markham said bitterly. "Can't they find some other piece of death and mayhem to bombard the public with?"

"This must be playing holy hell with national morale," Harrel said.

"It is," the president agreed. "And the answer is, what? Invoke government censorship?"

"This is war, Mr. President," Harrel said.

"Those days are long over," the president said. "Even if we could censor the netnews—and I'm not sure we could—the people would just get their news from outside the country, and you know the spin *they're* putting on things." He gestured at the screen. "At least they know they're getting an honest account here, and we'll need that when the tide turns." He looked at Gray. "We can expect a turning, can't we, Admiral? Please tell me there's a bright side to all of this."

"We expect a break in the attack soon, Mr. President," Gray said. "Our estimates of the number of missiles in their stores suggest they can't keep up this level of bombardment for much longer. They'll need time to rearm and reequip. The likeliest scenario has them announcing a dramatic cessation to the bombardment after today or possibly tomorrow, and giving us a chance to think things over. Their ultimatum still stands. They'll want some kind of a reply to that."

"And if we don't?"

Gray shrugged. "They'll continue the bombardment, I suppose, until we comply."

"There is a chance, Mr. President," the national security advisor added, "that they will escalate in the next phase."

"Nukes?"

"It's a possibility. The DCI says they might try using one or a very few tactical nukes as a demonstration against military bases, or possibly our launch facilities at Canaveral and Vandenberg. It is not likely, at this juncture, that they will resort to chemical or biological weapons."

The president grimaced. " 'Not likely.' But it'll happen sooner or later, if I don't back down."

Gray found himself holding his breath. The UN ultimatum had been blunt and to the point. The United States was to disarm completely. Its military forces were to stand down, its aircraft to remain grounded, its bases open to UN inspection teams and occupation forces. A United Nations Special Governing Committee was to take charge of the Washington bureaucracy; elected officials would remain in power, but subject to UN directives. It was nothing less than a blueprint for complete and unconditional surrender.

And Admiral Gray was afraid that Markham was going to agree to it.

"What kind of a chance can you give us, Admiral?" Markham wanted to know. "Tell me you have a secret weapon or two squirreled away that I don't know about."

"Well, sir, we don't have anything like that, but we can buy us some time. Operation Freedom is on track. Launch is scheduled for 0700 Pacific Time Tuesday. We're in the process of nudging Shepard into a better orbit, so they can provide backup and fire support."

"Operation Freedom. That's the ISS mission?"

"Yes, sir."

"And how is that going to help us?"

Gray drew a deep breath. "It's a symbol, Mr. President." He nodded toward the screen, where the destruction of the US Capitol Building was being played out again. "Most of their strikes, so far, have been against high-visibility, newsworthy targets. Public buildings. State capitols. Things with propaganda value, that demonstrate that we can't protect ourselves from this kind of attack."

The White House had been badly damaged several hours ago. A near miss had damaged the Washington Monument, too, though it was still standing.

"Go on."

"The International Space Station is also a symbol, Mr. President. A station that passes over our heads every ninety minutes or so and proves that we can't protect our interests in space . . . an area where America historically held a strong lead over everyone else."

"Hell, we were giving up on space," Harrel pointed out. "At least until we found that alien shit on Mars."

"That 'alien shit,' as Mr. Harrel calls it, may well be the key to this whole war," Gray said. "It's Ken Morrow's contention that Mars is the main reason the UN jumped us. Not Aztlan. And not US unwillingness to go along with the UN's agenda."

"I know," the president replied. "He's been telling me that every day now for the past week." He shook his head. "Tell me, gentlemen. Is anything we find on Mars worth *that*?" He gestured at Braun's oversize face on the wall screen.

"We won't know that, Mr. President, until our people have a chance to excavate the site a bit farther," Harrel said. "But it does appear that the UN forces on Mars launched this adventure because they wanted to shut us down there."

"Shut us down?" Gray said, thoughtful. "They could have done that as soon as their troops reached Mars, seven months ago. I think our people might have found something specific, something the UN didn't want broadcast. Otherwise, why wait until now?"

"They might've just been waiting until they were ready," Harrel suggested.

"Maybe, but the attack seemed rushed. As though it was being hurried along by events elsewhere. Mr. President, I think we have to assume that our most important battle right now is the one on Mars."

Markham gave a wan smile. "The one we can't do anything about."

"Well, sir, we can start by getting the ISS back. If the Marines win on Mars, we need a working spaceport on this end to pick them up when they return. The ISS is also the center of Spacenet, which handles all communications off of Earth. We'll need to secure that if we're to have a hope of finding out what's going on up there."

"Hence, Operation Freedom," the president mused. "The problem is, gentlemen, that even if we get the space station back, it'll be months before our people on Mars can return on the cycler, right? In the meantime, what am I supposed to tell the American people? That we're sitting through this bombardment so our people on Mars can dig up rusty alien spaceships?"

"That's why we're emphasizing the propaganda value of the ISS op, sir," Gray said. "You could think of it like the Doolittle bombing raid against Japan, a century ago. It won't hurt the enemy materially that much, but it sure as hell will hurt his pride."

"Mmm. That sort of gesture can only sustain us so far. We've got to hit the bastards back here on Earth, hit 'em hard, or else throw a big enough scare into them that they back off and leave us alone."

"The Tenth Infantry Division has deployed from Fort Drum," Gray pointed out, "and has been engaging the Quebeckers outside Plattsburgh Aerospace Force Base. We stand a good chance of winning that one, especially since the 380th Bomb Wing out of Plattsburgh has started hammering Montreal. We're also holding the Mexicans and the Colombians at San Diego. Our reserves and the National Guard are almost at full mobilization. Once the enemy attacks run out of steam, we should be able to go over to the offensive, both in Quebec and in northern Mexico. We'll also be able to start coordinating things with our allies. The Russians seem to be doing okay against the Manchurians. England is taking heavy cruise missile attacks from across the Channel, but they're holding. We actually stand a very good chance of holding them at our borders, and once—"

"That's just the problem, Admiral," Markham interrupted. "We've got to do more than just *hold* them. We've got to hit back. Hard. Before they decide to escalate to something nastier."

"It's possible, Mr. President," Harrel said softly, "that our hitting back harder would precipitate an escalation."

"I know. So the secretary of state told me." The president paused. "John Matloff offered me his resignation this morning. Did you know?"

"No, sir," Gray and Harrel said, almost in unison. Gray was surprised. Matloff hadn't struck him as the sort to make dramatic gestures, especially where his career was concerned.

"I refused it," Markham said. "Told him I wasn't going to let him start a stampede. The government has to be together on this. Present a united front. For the people. And for the rest of the world. Am I right?"

"Yes, Mr. President." Again, they spoke almost as one.

"I've authorized Operation Freedom, Admiral Gray. I'm not sure how much help it's going to be to us in the short term, but it's a good long-term gamble, and you're right about it being a symbol. We win a victory up there, in orbit, and we're letting the world know we still have the high-tech know-how to command space. But . . ." He stopped suddenly, one finger raised for emphasis. "But. If Operation Freedom doesn't come off as advertised, we are going to be in an extraordinarily vulnerable position. The people will see us throwing away lives and equipment in space when enemy forces are marching through our backyards and giving us one godawful shellacking. They might not sit still for that. I may be forced to sue for peace, while I still have the option. So I want you gentlemen to make this thing work. Clear?"

"Yes, sir."

"Keep working at ways of intercepting those missiles. The people won't support a government that can't protect them."

"Overall popular response has been good, Mr. President," Harrel said. "Surprisingly good, under the circumstances. The bombardment seems to have united most of them."

"I would remind the president," Gray said, "that an outside attack like this usually doesn't have the effect on the morale of the target population that the attackers hope. The Germans learned that when they tried to bomb England during the Blitz. We learned the same thing in Vietnam a generation later."

"Agreed. But it's been a long time since Americans have been involved directly in a war like this, gentlemen. Unless you count a few shells from U-boats and Japanese subs in World War II, we've never suffered a bombardment . . . and the last time enemy troops were on our soil was the War of 1812. These attacks on our government buildings and institutions are designed for three things, as I see it. They want to demonstrate they can hit us, and keep hitting us as long as they need to. They want to break our morale. And they want to drive a wedge into our people, between the Nationalists and the Internationalists. The Internationalist Party, you know, has already come out in favor of a negotiated truce and immediate incorporation into the UN World Government. They could gain a lot of converts if this bombardment goes on. If we can't show the people a damned positive turn in the battle, and *fast*, well . . ." He didn't finish the sentence.

"Operation Freedom is the way to go, sir," Gray said quietly. "Once we have control of Earth orbit, we've got the high ground, as it were. The Hecate laser aboard Shepard Station proved its effectiveness this morning. We'll be able to turn it against enemy launch sites . . . maybe hit those European arsenal ships that have been tossing cruise missiles at us from the North Atlantic. We might even consider laser attacks against their capitals . . . or against the UN building in Geneva."

"Who's on the Freedom op?"

"The Marine commandant himself is running the show, Mr. President. He's already left for Cheyenne Mountain. The unit tagged for the mission is First Platoon, Alfa Company, First Marine Strike Battalion."

"They're good?"

"The best. They're the unit that brought our people out of Mexico City. They're at Vandenberg, where they've been training for orbital combat operations."

"Who's in command?"

"A Lieutenant Fuentes, sir. CO of the rescue team at the embassy."

"Well, I hope to hell he can pull it off."

"Fuentes will do it if anyone can, Mr. President." Gray decided not to tell Markham that Carmen Fuentes was a woman. Sex had stopped being an issue in the American military decades ago, but even now there was the unspoken but very evident assumption in government and in the chain of command that a *man* was needed for a man's work. So far as Gray was concerned, Fuentes had proved herself and then some at the US

Embassy in Mexico City. Warhurst trusted her . . . and, more to the point, the men and women in her platoon trusted her. He wasn't going to risk interfering with *that*.

He just hoped she had what it took to pull off her mission. Right now, it looked as though the very existence of the United States of America was hanging by a thread.

NINETEEN

The Star Eagle *Michael E. Thornton*, a single-stage-to-orbit SCRAMjet transport, had cleared the lower reaches of Earth's atmosphere and was accelerating now on her rockets, thundering through the fast-thinning traces of air toward the sunrise. Lieutenant Carmen Fuentes, encased in Class-One/Special armor and riding in what by now was effectively vacuum, couldn't hear the rockets so much as *feel* them. The passenger module was a quick design that Marines jokingly referred to as "economy class," with thin padding over hard steel skeletons of chairs.

It was not the most comfortable way to ride to orbit.

The last whispering rumble of the rocket engines died away, leaving Lieutenant Carmen Fuentes and the twenty-two men and women with her in the Star Eagle's passenger compartment in the free-falling light-headedness of microgravity. The green light at the head of the compartment winked on, indicating that it was safe to move about. Fuentes unsnapped her harness, grabbed a handhold on the overhead, and pulled herself around to face her people.

"Listen up, everyone," she said over the platoon channel. "I want all of you to stay strapped in. There's nothing to see in this tin can, so you might as well stay buckled. You've all got your TD-patches, so you shouldn't be spacesick. Any of you do feel sick, use your barf bags. Just remember, it'll be a long time yet before we can unsuit."

The passenger compartment for this flight of the *Thornton* was deliberately unpressurized, which meant the Marines had to stay sealed in their armor all the way up.

"I got the word a few minutes ago," she continued, using the general talk frequency. "The *McCutcheon*'s lifted off from Florida and is on her way. We'll have our backup at the target."

She could almost sense the relief among the armored forms facing her. The *Keith B. McCutcheon* was another Star Eagle, identical to the *Thornton*, but she was coming to orbit with only a few Marines and technicians on board, riding in a pressurized passenger compartment. There would be doctors on board, and a small, microgravity surgery; most important, it would provide the Marine assault team with a place to go, shuck their suits, and stand down for a while. The op at the ISS was expected to take a long time, longer than their suits could carry them.

Fuentes resumed her seat. There were no windows, no display screens, and nothing to see but the cargo bay interior. From time to time, *Thornton*'s captain called back from the Star Eagle's cockpit, updating her on their status.

"Lieutenant?" the ship's captain said eventually. He was a Navy commander named Bryan Mason. "We're coming up on the target. I'm cracking your overhead now. Make sure everybody's tied down back there, and watch the light."

"That's a roger. We're all secure here."

"Copy. Opening up."

Like the old shuttles, the Star Eagle possessed long, twin doors above the cargo area, and those were slowly opening now, the movement completely silent in the vacuum, though Fuentes could feel the vibration through the hull when she touched it with her glove. She looked up and watched the dark gray hatch panels sliding apart, revealing the inexpressibly lovely, deep blue of the Earth hanging above their heads. She glanced back down at her platoon, watching for the signs she'd been warned about . . . thrashing about, shaking, any of the possible physical reactions indicating that someone might be going into panic.

There were none. The platoon had been well briefed and well trained.

As the doors swung aside now, sunlight blasted into the interior, darkening the polarized visors of every Marine in the bay. Earth was impossibly blue, impossibly brilliant, a swirl of azure ocean, white dapplings and currents and sweeps of clouds, and a tawny patch of desert. Fuentes had thought she knew her geography well, but she found she couldn't recognize any part of the planet suspended above her head.

"Range to target," Commander Mason's voice said in her headphones, "one hundred meters. We have hostiles in sight."

"Roger that. Thanks for the ride."

"Any time, Lieutenant. Fly Navy."

"My Ass Rides In Navy Equipment, Sir," she replied jauntily, using the old MARINES acronym. She switched to the platoon frequency. "Platoon! Unhook and disembark! By the numbers! First rank . . . go! Second rank . . . go! Third rank . . ."

Line by line, the Marines floated out of their seats, leaving belts and gleaming belt buckles magically adrift in zero G. Fuentes reached across with her right hand, touched the thrust control on her left arm, and felt the slight, upward nudge of her MMU's high-pressure nitrogen jets.

Class-One/Special armor, as the designation suggested, was a special adaptation of standard full armor.

The suit part was basically unchanged, hard-shelled and coated in active camouflage surfacing, with helmets made insectlike by the lenses of cameras and headlights arrayed just above the dark-tinted visors. The principal change was in the life-support backpack that each Marine wore like half of a mattress strapped to the armor's back. Derived from the Manned Maneuvering Units of the early days of the Space Shuttle, these MMUs served as miniature, one-man spacecraft, providing power, life support, and maneuverability for up to twelve hours at a time.

As Fuentes cleared the passenger module, she touched another thrust control, canceling her upward momentum. She was hanging now twenty feet above the gaping cargo bay of the Star Eagle. Above and around her were the other twenty-two men and women of her platoon. Directly ahead was the International Space Station, a glittering structure of interconnected cylinders, cans, and spheres, stretched along spidery struts between the gorgeous black-purple spread of its winglike solar panel arrays.

Mason was right. She could see armored figures, dwarfed to near insignificance by the size of the ISS structure, moving along the struts. It looked like the UN troops—some of them, at any rate—had come out to play.

She saw a twinkling of tiny lights in the shadowed side of the ISS and realized with a curious detachment born of her eerie surroundings that they were firing at her.

"Space Strike One, this is Eagle," Mason's voice said. "We are taking projectile fire from the target. Be advised that Hellfire is in position to deliver covering fire."

"Platoon!" she rasped out. "Watch your vision! Okay, Eagle. Let's have that cover fire!"

Hellfire was Shepard Station, nudged from its lower, faster orbit to a position in the same orbit as the ISS, trailing it by about twenty kilometers. A moment later, a portion of the space station's hull grew briefly, intolerably bright.

The ISS battle represented an odd balancing of forces and tactics. The station itself was unarmed, so the only way the defenders could hold off the Marines was to send armored troops outside and engage the attackers one-on-one. The Marines, in turn, were hampered by the fact that they couldn't just find an airlock and smash their way in. It took time to cycle through a lock, and by the time a handful of Marines could squeeze into an airlock and match pressures with the station interior, they would find a large number of UN troops on the other side, waiting for them to crack in the inner hatch and start moving through one at a time.

Neither could the Marines simply find a spot on the side of the station, blow a hole through, and storm inside. There were at least eight hostages aboard, including five Americans. Fuentes's orders stated bluntly that her first priority was to secure the station, but indiscriminately slaughtering hostages and enemy troops alike was not going to help the US cause much, any more than it would advance her own career.

The plan that they'd arrived at was a compromise at best, but one that offered a fair chance of success if they could clear the ISS framework of enemy troops. Unlike Shepard Station, the International Space Station was not powered by a nuclear reactor. All power came from the solar array, which converted sunlight directly to electricity and channeled it through a series of heavily shielded cables to the battery compartment at the station's midships area. Fully charged, those batteries could keep the ISS powered for an estimated forty-eight hours, a time period that could be extended somewhat by shutting down nonessential systems.

The Marine plan depended on being able to clear the enemy from the station's struts and rigging in order to gain unrestricted access to the power conduits from the solar panels. Cut those cables, and the station would be helpless, forced to draw on battery power for temperature control, communications, oxygen recycling, and scrubbing excess CO_2 from the air. The problem, then, would be waiting them out. The UN troops could afford to sit tight knowing the Marines couldn't storm inside and root them out; if the UN could get reinforcements to the station, the Marines would have to withdraw and the siege could be lifted.

And that, of course, was where Shepard and its laser came into the picture. Without reinforcements, sooner or later the ISS would have to surrender. And no reinforcements could approach the ISS so long as Shepard remained intact, with the Hecate HEL. In addition, Shepard could give the Marines a much-appreciated hand by sweeping snipers from the station's struts and rigging. By timing the HEL pulses to a fraction of a second, the laser wouldn't damage the station, but any enemy troops who happened to be looking in Shepard's direction would be blinded.

"Forward, Marines!" Fuentes cried, touching her forward thrust control and holding it, letting her velocity build. There was no sensation of motion save for the slow growth of the ISS in her field of vision, and the steadily dwindling green numbers flickering on her visor HUD at the edge of her field of vision, counting down the meters as measured by her helmet's laser ranger. Carefully, she unstrapped her ATAR, moving slowly to avoid going into a spin, and planted the rifle's butt plate squarely in the slot built into the armor just about over her navel. She touched a button on the rifle's side; a yellow crosshair appeared on the inside of her visor, together with a tiny, inset video image on her HUD's lower left field.

What she was about to do *ought* to work, but it had never been tried before . . . at least, not outside of the microgravity combat training simulators at Vandenberg. She selected a target, a blue-helmeted soldier clinging to an antenna guy, and moved her rifle until the crosshair was centered on his chest.

Lightly, almost delicately, she squeezed the trigger.

Every action has an opposite but equal reaction, and a rifle firing in zero G acts precisely like a small rocket, hurling mass in one direction and kicking the shooter in the other. Each bullet's mass was tiny compared to Fuentes and her hundred kilos–plus of armor and MMU, but moving very quickly, enough to give a noticeable recoil, enough to slow her forward velocity somewhat . . . but not enough to stop her or knock her off course. Most important, the center-of-mass-firing technique pioneered in the simulators at Vandenberg worked. If the rifle was badly positioned, the recoil could set her spinning. Careful firing from the center of mass, however, simply slowed her in her headlong charge. All of the Marines in the strike force had practiced firing from free-pivoting microgravity simulators, gangling contraptions made of struts and wires from which an armored Marine could dangle in a frictionless approximation of zero G.

She just hoped the rest of her Marines remembered their training. If one of them went spinning off into the void now, there'd be no way to recover him.

She'd been so concerned about not sending herself into a spin that she hadn't noticed what had happened to her target. The man was tumbling away from the space station now, arms and legs cartwheeling, a fine white mist of freezing air trailing like a tiny contrail. A second blue-top appeared to her left, but she couldn't fire at him without turning in place, a maneuver she wasn't about to try now. She concentrated instead on the part of the ISS she was going to hit, a smooth, curved, surface that was growing from a piece of a Tinkertoy construct to a vast white wall dead ahead. She triggered reverse thrust, then fired off a burst from her ATAR for good measure, reducing her forward velocity to a slow drift.

She hit with a clang that resounded through her helmet, rebounded, and went into a slow, almost graceful spin. For a moment, panic struggled with training; there was no up or down, no easy means of orienting herself. Then as she'd been taught, she put out her left arm to counter the rotation; that slowed her down enough that she could grab a handhold, coming to a bouncing halt.

She'd made it. "Fuentes on target!" she called over

the general com circuit. The idea was to keep everyone apprised of where everyone else was, but she could already tell that the sheer confusion of the situation was going to overwhelm any attempts at organization or battle management.

Turning herself about, she tried to reacquire the UN trooper she'd glimpsed on the way in, but she was confused. Not that way . . . *damn*! He could be behind her for all she knew. She turned again. The sky was filled with incoming Marines; a few blue-tops clung to station rigging or used handheld jets of some kind to propel themselves along the station's length toward one of the airlocks. Earth was enormous, a blue-white arc across half the sky. Over her headset, she could hear the crackling calls of her Marines.

"Wheeoo! Comin' in!"

"Watch it, Sandy! Bad guy on your four o'clock!"

"I got him!"

"I'm down! Ortega on target!"

"Help me! This is Kelly! I've got a malfunction! Someone help me!"

She looked around for Private Kelly but couldn't see him. The battle was a tangle of confusion, with unfamiliar shapes and movement in unexpected directions. She had an excellent vantage point, midway along the length of the ISS, somewhere in the vicinity, she thought, of the computer module. The station's keel—a massive structure of zigzagging struts and long, aluminum beams supporting the modules—was just over *that* way . . . and she could see the great, black wings of the solar panels when they eclipsed the glare of the sun.

That gave Fuentes her bearings, and she started moving toward the station keel.

Other Marines around her were doing the same, their active camo armor showing odd, almost abstract designs of black and white. The camo, she thought, worked well in space; it was hard to recognize anything *human* in those shapes, though the MMUs, which were not camouflaged, provided anchor points for the eye that helped her pick out individual features like helmets, gloves, or ATARs.

Several Marines, she saw, had reached the station dead, their armor torn open, a frosting of frozen water or atmosphere forming around gaping entry or exit holes. Others had missed the station and were receding into the black void beyond. She called up a visual on her platoon life-support readouts. It looked like five dead out of twenty-two . . . not good, but not as bad as it could have been, and there was always the tiny but defiant hope that some of those listed as dead were alive, but with damaged transmitters.

"Eagle, this is Marine One," she called. "We're down to eighteen effectives, but we're on the station. Can you clarify the tacsit, over?"

"Ah, copy that, One. Sorry, it looks like a real furball from here. Can't see much of anything."

"Rog." It was up to the Marines, then. Up to *her*.

As she rounded the curve of the station module, she spotted a blue-helmet clinging to the rigging in the distance. It was impossible, she found, to estimate ranges. Things seemed closer in vacuum, without the slight haze of an atmosphere to give subconscious clues to distance. No matter. She didn't even need to check the range on her HUD. Combat here was strictly point and shoot.

A patch of the station hull a few meters away suddenly and silently acquired a bright silver smudge; a bullet had just grazed the structure's outer skin. She dragged her ATAR around until the crosshairs were centered on the enemy, then squeezed the trigger. Recoil bumped her back, setting her adrift from the station as the UN soldier flung his arms out and lost his rifle as he drifted clear of the station rigging.

She used her MMU to stop her backward drift, then accelerate forward again. She skimmed past the station hull, her boots centimeters above the white-painted surface. She saw several more UN bodies, some drifting equipment, but no more active targets.

"Marine One, this is Eagle," crackled in her headset. "It looks like you've got 'em on the run. We can see five . . . no, six blue-tops making for an airlock at the Alfa end. Looks like you've got 'em bottled up.''

"Copy that, Eagle."

She was panting, breathing hard, though whether from exertion or excitement she wasn't sure. She used her suit controls to adjust her air mix, upping the O_2 content a bit, then set to work rallying her people. At her command, four Marines jetted over to the connector joints, where the solar panel arrays were mounted to the station's keel by large, rotating joints, and began placing their cutting charges at key points.

The first stage of the battle, at least, was over. Now the game became one of cat-at-the-mousehole, and they would have to see who broke first.

TWENTY

Candor Chasma
Sol 5651: 1830 hours MMT

"So," Mark Garroway said in what he'd intended to be a conversational way, but which came out more like a grunt. "What's so damned important about this shit you found at Cydonia?"

He was sitting in the Mars cat's lounge, tightly wedged in between Sergeant Knox on his left and Lieutenant King on his right, with David Alexander squeezed in with Pohl and Druzhininova on the other side of the vehicle.

His lips were dry and cracked, making conversation difficult. The entire force had gone on short rations of water four days ago, when two of the cat's fuel-cell recycler condensers had gone bad. Water was more important for power now than even for drinking. Without power, the cat would die, their armor life support would fail a few hours later, and they would be stranded, dead unless a UN patrol happened to find them.

"That's rather a difficult question to answer, Major," Alexander said. His voice cracked. "Obviously, it has a bearing on what Man is, where he came from, how he evolved. I'd say the question touches on just about every

278

aspect of human history, physiology, psychology, and evolution.''

"Isn't that what science is all about?'' Druzhininova said. She shrugged inside her suit. "To find out who we are, where we are going, and why.''

"Not necessarily *why*,'' Pohl said. "I've always thought that was a question for the theologians and the philosophers.''

"There is no question that can be excluded by science,'' Alexander replied. "Not if there is hard evidence that allows us to look at the question in the first place.''

The walls of the Mars cat shuddered, and all of them looked up. A full-blown dust storm was howling outside. Technically, it was daytime, but the black pall of dust thrown up by the winds screeching across the Martian surface had blotted out the sun as effectively as nightfall, forcing them—yet again—to halt their journey. The Marines on watch outside were all gathered, at Garroway's orders, in the narrow space beneath the Mars cat, taking advantage of a new technique they'd developed almost a week ago. By digging into the sand beneath the vehicle, the Marines forced to stay outside could huddle together in a narrow space that quickly warmed with the heat radiated from their armor and from the bottom of the crawler. It still wasn't comfortable, exactly, but they wouldn't freeze.

And in a howling Martian dust storm, it meant the others would know where to dig when the thing was over.

Dr. Druzhininova had pointed out that some Martian dust storms during the early summer could cover the whole northern hemisphere of the planet and last for months. If that happened, the MMEF and their civilian charges would die here, and their mummified bodies would remain for some far-future archeologist to wonder at.

Garroway reached up and scratched the bristle at his chin. The last tube of nobeard had given out five days ago, and all of the men were showing the effects now. There wasn't water to spare for shaving, and the male members of the MMEF were beginning to take on a distinctly piratical air as their beards started growing out.

Alexander's beard was fuller, almost neat-looking. He and Dr. Pohl had stopped using facial depilatories from the start and now looked like something halfway approaching distinguished.

Garroway was thoughtful for a time. "How long would it take you, Doctor," he said finally, "to write up a paper on the subject? Something you could transmit over the Spacenet?"

Alexander's face worked for a moment behind his sandy beard. "You mean . . . publish? It's what I've been dreaming of. You know that. But, well, I don't have much to say, yet. It'd be premature."

"You discovered those bodies back at Cydonia. That seems to be what the UN scientists want to keep under wraps. Can't you just publish that?"

"Well, yes. Certainly. But, well, we don't know anything about who those . . . those people were, or why they're on Mars. How they got here. I'd want to do a lot of excavating first, just to see if we could come up with any preliminary hypothesis."

"We find dead humans, or . . . what did you call them?"

"Archaic *Homo sapiens*," Druzhininova said. "Or possibly very modern *Homo erectus*."

"That's part of what we need to do more research on," Alexander added, "to nail down just what it is we're dealing with here."

"It strikes me, Doctor," Garroway said carefully, "that just the fact that ancestors of ours were brought here to Mars, that they seem to have been living here when the climate was, hell, a shirt-sleeve environment . . . wouldn't that warrant some kind of initial wake-up call? 'Hey, Earth! Mankind's prehistory is a lot different than you thought it was!' "

The others chuckled.

"You could write it up there," he said, nodding at the cat's comm center. "I can encode it, slip it in with some housekeeping traffic using the Phobos relay, and drop it in my daughter's e-mail box back on Earth. If you include instructions for where you'd like to see it published, she can take care of that.''

"It might work," Alexander said, nodding. "Lots of scientific papers are published over the net these days. Most of 'em, in fact. Used to be you needed to present it in a scholarly journal for peer review."

"That's what I was thinking," Garroway said. "Us shaggy-headed electronics types publish on the net all the time."

"So, what's your take on this, Major?" Alexander wanted to know. "Why are you in such a hurry to see us publish?"

Garroway pursed his lips. "I don't know. The fact that the UN wanted to suppress your discovery, for whatever reason, seems good enough reason to me to see it shouted from the housetops. Don't you think?"

Alexander nodded slowly. "You know, I think you're right."

                                2130 HOURS GMT

Tanegashima Space Center,
Osaki Launch Site
0630 hours Tokyo time

". . . roku . . . go . . . yon . . . san . . . ni . . . ichi . . . ima!"
Acceleration crushed down on Yukio's chest, pressing him hard against his couch as the powerful *Ikaduti* booster ignited, hauling the sleek *Inaduma* space fighter aloft from Pad Nine. His heart was pounding, and only partly from the building Gs of lift off. He was on his way to space. *On his way to space at last . . .*

Ikaduti and *Inaduma.* Thunder and lightning. Booster and spaceplane were well matched, the pinnacle of a long line of Japanese successes in spacecraft design and engineering. The thunder built steadily, though the actual sound seemed to be dropping away behind as the spacecraft climbed into the clear azure sky.

The *Inaduma* space fighter could carry a crew of four, though on this run there were only three aboard. *Sho-sa* Kurosawa was mission commander, *Tai-i* Iijima was pilot, and *Chu-i* Yukio Ishiwara was aboard as computer technician and radar operator, a position roughly analogous to the Radar Intercept Officers used aboard some American dual-seat military aircraft. Conditions in the *Inaduma*'s cockpit were cramped; Yukio's acceleration couch was jammed in immediately behind and slightly below the tandem couches of commander and pilot, while the fourth seat had been removed to accommodate an additional bank of electronic sensory equipment.

The roar of the main engines continued to fade, but the crushing sensation of weight on his chest and stomach actually increased. As the mighty *Ikaduti* booster burned up more and more of its fuel, the rocket's mass dwindled, increasing acceleration.

Yukio studied the radar intercept console beside his couch, struggling to focus on the main screen. Yes . . . the second fighter was there, rising from Pad Twelve thirty seconds behind them. *Taka* Flight—the word was Nihongo for *Hawk*—consisted of two spaceplanes, Yukio's *Taka* One, and *Sho-sa* Ozawa's *Taka* Two.

The *Inaduma* was small as manned spacecraft went, barely twelve meters long and shaped like a blunt, round-nosed arrowhead. The tips of the delta wings were set in a gentle curve, like a smile when seen from head-on, and the cockpit clung to the ship's back like a dark, glassy droplet of oil. Launched vertically, strapped to the side of the Thunder booster, it could easily reach LEO in a single-stage-to-orbit launch, carry out a variety of missions, and reenter like the old shuttle orbiters, bellying down on a meteoric blaze of incandescent reentry gases.

The sky ahead, just visible from Yukio's aft position between the heads of the commander and pilot, was swiftly deepening from cloudless, early-morning blue to deepest ultramarine. The spaceplane was angling over now, hurtling downrange across the Pacific into the sunrise, speed still building as it hurtled toward the tiny window of opportunity that would give them one shot, and one only, at the target.

Major Kurosawa was giving the countdown to booster separation now, his voice straining a bit beneath the pressure of almost five Gs of acceleration. *"Go . . . yon . . . san . . . ni . . . ichi . . . ima!"*

With a savage thump, the *Ikaduti* booster separated, dropping away from the *Inaduma*'s belly like an oversize bomb. For a blissful moment, all was silence and falling, and then the spaceplane's twin Mitsubishi engines cut in, hammering the stubby craft into space.

Yukio found himself unexpectedly amused by one aspect of the countdown. Japan took an exceptional pride in her space program, adopting all of the trappings of the Russian and Western programs with relish . . . right down to the countdown which, as he understood it, had first been added for dramatic impact to a 1929 German science-fiction film, *Die Frau im Mond*. Japan's national love affair with space stemmed at least partially from her justifiable pride in her technological accomplishments. Rising from the utter devastation at the end of the War almost a century ago to a spacefaring Great Power, *this* was Japan's destiny and her heritage, and she'd been pursuing it relentlessly into the twenty-first century, through her participation in the ISS, through her first manned shuttle in 2010, to her position now as one of the two major spacefaring powers in the United Nations.

The Western part of Yukio's mind, however, couldn't help but notice Kurosawa's routine substitution during the countdown of the word *yon* for *shi*, the numeral four. As a language, Japanese lent itself well to puns, for there were numerous words and syllables that sounded exactly alike and yet meant vastly different things. *Shi* not only meant "four." It was also the Japanese word for *death*, and in a lingering swirl of ancient superstition no hospital room or ward in Japan was numbered four, one never purchased gift sets with four items, the numeral itself was thought to be unlucky, and the safe word *yon* was almost always substituted for *shi* . . . *especially* in

something as critical and as auspicious as the countdown
for the launch of a spacecraft!

Well, superstition was a part of being human and was
scarcely restricted to the Japanese. The Americans
hadn't numbered a spacecraft "13" since the explosion
aboard the Apollo 13 spacecraft in 1970—launched at
1313 hours Houston time, on April 11, 1970 . . . an interesting date in itself since the individual numerals in
4/11/70 added up to 13, while the actual explosion
occurred on Monday, April 13. . . .

Yukio laughed, partly at the superstition, partly at the
sheer, heady joy of being in space at last, leaving his
mind in a racing, leapfrogging whirl.

"You said something, Radar Officer?" Kurosawa
asked over his headset phone.

"Ah, no, sir. Excuse me, please. I laughed. . . ."

Iijima chuckled. "His first time."

"I don't mind if you enjoy the flight, *Chu-i-san*,"
Kurosawa said. "But perhaps you should also see about
acquiring the target, *neh*?"

Yukio glanced again at the panel beside him. Except
for *Taka* Two, the sky around them was clear. "They
are not yet in range, Commander," he replied.

It was harder to speak now, as acceleration continued
to increase. The *Ikaduti* booster was patterned on the
monster Energiyas of the Russians and was fully capable
of hurling the spaceplane into orbit on a single stage.
Taka Flight was gambling on the extra velocity to put
them into a short, direct, interception course with the
target, one that would take them past the target in minimum time, then swing wide into a long, highly elliptical
orbit.

And then, the last of the thunder and the bone-rattling
vibration was gone. "Orbital velocity," Kurosawa announced. "We have attained orbit."

Yukio almost laughed aloud again at the slightly
queasy, swift-dropping sensation of weightlessness, a
delightful sensation that he knew he would come to enjoy quickly, if he had the chance. He just wished the
fighter had a roomier cockpit, with space enough to un-

buckle his harness and float around. Experimentally, he plucked a pen from his flight-suit pocket and let it hang, gleaming and silver, in midair before his face.

He had to snatch it back again, as Captain Iijima made some adjustments to his controls and the fighter gracefully rolled to port, bringing the vast and awe-inspiring blue majesty of the Earth "above" the spaceplane's cockpit. Yukio's view of the planet, stretched like a blue and cloud-mottled sky overhead, was partly blocked by the opaque hood over the afterpart of the fighter's cockpit, but he could see enough that it caught the breath in his throat and transfixed him with its impossible beauty.

The launch from Tanegashima had hurled the *Inaduma* far out over the Pacific, and he could see no land at all . . . nothing save the spirals of the great, cloud-folded weather patterns. Yukio was surprised to see how three-dimensional the clouds appeared, even from this height. He'd thought they would look flatter, like white brushstrokes against a blue backdrop. Instead, he could easily see their three-dimensional character, could make out the ripples in their upper surfaces, like wavelets in a pond, and see the shadows cast by the highest of the cloud tops, like shadows thrown by mountains in the early-morning sun.

If only Kaitlin could see. . . .

As though a switch had been thrown, his joy evaporated. It wasn't just the thought of Kaitlin. The view of Earth, that magnificent blue Earth, seemed so completely antithetical to their mission. The thought that they were here to try to kill people . . .

Don't think about that! You have your duty. Concentrate on your duty. . . .

But there was no way to deny the thoughts, rising unbidden and furious. Yukio had had trouble believing his orders when he'd first seen them. *Taka Flight is directed to launch at the earliest possible time in order to intercept American forces now attempting to capture the ISS, currently controlled by our UN allies. Your primary target is the American military space station* Shepard *and its high-energy laser, which is being used in support of American operations at the station. After the primary target has been neutralized, you will maneuver close to the ISS and render direct military support to UN forces aboard.*

"Direct military support." That meant, of course, attacking the American troops now outside the ISS.

Yukio had no wish to kill Americans. He felt trapped, trapped between his orders and that Western part of his soul that loved the United States and Western clothes and the freedoms of speech and thought that Americans took for granted . . . and Kaitlin.

Kaitlin, forgive me. . . .

But for the smallest of cosmic accidents, her father might have been among the troops attacking the ISS, and one of his targets. In a way, he *was* attacking her father, since the ISS was Earth's only orbital spaceport, the only way for him to come home when he returned from distant Mars.

For a time, he stared at the blue curve of the Earth ahead, agleam beneath the sun. For Nihonjin there was but one way to resolve the irresolvable, and that was by clinging to duty, to honor, and to family.

Gimu. Duty.

Shikata. It is the way things are done.

Shikata ga nai. There is no other way. The concept of *shikata* was a peculiarly Japanese sentiment. For Nihonjin, it was attitude first, then effort, and finally result. "It's not whether you win or lose, but how you play the game" might easily have been an aphorism first voiced by a Japanese sage.

With a decisive movement, he rotated the console at his side and locked it in place in front of him. He was picking up targets now on the screen, a cluster of objects of some size nearly five hundred kilometers ahead and one hundred kilometers above them.

"I have the cluster on screen, Commander." His gloved fingers tapped across his touch pad. "Working on best firing solution."

"Very well."

The cluster was the main group of manned space stations in low Earth orbit. That big one near the center was the ISS, and the smaller mass near it was an American Star Eagle transport. They were still too distant to pick up the American troops reported to be moving around outside of the station.

Other, smaller targets in the area were free-flying satellite facilities, research platforms, independent space stations owned by the ESA and Japan, sharing an orbit for mutual safety and comfort.

That blip, though, trailing the others by twenty kilometers, was the one *Taka* Flight was interested in. When he touched it with his cursor and clicked the query spot, the Romanji characters scrolling down the screen told the story: US INDEPENDENT RESEARCH SPACE STATION SHEPARD.

Though her engines were shut down, the fighter continued climbing, hurtling along the outward leg of her elliptical orbit. The launch had been timed perfectly; with only a few gentle course corrections, Iijima had put *Taka* One into a path that would neatly intercept Shepard in another . . . twenty-one minutes.

The only difficulty, of course, was that the Americans by this time knew that they were coming.

TWENTY-ONE

Shepard MOP
2223 hours GMT

"Cheyenne Mountain, Shepard," Colonel Dahlgren said, peering into the telescopic display. "We definitely have visitors . . . at least two *Inaduma*-class fighters on intercept. Over."

"Roger that, Shepard. We concur. We are tracking two birds, launched fifty-three minutes ago from Tanegashima. Intelligence sources report they are definitely hostile . . . repeat, hostile." There was a long pause, filled by the hiss of static. "Shepard, you are cleared for defensive operations."

Dahlgren drew a deep breath. "Copy, Cheyenne. Initiating defensive operations."

Defensive operations. It sounded so . . . sterile. Like "force package" or "direct action." Like a problem in air-combat maneuvers back at the Aerospace Force Academy, a few million years ago. . . .

He looked at Fred Lance, who was listening in on his own headset. Fred shrugged, then looked away. They'd been speculating for hours now on what Japan was going to do. It looked like they had their answer.

So far, Japan had not been an entirely eager participant in the UN campaign to bring the United States to its knees. The Japanese remained one of America's most active trading partners, despite the various UN-declared embargoes, and they'd argued forcefully in the General Assembly against military action.

Still, the Charter of 2025 required member nations to participate in "military police exercises" at the behest of the UN World Security Council. While Japan maintained the fiction of its so-called Self Defense Force, which it sent abroad only in very special and very carefully controlled situations, the fact remained that Japan's military space force was as good as or better than that of the ESA. There'd been some question as to whether Japan would honor its treaty commitments to the Charter.

That question, evidently, had just been answered.

"Fire up the program, Fred," he said. "Let's see how this sucker works on antiaircraft mode."

"We're tracking 'em. Hecate Program running. HEL powering up. Full charge in thirty seconds."

Dahlgren peered into the display. Even at full magnification, the approaching fighters were hard to see, for they were several hundred kilometers astern of Shepard. But they were also at a lower altitude and, therefore, silhouetted against the vast, sky-blue expanse of the Pacific Ocean. He set the telescope's crosshairs on the lead fighter and touched the keypad panel, locking in.

"We have full power, Colonel."

"Fire."

The bulk of the large and delicate Hecate High-Energy Laser was inside the lab compartment. The beam was channeled through a special port in the station's hull and out into space, where it struck a mirror on the end of a twenty-meter strut. That mirror, controlled by the Hecate AI Program, could be precisely adjusted to give the laser a full field of fire across nearly the entire sky. The beam itself was invisible in the empty vacuum of space, but for an instant, backscatter from the mirror illuminated half of the space platform like the rising of a second sun. . . .

Taka One
2225 hours GMT

"*Kuso!*" Kurosawa snapped. "What was that?"

There'd been no sound, no shock, but abruptly a patch of violent, intolerably bright incandescence had flared on the craft's nose, a few meters below the cockpit. Iijima hit the craft's roll jets and added some yaw, nudging the craft clear of that deadly beam before it could more than blacken *Taka* One's coat of reflective white paint.

"Laser, Commander," Yukio replied, checking his instruments. "I read it in the half-megawatt range. We are being fired on."

A moment later, the beam struck again, this time on the wing, clawing at the hull long enough to explode a puff of vapor into space, the jet kicking them sharply to the right. Iijima responded by rolling back, clearing the beam, and accelerating.

"*Taka* Two reports they are taking fire as well," Kurosawa said after a moment. "The bastards are shifting between us. First us. Then Ozawa. They're trying to cripple us before we can get into missile range."

A decent tactic, Yukio thought. *It could work.*

For five more minutes, they played this deadly and uncomfortable game. The laser would play briefly against the *Inaduma*'s hull, the beam itself invisible but the effects startlingly clear. As light flared, as flecks of hull material snapped away or vanished in puffs of glowing white vapor, the pilot would fire the ship's maneuvering jets, tossing them left or right, up or down, seeking to evade that deadly, clawing beam. For a time, they would be in the clear.

And then the beam would find them once more.

"Range to target," Yukio said calmly. "Three-two-three kilometers, and closing." He consulted his main display, where an intercept program was running with a rapidly shifting interplay of numbers representing relative velocities, delta-v, acceleration, time, and distance.

"Time to best firing solution on this vector . . . three minutes, twelve seconds."

The *Inaduma* carried two *Hayabusa* missiles mounted in internal bays, one fitted inside each thick wing. The name was a poetical form of the word for the peregrine falcon, a swift bird of prey and a deadly hunter. In aerial combat they had a range of well over 150 kilometers; in space, technically, their range was unlimited, though a firing solution involved higher or lower orbits and the complexities of orbital intercepts.

The real problem was gauging the best range at which to fire. Obviously, the Defense Intelligence report that Shepard Station was testing a powerful new space-based laser was all too accurate. Launch from too great a distance, and that laser might burn the missiles out of orbit; try to get too close, and the laser would burn the space fighter out of orbit. The program running on Yukio's console was designed to pick the best of several bad options.

The fighter lurched again, and for a moment, the huge blue Earth seemed to tumble around the ship, alternately flooding the cockpit with turquoise light and plunging them into darkness.

"*Unko!*" Major Kurosawa snapped. "Stabilize us, pilot-*san!* Thrusters five and seven! Do it!"

Slowly, the hard roll to port slowed, then stopped. Yukio chanced a quick look forward, past the seats of pilot and commander at the blackness of space beyond. He still couldn't actually *see* the American space station, not with the naked eye. It was a strange kind of warfare. . . .

"*Taka* One, this is Tanegashima Control."

The voice sounded in Yukio's headset, but Kurosawa answered it. "Tanegashima, *Taka* One. Go ahead!"

"*Taka* One . . . *Taka* Two is no longer in communication. It appears to be tumbling on free trajectory. We must assume it has been destroyed."

Yukio felt cold. *Just like that. A ship and three men, killed. . . .*

"Tanegashima, *Taka* One," Kurosawa said. "We

copy. We are proceeding with the attack.''

There was no alternative, of course. They were committed now. Even if they'd wanted to break off and return to Earth, the deorbit maneuver would simply drop them into a lower and faster vector. The enemy would assume they were still attacking.

Besides, honor was involved, and the workings of *wa* and *bushido*. To flee now, even if they could, was unthinkable.

Laser fire clawed at the spaceplane's nose again, the glare off vaporizing hull metal dazzling through the cockpit window. Captain Iijima jinked the spacecraft hard to the right, the sudden acceleration slamming Yukio against his seat. The laser found them again with unerring accuracy.

"*Chikusho*!" Kurosawa shouted. "*Chu-i-san*! Give me a solution!"

Yukio was struggling to plug new numbers into the equations, taking into account the last violent change of lateral vector. Whatever drift to left or right the fighter had, the missiles would possess as well. He bit off a curse. They were still a long way from the American station . . . but it would take too long to try to work closer. "Firing solution!" he announced, fingers stroking the touch panel on the console as he programmed both missiles. "Missiles programmed and ready to fire!"

"Missile release!" Kurosawa announced. Yukio felt the slight hum and thump as the underside of *Inaduma*'s wings opened wide, and the sleek, three-meter white arrows drifted free.

"Missiles clear, Commander," Yukio announced. "You may trigger ignition."

"*Banzai*!" Kurosawa shouted, and the others in the cockpit joined him to complete the traditional chorus of three. "*Banzai! Banzai!*"

Yukio glanced forward again in time to see two brilliant suns whip out from under the *Inaduma*'s nose and dwindle rapidly into the blackness ahead.

"Tanegashima, this is *Taka* One," he said. "Missiles away. . . .''

The three men waited breathlessly as the missiles continued their run. At least the enemy laser fire had ceased. Shepard's radar would have announced the launch of the two missiles, and the Americans would have shifted targets. After nearly a minute, Yukio read the telltale flicker of numbers on his screen and shook his head. "Missile one has been destroyed. Objective is shifting the attack to missile two."

It wasn't going to work. With four missiles, Shepard's defenses might have been overwhelmed . . . but *Taka* Two had been knocked out of action before they could get their *Hayabusas* into the game. If the Americans destroyed both of *Taka* One's missiles, they would have to attempt to close and engage the enemy with the gatling cannon in the spaceplane's nose, an attempt that would almost certainly be fatal.

"Stand by to detonate the warhead, *Chu-i-san*," Kurosawa said.

"*Hai!*" Yukio had already flipped open the second of two large, yellow-and-black-striped protective covers on his console, exposing a large, red button. His thumb hovered above it, waiting . . . waiting . . .

"Range to target, two-five kilometers," he announced. "Target has acquired the missile."

"Trigger the warhead," Kurosawa said. "Now!"

Yukio pressed the button and, hundreds of kilometers ahead, the *Hayabusa*'s warhead detonated.

The warhead was a special type designed for antisatellite warfare, with explosives packed behind a cluster of heavy, steel ball bearings. The explosion hurled the bearings forward in a large and deadly cloud, like the blast from a titanic shotgun. By detonating the warhead far short of the optimum range, Major Kurosawa was taking a chance, gambling that enough of the ball bearings would still hit the target to do critical damage. Like an actual shotgun blast, the shot began spreading as soon as it was fired; where detonation at a range of several hundred meters would have fired nearly one hundred steel balls into the target with a velocity difference great enough to shred the Shepard Station's hull, detonation at a range of almost twenty-five kilometers meant that *Taka* One would be lucky if they hit with ten. Or five. Or even one. . . .

It also meant that the software AI running the enemy laser was momentarily confused. One large and deadly target on an intercept course had just been replaced by a hundred tiny targets, each one relatively harmless by itself. For nearly one second, the program analyzed courses and drift, arriving at the conclusion that not more than eight of the oncoming spheres would collide with the station proper.

It therefore gave the projectiles a lower threat rating and shifted aim back to the original target . . . the *Inaduma* spaceplane still approaching on an intercept vector.

Aboard *Taka* One, Yukio was just about to report that the missile had detonated successfully when the cockpit abruptly filled with a heavenly, glorious light, a blinding, blue-white radiance unlike anything Yukio had ever seen before. He had no time to scream, no time even to feel pain as his helmet visor cracked and his eyes melted and most of his skull burned away.

Then, a tenth of a second later, uneven heating of the cockpit surface shattered the tough plastic, the space-plane tumbled forward, and the half-megawatt beam ate through to a large tank of liquid oxygen—part of the craft's fuel-cell reserves—just below and aft of the crew compartment.

2228 hours GMT

The explosion was clearly visible to the men aboard the American military station, even without the telescope, a silent flare of white light against the peaceful blue backdrop of Earth. "Got the bastard!" Dahlgren cried.

Moments later, six projectiles the size of ball bearings smashed through Shepard's thin hull like bullets fired through cardboard.

Marine Orbital Strike Force
International Space Station
2235 hours GMT

Fuentes was not outside when the Japanese Lightnings were destroyed. The SCRAMjet transport *McCutcheon* had arrived on schedule, and half of the Marines standing watch over the ISS had gone aboard. A rotation schedule had been set up, allowing the Marines of the MOSF to spend six hours at a stretch inside a pressurized environment where they could take off their armor and enjoy some downtime. Fuentes had stayed outside for as long as her life support could take it, then gone inside with the last rotation.

The initial battle had been savage but mercifully brief, a necessary result of the sheer deadliness of combat in vacuum. Five Marines had been killed. Three more had missed the station in their headlong charge across space or been knocked away by careless bursts from their ATARs, but all of them either had managed to reverse course and make it back to the ISS or, in the case of Private Bagley, had been picked up by the *Thornton* on Search and Rescue and brought back to the *McCutcheon*.

The exact number of UN combatants at the ISS was unknown. Three bodies had been recovered, but it was believed that at least two others had been killed as well. The fighting, Fuentes thought, had been eerily like something out of eighteenth-century naval warfare and the very beginnings of the Marine Corps's history, with troops clinging to the rigging and spars of the station to blaze away at one another, sometimes at almost point-blank range.

With the enemy withdrawn inside the station, the battle had reverted to something out of an even earlier time, the siege of a medieval castle. The attackers couldn't get in without destroying what they wanted to capture; the defenders couldn't get out without risking being overwhelmed. Intelligence reports relayed to the Marines from Cheyenne Mountain indicated that a European

SCRAMjet orbital transport was apparently being read-
ied at their primary CSG launch site at Kourou in French
Guiana.

That transport would have reinforcements—probably
too many for the MOSF to handle. Only the presence of
the High-Energy Laser aboard Shepard Station was dis-
couraging them from launching. Cheyenne thought that
the Japanese fighter attack had been intended to knock
Shepard and its laser out, clearing the way for the arrival
of UN reinforcements.

And there was one piece of extremely disturbing
news. While the rest of the Marines aboard *McCutcheon*
were still cheering the news of the destruction of the
Japanese fighters, Captain Fitzgerald, *McCutcheon*'s
commander, had taken her aside and quietly told her that
Shepard Station's radio was off the air—knocked out,
apparently, by the impact of several projectiles fired by
one of the Japanese space fighters during the attack. That
could mean simply that their communications had been
knocked off-line. It could also mean, however, that Colonel Dahlgren and Major Lance were dead, the station's
HEL smashed, and the Marine Orbital Strike Force's one
ace in the hole permanently out of the game. There was
no way to tell just by looking at the station; it continued
to trail the ISS by about twenty kilometers.

But all radio messages from Dahlgren had ceased
abruptly at the moment projectiles from the detonated
Japanese warhead had swept past the station.

The biggest danger now was that the UN would pick
up on the fact that Shepard had fallen silent. According
to Fitzgerald, even moving the *Thornton* over to the
Shepard's vicinity to check out the damage might call
unwanted attention to the fact that the laser seemed to
be off-line. If the UN decided that it was safe to proceed
with the SCRAMjet launch from Kourou, it would only
be another hour or so before local space was swarming
with enemy troops . . . or possibly some more fighters
similar to those downed by Shepard. The Marines would
have no alternative then but to pack up and head back
to Earth.

Fuentes had all of this in mind as she suited up once more and passed through the *McCutcheon*'s airlock into space. Seven Marines were on station outside the ISS at all times now, and care was taken to change the guard at staggered intervals, to avoid providing an attractive target for the UN troops penned up inside.

"Okay, Carlotto," she said, jetting gently across the intervening emptiness toward the station. "Time for you to go take a load off."

"Yessir," Private Carlotto replied. "Man, it stinks inside this armor, y'know?"

"It's getting about that bad on the *McCutcheon*," she said. "Just think about hot showers when we get back to Earth."

"What're you tryin' to do, L-T?" Gunnery Sergeant Walsh told her. "Ruin morale? I've been doing nothing for the past three hours but float here thinking of hot showers."

"That's what we're fighting for, Gunny," she replied. "Hot showers and all the soap we want."

Walsh rose on silent pulses of his MMU jets, his armor changing swiftly from ink black to mottled silver and blue as he cleared the station's shadow and began picking up some of the light reflecting off the Earth and the lit portions of the station. With Walsh at her side, Fuentes let herself drift slowly along the length of the ISS, her boots less than two meters from the uneven white surface. The central part of the ISS was a jumble of lab modules, some showing various flags of participating countries, including Japan, France, and Russia. The largest structures were converted Shuttle II external tanks, most of which were currently being used for storage of either consumables or rocket fuel or water hauled up from Earth. The end facing Earth included the ISS bridge, a turretlike structure with several windows set just above the main docking collar, where a European Hermes remained docked to the station. The lights inside had been shut down, and there was little to be seen through the windows.

Fuentes continued drifting along the station's length,

past the vast, black expanse of the solar panels, where Marines had successfully cut the power cables and robbed the ISS of its main source of energy. The far end of the ISS, away from the Earth, was the original Alfa module. There were five separate airlocks on the station besides the one currently occupied by the European shuttle, each of them guarded by at least one Marine. Three of those five locks were located on the Alfa complex, however, and if UN troops were going to attempt a sortie, that was a good spot to try it from. The big trouble in attacking either into or out of the ISS was the bottlenecks imposed by the airlocks. If only a couple of troops at a time could pass through them, it would be simple for the other side to pick them off one at a time.

She was floating above the Alfa complex when something struck the side of her armor.

At first, she couldn't see what was happening. Then she realized with a start that part of the Alfa assembly was drifting away from the rest.

No, it wasn't a part of Alfa, not quite. A lifeboat, one of the original winged pods intended as escape capsules in case of orbital disaster, had been nestled against the last module in line. Now, however, the lifeboat was drifting clear; the fragment that had struck Fuentes's armor was a bit of metal or paint thrown clear by the silent detonation of a small explosive charge of some kind. And in the next instant, she knew what was happening.

"Heads up, Marines!" she called over the general frequency. "The bad guys are coming out, Alfa-end!"

"Minsky! Ortega!" Walsh added. "Everybody! Get your asses down here! They've blown the lifeboat clear and are using the whole damned Alfa complex as a giant lock!"

As he spoke, the first blue-helmeted troopers drifted into view, rising out of the widening gap between Alfa and the escape pod. Hell, they must have depressurized half of Alfa, crowded as many troops inside as they could, then blown emergency release charges on the lifeboat to open up. There could be a lot of soldiers coming out in one big mob.

Fuentes braced her ATAR, acquired a target, and fired. She missed, and a slight imprecision in her aim set her tumbling to the left. Reaching out, she managed to snag a guy wire bracing part of the keel structure, arrest her tumble, and anchor herself against a keel strut. With her legs gripping the strut, she was able to raise the ATAR in both hands without worrying about balance, drag the crosshairs on her HUD's video inset across an oncoming armored figure, and squeeze the trigger.

The effect was satisfactorily gory, with the UN trooper's helmet torn open and a pink haze of freezing blood and air spilling into nearby space, as the man's body spun in the opposite direction. A second UN soldier came in behind the first, firing as he moved and doing a pretty good job of keeping the weapon's butt plate squarely on his center of mass. Fuentes felt the shock as bullets struck the strut she was clinging to, but she acquired target and returned fire without flinching; there was no place to duck in this alien battleground, no foxholes, no protective cover.

Walsh floated in and anchored himself nearby. "Think they'll add a verse to the Marine Corps Hymn?" he asked, squeezing off a short burst.

"Hell, they'd better," Fuentes replied, adding her fire to his. "I don't like the unsung hero bit."

"Me neither." He fired again. "Everyone who can make it is on the way. If we can hold 'em—"

But there were blue helmets everywhere she looked, and they were closing in. There were only three or four Marines on this end of the ISS, counting the two of them, and they were badly outnumbered.

Which, of course, would have been the UN commander's plan. Storm out all at once, overwhelm the few Marines you find around your exit point, then disperse and gun down the rest as they approach. A simple, almost elegant solution to what must have seemed like an insoluble tactical problem.

But Fuentes was determined to screw up their plan *somehow*.

With the strut as an anchoring point, she could be a lot freer with her gunfire, while the approaching blue-tops had to be careful with their bursts lest they set themselves spinning or tumbling out of control. Several of them were already out of the fight, at least for the moment, because of an incautious burst from their rifles. Fuentes ignored them, concentrating on the armored figures who seemed to be handling themselves well in microgravity. One emerged from beyond the end of Alfa carrying what could only have been a bulky, backpack-powered laser rifle; she drew careful aim on that one before he could bring the weapon into play, sending a long, savage burst ripping through his torso armor and helmet and nearly tearing him in half.

Then the rest of the Marines were arriving, drifting in on high-pressure nitrogen jets as fast as tiny fighter planes, giving no thought to slowing, to hiding, to anything except breaking that enemy formation. Two more UN blue-helmets tumbled out of the battle like string-cut puppets . . . followed by a third. Several more were taking cover amid the struts and crossbeams of the ISS keel, trying to anchor themselves to return fire on the advancing Marines, but enough of them had been hit or panicked that their fire was scattered and inaccurate.

When she turned, Fuentes saw the *McCutcheon* bearing down on them, a huge black-and-white, flattened dart casting a black shadow across half of the ISS as it edged forward, spilling additional Marines from its airlock as it came. Fitzgerald had recognized the danger, and the Marines on board were suiting up as fast as they could, entering the battle as Fitzgerald brought them closer despite the wild gunfire from the UN defenders.

Gunny Walsh turned to face Fuentes. She could see his grin through his dark helmet visor. "Well, Lieutenant," he said. "I think we—"

His helmet visor starred, a white, frosted slash appearing across the dark plastic like a shocking splash of paint; a UN round had passed between them, just grazing his visor. Somehow, miraculously, the thin, tinted plastic didn't crack . . . yet. But tiny flakes were spilling from

the frosted surface, and she could see Walsh's eyes wide
with shock and fear beyond.

"My helmet!" he screamed in her headset. "Christ,
my helmet! It's going to—"

"Quiet, Marine!" she shouted back. "Don't panic!
Don't *move*!" Almost without thinking, she grabbed him
by the arm, pivoting them both in space until he was in
front of her, then triggering her MMU jets and setting
them both in motion. A round hit her suit—she felt a
violent blow above her left hip that kicked her to one
side, but she still had air and she ignored it, steering the
two of them toward the open end of the ISS.

It was, she reasoned, the closest airlock, and the most
accessible. There might be another twenty UN troops
inside, waiting for some Marine to pull just such a dumb
stunt as this, but she wasn't going to float helplessly by
and watch Gunny Walsh's helmet explode.

She didn't decelerate. Holding tight to Walsh's MMU,
she stretched out with both feet and snagged the lip of
the Alfa module with her boots, pivoting sharply, swinging heads over until they were facing the gaping, cave-
like entryway that had been occupied moments before
by the lifeboat.

Her toehold broke free and the two of them drifted
past the end of the station, falling into a gentle tumble.
Somehow, she managed to jockey her MMU jets until
the tumble was arrested and they were moving forward
once more, this time into the deeply shadowed interior
of Alfa.

Both doors of the docking module lock were open,
and Alfa's interior was open to space. The first compartment, eerily empty, dark, and still, was unoccupied;
a closed hatch at the far end beckoned, just visible beneath a small, orange emergency light.

"It's no good, Lieutenant." Walsh's voice was harsh,
close to cracking. "I'm losing pressure. The inside of
my helmet is frosting over. You'd better leave me."

"*Fuck*, no!" she shouted, her voice sounding loud
and hollow inside the confines of her helmet. She still
remembered Captain Warhurst on the embassy roof, still

had nightmares about him going down as her Peregrine
lifted into the sky.

She wasn't *about* to leave one of her people.

That frost inside his visor was a bad sign, though. As
air expanded, it cooled. The air in Walsh's helmet must
be expanding fast as it leaked through the myriad crazes
and cracks in his visor and into space. He had only seconds now. . . .

She didn't know if anyone was waiting for them on
the other side of that hatch, and at the moment, she
didn't care. The hatch opened the old-fashioned way,
with a locking wheel. She released Walsh long enough
to throw herself against the wheel, bracing her feet on a
deck grating for leverage. If there was pressure on the
other side . . .

There wasn't. The hatch swung open gently. Grabbing
Walsh, who by this time was completely blinded by frost
and might be close to blacking out, she shoved him
through the open hatch and dove through after him.

The next chamber was a small airlock with four
hatches, a kind of joiner module that connected three
other modules to a fourth. With the hatch dogged down
behind her, she turned about desperately, looking for a
pressurization control, unable to find one—

She turned Walsh, intending to move him aside in the
cramped quarters, and saw with horror that a piece of
his visor the size of her hand had shattered, the pieces
of tinted plastic and ice scattering in a glittering, tumbling cloud. His eyes stared at her, bugging from his
face in terror, his mouth wide-open, the lips bright blue
as he tried to draw breath. Too late! *Too late!* . . .

And then she realized that there was something
strange. He was breathing. With difficulty, yes, but he
was *breathing*, his mouth gasping like a fish on land as
he gulped down lungfuls of air. Only then did her armor's external mikes pick up the faint but growing hiss
of air pouring in through a duct close by their heads.
She hadn't found the control; someone inside must have
seen them coming in and triggered it for her.

Her suit's visor advised her moments later that there

was breathable atmosphere outside, standard temperature and pressure. With a creak and a bang, the hatchway opposite the one they'd come through swung open.

Fuentes still had her ATAR, attached to her suit by its lanyard, but she hesitated in bringing it up. She didn't know at the moment whether it would be better to storm through firing or go ahead and surrender; the whole purpose of this exercise, after all, had been to get Gunny Walsh into atmosphere, and this she had done. It grated, though, to simply turn over her weapon and give up. . . .

A young, tanned, blond, male face peered through the open hatch at her, just visible by the wan light of an emergency lantern. "Come on aboard, Marine," the man said. "We've been expecting you."

She wiggled through the narrow hatch. There were three men on the other side, one holding an automatic pistol. A fourth man floated in a corner, blood smeared across his face.

"I'm Colonel Gresham," the man with the pistol said. "US Aerospace Force."

"Colonel Gresham?"

"Commander of this station," he said. "Welcome aboard . . . and I mean that, very sincerely!"

She unfastened her helmet. It was steamy hot inside the station, a testimony to the effectiveness of the Marine siege and the cutting of power. There were no lights on at all save for small emergency lights at key points. "What's the tacsit?"

"Nearly all of them went out that way a few minutes ago," Gresham replied. "There are only two or three UNers left aboard, I think." He jerked a thumb at the body in the corner. "He was on guard here and was going to leave you in the lock, but we persuaded him otherwise."

"Thanks," she said. She was floating next to Walsh, checking his breathing. The gunnery sergeant was conscious, still breathing hard but able to nod at her when she touched his face. "For both of us."

"It sounded like their attack was a last effort," Gresham said. "I think they knew they weren't going to get any help from Earth, and decided on a last do-or-die charge.''

''It almost worked,'' she said. She pointed at a radio on the bulkhead. ''You have power enough for that?''

''Sure do.''

''Okay. Use Channel 15. Talk to the Marines outside, and have them start coming in through here.''

''While you? . . .''

''Have a chat with the people at the other end of this thing.''

Gresham hefted the pistol he'd taken from the UN soldier. ''I'll come with you.''

''Right.'' She put her helmet back on, switching on the headlamps to cast a harsh, yellow glow in the direction in which she was looking. They left Walsh with one of the Americans, while the other took Walsh's ATAR. Close together, in single file, the three made their way through the silent, stifling space station, getting all the way to the other end before they encountered anyone. Fuentes saw a movement against a lighted window and called out, ''Hold it! US Marines!''

She heard a Gallic sigh in the darkness. ''I suppose it had to be. Very well, US Marines. We surrender.''

There were just two UN troops left, Colonel Cuvier and his aide, a Captain Laveau, not counting the members of the regular station crew.

It seemed like anticlimax. Fuentes's heart was still hammering beneath her breastbone, and she was keyed up with a battle lust unlike anything she'd ever felt before in her life. As Gresham held the prisoners at gunpoint, she made her way to the control-deck radio. ''Cheyenne Mountain, Cheyenne Mountain,'' she called. ''This is the American Space Station Freedom. The Marines have landed and have the situation well in hand.''

She'd always wanted to say that. . . .

TWENTY-TWO

Garroway
Candor Chasma
Sol 5656: 0838 hours MMT

They'd broken out of the narrow canyon that stretched across the Martian desert from Tithonium eighteen days after leaving Heinlein Station, and then, at last, the MMEF had started to move. On the desert flats beyond the canyon, they'd raced along at a relatively high speed, their drag sled raising a whirling cloud of dust behind them as they ground across endless sand flats and dunes beneath the towering expanses of red-and-tan-banded cliffs four kilometers high.

After three weeks, to say they all were tired, dirty, hungry, or thirsty would have been grievous understatement. Some of them could barely stand, so bad were the blisters and contact sores at various places on their bodies, where the armor had been rubbing almost constantly. Their destination, however, was nearly in sight.

Early in the predawn hours of the twenty-first sol of the march, they deployed from the Mars cat. Four of the Marines—Lazenby, Hayes, Petrucci, and Follet—no longer had working armor. For a time, they'd tried trading off with other Marines, but space was so cramped it was easier to simply take them off the watch list and let them enjoy the relative luxury of living in their fatigues again. Two more, Kennemore and Witek, had such bad sores on their legs and backs that Doc Casey had recommended both men be taken off duty and out of their suits.

Those six, then, plus the three civilians, all remained with the Mars cat, with Corporal Hayes at the controls, while the rest of the Marines clambered out through the airlock for one last time and trudged their footsore way across the sand, leaving the crawler behind.

Garroway and King had carefully checked the terrain ahead using the maps left aboard the crawler. Mars Prime was located two hundred kilometers from the point where the narrow, straight-line fault canyon opened into the far vaster and emptier basin known as Candor Chasma. They'd already traversed about 180 of those kilometers in just the past two days, making a brisk eight to ten kilometers per hour. They now estimated that the base was less than twenty kilometers ahead.

Twenty kilometers. About twelve miles. They could *walk* that far if they had to.

Once the Marines were moving ahead on foot, Hayes started up the Mars cat again and followed, but slowly, meandering along at a stately three kilometers per hour, a speed so slow that even with blisters the Marines outside could easily outpace the cat. The sled, empty of people now but still weighted down with crates and canisters, raised its signature cloud of dust as it dragged along in the crawler's tracks. It wasn't too long, then, before Sergeant Jacob, on point, spotted an answering cloud of dust to the east. He signaled the rest of the Marine column, which swung to the south and took cover behind a low, sandy ridge. Twenty minutes later, as the Mars cat trundled slowly past the ridge, two more Mars cats appeared out of their dust clouds, racing along at 20 kph from the direction of Mars Prime.

The Marine crawler halted, dust still hanging in a red-

gray pall above and behind the gently purring vehicle.
The two new crawlers halted as well thirty meters away.
A few moments later, airlocks opened, and blue-
helmeted troopers began filing out.

0946 HOURS GMT

Kaminski
Candor Chasma
0905 hours MMT

Lance Corporal Kaminski lay on his stomach at the top
of the ridge, watching through his rifle's sighting camera
with a vid-feed to his helmet's HUD as the UNdies ex-
ited their tractors. It looked like there was a total of
about fifteen UN troops, all armed. That put the Marines
at a serious disadvantage; of the twenty-one Marines on
the ridge, only four had ATARs, rifles taken from their
former guards so long ago at Heinlein Station.

Surprise, however, counted for a very great deal. Kaminski turned his helmet so that he could see the major,
crouched behind the ridgetop a few meters away.

By this time, Kaminski didn't know a single man or
woman in the platoon who wouldn't have died for the
old man on the spot if he'd given them the word. Something about the shared hardships of the past three weeks
had welded the platoon together in a way unimaginable
before, even after the seven months of sardine-can duty
aboard the cycler. If anyone blamed the major for the
pain and danger of the march, he wasn't saying a word,
and a good thing, too. The platoon was definitely gung
ho—a Corps term from duty in China over a century
before that, very roughly, translated as "all together."
The MMEF platoon was *definitely* gung ho in that sense
and wouldn't have tolerated anyone knocking their new
CO.

Kaminski returned his full attention to the rifle. Garroway had run trials out in the desert a week ago, as-
certaining that the four best shots under Martian
conditions were Ostrowsky, Knox, Caswell . . . and him.

The discovery filled him with a galloping pride. The others were all seasoned vets and senior NCOs; you'd *expect* them to be crack shots. The fact that he'd beaten out everyone else definitely gave him bragging rights.

He liked it. After he'd turned over his carefully hidden flag, back at Heinlein Station, in fact, some of the other Marines had started talking about him like he was some sort of super Marine, a real lifer. That was nonsense, of course. He was still getting out as soon as he hit Earth again. But it was a real kick to get to do the John Wayne bit. He and the three NCOs had been given the platoon's four ATARs and spaced evenly along the ridge so that their fire would hit the UN troops from front and rear as well as from their left. Now they were just waiting for the—

"*Now!*" Garroway's voice said in his headset, breaking the carefully preserved radio silence.

Kaminski already had the green crosshairs on his HUD centered over one of the UN troops. His glove clamped down on the rifle's trigger, and he felt rather than heard the silky hiss of five rounds snapping from his muzzle. The man in his HUD display staggered, then flopped forward. Kaminski was aware now of the sound of gunfire, a harsh snapping in the thin Martian air. Two more of the UN troops fell . . . then a third. The others stared around wildly, trying to find where this sudden storm of death was coming from, and a fourth spun, threw up his hands, and crumpled onto the sand.

The rest dropped to the ground, still trying to find targets at which they could return the fire. Several opened fire at the Mars cat, but Hayes already had the vehicle in motion, gunning it forward at high speed, treads whirling, flag fluttering from the whip antenna, sand and dust boiling into the sky like an impenetrable smoke screen.

Hayes steered the cat in a wild, slewing arc that took it between the hidden Marines and the UN troops; as soon as the dust cloud blocked all view of the enemy, Garroway stood up and waved. "Come on! After me!"

Kaminski rose, aiming from the hip and squeezing off

another five-round burst. All along the sandy ridge, weary men and women in armor showing the red-ocher hues of the Martian landscape staggered to their feet and started jogging down the north slope of the ridge. Everyone in the platoon had volunteered to make the charge; even unarmed, they might be able to draw fire from the Marines with rifles . . . and if a rifleman fell, there would be someone to pick up his weapon and carry on.

With jolting, sand-slipping bounds, Kaminski rushed toward the lead tractor. A figure materialized out of the dust ahead, little more than a shadow, then stumbled and collapsed as Ostrowsky sprayed it with a burst of caseless rounds. Kaminski slowed as they entered the dust cloud, watching each step . . . and careful now to identify targets before shooting randomly.

"*Ooh-rah!*" Kaminski bellowed over the tac channel, an ancient Marine battle cry. "*Marines!*"

0950 HOURS GMT

Garroway
Candor Chasma
0909 hours MMT

Garroway reached the UN Mars cat, putting out one hand to touch it. A SIG-Sauer P-940 pistol with the trigger guard removed lay on the sand and he scooped it up. The fight, though, was all but over. Other Marines were finding ATARs and lasers on the ground next to dead or dying UN troopers; the four armed Marines became six, then ten. A brief, savage exchange of gunfire in the smoky darkness of the dust cloud killed two more UN soldiers and sent a round through Sergeant Steve Abrell's right arm. Air was shrieking through the bloody holes punched in his armor, but Casey reached him in time with a roll of vacuum-seal duct tape, winding the heavy gray plastic around and around the damaged area until the air stopped leaking. Abrell was unconscious, but his armor readout showed he was stabilizing as Casey fed him more O_2 from his life-support pack. He would be okay, if they could get him into a pressurized environment soon.

"*Nicht schiessen! Nicht schiessen!*"

"Don't shoot! I surrender!"

The dust was settling out of the air now, the cloud thinning. The few blue-tops still standing were surrendering, dropping their weapons and raising their hands high. Ostrowsky and Knox, both according to plan, each entered a different UN cat and took the drivers prisoner. In seconds, then, the skirmish was over, the surviving UN troops disarmed and sitting on the ground.

Twenty-one US Marines, with a little help from the decoy Mars cat, had killed nine UN-service Foreign Legion troops and captured eight, at a cost of one man wounded.

It was, Garroway thought, a fitting end to an epic march that ought to be remembered right there alongside the Corps's saga of O'Bannon and the Marines at Derna.

The recapture of Mars Prime was a relatively simple and straightforward affair. Questioning the prisoners separately, Garroway learned that there were only five UN troops left at Candor, while all of the rest—a total of some thirty troops plus the European scientists working for the UN—were at Cydonia.

It was a foregone conclusion that one or both of the UN cat drivers had gotten a warning off to Mars Prime, and by now, Cydonia would be alerted as well. The Marines would have to move fast.

They were able to drive right into the Candor base, steering all three cats to the vehicle bay where they parked them. Garroway had half expected a fight at the vehicle bay airlock, but when the Marines rushed through, weapons at the ready, they encountered only a curious crowd of scientists, NASA workers, and Russian technicians. As the Marines staggered into the base proper and began pulling off their helmets, the crowd burst into spontaneous applause, an applause that swelled rapidly to cheers and shouts until the large base entry foyer started taking on an almost carnival atmosphere. Several of the Marines got kissed by female techs and scientists, despite their clumsy armor and the inescapable stink of twenty-one days without washing or even shedding their armor. Some of the techs had managed to hand-letter crude signs on cardboard: WELCOME US MARINES! and USA! were the most prevalent.

The lounge area was a kind of solarium, with translucent ceiling panels that flooded the converted external tank with warm, morning light; it was equipped with foam-molded chairs and tables that gave the place an almost homey feeling. The Marines were met at the table by a smiling Captain Gregory Barnes, the MMEF's supply officer, plus the two Marines who'd volunteered to hop back to Candor to assist him, Corporal Jack "Slider" Slidell and Lance Corporal Ben Fulbert.

"Hello, Greg," Garroway said, extending a hand. He was still wearing his torso armor, but he'd left arm and leg pieces in the cat, along with his helmet. He was already beginning to harbor fantasies about never having to wear that hated Class-One armor again. "Haven't seen you in an age or two."

"My God, Major!" Barnes replied. "It's good to see you! You were reported lost and presumed dead, you know."

"No, I didn't."

"As you can imagine, sir," Ostrowsky added, "we've been kind of cut off from the news."

"The UN people running the show, well, they didn't admit you people had left the base where they'd marooned you, at first . . . but they brought those two scientists, Vandemeer and Kettering, back here, and after a while the word was out that you people had pulled a vanishing trick right into the desert."

"Glad to hear those two made it back, anyway. I was worried about them."

"Oh, they're fine. Holed up with their UN buddies now, I imagine, up in the commo shack. Anyway, everybody knew you were out there, though the UN brass wasn't saying a word. Then a couple of weeks ago there was a big dust storm . . ."

"Yeah. It nearly buried us for good."

"Well, there'd been a lot of activity out of here, Mars cats on patrol and shuttles going out and back. I think they were hunting for you pretty thoroughly. Then they made the announcement, usual rigmarole, that they regretted to inform us that Major Garroway and twenty-four Marines and three civilian scientists had all been lost in the storm after leaving a shelter without authorization or proper equipment. That was the last any of us heard . . . at least until all the excitement this morning."

"Well, we rode out the storm all right," Garroway said. "Maybe they really thought we were dead. Or they just didn't want any of you going out and looking for us."

"That could be. We haven't been prisoners, exactly. . . ."

"But?"

"Yeah. *But*. They took over Control and the commo shack. They claimed there were communications problems with Earth, but everyone knew that was a lie. They put us Marines in a separate cubicle where they could keep an eye on us. Told us we could communicate with Earth 'when the political situation there is clarified.' Yeah. Right."

"What is the political situation, sir?" Lieutenant King wanted to know.

"Damfino. They haven't told us shit."

Suddenly Garroway was possessed by an overwhelming feeling of utter exhaustion. He wiped his face and felt the grime caked there. "We'd better take care of those UN holdouts," Garroway said. "And after that, I think we need to arrange for showers, some serious rack time, and some new uniforms. Oh, and we'll all need med checks. Most of us are carrying some pretty nasty bed sores, from wearing that armor for so long."

Barnes nodded. "I think we can fix you up on all counts. I've already notified Dr. Rybinov." He hesitated, his nose wrinkling. "I hope you'll pardon me saying so, sir, but, God, you *stink*!"

"I think my nose stopped working about three weeks ago, Greg. All I really want right now is a shower, a drink, and a real bed . . . and not necessarily in that order.''

"Begging the major's pardon, sir," Corporal Slidell said, stepping forward, "but, ah, maybe this would help?" He held out a can wet with condensation.

"Slidell—" Barnes said, an edge to his voice. "I warned you. . . ."

Garroway eyed the can suspiciously. "Is that what I think it is, or am I hallucinating?"

"Genuine article, sir," Slidell said proudly. He turned the can so that Garroway could read the label. It was a beer. An honest to God Stony Brook beer.

Gently, Garroway reached out and accepted it, as though afraid it was about to disappear. "So, tell me, Slider," he said, his voice soft. "How is it we seem to have stumbled across the only beer in a hundred million miles?"

Slidell managed to look both embarrassed and smug. "Well, ah, it's sorta like this, sir—"

"These sons of bitches managed to stash a quantity of beer on board the cycler, Major," Barnes said matter-of-factly.

"Smugglers, huh?"

"Aw, shit, sir!" Slidell said. "We just thought, I mean, Ben and me, well, we thought you would like a cold one, comin' in off the desert!"

"You, ah, better have enough of these for everyone who wants one, Corporal."

Slidell's face fell, then brightened again. "Well, sure, sir. I think I could swing that."

"Let's see 'em."

"Yessir! C'mon, Ben. Gimme a hand."

As the two corporals hurried off, Garroway asked the question of Barnes with his eyes.

"It's, ah, kind of a long story, Major."

"I can imagine." He looked at the beer can, turning it over in his hands. "This only violates about twenty or twenty-five Marine and NASA regulations that I can think of offhand." He held the can up close, reading the fine print. " 'Packaged in USA.' I've always known about the penchant Marines have for putting together stills in out-of-the-way locales so they can brew their own. This is the first time I've run into their importing the stuff. How much did they have?''

"About five hundred cans, sir."

"What?"

"Yes, sir. Five hundred cans. In sealed, refrigerated, pressure-sealed cases marked 'BATTERIES, GERMANIUM-ARSENIDE, SERIAL NUMBER 8373635, USMC, DO NOT OPEN.' ''

"And, ah, what vital components were left behind to make room for these batteries, germanium-arsenide?"

"As far as I can tell, sir, none. The listing appears in the regular manifest and was factored in with all the rest. Total mass, two hundred kilos, plus another fifty kilos for the packaging. All I can think is that one or more of these guys had access to the supply depot back at Vandenberg."

Slidell and Fulbert returned a moment later, dragging a large chest filled with cold beer. Garroway knew that he was adding a few violations of his own to the list already accumulated, but right now he didn't give a damn. "Okay, ladies and gentlemen," he said. "Help yourselves, one to a customer."

Only when the beers were being handed out, accompanied by delighted shouts, cheers, and outright laughter, did Garroway pop the top on his and allow himself a cautious sip. Normally, he disliked beer. He'd tried it a time or two when he was younger, more to fit in with his buddies than anything else, but somehow he'd never managed to acquire the taste for the stuff.

This one tasted like pure, sweet, cold nectar. After several small swallows, he studied the can carefully. He was thinking of Lloyd's words back at Cydonia. "Never trust a Marine who volunteers for shit details."

"So, Captain Barnes. Why do you think this man did it?"

"Well, sir, I gather the idea was, if they were going to be stuck on Mars for a year or so, they'd have enough beer squirreled away to let 'em have a cold one every so often. Either that, or they could buy a hell of a lot of favors from the other Marines.''

''Hell, sir, it wasn't nothin' like that!'' Slidell insisted. ''It was just, you know, to kinda remind us of home, and everything.'' He sounded hurt. ''It wasn't like we was smuggling drugs or hustling our buddies or anything.''

Garroway stared at the man. ''You were aware, weren't you, son, that every kilo brought to Mars is precious? I'd guess you have several tens of thousands of dollars of beer here, if you go by the cost of boosting it up from Earth and then hauling it all the way out here on the cycler.''

''We've been over this already, sir,'' Barnes said. ''I found him and Fulbert here sneaking a couple of beers a week ago and got the story out of them then. Maybe I should've put 'em both under arrest, but, well, I couldn't see turning them over to the UN, and, well—''

''You did right, Captain,'' Garroway said. ''Marines take care of their own.''

The way he said the words had a chilling effect on Slidell. ''Uh, really, Major, we didn't mean—''

''Stow it, Marine. For now, consider yourself, both of you, on report. Who else was in this with you?''

''I was, sir,'' Kaminski called out. He looked miserable, his eyes very white within the grime and dirt smearing his face. The only other clean part of his face was the skin around his lips, where a long swallow of beer had washed it off. ''It was the three of us. Nobody else.''

He stared at the man for a long moment. ''I'm disappointed in you, Ski,'' he said. ''You show real potential as a Marine.''

Kaminski's face fell, but Garroway pressed on. Discipline—and even-handedness—were all-important. ''Very well. You're on report, too.'' He allowed himself another sip. God, it *did* taste good. . . .

He drained the last of the beer. He'd been drinking bottled and recycled water for so long that he'd forgotten that anything liquid could have any taste at all. He felt light-headed and wondered if the alcohol of a single can could affect him. Well, maybe it could. He was probably pretty dehydrated, and his stomach was empty. But he was feeling okay.

"All right," he said, setting the empty can back on the table. "You said the rest of the UN people are in the commo shack?"

"Yessir," Barnes replied. "I think someone in one of those crawlers they sent out to bring you in must have called in that things weren't going so well for 'em. The word went out over the PA for all UN personnel to report to the comm room, and that's the last we've seen of any of them."

"Well, I'd say it's about time we paid them a visit, don't you?"

"Sounds like a plan to me, sir."

The UN troops and personnel in the commo shack surrendered without a shot being fired or anything, in fact, stronger than a threat to blow the door in. As they were being led out, Garroway walked in and checked the consoles. It wouldn't take long, he thought, to plug in a new set of encryption keys and get full communications working once again with Earth.

"You might as well surrender now, Major Garroway."

Garroway looked up, surprised. Colonel Bergerac's clean and clean-shaven features stared down at him from the comm center's main screen. He was suddenly aware of just how dirty, disheveled, and out-and-out seedy he must look. "Hello, Colonel," he said. "How do you figure *I* should surrender to *you*?"

"Obviously, you were able to ambush my men in the desert this morning, but you cannot think you could do that again, with me. I have thirty men here, and we will know when you are coming." He smiled. "Unless, of course, you'd care to try the overland route once more. I don't think, somehow, you would find five thousand kilometers as easy to cross as 650. You certainly don't look as though you would survive!"

"Don't bet on it, Bergerac," Garroway growled. "We have the main base now. You're cut off. Surrender now."

"You don't understand, my friend. We have plenty of food here, and extensive permafrost to provide us with all the water and fuel we need. We have more troops on the way, and they'll be here in five months." He gave a Gallic shrug. "In the meantime, we have the ruins here, the whole reason for Man's presence on this planet, under our control. And, not to put too fine a point on it, we have two Marines here, including your commanding officer, as well as a number of American civilians. I suggest that everyone would be spared a great deal of pain and trouble if you would submit to United Nations authority on this."

"And let you dump us back in the desert? Not damned likely!"

"Perhaps that was a mistake, monsieur. We can work out another arrangement."

Garroway was too tired for subtlety. "The hell with it. I'm coming after you, Bergerac, you and that Joubert bitch, and when I catch you I'm going to kick both your asses." He raised a finger, in warning. "And if any of our people are harmed, I, as acting military governor of this base, will declare you and all of your people to be in violation of the UN Act to Condemn International Terrorism. You will be tried as terrorists and summarily executed. My recommendation will be that you just be tossed out the nearest airlock. Have you seen people die of asphyxiation on the Martian surface? I have, and it's not pleasant. I'd really hate to see that happen to you. . . ."

"Empty threats, Major. You have done well, but you can do no more. If you elect to wait until our reinforcements arrive, you will find yourself in a box, with no way out."

"I'll see you at Cydonia, Colonel." But the channel was already closed.

Garroway stared at the blank display screen for several long seconds, lost in thought. Lieutenant King appeared at his side. "You think the bastard meant it, sir?" he asked. "Would they hurt the colonel?"

"I doubt it, Lieutenant. But the fact remains, Marines don't leave their people to the enemy. I *want* Cydonia."

"But if they know we're coming, sir. . . ."

"Yeah, that is a problem." He was silent for another several moments. "Okay. Pass the word for me, King. I want all our senior people up here for a planning session. And . . . ask Dr. Alexander to come, too."

"Shouldn't . . . shouldn't we let our people get some rest, sir?"

"We'll get our rest. But I want to talk to them first. See if you can scare up a map of Cydonia for me."

"Aye, aye, sir."

He wanted another beer. He wanted it very badly. A plan was forming, and he didn't know if it was rising from his exhaustion or from the unpredictable effects of alcohol on his dehydrated system. He was betting that it was the alcohol, though, and another beer might jog the thing to fullness.

At least, he was going to give it a damned good try.

TWENTY-THREE

Kaminski
Mars Prime
Candor Chasma
Sol 5657: 1530 hours MMT

Thirty hours after the MMEF's triumphant return to
Mars Prime, all of the Marines on base, with the exception of those on radar or comm watch or outside on
perimeter sentry duty, drew up in formation in the
lounge area near the main lock. Kaminski, clean and
depilated now, stood at parade rest in his freshly laun-
dered BDUs between Slidell and Fulbert. In front of
them, behind a plastic table, Major Garroway sat with
his PAD and an unopened can of beer in front of him.
Kaminski tried not to look at Garroway but kept his eyes
carefully fixed on an imaginary point somewhere above
and behind the major's head.

In addition to the three Marines, the proceedings this
afternoon had drawn quite a large crowd of civilians.
The novelty of having US Marines at the base, evidently,
hadn't worn off yet.

"Very well," Garroway said, studying the three.
"Corporal Slidell, Lance Corporal Fulbert, Lance Corporal Kaminski. You three have a choice. You can vol-

untarily accept nonjudicial punishment, right here, right now, before me. Or, if you prefer, your cases will be held over for further investigation at such time as we return to Earth. At that time, depending on the findings of the Judge Advocate General's office, you may be remanded for court-martial. What's it going to be?''

What he was offering them was a choice between accepting whatever punishment he chose to give them, and going the whole trial route, complete with lawyers and the possibility of a much heavier punishment at the end.

"Uh, we'll go along with the NJP, sir," Slidell said.

"Fulbert? Kaminski? You both agree to this?"

"Yes, *sir*!" Kaminski replied, chorusing his answer with Fulbert.

"Very good. I think we can sort this thing out pretty simply. You've all three been charged with a variety of crimes, including negligence, reckless endangerment, possession of a controlled substance, unauthorized access to company records, fraud, dereliction of duty . . .''

He stopped, pausing to read something on his PAD, probably their service records. Kaminski was sweating, despite the cool temperature in the compartment. "Under the circumstances," Garroway continued, "I have decided to drop all charges except one, and that is conduct prejudicial to good order and discipline."

Kaminski's knees sagged, and his heart gave a surprised leap. If Garroway had wanted to, he could have hit them very hard indeed on the smuggling and reckless-endangerment charges. Conduct prejudicial was the age-old catchall charge, the one that could be stretched or chopped to fit just about anything the commanding officer wanted.

"Now," Garroway said. "Where did the beer come from in the first place?"

"Uh, we bought it, sir," Slidell said. "We all chipped in and bought it before we left Earth."

"Do any of the three of you have anything to say in your own defense?"

"No, sir," Slidell said.

"We did it, sir," Fulbert said.

"No excuse, sir," Kaminski added. He was relieved that Slidell was behaving himself. The guy had a sea lawyer's attitude that could have gotten them all in real trouble. A couple of hours ago, though, Fulbert and Kaminski together had gone to Slider and told him in no uncertain terms that they weren't going to go along with his nonsense, not this time. They would take their lumps and not try to wiggle out. Somehow, he didn't think they could put much of anything over on Major Garroway. The guy was *sharp*.

"Anybody else have anything to say, one way or the other?"

"Uh, Major," Captain Barnes said. "I'll just say that these three are good men and hard workers. Neither Slidell nor Fulbert gave me any trouble while they were assigned here."

"I've taken their records into account, Captain." He looked at the three, then reached out, picked up the unopened can of beer, and brought it down sharply on the tabletop. "I find you three guilty as charged under the Uniform Code of Military Justice. All three of you are reduced in rank one grade, and restricted to base, save for necessary military duties, for fourteen days. You are also assigned extra duty for the next fourteen days, at your commanding officer's discretion. The, ah, contraband, of course, is forfeit."

Slidell's face fell at that, but at this point, Kaminski didn't give a damn about the beer. The major had all but let them off with a slap on the wrist.

"Do any of the three of you have anything to add?"

They didn't.

"Your first assigned extra duty will be to load the contraband—all of it—on board *Harper's Bizarre*. Captain Barnes will tell you what needs to be done. Dismissed!"

Fourteen days restriction, when there wasn't a damned place to go on this planet anyway? A one-grade reduction when enlisted rank was all but meaningless anyway? They'd gotten off scot-free!

Then he realized that he and Fulbert were now the

only PFCs in a platoon heavy with corporals and sergeants, a private's natural enemies.

And two weeks of cleaning out the heads. Maybe they hadn't gotten off *completely* free. . . .

                                        1705 HOURS GMT

Garroway
Mars Prime
Candor Chasma
1537 hours MMT

As the three turned and walked away, Alexander unfolded his arms. "You went pretty easy on them, didn't you, Major?"

"I'll say he did," Sergeant Ostrowsky said, laughing. "Being restricted to base on Mars doesn't mean a damned thing when there's no place else to go anyway!"

"There's no real point," Garroway said. "Technically, I suppose what they did constituted reckless endangerment, but we had a big enough safety margin in what we brought along and in our assigned mass allotment that no harm was done."

Captain Barnes nodded. "They also didn't go and get blind drunk, which some in their situation might have done. In fact, about the only thing I see they did that was really reprehensible was the two of them volunteering to come down here and give me a hand."

"Yes," Garroway said, grinning, "and in so doing, missing out on getting captured and going for a long walk in the Martian desert." He shook his head. "I may never forgive them that one."

"So why the nice-guy routine, Major?" Gunny Knox wanted to know. He rubbed his newly beardless chin. "Hell, back in the *old* Marines, those three'd've been skinned alive and hung out to dry."

"The way I see it, Gunny, those three have contributed significantly to our effort here. In fact, they may

have provided us with exactly what we need to beat
Bergerac and his people.''

"What, sir?" Ostrowsky said, puzzled. "We're going
to give the UNers beer in exchange for the colonel?"

"Not quite, Sergeant. But we now have something we
need very badly."

"What's that, Major?" Alexander asked.

"What every Marine prays for." Garroway grinned.
"Close air support."

                                    1833 HOURS GMT

Mars Prime
Candor Chasma
1625 hours MMT

David Alexander was on his way to the base communications center when someone called to him from behind. "Hey! David! Wait up!"

He stopped and turned. It was Craig Kettering.

"Hello, Craig."

"I've been looking for a chance to talk to you! Welcome back to civilization!"

"It's good to be back." He closed his eyes for a moment, shaking off memories of thirst, crowding, and discomfort. Most of all, there'd been the never-ending,
grinding fear that something else was going to go wrong,
that they weren't going to make it. He opened them
again. "How long have you been here?"

"Oh, they came by and picked us up a couple of days
after you left. The grunts really had them ticked, too.
They had all of the shuttles fitted out as lobbers, taking
short, suborbital hops back and forth looking for you.
Anyway, we're glad you made it."

"So am I." He turned away.

"Hey, hey! Wait! Where you going!"

"Comm shack. I've got something to send to Earth."

Kettering's face darkened. "Not . . . ah . . ."

"I'm sending a report on what we found at Cydonia."

The other man looked thunderstruck. "David! You can't—"

"I've already published, Craig. Last week, on Usenet."

"*Damn* you!" Kettering exploded. "How could you?"

Alexander folded his arms. "The UN is trying to suppress the find, Craig. I'm letting the world know about it."

"How irresponsible can you be? You've ruined it for all of us!"

Alexander was fascinated by Kettering's anger. Obviously, the man had a personal stake in this. "You've been talking to Joubert, haven't you?"

"Mireille is a professional, a responsible scientist," Kettering replied. "You should have listened to her."

"They're trying, *she's* trying, to stop us from publishing the truth!"

Kettering reached out, placing one hand on Alexander's arm. "David, look. I know you were upset. I know you thought the UN Scientific Authority was trying to usurp your work. I think you have a legitimate complaint, something to take up with them when we get back. But, damn it, David, don't you see that they have a point? A good point? This information should be classified, should be kept classified, so that it can be studied by responsible experts."

"You keep using the word 'responsible,' Craig, and I'm getting a little sick of it. It's irresponsible of these so-called experts to withhold the truth from people. What happened here half a million years ago is important! It may have shaped us, who we are, how we think!"

"And what is the truth? Sorry. I sound like Pilate, I know, but what have we got? Some bits and pieces, some fragments. You know as well as I do that archeology is like trying to assemble a thousand-piece jigsaw puzzle, when all we can find in the box is a couple of hundred random pieces. The picture we come up with is subject to interpretation, to judgment. We see a little bit here, a flash there—''

''So what's your point?''

''My point, David, is that the *people* you keep calling on don't know what to do with the information we uncover. All you have to do is look at the record! Archeology gave to modern civilization the story of the Incas, of the Mayas, of Angkor Wat, of Sumer, of Xian's buried warriors. And what do the *people* believe in? Von Daniken's chariot-spaceships. Pyramidiots with their numerological interpretations of Giza. Little men from Mars who raised the heads on Easter Island, built the Great Pyramid, and shot John F. Kennedy for good measure. They believe in *astrology*, for God's sake. In the Biblical Flood. In crop circles, flying saucers, and gods from outer space! Can't you understand that what we've found here is just going to fuel all that nonsense? Every nation on Earth is being torn apart right now by conflicting cults, churches, and crackpot theories, and they've all been started or made crazier by the discovery of that damned Face. Hell, half the people on Earth think the Cydonia complex was built by gods who also created humans. The rest think they were demons, out to destroy God's Word.''

''What does all of that have to do with how we do our job? There are always crackpots and fringe elements, Craig. You know that. Our job is to learn about Man's past, to dig up the dinner leavings and the garbage and the art that'll let future generations of archeologists put together a few more of those jigsaw pieces. It's not to worry about how what we learn is misused.''

''I disagree,'' Kettering said. ''Mireille disagrees.''

''How long have you two—''

''*That's none of your damned business!*''

''Sorry. But I understand. She can be ... persuasive in her arguments.'' He shrugged. ''Excuse me, Craig. As I said, I've already published on Usenet. I've been asked to follow up with a piece for *Archeology International*.''

''And are you willing to accept the deaths the pre-

mature release of this information will most certainly
cause?''

Alexander raised his eyebrows. ''Deaths?''

''The bloodiest wars of history, the most savage
butcheries and massacres, the worst bloodshed have always been wrapped up with religious differences, one
way or another. We are looking at a century or more of
religious warfare, Dr. Alexander. Religious warfare that
will make the Hundred Years' War and Ireland and the
Jewish pogroms all look like Sunday teas. And you are
contributing to the bloodshed by giving these fanatics
and crackpots the ammunition they need. It'll all be on
your head!''

''The bloodiest wars,'' Alexander replied quietly,
''are the ones brought on by *ignorance*, Dr. Kettering.
That is the enemy we should be fighting. And I'm
damned if I'm going to be guilty of aiding and abetting
that enemy.''

Angry, he turned and strode off toward the comm
shack.

                              TUESDAY, 19 JUNE: 1500 HOURS GMT
Cydonia One aboard MSL
Rocky Road
South of Cydonia Prime
Sol 5658: 1215 hours MMT

Garroway caught hold of an overhead grabstrap and
leaned across the seated, armored forms of Sergeants
Jacob and Caswell so that he could see out the tiny porthole in the ship's bulkhead. The shuttle *Rocky Road*,
piloted by a former NASA astronaut named Susan Christie, had been put into its lobber configuration the night
before, then launched in a high-trajectory suborbital
jump that was bringing the bulk of the MMEF down on
the Cydonian plain just a few miles south of the archeological base there. They'd been in free fall for nearly ten
minutes, and only a few moments ago Christie had cut
in the main engines to gentle them in toward their land-

ing site. There was very little sound, nothing much at all save a far-off whisper from the engines. They were making the suborbital hop "hollow," meaning depressurized. It was easier to have everyone suited up and ready to bounce from the moment they touched down. Besides, if the bad guys were waiting for them with a surface-to-air missile, or even a decent heavy machine gun . . .

They were descending fast and passing now, he saw, their primary navigational checkpoint, the imposing bulk of the D&M Pyramid.

From this vantage point, the thing was enormous . . . a titanic structure that dwarfed the tiny lobber to an insignificant mote. It was a mountain, just over three kilometers across from north to south, two from east to west, and reaching nearly a kilometer into the sky. It wasn't a classical pyramid in shape, of course, since it was five-sided instead of four. The term pyramid had stuck, however, because of the markedly smooth and regular sides. Even though it had almost certainly started out as a mountain, the thing had an uncannily artificial feel to it, a precision of orientation and regularity that suggested it had been reshaped by intelligence, just as the far more famous Face twelve kilometers to the northeast had started off as a mesa but been reshaped by means now unknown. Desert winds can carve natural pyramids, called vents, but those tended to have three sides only, with the sharpest angle facing into the wind; the D&M Pyramid had five sides, with gigantic buttresses at each corner. The surface was eroded so far that it was impossible to tell what it had looked like originally, but the unmistakable hand of intelligence still showed in the design and in its looming, brooding presence.

Most telling of all, though, from Garroway's point of view, were the signs that the D&M Pyramid had been *deliberately* destroyed. Almost directly below the shuttle, a few hundred meters from the pyramid's eastern face, a tunnel plunged into the depths of the Martian surface, a crater . . . but not a natural one. Something had struck the surface there millennia ago, tunneling deeper into the ground than a typical meteor, then detonating far below the surface. Part of the eastern face of the pyramid had bulged slightly, and a great deal of debris had cascaded down those unnaturally smooth sides.

Garroway looked up and spotted Alexander in his civilian EVA suit, pressed up against another porthole nearby. The archeologist had volunteered to serve as guide in unfamiliar terrain, and Garroway was happy to have the man along. He'd talked some with the scientist about the evidence indicating that the Monument Builders had been attacked. Archeological teams had made initial surveys of the D&M area, but outside of confirming that the structure appeared to have been destroyed by an interior explosion—and that the tunnel-crater was now blocked with fused debris—little was known either of the structure's original purpose or of who destroyed it, and why.

Alexander, Garroway thought, was a man with a crusade, determined to seek out and publish the truth, no matter what the cost to himself . . . or to others. That was fine with Garroway, who'd always stood by the principle that the truth was better than a lie. *I wonder, though,* he thought, *what we've unleashed back on Earth.* The UN was damned sure they wanted Alexander's discoveries buried, and they must have their reasons.

The hell with it. If this is a fight between suppressing free speech and free scientific inquiry, and shouting the truth to the world, I know which side I'm on.

With a savage jolt, *Rocky Road*'s pilot increased thrust on the lobber's engine, slowing their rapid descent toward the desert. Garroway had to straighten up away from the porthole to keep his balance. Outside, red dust exploded upward past the window, sharply cutting the golden sunlight streaming in from the west.

Then there was a bump, and they were down.

"All right, Marines!" Lieutenant King called out. "Hit the beach!"

"Let's go, let's go, let's go!" Sergeant Jacob added. "Haul ass, Marines!"

They swung out into the central corridor, awkwardly grabbing the ladder rungs and clambering down toward the cargo deck. Garroway allowed himself to be caught up in the rush, descending rapidly, threading his way through the cargo bay, then down the ramp and onto the Martian surface.

Garroway trotted onto the sand, his ATAR—freshly drawn from the recaptured stores at Candor—at port arms, and took a wondering look around. He'd thought his weeks in the Valles Marineris had cured him of any awe over something so commonplace as scenery. The Cydonian landscape was, in a way, the opposite of the canyons and rilles on the equator, however. There, you felt hemmed in by four-kilometer vertical walls of red rock; here, the horizon was flat and far, but the various mesas, mountains, and, above all, the black-gray bulk of the D&M Pyramid thrust up into the pink-red sky like giant's teeth, monuments to human insignificance.

The Marines spread out into a broad, defensive perimeter as soon as they hit the beach. After a moment's careful check with various sensors, both in their suits and aboard the *Rocky Road*, Lieutenant King trotted up to Garroway. "The area looks clear, sir. Maybe we caught 'em napping."

Garroway grinned behind his visor. "Well, if they were, they're awake now. C-Prime has a pretty decent traffic-control radar system, as I recall. They'll've seen us coming and know exactly where we touched down. Let's get our people moving."

"Aye, aye, sir!"

"Sergeant Jacob!"

"Sir!"

"Set the beacon."

"Aye, aye, sir!"

They'd touched down about a kilometer north of the D&M Pyramid. Cydonia Prime was seven kilometers to the north, though Garroway fully expected to be stopped long before they got that far.

That, after all, was a part of the plan. He checked his suit's clock. 1229 hours.

He hoped *Harper's Bizarre* was on sched. If she
wasn't, Bergerac's prediction about the outcome of this
little outing was going to become entirely too accurate.

Cydonia Two aboard MSL
Harper's Bizarre
Over the Face
1412 hours MMT

"You two tucked in okay, back there?" Elliott's voice
said over Knox's headset.

"Yeah," Knox replied wryly. He turned and checked
the armor-suited form of Staff Sergeant Ostrowsky, lying in the acceleration couch next to his. She grinned
and gave him a thumbs-up. "Tucked in is one word for
it, I guess. I never figured I'd end up as bombardier on
an air strike, though."

Captain Harper Elliott laughed. "And I never thought
I'd be flying close support for a bunch of jarheads. Hang
on. This could be a bit bumpy."

With a shrill roar, the Mars shuttle's nuclear engines
fired, converting methane to white-hot plasma and kicking the ungainly transport into the sky. Knox felt the
familiar, smothering weight of high acceleration, a
weight that faded away seconds later as *Harper's Bizarre* entered her suborbital trajectory. Now they were
skimming across the Martian desert at an altitude of
about a thousand meters.

They'd left Candor Chasma just behind the *Rocky
Road*, but they'd followed a different flight path, landing
thirty minutes later inside a crater in Deuteronilus, some
one hundred kilometers east of the Cydonian Complex.
There, Captain Elliott had spent the last hour refueling
the main reaction mass tanks from strap-on spares,
which were discarded once they were empty. This gave
Harper's Bizarre a full fuel load for the final leg of the
mission.

They were going to need it. Instead of making a second high-trajectory lob, they were staying closer to the Martian surface, barely clearing some of the higher mountains, and using the shuttle's main engines to kick them a bit higher from minute to minute, to keep them airborne in a nearly flat trajectory. It took more fuel that way, but it also reduced the chances that Cydonia Prime's radar would pick them up on the way in.

Time passed. Knox tried not to think about it. Everything was riding on *Harper's Bizarre* and her mission. Eventually, though, Elliott called down again from the cockpit. "Okay, guys, we're coming up on the final leg here. I've got the beacon."

"Outstanding!" Ostrowsky said. "The op's a go, then!"

"Looks that way," Knox said. The beacon meant that Garroway and his people were down and now walking toward Cydonia Prime. If there'd been no signal, they would have aborted and landed in the desert.

"I can promise you another few minutes without too many bumps," Elliott said, "so you'd better get set up and ready now."

"Roger that," Knox replied. "Let's go, Ostie."

"I'm with you, Gunny."

Carefully, he clambered down the ladder and into the lobber's cargo bay. The main cargo doors had been removed, and he could look out through unobstructed emptiness to the desert and mountains drifting along below.

"Five minutes, Gunny," Elliott called down to him from the cockpit. "You ought to be able to see 'em now."

Clutching his safety line, which held him secure to a bulkhead support, Knox leaned out of the open hatch just enough to look ahead and down. They were traveling west, toward the sun; southwest, the impossible, smooth-sided shapes of the Cydonian pyramids rose black and mysterious from the crater-pocked sands. He looked straight down and suppressed a start. The Face, in all its astonishing, scale-of-giants weirdness, lay less than three hundred meters below. Eyes, each with the surface area of a football stadium, stared sightlessly up at the tiny NIMF lobber as it traveled overhead. The mouth, lips slightly parted, showed irregular plates that might have been intended to represent teeth, each the size of a city block.

The sight shook Knox. This close, the countless imperfections and irregularities in the rock conspired to make the mountain-sized artifact look more natural, less like something deliberately carved from a mesa by alien engineers. It was almost possible to imagine that the people who still insisted that the Face was of natural origin were right.

Gunnery Sergeant Knox was not a particularly imaginative person, and he didn't tend to see faces in clouds or rocks or chance combinations of smudges on Rorschach tests or the grime on a linoleum tile floor. It still looked like a face to him, though, in a heavy-browed, blunt-muzzled way, and its stare from this range was distinctly unsettling, making him feel like a dandelion seed slowly drifting over a reclining human's head.

Nonsense! Hell, the damned thing probably was a freak of nature. It was strange, yeah, but he'd seen strange things on Earth, too. Not as *big*, maybe.

What was it about that thing that had made the UN willing, even eager, to go to war? It didn't make sense. . . .

Knox tore his eyes from the compelling, Sphinx-like skyward gaze of the Cydonian Face, staring instead along the shuttle's line of flight. Eight miles ahead, he could see the oddly rectilinear walls of the Fortress and the enigmatic, DNA spiral of the fallen Ship. There was no denying the alien origin of that thing, though half a million years had reduced it to little more than a twisted, spiral-staircase skeleton half-buried in sand and rubble.

Elliott was guiding the shuttle along now with the main engines throttled way back, the lobber canted over at very nearly a forty-five-degree angle both to give it forward momentum and to keep it airborne. With the cargo-hold door open, Knox could step out onto what the NASA people called its "front porch," a term that had come down from a similar platform built out from the hatch in the front of the lunar landing modules of seventy years ago. Carefully, he began clipping a set of web-belt harnesses to his armor, anchoring himself to the structure just outside of the hatch. The west escarpment of the Face fell away abruptly as he worked, giving him an uninhibited view straight down to the desert floor, seven hundred meters below.

"Okay, Captain," he said. "I'm in position and ready for the run."

"Roger that. Three minutes now."

They were closer to the enigmatic spiral-shape of the Ship, now, where it lay half-buried in the ruin of the incomplete or blast-damaged pyramid that the scientists called the Fortress. Cydonia Prime, their objective, rested on a clear sweep of desert half a mile south of the Fortress. It looked out of place amid so many titanic monuments made ancient and smooth by windblown sand and the passing millennia, and nearly lost by the sheer, vast size of its surroundings.

"You ready for me out there?" Ostrowsky called over the intercom channel. "Or are you sight-seeing?"

"All set, Staff Sergeant," he replied. "Watch your step, though. It's a long way down."

A moment later, Ostrowsky's bulkily armored form appeared in the open cargo hatch. Knox braced himself across the opening as she carefully attached her own harness restraints. "Well, Gunny?" she asked. "Ready to party?"

"Yup. Let's rock and roll. Hand me your ATAR."

She unhooked her rifle from her suit and handed it to him. He switched on the imaging system and raised it to his shoulder. The inset TV picture on his HUD showed a magnified image of the base, half-buried external tanks, microwave mast, scattered Mars cats and wellheads, fuel farm and landing pad, assembly crane and storehouses and all the rest of the clutter attending Man's first large-scale exploration and exploitation of another world.

He touched a control, increasing magnification. He

could just make out the UN troops now, tiny, red-brown figures emerging in groups of five from the Cydonian base's main hab and scattering across the desert.

Knox shifted aim, looking south toward the black loom of the D&M Pyramid, seven miles or so south of the Fortress. He couldn't see the other lobber, which should have touched down a couple of miles north of the pyramid over two hours ago. He scanned the desert between Pyramid and Fortress, looking for some sign of the major and the rest of the MMEF, but couldn't spot them. Well, no surprise there. Their active camo armor would let them blend into the desert damned near as well as the sand and rocks themselves. It was pretty clear that the UN troops knew they were coming, though. He could see them deploying behind a low ridge a mile south of the base. In fact, they appeared to be using entrenching tools to dig in.

He switched off the rifle and studied the area without the electronic enhancement. "Incredible," he said. "Almost halfway into the twenty-first century, and the UN is resorting to trench warfare."

Ostrowsky chuckled. "The major sure as damn-all called it right, huh?"

"I guess he damn well did." It seemed obvious now, but when they'd been planning this operation, Knox had wondered how Garroway could so confidently expect the Foreign Legion troops to do exactly what they were doing. In Knox's experience, the enemy never did what you thought they were going to do.

This time, though, Bergerac and his UN troops really had no choice. If they'd tried to mount a long-range assault against the Marines at Mars Prime, they would have found themselves attacking a prepared enemy. Far better to wait and let the enemy come to you. The only real option open to them was to wait until the Marines landed nearby, then rush out and form a defensive line, blocking the Marines' advance. If the Marines landed smack in the middle of things, the Foreign Legion troops would emerge from the habs and attack them as they climbed out of the lobber. If the MMEF landed farther away to protect the lander, the UN forces would create a defensive line . . . exactly what they were doing now. To Knox's eye, it looked like about half of the blue-helmeted troops were climbing into several Mars cats parked near the habs. Those would be Bergerac's mobile forces. Once the Marines were pinned, those cats could swing wide around Garroway's flanks, drop off their troops, and either surround the Marines or pull an end run and go capture the lobber, the MMEF's only tie to Mars Prime. There was no activity that he could see around the two lobbers parked at the landing pad, and that fit with the major's expectations as well. Bergerac wasn't likely to risk his shuttle-landers in battle.

At least, not the way Garroway was risking his.

"Hang on out there!" The engine kicked them with a hard burst, and Knox grabbed a stanchion to keep from being flung against his harness. Elliott was bringing the lobber down now, balancing against the steady thrust of the NIMF's nuclear plasma engine. Ostrowsky, working just inside the cargo bay, picked up one of the large, plastic parts-transport containers—about the size and shape of a picnic ice chest, complete with handles and hinged lid—and dragged it over to a spot on the deck just inside the hatch. They waited, then, watching Elli-ott's final approach with something more than a merely academic interest.

"I'm getting waveoffs and warnings from the base command center," Elliott's voice said over the intercom. "I told 'em we're a scientific explorer team returning from Utopia Planitia, but I don't think they believe me."

The story about a science team had been concocted as a means of buying time. Bergerac couldn't be sure he had up-to-date information on all of the research teams on Mars, and it was at least plausible that one, over-looked, had been camping out on the other side of the planet since before the UN troops had even arrived.

Before long, though, he would either use the base computer logs to verify that no such research team existed . . . or he would decide he couldn't take the chance and order his people to open fire.

It wouldn't be much longer now, one way or the other.

TWENTY-FOUR

Garroway
Cydonia One ground position
One kilometer south of Cydonia
Prime
Sol 5658: 1421 hours MMT

"Down!" Caswell cried, throwing herself facedown into the sand. "We're taking fire!"

Garroway ducked instinctively, then rushed ahead, dropping to his belly behind the low ridge of hard-packed sand a few meters to Caswell's right. He couldn't hear shots, not in this thin air, but he could see dark shapes scurrying along another ridgeline a couple of hundred meters to the north. Beyond, just visible on the horizon, he could see the tops of several habs, the microwave tower, and the obelisk of the shuttle *Ramblin' Wreck* standing on its apron. A blue UN flag hung listlessly from a pole.

Sand splashed from the crest of the ridge less than a meter away, and he slid farther back behind the dune's protective rise. Several of the other Marines returned fire, but Jacob and the other noncoms yelled at them to drop.

Lieutenant King dropped to the ground next to him. "Here we go," he said.

337

"Yeah," Garroway replied. "Now we start praying for air support."

1709 HOURS GMT

Cydonia Two aboard MSL
Harper's Bizarre
30 meters above UN Positions
South of Cydonia Prime
1424 hours MMT

Knox took another look out the cargo hatch. They were less than one hundred feet up now, close enough to see individual blue-helmeted troops scurrying about on the ground or ducking for shelter behind the three Mars cats parked near the base's main hab. He saw a flash as someone took a shot at them and something jarred the lobber's hull . . . then again.

Fortunately, the lobber's appearance had rattled the base defenders, and their fire was less than accurate. Some of the blue-helmets ran for cover. Others stood in the open, rifles dangling at their sides, as they stared up at the huge, four-legged apparition that was bearing down on them from this unexpected direction. The jet of plasma from the lobber's engine was invisible, but the heat waves shimmering beneath warned of high temperatures and a possible radiation hazard. Some of the defending troops hesitated before firing, fearful perhaps that they would bring the thing down on top of them.

"Okay, Captain Elliott," Knox said, leaning out from the cargo bay as far as he could so that he could see. "Let's take that near Mars cat, the one with hull number 357." There were five blue-helmeted troops huddled together in the shadow of the crawler.

"That's number 357, rog," Elliott replied. With a thump, the lobber changed course slightly, drifting toward the target. Knox reached down and picked up his end of the ice chest, and Ostrowsky, opposite, did the same. Carefully as the lobber bounced and jolted, he unsealed the pressure-tight lid with a sharp hiss and opened it. A simple latch arrangement kept the lid locked open, back and out of the way.

Inside, set in loosely packed array, were thirty cans of Stony Brook beer.

They were fifty feet above the Mars cat now and perhaps fifty feet to the side, drifting along, Knox estimated, at a man's walking pace. "Ready?" he asked.

"Ready, Gunny," Ostrowsky replied.

"And . . . three, and . . . two, and . . . one . . . "

With each number, they swung the chest out, then back, working up the rhythm and the momentum.

". . . and . . . *now*!"

"Bombs away!" Ostrowsky yelled. They released the ice chest on the up-and-out swing, tossing it clear of the drifting lobber. Its lid latched open, it sailed through the air, turning end over end and scattering a cloud of small, metallic cylinders that glittered and flashed in the afternoon sun.

The cans fell, spinning, and long before the first one reached the ground, some of them had already exploded in a glorious, golden spray that sparkled as it fell. . . .

                                        1709 HOURS GMT

UN Positions
South of Cydonia Prime
1424 hours MMT

Lieutenant Jean-Michel Dutetre was aiming his FA-29 rifle at the splay-legged apparition backlit against the sky overhead when the case sailed out into the air, spilling its contents across the UN position. His first thought was that it was some kind of cluster bomb, a projectile designed to scatter a cloud of smaller bomblets, even though UN intelligence had reported that the US Marines on Mars possessed no such specialized munitions.

His thought was confirmed an instant later when some of the falling cylinders struck one another or simply exploded; a rain of gold liquid splattered down across the sand, the Mars cat, and the men crouched behind it. Each drop that touched the ground seemed to explode in a puff of white gas and ocher dust. At the same time, whole cylinders were hitting the ground with distinct, hollow-sounding pops, exploding and hurling streamers of liquid and white gas in every direction.

The empty case struck the top of the Mars cat's cab, bounced off, and landed on the sand a few meters away. Several UN troops went to their knees, scrabbling desperately at the liquid that clung to their helmet visors like hot-smoking glue.

One can struck Private Benz squarely on his blue helmet; the liquid splattered across his armor and Dutetre's armor as well, and when it hit, it clung and smoked, steaming furiously like some kind of unimaginably powerful acid. . . .

Dutetre dropped his rifle and began trying to brush the liquid off. It was boiling and freezing at the same time, the liquid bubbling furiously and giving off clouds of white smoke even as it congealed to a thick, icy frost that clung to whatever it touched. He couldn't imagine what the stuff might be . . . but he was terrified that whatever it was must be eating its way through his armor.

"Chemical attack!" Dutetre screamed over the general command frequency. "Chemical attack!"

"It's acid!" someone else yelled. "It's eating my suit!"

"Help me! It's all over my visor! I can't see! *I can't see!*"

1711 HOURS GMT

Cydonia Two aboard MSL
Harper's Bizarre
30 meters above UN Positions
South of Cydonia Prime
1426 hours (MMT)

". . . and two, and . . . one, and . . . *now*!"

Together, Knox and Ostrowsky hurled another case of

Stony Brook from the shuttle's cargo bay, nailing the third and final Mars cat, engulfing the vehicle in swirling steam.

They'd tested the idea back at Mars Prime before loading the beer aboard the lobbers for the voyage north. The beer cans were actually fairly stable in the Martian near vacuum, though they were under high pressure. The pressure increased rapidly as the beer cooled enough for the water content to start to freeze, expanding against the confines of the thin aluminum walls of the can.

All of this meant that any sharp, hard shock—such as striking another can in flight, or smashing into the ground or the cab of a Mars cat or the top of a blue-painted space helmet—guaranteed an explosive release of pent-up pressure, and the moment beer hit the Martian atmosphere, several things happened all at once. The carbon dioxide in suspension in the liquid came out of suspension very quickly, as foaming bubbles, and as gas that turned as visible and as white as smoke as it chilled. The liquid froze almost as soon as it touched the cold outer layers of armor or vehicle windscreen; everything it touched was swiftly coated by a thin scum of water ice and sublimating carbon dioxide.

And where the liquid touched the Martian ground, the effect was even more spectacular. Most of the surface regolith was so dry it made the sands of the Sahara Desert seem like wetlands in comparison. When liquid water hit it, as the Viking landers had demonstrated decades before, it released a large amount of oxygen . . . enough to create a sharp fizz and enough of a pop to fling a cloud of fine, dry dust into the air. Enough liquid hitting the ground all at once created the *impression*, if not the fact, of an explosion. . . .

Garroway had first considered tossing the beer cans individually, like hand grenades, but he'd rapidly discarded that idea. One can exploded by itself made a small mess but simply wasn't that spectacular. Besides, Marine armor was not designed for throwing hand grenades—a serious deficiency, so far as Knox was concerned. A large number of cans, however, spilled all at once from a hovering lobber across a large area, created a truly spectacular effect.

The devastating and totally unexpected nature of the attack had thrown the defenders into complete panic. In an instant, the discipline of the UN troops had vanished, as case after case of chemical bombs was flung from the hovering cargo shuttle, scattering their contents across broad footprints of desert. Some troops stood their ground, continuing to fire up at the lander; most fled, many of them dropping their weapons as they either scattered into the desert or ran in an ungainly mob back toward Cydonia Prime.

"What'll it be, folks?" Elliott called down to the two bombardiers. "The trench or the UN's HQ?"

"The trench, Captain," Knox replied. "We want to open a hole for the major."

"Hang on to your beer," Elliott replied. "Coming around to the south now."

The lander's engine flared, jolting Knox and Ostrowsky as they clung to the cargo bay's framework.

The trench was about a half kilometer or so away.

                                        1711 HOURS GMT
Cydonia One ground position
One kilometer south of Cydonia
Prime
1426 hours MMT

More high-velocity bullets slashed into the sand dune, hurling up meter-high gouts of dust as the Marines tried to bury themselves just a little deeper in its welcome shadow. Garroway held his rifle up above his head, using its optics to transmit a magnified image of the enemy line to his helmet HUD display. He could just make out the line of the next dune on the horizon, 185.4 meters distant according to his rifle's laser ranger, and occasional black spots that might be the heads of the enemy.

"Pretty damned hot, Major," Lieutenant King said, crouching in the sand next to him.

"They're dug in and they're waiting for us," Garroway replied. He brought the rifle—and his arms—back down under cover. Every Marine there was well aware that what might be a light wound on Earth would, here, almost certainly mean death as the armor's air poured out through a bullet hole. "We can't take them frontally."

"Hey, you think the beer-bombing idea's gonna work, Major, sir?" Corporal Slidell asked. He was lying on the ground on the other side of Lieutenant King.

"It damned well better, Slider," Garroway replied. "If it doesn't, we're in a hell of a fix . . . and we'll have thrown away the only beer within a hundred million miles."

"You can say that again," Slidell said. "Sir."

King held his own rifle above the embankment for a look. "Hey, Major!" he said. "Have a peek!"

Garroway raised his rifle again, careful not to lift it far above the dune. This time, he could see a lobber drifting through the sky just beyond the enemy lines. As he watched, a tiny object flipped out of the lobber's side, spilling dozens of smaller objects as it fell. The reaction in the UN lines when the objects hit was immediate and spectacular. Men were leaping out from behind the low ridge, some slapping at themselves, others firing at the lobber overhead, and the rest running as fast as their cumbersome armored suits would allow.

"You know," King said, "I think we've just added a new secret weapon to the Corps's inventory. Beer bombs!"

"Yeah," Slidell added. "*My* beer! . . ."

"Sacrificed in a good cause, Slider," Garroway said. "We were not issued ordnance sufficient to the needs of this mission. We therefore improvise, adapt, and overcome!"

"Yeah, I guess. Look at them blue-tops run!"

A ragged volley of gunfire snapped out from the Marine lines, tearing into the UN troops who were shooting at the lobber. Several toppled over backward, falling back into the trench. Others dropped their weapons and started to run.

"Let's go, Marines!" Garroway shouted. Rising, he struggled up through yielding sand to the top of the dune, then lurched over the top. A bullet struck his armor with a sharp *spang*; he pivoted, targeting the UN soldier who'd fired, and sent back an answering burst. The man tumbled back out of sight, dead or simply knocked down, there was no way to tell.

Not all of the UN troops had run, and those still in place opened up with a devastating volley. Their line was broken, however, by the sudden attack by the lobber, and as the Marines charged, those in the trench wavered, then began falling back.

One Marine to his left—Marchewka, he thought—flung up his arms and pitched back down the face of the ridge. An instant later, Corporal Hayes's helmet exploded in fragments and pink-tinted white vapor. For seconds, the charge wavered . . . and then the Marines were surging forward, firing from their hips as they jogged across the sand.

Ahead, another case was flung from the lobber, scattering cans of beer in a terrifying bombardment of steam and ice and sticky, golden liquid.

Broken, panicking now, the UN troops were running. . . .

1714 HOURS GMT

Cydonia Two aboard MSL
Harper's Bizarre
50 meters above UN Positions
South of Cydonia Prime
1429 hours MMT

"We've got about five more minutes of fuel at this rate, guys!" Elliott called over the intercom. "You'd better think about where we're gonna set down!"

Knox looked at the remaining cases of beer in the cargo bay. There were three left, and he hated to break off with bombs still on the racks. "Bring us around to the base, Captain," he replied. "One more pass, and we can touch down by the Fortress."

"Roger that. Hold on. I have to grab some altitude."

The lobber's thrust increased briefly, boosting them higher. Below, he could see at least a dozen UN soldiers, fleeing their trench line and jogging north as fast as they could, leaving several bodies and a large number of weapons lying in the sand.

The Marines were swarming over the former enemy works now. Some of them were stopping to pick up discarded weapons; there'd not been enough to go around, of course, and some of the Marines had charged the UN works unarmed.

They all had weapons now, however, as they continued to pursue the Foreign Legion troops toward Cydonia Prime.

As the lobber began descending again, Knox saw a small mob clustered around the outside of the main hab's airlock. Most of them, he thought, were UN troops caught in the earlier attack against the parked vehicles, trying to get back inside.

The mob was an easy target; a case of chemical bombs flung high over the cluster of running, armored men spilled its contents across them all. Explosions of bone-dry dust suddenly reacting to liquid water and alcohol, the sticky splash of rapidly gelling beer, the stark confusion of running men and panicked radio calls served to dissolve the last remnants of any unit cohesion the UN troops might have had.

1715 HOURS GMT

UN Positions
Cydonia Prime
1430 hours MMT

Somebody collided with Dutetre from behind, knocking him down. Growling a harsh, Gallic curse, he rolled over and started to rise. Something caught his eye.

He was only just beginning to realize that the projectiles launched from the cargo shuttle were not doing that much damage when they struck. The explosions were spectacular, certainly, but the shrapnel traveled so slowly it bounced off combat armor without effect. The liquid inside, for all its steaming and bubbling, didn't seem to be doing anything except make a mess of the men's suits . . . and blind the ones who got the stuff on their helmet visors. A few meters away, he saw one of the cans lying empty on the sand.

He picked it up. The top had blown off, but the rest of the can was nearly intact. Dutetre's English was poor, but he could puzzle out the words, scraping at the thin metal with his glove to rub the ice off.

Stony.

Brook.

Beer.

Mon Dieu! *Bière*?

Angrily, Dutetre looked up suddenly at the cargo shuttle hovering above the base. Bastards! They've been dropping cans of *beer*!

Reaching down, he snatched up an FA rifle dropped on the sand, took aim at the hovering lander, and squeezed the trigger. Set on full automatic, the weapon sent a long stream of high-velocity penetrators snapping toward the target.

                                        1716 HOURS GMT

Cydonia Two aboard MSL
Harper's Bizarre
20 meters above UN Positions
South of Cydonia Prime
1431 hours MMT

Knox felt the heavy thuds of rounds striking the lobber, and twice something struck sparks from the support struts to either side of the *Bizarre*'s front porch. He ducked back, throwing out one arm to shove Ostrowsky back as well. Until now, only occasional rounds had come their way, either because the UN troops didn't want the lobber to crash on top of them, or because they'd been too demoralized by the beer run to even think of shooting back.

They were shooting back now, though. Several of the troops down there were holding their ground and blazing away. They looked mad, Knox thought, as though they'd just learned the nature of the joke played on them by the Marines.

The lobber's fuel tanks were heavily wrapped in foil insulation, and more padding—plastic sheeting, blankets, even mattresses—had been tied over the lower tankage assembly to provide some added protection from bullets, but judging from the hollow thunk of some of those impacts, and the way a thick white mist was starting to spill from behind the padding, at least a few rounds were drilling clean through.

"We got problems, people!" Elliott called. "I'm losing fuel damned fast!"

"We're taking rounds in the storage tanks, Captain," Knox called back. "You'd better get us clear!"

"Hell, I'm going to be lucky if we set down in one piece!"

The shuttle was faltering now, its plasma jet already giving out. "One more?" Knox asked Ostrowsky.

"Hell, yeah!" Together, they picked up one of the two remaining ice chests, opened and latched the top, and tipped it off the front porch in a glorious, spinning avalanche of brews. The lobber was falling quickly now, rotating clockwise as it fell. Elliott was apparently trying to guide them past the main hab and the other pressurized base facilities, but *Bizarre* had suddenly developed all of the aerodynamic proficiency of a very large rock.

"If you can, people," Elliott told them, "try to jump clear before we hit!"

Together, Knox and Ostrowsky started unbuckling their safety harnesses. Elliott's warning was a good one. If they jumped, they might hit soft sand and manage a roll. Stay aboard, and they could be caught between the deck as it slammed up at their feet, and the upper part of the shuttle as it slammed down from above.

He didn't need to ask about Elliott. She was obviously still trying to coax a bit more thrust from the dying engine and wasn't going to abandon her charge. "Ready?" he asked Ostrowsky, and he saw her answering nod. He made sure the ATAR was securely fastened to his armor, took Ostrowsky's gloved hand, and waited a couple of seconds as they spun closer to the ground.

They were still four or five meters up when they jumped.

1716 HOURS GMT

Garroway
Cydonia Prime
1431 hours MMT

Garroway was running toward the main hab when Caswell shouted, "Hey! The bastards nailed the lobber!"

He stopped, looking up and toward the right, where the squat shape of the shuttle was dropping rapidly toward some storage habs close to the main structure.

"First Section!" he yelled. "With me! The rest of you, hit that main hab!" He started running toward the falling shuttle as fast as he could manage, loose sand flying with every step. Most of the UN troops, he noted, had stopped fighting. Some were standing about with hands raised. Others were simply standing. More and more of the MMEF Marines were having to stop and take charge of prisoners.

But some were still very much in the fight, and Garroway wanted to get to the shuttle before they did.

1717 HOURS GMT

Knox
Cydonia Prime
1432 hours MMT

They jumped. For a dizzying moment, Knox and Ostrowsky, still holding hands, fell with the fairy-tale slowness of falling bodies in one-third G. When they hit a moment later, they struck sand, hitting hard but rolling apart as their legs gave way beneath them. Knox ended up on his back, staring at the huge, spidery shape of *Harper's Bizarre*, which seemed poised to come down on top of his head.

Then it passed him by, one landing leg colliding with a nearby ET module, which knocked the vehicle askew and sent it toppling onto its side. He half expected to see the ship burst into flame, but without oxygen it simply crumpled, its lightweight framework giving way beneath the impact. He tried to rise and his left leg shrieked pain . . . broken or sprained, he couldn't tell. Dropping again, he turned to look toward the south, where a number of angry-looking blue-helmets were rapidly closing on his position.

"Oh, shit." He grabbed his ATAR and took aim, squeezing off a short burst . . . and another . . . and another, shifting aim each time to a different target. Two of them dropped. The others wavered as he continued his one-man stand, some of them trading fire with him, until, as though by common consent, they scattered and broke for cover.

"Ostie!" he yelled over the general comm channel. "Ostie! Can you hear me?"

No answer. He saw her lying a few meters away, unmoving. "Captain Elliott! Do you copy?" No answer there, either.

A round careened off the side of his helmet, a glancing ricochet. He turned his attention to the front again, returning fire with deadly precision and grim will. Another running blue-top spun wildly, collapsed, and lay still.

Kaminski
Cydonia Prime
1432 hours MMT

PFC Kaminski froze in place just outside the main hab. A UN soldier had just stepped through the airlock and was hurrying toward the fighting . . . but he'd not seen the Marine standing rock-still just ten meters away. *Let's hear it for chameleon armor*, Kaminski thought, as he pivoted his ATAR into line with the man and squeezed the trigger.

The UN soldier spun, collided with the slender flagpole in front of the hab, and collapsed. The battle was sputtering out now, with many of the surviving UN troops raising their hands. Kaminski looked up at the blue UN flag hanging from the pole and shook his head. *That* would never do. . . .

"Hey, Slider!" he called. "Fulbert! Gimme a hand!"

Together, they grabbed the flagpole and hauled it up and out of the hole dug in the frozen ground to receive it. Ellen Caswell and Doc Casey trotted over to help, and in seconds, the pole came down, dragging the blue flag aflutter behind it.

Kaminski was prepared. He'd recovered the grit-scoured US flag that had flown from the Mars cat for the past three weeks and packed it in his armor's thigh pouch. With a couple of lengths of vacuum tape supplied by Doc, he began to fasten the flag onto the pole, while Caswell yanked off the UN banner.

More gunshots sounded close by, and a round slapped into the sand by their feet, but they kept working. . . .

Knox
Cydonia Prime
1434 hours MMT

Knox ducked and rolled as a stream of rounds slammed into the side of the Mars hab close by. He came to his knees, taking aim once more, when a blur of motion from his left caught the ATAR and ripped it out of his hand. He rolled to the side, looking up; an armored figure in a blue helmet loomed above him, a French rifle aimed at his head. "Do not move, American," the man said, his accented voice sounding over the Marine frequency. Knox remembered the voice, as he remembered the name stenciled on the armor: Bergerac. A second man trotted up behind the first, and Knox heard a torrent of French.

"*Pas de problèm*, Lieutenant Dutetre," Bergerac said. "We will use them as hostages for—"

A silvery something struck Bergerac in the side of his helmet, bursting in a golden spray. Knox rolled to the side, snatching at his ATAR, bringing it up just as Dutetre took aim at another figure standing in front of the crumpled wreckage of the ship. Elliott! She'd dragged herself clear of the wreckage and thrown a can of beer at Bergerac, and now Dutetre was about to shoot her down.

He squeezed the trigger, not even aiming, but simply pointing the ATAR's muzzle and loosing a long burst into the French lieutenant's chest, knocking him back. Bergerac spun toward him then, firing despite the smear of ice and steaming liquid clinging to his visor, the rounds stitching through the sand toward Knox's head.

A clatter of thin, high-pitched gunshots slammed Bergerac forward, lifting him onto his toes and pitching him down and across Knox's legs. Knox screamed as the weight smashed his injury.

"Gunny! You okay?"

It was Major Garroway, trotting toward him with his ATAR at the ready. "Shit, Major, am I glad to see you!'' He turned so that he could see Elliott, limping heavily as she made her way to the scene of that last desperate fight in the sand. "You pitch a mean beer, lady," he said admiringly. "Can't land a spaceship worth shit. . . .''

"Hey, any landing you can walk away from, jarhead."

He tried to sit up. "Gotta check on Ostie. She's down."

"M'okay," Ostrowsky said. She sounded dazed, a bit shaken. "Had the wind knocked out of me, is all."

"How are *you*, Gunny?" Garroway asked. Stooping, he rolled the French colonel's body clear.

"Dinged m'leg in the landing. Major, we *gotta* do something about these Navy drivers!''

Knox looked past Garroway at the plain south of the base. The fighting, it appeared, was almost over. Gunfire continued to snap across the plain or kick up geysers of sand, but most of the UN troops were dropping their weapons now and surrendering.

"Hey, guys!" Elliott called, pointing. "Look at that!''

They all turned to see what she was pointing at. Five of the MMEF Marines had knocked down the UN flag above the base and now were raising the five-meter length of pipe once more. Kaminski's American flag was fastened to the top, while Alexander stood nearby with an EVA camera, taking pictures.

Despite the obvious and deliberate parallelism to another Marine flag-raising, that one on a speck of volcanic rock in the Pacific nearly one hundred years before—Knox's eyes filled with tears at the sight . . . an inconvenience in full armor, when you couldn't wipe your face. Unwilling to let others hear his throat-rasping emotion, he dropped his voice to a growl. "So, is that it?" he said. "Did we win?"

"We won," Garroway said. Without ceremony, he raised his right arm, touching his glove to his helmet in salute, dropping his hand as the flagpole reached the vertical and was anchored in place at the base.

"Ooh-rah," Knox said. "What'd we win?"

"That, I'm afraid, has yet to be determined."

"Oh, I don't know," Elliott said. Knox could hear the grin in her voice. "These two missed a case when they were chucking the beer overboard. At least we have that!"

Garroway laughed. "It'll do for now, people. It'll do for now."

Behind him, the American flag flew from its make-shift pole in the golden light of the Martian afternoon.

TWENTY-FIVE

Warrenton, Virginia
0940 hours EDT

Kaitlin was on the floor in the den playing chess with twelve-year-old Jeff Warhurst when the call came through. "Kaitlin?" Stephanie Warhurst started speaking before she was fully in the room. She sounded concerned. "It's a vidcall from Monty, at the Pentagon, and he says it's on a special line. I don't really know why he's calling you. . . ."

"It's okay, Mrs. Warhurst. Can I take it in the E-room?"

"Of course, dear. I'll transfer the call there."

"Hey, Kaitlin?" Jeff said, looking up from the board.

"Yeah?"

"Are you gonna be a Marine someday, like my grandpa . . . and my dad?"

The question, coming out of nowhere, shook her. She'd thought about it a lot, of course . . . and she'd been thinking about it again ever since her return from Japan. But . . .

"I don't know, Jeff," she said. "Why?"

"I dunno. Just wondering, I guess. I'm gonna be a Marine, you wait! And the UNers better watch out!"

354

There seemed to be no proper answer to such an assertive statement. She rose and started to follow Mrs. Warhurst.

"Oh, and Kaitlin," Jeff added.

"Yes?"

"Just thought I'd warn you. Your queen's a goner."

She grinned. "Take another look, sport. If you take my queen, I've got mate in five."

"Huh?" Jeff looked incredulous.

"Sometimes sacrificing a piece can give you a significant advantage. See if you can figure it out by the time I get back."

The Warhursts' entertainment room was large and comfortably furnished, with a circular sofa in the sunken floor, and a Hitachi wallscreen that literally covered an entire, eight-meter wall from ceiling to floor. She sat down behind the low, central table and slid open the polished top, exposing the keyboard, touchscreen, and gaming controls. She touched the accept key.

The screen came on, and Montgomery Warhurst's craggy face looked down at her, huge and imposing. "Hello, Kaitlin," he said.

She touched a control that stepped the screen's active area down a bit, so she didn't feel like she was standing in front of the Face on Mars. "Good morning, General," she said. "What can I do for you?"

"Kaitlin, I've just had the damnedest call. Came through from an old friend of mine . . . who also used to be our ambassador to Japan. It seems a Japanese friend of his has been trying to get in touch with you, and, well, with the war and everything, he had to resort to some pretty sneaky back channels to carry it off."

Kaitlin's heart leaped. A Japanese friend? But, no . . . it couldn't be Yukio. Yukio's father might know the American ambassador as a friend, but not Yukio.

And in that moment, she knew who the call was from, and what it was about.

"Anyway, we've set up a special comm channel for him. It's, ah, it's the Japanese minister of International

Trade and Industry, and he wants to talk to you. In private. Will you take the call?''

Kaitlin felt very cold . . . and detached. It was as though she were listening to someone else, a stranger, say, ''I'll take it.''

''Okay.'' He turned his head, looking at another screen. ''I'm putting you through, sir.''

The face that appeared on screen a moment later was not Ishiwara's, but a younger man sitting cross-legged on a tatami behind a low table with a PAD. It was *Hisho* Nabuko, the man she'd spoken with the day she left Japan.

He bowed formally. ''Good morning, Miss Garroway,'' he said in only slightly accented English.

She stood, then bowed in reply. ''*Konichiwa, hajimemashte, o-hisho-san.*''

''I am well, thank you. The minister would like a moment of your time, if you would be so kind.''

''Of course. I would be delighted to talk to him.''

Her stomach was twisting, her eyes blurring through the tears. Slowly, she slumped back to the sofa, then let herself slide to the floor, kneeling next to the table. *Oh, God, no! Not Yukio! Not Yukio! . . .*

Ishiwara appeared, wearing a silk robe and seated on the floor behind a low table and PAD identical to his secretary's. He was seated in one of the almost bare rooms of his home, and she wondered what he must think of the lush, cluttered, and very Western decor at her back. Well, he was used to dealing with Western *gaijin*. More surprising was the very fact of speaking face-to-face with a member of the Japanese government . . . when the United States was at war with Japan.

What, she wondered, would her father think?

With a small, jarring shock of recognition, she saw that a small niche in one wall was occupied now by her house present, the sleek and elegant little model of the *Inaduma* fighter, a black-and-white, dart-shaped minnow clinging to the back of the whalelike *Ikaduti* booster.

''*Konichiwa, Kaitlin-san,*'' Ishiwara said. ''*Genki des ka?*''

He was addressing her as a younger friend, asking her how she was.

"*Genki des, domo, o-Daijin-sama*," she replied, giving the traditional *za-rei*, or seated bow, three large fingers of each hand on the floor, thumbs touching little fingers in circles. "*Konichiwa, o-genki des ka?*"

"I am . . . in good health, Kaitlin-san," he said, switching to English. "I fear, however, that I have very bad news. Nine days ago, Toshiyuki-san . . . he failed to return from his mission."

Somehow, *somehow*, she kept her face as impassive as his. "I am very sorry to hear that, Ishiwara-sama. The loss of your son . . . of *Yukio* . . ." She couldn't stop the tears streaming down her face. She reached up and brushed them away. "I am very sorry for you, for your loss."

Ishiwara smiled, the expression jolting Kaitlin for an instant, until she remembered that in Japan, a smile, a pleasant face, was expected to cover any emotion. When she looked into his eyes, however, she saw there the truth.

"First, *Kaitlin-chan*, let me tell you that Yukio loved you very deeply. We talked often about it, about you. I know this to be true."

Kaitlin was still recovering from the shock of hearing Ishiwara use the honorific *chan* instead of *san*, an affectionate diminutive usually reserved for family members or intimate friends. She could say nothing . . . *do* nothing but try to match Ishiwara's smile.

"I must tell you frankly," Ishiwara continued, "that I was against your relationship. Not your friendship, perhaps, but there could be no thought of the two of you marrying. I was, frankly, most relieved when I received your message that you had to return to your country. The two of you were from worlds vastly more alien than Earth is from Mars. One or the other of you would have had to deny himself, to deny his very soul in such a union."

Kaitlin wondered why Ishiwara was telling her this.

He doesn't need to justify himself, she thought. *Not now, not to a* gaijin.

"We had many long talks, my son and I," he continued, still smiling. "He told me much about you, about your thoughts. He told me, just before he left for Tanegashima for the last time, that he felt the war between our countries, yours and mine, was a serious mistake, that we were fighting the wrong people at the wrong time for the wrong reasons. I suspect that your feelings were at least partly responsible for his belief."

"I am . . . sorry if I gave offense, *Ishiwara-sama.*"

"Offense must be accepted as well as given. You expressed your heart, as did he. In any case, *Toshi-chan*'s convictions have been . . . weighing heavily, these past few days. Soon, I must address my government and tell them what I feel about this war. I wished to tell you, Kaitlin-chan, that a part of you, and a part of *Toshi-chan,* will be there with me when I address the prime minister."

He hesitated then, and Kaitlin wondered if he was waiting for a response. She had none to give. She could say nothing. She still didn't know why Ishiwara was telling her these things. Her grief at knowing that Yukio was dead left her numb to thoughts of governments, prime ministers, and cabinet meetings. *Oh God oh Christ I hate this war,* she thought, and her fists clenched until her nails bit the palms of her hands. *I hate this damned, stupid war!* . . .

"There is something else," Ishiwara continued. "Something . . . something deeply and personally embarrassing to me. I must apologize deeply, *Kaitlin-san.* In your farewell message, you enclosed a message for me to give to *Toshiyuki-chan.* I am very sorry to tell you that I never gave it to him. The fault is mine. I thought . . . I thought it best not to give it to him, since I feared encouraging you to continue your relationship. I feared that it might affect the performance of his mission. It was wrong of me, and I apologize." He bowed, deeply.

"Please don't be sorry," she said. Pain churned within her. *He never got it. He never knew.* "You were right. You were right, after all. It couldn't have worked out with us. I know that now." *It'll never work so long as people keep acting so damned stupid,* she thought fiercely. *It'll never have a chance of working until we can start all over, someplace else, away from this damned black hole of old cultures and old customs and old notions of what's proper and what's acceptable and what's right. Damn, damn,* damn *this war!* . . .

"I'm not so sure that I was right, *Kaitlin-chan.*" He sighed. "In any case, I apologize for keeping back the letter. And this, you see, brings me to another subject. After . . . Toshiyuki's final mission, the base commander sent me a memclip. It had been found among his things, along with instructions to transmit it to me, if . . . if he failed to return. One of the items on that memclip was a vidmessage for you. I have not seen it . . . but I have arranged to have it transmitted over this channel, if you wish to see."

"I would. *Domo arigato gozaimasu.*"

"I will leave you then. I'm very sorry for any sadness I have given you."

"And I am sorry, Ishiwara-sama, that you have lost your son."

"Perhaps there is yet good to come of it. *Sayonara, Kaiti-chan.*"

The word sayonara, in Japanese, was abrupt for the language, a word tinged with sadness that the two who were parting might never see one another again. Kaitlin bowed deeply and chose a more informal closing. "*Domo arigato gozaimasu, Ishiwara-sama,*" she said. "*Dewa mata.*"

Her good-bye meant something more like "Well, see you again sometime."

For the briefest of instants, she thought she detected a flicker of surprise behind those dark eyes, and the rigidly controlled emotions dwelling there. He bowed, and the screen went blank.

And a moment later she was looking up at Yukio. He was wearing a black Space Defense Force uniform with the chrysanthemum pips of a *chu-i* on his collar. He appeared to be in a booth of some sort; at his back, blurred and out of focus, was some sort of recreation hall. She could hear laughter in the background, see the shadowy shapes of other young men gathered around a table, standing and talking, playing Ping-Pong. *The enemy. . . .*

He smiled at her. "Hello, Chicako. Look, I'm not very good at this, and I don't want to seem overly dramatic or anything, but, well, if you're seeing this, I guess that means I'm dead." His smile stayed in place, but the eyes were dark and terribly serious.

"When we were together here," he went on, "I felt . . . strange. Divided. I guess I was having some trouble reconciling the Western part of me with the Nihonjin. And, maybe I was wrong, but I thought I was sensing the same sort of struggle going on in you. When my father told me that you had returned to America, I figured you had probably decided it had all been a terrible mistake."

He didn't know. He never got my message.

"You know, Chicako, it wouldn't have been easy. I couldn't have just turned my back on my family. And, well, you must feel the same way about your father. And your country. I don't know how we were going to work it out.

"I just wanted you to know that we *would* have worked it out. You taught me that, Chicako. Anything's possible, with enough love.

"By now, you'll know that the UN has ordered us to join the fight against the United States. I hate that order, with every fiber of my being, but because I am who and what I am, I must obey. It's, well . . . my heritage, I guess you would call it. *Samurai.* I will do what I have to do. And die doing it. But I want you to know that I love you with all my heart, that I'll be thinking of you out there . . . and that I know we would have found a way, if fate had been just a little kinder.

"Remember me, Chicako."

"*Ah, Toshi-san!*" someone called out from close by. "*Isho-ni konai?*"

Yukio turned his head. "*Ima iku!*" he called. He turned back to the screen. "I've got to go now. I just wanted you to know . . . I love you. Always. *Sayonara, Chicako.*"

Much later, Jeff Warhurst came to the E-room to find Kaitlin. After figuring out her queen gambit, he'd spent the next hour looking for an alternate plan that didn't involve capturing her queen but would still give him a fighting chance. He'd thought he'd found one, and he was eager to check it out, but when he looked in the room, he saw Kaitlin, still on the floor, head down on her arms on the tabletop, sobbing quietly. He hesitated, wondering if he should go in, then changed his mind and quietly closed the door, giving Kaitlin some time alone with her grief.

After his dad had died, he'd learned about grief himself. He knew about being alone.

WEDNESDAY, 4 JULY: 0343 HOURS GMT

Cydonia Prime
Cydonia, Mars
Sol 5672: 1510 hours MMT

Major Mark Garroway emerged from the main hab at Cydonia Prime. It was midafternoon, and the Cydonian Plain stood golden in that astonishing clarity of the thin Martian air.

It was, he was forced to admit, beautiful . . . in a stark and oceanless way. . . .

Strange. Garroway was beginning to like Mars . . . like its solitude, its stark beauty, its magnificent vistas of sand, rock, and color. It couldn't compare to the ocean, of course, and he was still looking forward to that marina in the Bahamas . . . but he thought he was going to enjoy the rest of his deployment here. Kaitlin, he thought, would be pleased.

He hoped she was all right. As soon as full communications with Earth had been restored after the battle, they'd started exchanging e-mail frequently. But then, a few days after the battle, she'd stopped answering him, and Garroway had been increasingly frantic. General Warhurst, finally, had mentioned a mysterious vidcall from the Japanese minister of International Trade and Industry—a private call for Kaitlin. Although the NSA had probably decoded and recorded the conversation as a matter of course, Warhurst didn't know what had been said, and Kaitlin had mentioned nothing about it, either to him or to Garroway.

"Damned if I know what it was all about," Warhurst had told him. "I do know that she was in Japan in May, just before the war started . . . and I also know that four days after the ITI Minister called, we got the first overtures from Tokyo that they might be willing to come over to our side if we guaranteed them a piece of what we find at Cydonia. You've got one hell of a special girl there, Mark."

A special girl? Yeah, she was all of that. He still wanted to talk to her, though, about what the hell she'd been doing in Japan of all places. Why was it that fathers were always the last to know? . . .

Thirteen more months on Mars . . . and seven more after that for the cycler ride home. He missed Kaitlin so badly he could taste it. Twenty more months before he could be with his little girl . . . who'd somehow and disconcertingly been transformed into a not-so-little young woman.

He *thought* he could wait that long.

The fighting on Mars was over, and for that, Garroway was grateful. While civilians might bemoan the idiocy of war, only someone in the military, someone who'd actually faced that vilest of the Four Horsemen, could truly appreciate war's ugliness, its terror, its sheer, blind stupidity, its colossal *waste*.

The war, he knew from Triple-N and regular comm reports, was continuing on Earth . . . but with the abrupt defection of Japan from the UN, it appeared that the balance of power had subtly shifted in favor of the US-Russian Alliance. The cruise missile assault had dropped to nearly nothing with the sinking of three UN arsenal ships—two of them by the Shepard Station HEL, newly repaired and recrewed. Fierce fighting continued in the northern Mexican desert, and Monterey had fallen to troops of the 2nd Armored Division on the twenty-fifth. In the north, Army forces had entered Longneuil, just across the St. Lawrence from the québecois capital of Montreal, and there were fairly substantial rumors that secret negotiations were under way that would result in Quebec's withdrawal from the UN and the war. With Japan out of the war, US forces had been able to transit the La Perouse Strait, cross the Sea of Japan, and land reinforcements for the beleaguered Russians near Vladivostok. Only hours ago, according to the last Triple-N download, US Marines of the 2nd Marine Division had landed at Matanzas, Cuba.

After that grim initial period of the UN bombardment, it was turning out to be one hell of a glorious Fourth.

The war showed no signs of ending yet, but the tide had definitely turned. That, at least, was the assessment of the Marines at Cydonia. They appeared confident and had greeted the word that French troops were on the way aboard the *Faucon* spacecraft with wry and optimistic good humor. The Marines now controlled every Mars shuttle on the planet; when the *Faucon* swept past the orbit of Mars a few months from now, how were the UN troops supposed to disembark? They would do so on the Marines' terms ... or not at all.

Even so, Garroway was making preparations, just in case the UN had allowed for that contingency by including a shuttle in the *Faucon*'s payload—unlikely, given the high fuel-to-mass ratio of a Mars Direct flight.

A century before, when Japanese forces had invaded tiny Wake Island shortly after the attack on Pearl Harbor, the story had circulated that the Marine commander on the doomed island had been asked if he needed anything else. "You can send us more Japs" was his apocryphal rejoinder. The incident almost certainly had never happened, but the Marines at Cydonia had dusted it off and begun circulating it among themselves. "The major e-mailed the Pentagon for recreational supplies,'' the current story ran. ''They're sending us more French.''

Outside the main hab, between the living facilities and the landing pad, the American flag still flew from a length of microwave tower support tubing driven deep into the sand. As on the Moon, a piece of wire kept the flag extended, though often there was wind enough here to unfurl the lightweight fabric.

As it turned out, the photograph David Alexander had taken of the flag's raising during the closing moments of the battle at Cydonia Prime had been uploaded to Spacenet. The shot of five Marines in their Class-One armor erecting the five-meter pole in the Martian sand had been so spectacularly reminiscent of the flag-raising on Iwo Jima that, at last report, the Marine Public Affairs Office back home was being swamped with requests for the picture, even though it was freely available on the net.

Garroway grinned. Not long ago, the very continued existence of the US Marines, perceived as an anachronism in this modern age of spacecraft, orbital lasers, and electronic warfare, was in serious doubt. He, himself, had been questioning his own contented service in a military arm with little real future.

When the flag had been raised on Mount Suribachi, on the embattled island of Iwo Jima in 1945, then–Secretary of the Navy James Forrestal had been watching from the deck of an amphibious command ship offshore. He was reported to have turned to Marine Major General Holland ''Howlin Mad'' Smith and said, ''Holland, the raising of that flag on Suribachi means a Marine Corps for the next five hundred years.''

It had only been ninety-six years since Suribachi. Maybe they needed a flag-raising like this one every century or so, just so that people would remember. . . .

The Face
Cydonia, Mars
1510 hours MMT

David Alexander stood at last on the top of the mesa,
the broad, red and brown expanse of the Cydonian plain
spreading out beneath his feet like a map. West lay the
pyramids of the City, the Fortress, the enigmatic strangeness of the Ship, and the tiny cluster of life and light
that was Cydonia Prime. Southwest, the D&M Pyramid
bulked huge against the pink sky, as protective of its
mysteries as ever.

He was standing atop the Face, symbol of all that was
still unknown about Mars, about the beings who'd lived
here half a million years ago, about Man himself, and
how he'd come to be. . . .

It seemed odd, but the features of the Face, so obviously artificial, so obviously artistic, so obviously the
product of conscious and intelligent design when seen
from high overhead, flattened into an expanse of ordinary sand-smoothed rock from this vantage point, from
the surface of the Face itself. After an hour's climb, he'd
reached this highest part of the mesa, the center of the
chin just south of the enormous crevasse that formed the
image's mouth.

Below, at his feet, were the quadrangular plates that
so resembled teeth; farther off, just visible half a mile
to the north, were the vast, bare, flattened mounds of
windswept rock that, from the sky, at any rate, looked
like eyes.

From where he stood now, it didn't look as though
the landform could possibly be artificial. Only from the
air did the overall cumulative effect of thousands of separate aspects, the convex smoothness of the eyeballs, the
planes of cheeks and jaw and ridged brow, even the
striations in the carving's headdress or helmet that gave
it such an eerie resemblance to the *nemes* of some pharaoh out of ancient Egypt, all come together, directly

challenging any assertion that this was the mindless accidental product of eons of wind, ice, and water.

Fifty-one sols on Mars, and he still felt no closer to the answers he was looking for than he'd been back on Earth. It was going to take years . . . no, *decades*, just to learn where to begin. The archeological teams continued to uncover mountains of weather-eroded equipment, enigmatic artifacts, and the ungraspable products of alien design philosophies. It was already clear that human manufacturing and materials-processing techniques were about to be revolutionized, and the teams hadn't yet gotten properly started. No one was willing to even guess what new surprises might still be in store.

And with all of this, the biggest questions were still stark and unyielding mysteries. Who'd built the Cydonian monuments, and why? Who were the humans whose remains were now being found everywhere throughout the region? What was their relationship with their cousins left back on Earth at the very dawn of the human spirit?

He sat down on a smooth-sculpted ridge, feeling the thin wind rattle against his lightweight EVA suit.

He liked it here on Mars, liked the freedom to pursue his studies without hindrance, liked the fact that the government, even though it was sponsoring his work, was far, far away. He'd come to terms with the Marine presence here; Garroway and his MMEF were what was making all of this possible, and he was grateful for that, as well.

Alexander was being hailed as a hero of the scientific community, the scientist who'd refused to acquiesce to the UN World Cultural Bureau's attempts at censorship. Well, he couldn't have managed that without the Marines. This war, he thought, more and more, was a struggle between those who would disseminate the truth, and those who would try to control it.

Control was the key, so far as the governments of Earth were concerned. No wonder, he thought, the UN had been so desperate to hide the secrets uncovered beneath the Cydonian plain. In the past weeks, according to the Net News vidcasts, dozens of new religions, new alien cults, new cosmic awareness groups had blossomed around the news that mummified humans half a million years old had been discovered on Mars. There were rumors that widespread riots in France, Germany, and Mexico were threatening to undermine those nations' war efforts. If their governments fell in the chaos of religious rioting and fanaticism, the war might well sputter to an end.

Alexander's published papers, both on the net and in *Archeology International*, were being hailed in the States as one man's bid for academic freedom, an end to scientific censorship, and a victory for truth.

Maybe. He'd gotten credit for the discovery, at any rate. And most of Mireille Joubert's team was working for him now, part of a genuinely international research project that had as its goal the discovery of the truth about the Martian ruins. Joubert herself was still sulking, but he thought she would come around.

He looked around at the bleak and rocky landscape of the Face and laughed. This Martian Sphinx was good at keeping its secrets . . . better, perhaps, than its far smaller cousin on Earth. The ancient humans discovered here remained the biggest mystery of all.

His original guess that the bodies he'd found were representatives of *Homo erectus* had been mistaken, it turned out. Several papers had already emerged in various journals and net professional posts discussing the images of the bodies uncovered so far, pointing out that their facial features almost certainly placed them in the group generally referred to as "archaic *Homo sapiens*." These were essentially modern humans with hang-on traits of their *Homo erectus* ancestors, like brow ridges and heavy musculature. Their brains were as large and as complex as those of fully modern humans; perhaps even more telling, the structure and placement of their larynxes were the same as modern humans, riding lower in their throats, and with larger pharyngeal cavities than the earlier *erectus*.

These people could talk. They could dream. They could imagine. They could create.

As with all good science, each new Cydonian discovery only increased the number of questions until it seemed there would never be an end to them. Who were these people? Who or what had brought them to Mars, and why? Had that agency, as some scientists were now suggesting, been responsible for creating *Homo sapiens* by genetically manipulating populations of *Homo erectus* . . . and if so, why? The humans—had they carved their own image into the titanic monument known as the Face? Or was the agency that had brought them to Mars the artist and, again, why?

And the dark question that more and more people on Earth were asking lately—who or what had destroyed the young colony on the Cydonian plain? Everywhere across this part of Mars, now, excavations were turning up more and more artifacts, shattered remnants of a vast city that had covered an ancient, once-subtropical coastline on the Boreal Sea, a city that had flourished for decades at least, and possibly for centuries, until some devastating force had struck from the sky and destroyed it all, probably within the space of hours. The D&M Pyramid was now believed to have been some sort of titanic apparatus for creating a warm and breathable atmosphere over a large portion of the northern hemisphere; its destruction had resulted in the rapid and inevitable bleed-off of the artificial atmosphere into space, the freezing of the ocean, the suffocation, freezing, and mummification of humans suddenly faced with Armageddon.

Who had attacked the Martian colony? Were they still out there, somewhere among the stars . . . and were they a threat to Earth and Humankind now?

Interesting. During the past weeks, more and more of the net's resources had been focused here, on Cydonia, instead of on the war. Was that, he wondered, the way to end war? Could it be as simple as that . . . providing the world with new frontiers, new horizons . . . and new sources of wonder?

Of course not. It was not, he realized now, the military that divided peoples and created wars, but *governments*, governments that lived only to serve themselves, no matter how democratic they might seem outwardly, governments that for survival needed to control the populations from which they'd emerged.

For Alexander, that was an astonishing revelation, as significant, perhaps, as the mummified bodies beneath the sands of Cydonia. So much human misery could be laid at the doorstep of human government and greed and monkey-band fear and the appalling ignorance that separated humans into mutually suspicious tribes.

Earth, Alexander suspected, was in the long run a lost cause. If there was a future for humanity, it was out here. Man's heritage, it seemed, lay somewhere among the stars.

He was going to have to go there to find out who he was, and why he'd come to be that way.

The sun had nearly reached the western horizon, and it grew dark swiftly on Mars. It was time for him to start back. A kind of rock-carved ramp ran down the left side of the Face, providing relatively easy access if you didn't mind the three-hundred-meter climb. Fortunately, it was all downhill from here. He could see the others waiting for him by the Mars cat below, almost lost in the east-reaching shadow of the Face.

On the way down, some moments later, the ground shifted slightly beneath his feet. Alexander put his gloved hand out to steady himself . . . and never realized how close he'd come to actually touching the cunningly concealed rock doorway leading to the Face's interior.

The Cydonian Face had clung to its secrets for half a million years, now. It could wait a little longer . . .

2042

EPILOGUE

Washington, DC
1230 hours EST

Marine Lieutenant Kaitlin Garroway walked through the automatic doors of the Golden Samurai, one of Washington's most distinguished and exclusive restaurants. Formerly known as Le Maison d'Or, the place had been widely known for its exquisite French cuisine.

Now, with Japan's formal entry into the war on the side of Russia and the United States, it was a Japanese restaurant. Kaitlin shook her head at the inaccurate *faux*-Buddhist wood carvings and decor above the ornamental *koi* pool in the dimly lit lobby. During World War I, she'd heard, it was treason in most parts of the United States to own a dachshund, and sauerkraut had been renamed victory cabbage. In World War II, thousands of Nisei, Japanese only by accident of descent and as loyal as any typical, native-born Americans, had been declared threats to national security and herded into concentration camps.

This time around, French, German, and Mexican restaurants were going out of fashion, even out of business, while Japanese and Russian restaurants flourished. Tacos were known now as "Martian sandwiches," and two

370

weeks ago the town of Paris, Texas, had formally voted to change its name to Garroway.

It was, she reflected, one hell of a crazy world.

The restaurant's sound system was playing the "Stars and Stripes Forever." That was another sign of the changing times. Patriotism was fashionable in America again, and patriotic music, especially Sousa marches and military anthems, could be heard in the unlikeliest of venues.

Kaitlin removed her hat and tucked it under her arm, then paused to tug the jacket hem of her blue dress uniform straight. She'd been a Marine for almost a year now; she'd joined two days after getting her degree at CMU and been on her way to ten weeks of OCS at Quantico ten days after that. People with her quals in computer science, she'd learned, were worth their mass in antimatter to the Corps . . . and the fact that she happened to be the daughter of "Sands of Mars" Garroway, hero of Garroway's epic march, had guaranteed her any ticket in the US Marines that she cared to write.

She'd considered changing her name. She wasn't going to go to the stars on her father's long and famous coattails.

"Lieutenant Garroway?" the maître d' asked, bowing slightly. He did not look in the least Japanese. Likely he'd been working here when the place had still been French.

"Yes?"

"This way, if you please!"

She followed him, bemused. She still didn't understand the point of this summons. "Meet me at the Golden Samurai for lunch," her father had told her the night before. "I'll have a surprise for you."

The problem was, no matter whether it was called the Golden Samurai or the Maison d'Or, this place was way above and beyond her budget. Hell, she wouldn't start collecting her space pay until she launched, two weeks from now. These places charged a hundred dollars for lunch and probably at least that much just for the privilege of looking at the dinner menu.

Well, if Dad was paying. He could afford it, certainly, now that he was back from Mars and an official, bona fide hero.

"Your table, Lieutenant. . . ."

She stopped cold, thunderstruck. Her father was there, resplendent in full-dress Marine blues, his chest splashed with colored ribbons, representing everything from the red-gold Martian Campaign Medal to the Navy Cross. The silver leaves of a lieutenant colonel winked on his epaulets. His face came alight when he saw her, and he rose to his feet.

But Kaitlin was staring wide-eyed at the man next to him. Tetsuo Ishiwara dropped his napkin and stood. "*Konichiwa, Chu-i-san,*" he said, bowing deeply. "*O-genki des ka?*"

"*K-konichiwa, Ishiwara-sama!*" she stammered back, bowing in return. "*Okagesama de, genki des.*"

"I am very glad to hear it," Ishiwara said, shifting to English. "Please, won't you join us?"

"What? . . . What? . . ." She turned and stared at her father as he held her chair for her, feeling as though the ground had just been yanked from beneath her feet.

On the sound system, Sousa had ended, and a different piece was playing now. A detached part of her mind recognized a currently popular Japanese patriotic song: "Washi Muttsu." The name translated as "Six Eagles"; the reference was to the six Japanese aviators who'd died in the brief war with the United States.

Kaitlin's eyes were burning. She couldn't speak.

"We're talking business, Chicako," the elder Garroway said, gallantly stepping in to her rescue. "Ishiwara-san is the Japanese ambassador to the United States now, did you know? I learned you two were old friends, and I thought you'd like to see him again."

"I particularly wanted to extend my congratulations," Ishiwara said, beaming, "on the honor of your promotion to *chu-i.*"

"Th-thank you!" She laughed. "Good God, sir, it's good to see you!"

"The pleasure is entirely mine, Kaiti-chan. I have

been talking to your father about his new assignment. Have you heard about it yet?''

She looked at her father, cocking her head to the side. ''New assignment?'' His current duty station, his assignment ever since his return from Mars, in fact, was the new Space Combat Training Facility down at Quantico.

''I just found out about it yesterday, Mr. Ambassador,'' he said. ''I didn't want to tell her until after you and I'd had our little chat this morning.''

''What new assignment?''

''I'm being transferred to Kyoto,'' Garroway told her. ''I'll be working with both the Ministry of Science and Technology and the Ministry of International Trade and Industry. Some really great new stuff is coming out of the Cydonian site. We'll be working together to start learning how to adapt it to our use.''

''There is astounding potential here,'' Ishiwara said, thoughtful. ''New types of materials and materials processing, lighter and stronger than anything we can manufacture now. Something that looks suspiciously like temperature-independent superconductivity. A new way of focusing magnetic resonance, that could allow guideless levitation.'' He shook his head. ''The list goes on and on. No one ever dreamed that archeology could be such a technologically productive, or such a *lucrative* science.''

''It sounds like the war is good for business,'' she said . . . and immediately wished she could retract the words. She was still bitter about the war, and Yukio's death still dragged at her sometimes, even now. But that didn't give her the right to be rude to Yukio's father. ''*Sumimasen*,'' she said. Literally referring to an obligation that never ends, the word was one of the more common terms that meant, ''I'm sorry.''

''Kaitlin—'' Garroway said.

Ishiwara raised his hand. ''War,'' he said, ''is a terrible thing. It destroys families. It destroys peoples. In the circumstances, a minor *shitsurei* is of no consequence.''

Shitsurei was a minor breach of etiquette, the equivalent of bumping into someone on a crowded maglev platform.

"*Domo arigato gozaimasu,*" she said, bowing.

"I asked your father to invite you here today," Ishiwara went on, as though nothing embarrassing had happened. "Partly, of course, I wanted to see you again. But I also wanted to extend to you an invitation. I understand that you are something of an expert in computers."

"I wouldn't say I was an expert, exactly," she said, uncomfortable.

"Of course you wouldn't say it," Ishiwara said, eyes twinkling. "You are too much the Nihonjin for that. But others would and do. I would like to offer you the chance to come to Japan, to Kyoto, to work on this new Alliance project with your father. It is supremely important work, and we are looking for the very best people in the field. Some of what we are developing . . . well, it is astonishing. One of the things your people at Cydonia have uncovered recently suggests a possible new approach to computer memory storage, using quantum gates and atomic matrices." He tapped the expensive Sony wrist-top on his arm. "It could make these as clumsy and as inefficient as the vacuum-tube ENIAC of a century ago. You could be part of the development team on that project."

She blinked. The offer was tempting. God, it was tempting! To be back in Japan, and with Dad . . .

"Thank you, *Taishi*-sama," she said. "Thank you more than I can say. But it's not possible. I've already got my orders."

"I can swing it with the Pentagon, if you like," her father said. "Just give the word. You know that ten thousand Marines would give their right arms and a month's pay for a shot at your new assignment."

She smiled. "Which is one reason not to give it up, right?" She looked at Ishiwara. "I've been assigned to the First Marine Space Assault Group," she said proudly. "Under the command of Captain Carmen Fuentes. And it's no secret where we're bound.''

"I've heard," Ishiwara said. "The Moon. . . .''

The UN base at Fra Mauro was the specific target. It would be a way of telling the UN that the United States now had absolute space supremacy in the war, and they were going to keep it.

"I appreciate your offer, sir," she added. "It's a great honor. But I'm a Marine, and I go where I'm ordered. I'd rather not get a free ride.''

"Told you," Garroway said. "That's twenty you owe me, Mr. Ambassador.''

"I understand, *Kaiti-chan*," Ishiwara said, bowing. "You must, of course, be true to yourself, as a Marine.''

Kaitlin turned to her father. "You know, we just had a new replacement arrive today," she said. "Bob Haskins broke an ankle in training, so they brought this new guy in. I was interviewing him, and it turns out he was on the Candor March with you.''

"Really?" Garroway said. "Who is it?''

"Sergeant Kaminski. He just signed his papers for six more years. A real lifer.''

"He's a good man," Garroway said.

The music playing on the sound system had changed again, Kaitlin realized. The yearningly sentimental "Washi Muttsu" had ended, and—possibly because of the two Marines among the clientele—the management was playing a rather artsy vocal rendition of the Marine Corps Hymn.

They'd reached the new verse, the one added just since the return of Garroway and the MMEF from Mars.

From the blue-white vistas over Earth, to the
ocher sands of Mars,
We are in the vanguard of Man's rise, from the
earth out to the stars.
As humanity spreads to other worlds and learns
what our heritage means,
We will proudly bear the banner of the United
States Marines!

She reached out and took her father's hand. She was crying—partly for Yukio, mostly, though, for happiness and pride.

Like him, she'd made a march of her own.

Like him, she was a United States Marine.

AVON EOS

RISING STARS

Meet great new talents
in hardcover at a special price!

$14.00 U.S./$19.00 Can.

Circuit of Heaven

by Dennis Danvers
0-380-97447-9

Hand of Prophecy

by Severna Park
0-380-97639-0

Buy these books at your local bookstore or use this coupon for ordering:
Mail to: Avon Books, Dept BP, Box 767, Rte 2, Dresden, TN 38225   G
Please send me the book(s) I have checked above.
☐ My check or money order—no cash or CODs please—for $_____is enclosed (please
add $1.50 per order to cover postage and handling—Canadian residents add 7% GST). U.S.
residents make checks payable to Avon Books; Canada residents make checks payable to
Hearst Book Group of Canada.
☐ Charge my VISA/MC Acct#_____Exp Date_____
Minimum credit card order is two books or $7.50 (please add postage and handling
charge of $1.50 per order—Canadian residents add 7% GST). For faster service, call
1-800-762-0779. Prices and numbers are subject to change without notice. Please allow six to
eight weeks for delivery.
Name_____
Address_____
City_____State/Zip_____
Telephone No._____   ERS 0298

AVON
EOS

PRESENTS AWARD-WINNING NOVELS FROM MASTERS OF SCIENCE FICTION

PRISONER OF CONSCIENCE
by Susan R. Matthews   78914-0/$3.99 US/$3.99 Can

HALFWAY HUMAN
by Carolyn Ives Gilman   79799-2/$5.99 US/$7.99 Can

MOONRISE
by Ben Bova   78697-4/$6.99 US/$8.99 Can

DARK WATER'S EMBRACE
by Stephen Leigh   79478-0/$3.99 US/$3.99 Can

Coming Soon

COMMITMENT HOUR
by James Alan Gardner   79827-1/$5.99 US/$7.99 Can

THE WHITE ABACUS
by Damien Broderick   79615-5/$5.99 US/$7.99 Can

Buy these books at your local bookstore or use this coupon for ordering:
Mail to: Avon Books, Dept BP, Box 767, Rte 2, Dresden, TN 38225   G
Please send me the book(s) I have checked above.
❑ My check or money order—no cash or CODs please—for $_____is enclosed (please
add $1.50 per order to cover postage and handling—Canadian residents add 7% GST). U.S.
residents make checks payable to Avon Books; Canada residents make checks payable to
Hearst Book Group of Canada.
❑ Charge my VISA/MC Acct#_____Exp Date_____
Minimum credit card order is two books or $7.50 (please add postage and handling
charge of $1.50 per order—Canadian residents add 7% GST). For faster service, call
1-800-762-0779. Prices and numbers are subject to change without notice. Please allow six to
eight weeks for delivery.
Name_____
Address_____
City_____State/Zip_____
Telephone No._____   ASF 0198